Irene Dische is a novelist and journalist whose work has appeared in *The New Yorker*. Her books, published in twenty-five countries, have included international bestsellers. She divides her time between Berlin and Rhinebeck, New York.

D1009279

Additional Praise for *The Empress of Weehawken*

"Brilliant . . . Discomfitingly funny . . . [Dische's] narrator is as winning and willful as any reader could wish for. . . . A marvelous exploration of honor and identity, greed, sacrifice, and just desserts . . . Just as Dische's staccato rhythms and deadpan sentences stretch into lyricism, so too what seems stark, even cynical, moves into an entirely unsentimental, deeply satisfying (and sometimes scary) love."   —*Newsday*

"I would tell you *The Empress of Weehawken* is my favorite book, but you'd think I was exaggerating. So let's just leave it at: it's perfect."

—Patricia Marx, author of *Him Her Him Again The End of Him*

"The Empress never stops talking, even after she's dead, and the wonderful part is that you're glad. She's funny, wise, and unpredictable. Her story spans three generations and two continents, and every page is a delight."

—Jane Juska, author of *A Round-Heeled Woman*

"Incredibly witty, beautifully written . . . *The Empress of Weehawken* is a potent stew of class, sex, and religion, as well as culture and generational clashes, and Dische crafts a glorious misanthrope in her fictionalized version of her grandmother."

—*The Star-Ledger* (Newark)

"Dense, dark family history—loosely based on the author's own— becomes relatable and funny through the no-nonsense narration of Elisabeth Rother, an upstanding Catholic German who marries a Jewish doctor before WWII."

—Jennifer Armstrong, *Entertainment Weekly*

The Empress of Weehawken

The Empress of Weehawken

IRENE DISCHE

PICADOR

FARRAR, STRAUS AND GIROUX

NEW YORK

www.picadorusa.com

Picador® is a U.S. registered trademark and is used by Farrar, Straus and Giroux
under license from Pan Books Limited.

For information on Picador Reading Group Guides, please contact Picador.
E-mail: readinggroupguides@picadorusa.com

Designed by Gretchen Achilles

ISBN-13: 978-0-312-42795-5
ISBN-10: 0-312-42795-6

First published in the United States by Farrar, Straus and Giroux

First Picador Edition: August 2008

D 10 9 8 7 6 5 4 3 2

AUTHOR'S NOTE

Certain events and characters in this novel were inspired by real people and events. But the actual events, characters, and dialogue depicted are all fictional.

My grandmother owes no one any explanations for her interpretation of events, but I am indebted to Charles Dische, Hans Magnus Enzensberger, Susan Golomb, Courtney Hodell, and Wieland Schulz-Keil for helping me so generously with mine.

Part
One

uch of what went kaput, as the Americans say, in the generations after mine can be blamed on Carl's low sperm count. He had murdered his men with heroism, the exact details later. As a result, he only managed one child. And that was the wrong sex. We tried and tried for another. He would plant himself inside me and till away. He worked hard, grunting and sweating—he was not a lazybones. Afterward, I remained on my back, hoisting my legs in the air over my head, the soles of my feet touching in prayer.

God did not hear my prayers. When nothing had come of our efforts for more than five years, and our child was already in school, I said, "Carl, according to the laws of the Church, one does this to make children. According to the Church, if it's not to make children, then you Must Not."

Carl had arguments up his sleeve about procreation as a form, with or without content, developed by God along with prayer as a ritual to be repeated as often as possible. His faith was deep and I loved him, and believed him, although my body didn't. Then one day, when I showed reluctance, he said, "The ancient Jews were commanded to lie with each other on the Sabbath, *because* the high point brought them closest to God."

"Jews!" I snorted.

"Not everything about the Jews is bad," he said. He was apologetic, a rare occurrence. I sulked for a while, and allowed him to take me again, it was my duty. I was gaining weight. Soon there was so much of me that it was hard to say where I began or ended, and he became discouraged, and left me alone. Even a surgeon can be surprised by the human body. The fact is that when we met, I was beautiful. I was the pinnacle of female beauty in our family; after that, it was downhill. Do not laugh at my conceit—I am being objective. In the first place, everyone always remarked about me and my favorite brother Otto that we were the most beautiful children. Adolescence did not alter this generally held opinion. In the second place I am not blind: we looked like German gods; we both had thick yellow hair, chiseled noses, eyes blue and commanding as planets, and almost perfectly fleshless lips. One could see plainly that our family had ties to the aristocracy.

Nowadays this doesn't count for much, especially in the less civilized world, like New Jersey. But it should matter. Because aristocracy is a chain of people passing along a sense of worth, handling it cautiously, so as not to lose any, from one generation to the next. My great-great-uncle was Joseph von Görres. I will not bother to explain who he was. In my youth, those syllables belonged to the syllabus of general education, not to mention countless streets and public squares, and anyone who knew us, knew as well that we were connected to Görres. Not a direct descendant, I admit: he married a distant aunt, who was a von Lassaulx, also a name of distinction. Generations followed, of doctors, lawyers, engineers, prelates. They weren't all Germans—some were Dutch, others French—but they were all Catholic. Over generations, my family, the Gierlichs, took one turn after another that led it into the middle class, but we never sank below that. Of course this was thanks to the women, who made sure there was no monkey business.

It is up to the women to keep up a family standard, men are not strong enough. Women must keep them in line, including lineage. I learned this from my grandmother, who instructed me that my very presence must influence, that when I enter a room the men must unconsciously move their hands to their trousers, to make sure they have not forgotten to button up; I was about seven years old.

The women were groomed to choose their husbands prudently. My grandmother turned down a rich aristocrat because he was lazy. He had a castle, but not a position. Instead, she married an energetic engineer, who soon rewarded her by building the railroad from Berlin to Petersburg. Czar Alexander was so grateful that he presented my grandmother with a set of onyx and diamonds, big pieces that really qualify one to say "family jewelry." I don't like the first syllable of that word, but this substance is one thing that I really enjoyed in my life: I inherited and was given a lot of it, and I took excellent care of it. Many decades later, I risked my life to smuggle Czar Alexander's generous gifts to safe shores—only to have my granddaughter auction them for a pittance at Christie's, under circumstances so demeaning they make our flight from Germany look like a Sunday excursion to Chadwick Beach. I will return to that later.

Because this gory little narrative concerns my granddaughter, the hows and whys of her, a kind of True Confession I have decided to write for her since she has just reached a spot that is as lonely as a vacuum. Her conscience is in there with her. She has A Lot on it. She is not entirely to blame. She had terrible role models: her mother and her father. And she was, by nature, not well equipped morally. Really, all the bad qualities that could be cooked up in the family genes were served to Irene. I will get to these, but not as an excuse. Because one can overcome, make the best of what one has. In any case, her background must be recounted, to make sense of the foreground. But where was I?

My appearance.

In our engagement photograph I look like a martyr about to be thrown to a lion. My future husband holds me in his arms, his wild creature poking at the barriers between us: our layers of clothing, the weeks until the wedding ceremony. Soon it would be released. Carl's eyes were even larger than mine, but black. His nose was large too, and beaked. His bones were large. His creature would not be small.

I am not suggesting that Carl was ever anything but honorable. He wore his military uniform to our wedding. With his medals for heroism, and his sword at his belt, he looked like the perfect German gentleman. His moral credentials were impeccable. But of course I was doing the Wrong Thing by marrying him. I aimed the family downward. I crash-landed the family. Love makes one careless. I argued with my parents that since he converted to my faith, just the way Gustav Mahler and countless other important people had, and was twice as Good as me, since goodness came to him without effort, whereas I always had to work at it (my parents nodded vigorously in agreement), he was a perfectly respectable choice in a husband. The alternative was no husband at all. This had been my sworn objective until I met him, Dr. Carl Rother.

We had met over a limb amputation, in an army field hospital.

I was one of the nurses, in a sterile gown, my hair hidden under a conical surgical cap. He was even more covered up. He wore a mask. I did not see the size of this nose until later. I saw his black eyes. And his quick, graceful hands, handling the saw with such familiarity. He cut and trimmed and sewed, all at great speed. His palm was square and muscular, his fingers long and tapering to small tips with round, neat fingernails. When the stump was all cleaned up and lay on the operating table looking like a giant salami, he sighed, stood back, and gazed over at me.

For a while, I would have none of him. I had already turned down all the eligible boys back in the Rhineland, where I belonged.

But I allowed him to kiss me. It wasn't so bad. He was very clean. He gave me a ring. I gave it back. He gave me another.

His father owned a hardware store in a small town in Upper Silesia. The men in the family wore yarmulkes, the women wigs. I accepted the ring. I told my family. My brother Otto said nothing. I mean: nothing; he wouldn't speak to me. My youngest brother Heinrich proclaimed himself concerned. Up till then, *he* was the family problem; he hadn't even finished high school and he seemed headed for a career in manual labor. Compared with me now, though, he was a shining light. He adored my predicament, and when I went home to discuss the wedding with my parents, he pretended to try to talk me out it. I was amused when he addressed me over a hastily called dinner, and my smile triggered his usual raging, his shouts of *"kleiner Idiot"* sprayed into the first course, a delicious *Milchkaltschale*, iced soup with beaten egg white floating in icebergs on top; it was the middle of the summer. My sisters looked at me, their souls doubled over in pain: betrayal. Together, we had danced our way through bourgeois Rhineland life, attended balls, dried our first bouquets, toyed with the officers and academics and higher forms of male being that invited toying, while exchanging, again and again, our childhood oaths to keep forever our virginity and to have, therefore, interesting lives. My decision shocked my sisters into a kind of submission to me. I had my way. A week after Carl was baptized, I married him. And I moved with him to the backwater where he had grown up.

I accepted his attempts at compensation—a boxer, a dachshund, and the biggest villa in town. It was larger than the Gierlich home overlooking the Rhine. It had high stucco ceilings, ornate parquet floors, an enormous kitchen, a wing for the servants, a nursery, and three bathrooms, two for the family, one for the staff. More compensation—I had a lovely sitting room, with a settee. I changed the slipcovering every season. Pastels in spring and summer, solemn browns and grays for autumn, and deep reds and greens for winter. A small table held my books, mostly biographies and travel guides, and the cookies, which changed with the seasons too. I looked forward to spring—flowery anise cookies; summer—airy waffles and *Löffelbiskuits*; autumn—*russisches Brot*; winter—*Lebkuchen, Spekulatius*. I could look out at the flowers or the snowdrifts in the back garden. The front yard had a high brick wall so that passersby could not stare in, but most of them were friendly, and many were related. I accepted Carl's family and enjoyed calling them my own, even if they were socially not on our level: four good-natured sisters who did not employ servants but managed all by themselves to keep clean houses and bake various pastries; three brothers, one a barber, the other a cantor in the synagogue, and the youngest, like Heinrich Gierlich, the family problem—worse: a thief.

The youngest children are usually the family problem, as Irene would turn out to be. I have asked around here why that is, and received no satisfactory answer. When I met Carl, Jacob Rother was only fifteen and so enterprising that he had already found his way into a prison. His crime was modest. He had found a broken camera in a scrap heap and polished it up. He set off into the countryside on a mission, to make portraits of the peasants and their families. They dolled up, assembled in front of the camera, and he solemnly clicked their pictures and took their coins. And that was the last they saw of him. Little Jacob came out of prison, claimed to be sorry, shocked us with his stories, and disappeared on another scam. Although he was the only other man in the family not running around in a yarmulke, Carl detested him. "I have enough brothers to go around, I don't need you, Jacob," he said, and forbade him to visit us.

I opened the back door for Jacob when Carl was not home. I fed him a big meal, and told him enough about Jesus, a parable a visit—Jacob ate very vigorously, so I had to speak up—to justify the invitation. Even if I was sowing into thorns, I enjoyed the company of this young version of Carl—as dark and muscular and nearly as smart—and sent him away with admonitions he would never heed, my heart happy. I also liked all the countless little well-behaved nieces and nephews that lived in town. They turned the dreary provincial town into a warm lap.

The biggest compensation—Carl was a big man in a little town, but he was also a fairly big man in a very big town. He ran the local town hospital as chief doctor, but he also taught at the university of Breslau. His title was not just Herr Doktor, it was Herr Professor Doktor, and I was his wife, and my name became Frau Professor Doktor, and that bit of recognition, in the large sense small, made up for a whole lot of strangeness and smallness that a worldly Rhinelander like me took upon herself moving to Upper Silesia. But apart from all that, I admired Carl more than I had ever admired anyone but my big brother Otto. My husband was just as intelligent, as morally upright. He had grown up praying to a different God, but he believed in Jesus all the more passionately, and securely, for having spent so many years without Him. Our child made him miserable, because it soon became obvious that it had grave flaws.

Flaw number one: it did not resemble me in the way that mattered. It had Carl's enormous dark eyes, his nose, and all on its own, I don't know where they came from, red, flashy lips. Also unlike us, our child had a noticeably weak chin, and that, said Carl, represented weakness of character. All this was not obvious when the baby was born, for nothing is, they all look alike, I find them somewhat disgusting. But I knew that, and I can't say it disappointed me. Something else. Flaw number two. A shock. I was unprepared: a girl.

It was bad enough being a girl myself, not being able to become an army officer, a hero of battles. Otto bathed naked but I had to take baths with my underpants on, so as not to see. I took my underpants off anyway, and my nanny smacked me. Father, I was impure. Constantly. All around me were shining examples. My sisters were in and out of the confessional in five minutes. Not me. Father, I was angry, envious, greedy.

It did not go unnoticed. I dunked the braids of the girl at the desk in front of me into my inkwell because her braids were thicker than mine. I had to leave the convent school. A girl spoke loudly in the confessional and I listened in and giggled; I had to leave the school. When our teacher fell from her chair, I claimed that we children had seen her underpants and she was therefore unfit to teach us. I had to leave the school. In the end, I had private tutors. A visitor gave each child in the family a heavy glass egg, with a figurine from the New Testament inside. But mine had a little chicken. A chicken! I hurled it out the window. My guardian angel nudged it off trajectory by one centimeter, so that it merely grazed the rim of a gentleman's felt hat rather than killing him. Sin of nearly taking someone's life. In living room and nursery and dinner-table confrontations they scolded that I was intransigent, my morals beyond repair because I was immune to scolding. I am afraid that I passed on my character to my granddaughter Irene. The difference between us is that all my life, I pitted my will to be good against my natural inclinations, while she saw no point in that. More about this later. I must explain about Otto. My brother Otto was pious, God-fearing, and quiet. We were often mistaken for each other. Otto was ten months older than I was, and exactly my height until he reached his teens. Then suddenly he grew much taller, he had a growling voice, while I kept the thin, piping one. He started treating me with disdain. He didn't like girls any more than I did, even as an adult. I happen to know that he preferred boys. Another tragedy for me: I was not a boy he could love and confide in.

So I longed for a son, as blond and fine as Otto, whom I could raise to be the perfect man, and instead I was given a dark-haired girl. Carl was pleased. He said she resembled the Virgin and wanted to name her Maria. I wanted to call her Renate, because the name—now more than ever—always struck me as so hopeful—"reborn," anything is possible. We compromised on Maria Renate, and soon, when her natural temperament came to the fore, making any association with the Virgin grotesque, we called her only Renate.

She proved to be much worse than I had been, because she had all these splashy talents—too much of anything is bad. By the time she was five, she was already distracting us with her intelligence, her ability to draw and to sing any song after hearing it just once. Was it not far more significant that she was up to no good? I missed countless opportunities to bend her character right. I can still hear her creeping into the house from outside. I could recognize a door closing too slowly, too silently, and sneaking footsteps. I leaped up out of my settee to see what was going on. She was trying to make the bathroom before I could get a closer look. I flung out my foot and blocked the door. I cried, "Renate, let me see!" She began to cry bitterly, she said she had fallen and had hurt herself. Her mouth and hands were covered with a thick scarlet paste. Without hesitation, I licked her hand. "I have sweet blood!" she cried. "It is sweeter than yours!" She began shrieking with laughter. I knew she had been stealing raspberries again. How could I not laugh too? That time, I collected myself. I went into the garden with a big bowl and scooped up the old worm-eaten raspberries lying on the ground. I forced her to eat them up. But she claimed that they tasted delicious. "Thank you, thank you, Mama!" And then she vomited all over my favorite carpet.

I sent her to the attic. I locked her in from outside. It grew dark. I waited for dinner. I had a headache. I thought I might have a brain hemorrhage from unhappiness. Was 1927 going to be my year of death?

"Her stubbornness must be crushed," Carl said.

I defended her then. "She will grow out of it, the way I did."

I went upstairs to fetch her. She came, quietly, exuding satisfaction. Triumph even. Years later, I knew why. She had prepared the attic for her prison terms. She had boxes of chocolates hidden there, tins of juice, a pillow, candles, and her favorite books. She did not eat dinner that night, because she was stuffed with sweets. We thought she was upset, and stubborn.

"It is not just stubbornness," Carl said, lying in bed, discussing our progeny. "It is a will to power. She wants to rule over us."

He cried, "We will not let her!"

In particular, she wanted to break her father's will. Whatever he did, she wanted to do better, to show him up. She lacked an older brother to show her to her lower place. She aimed for her father's position. Carl was the first one in his family to stay in school beyond the eighth grade, to play the piano. He taught himself to read notes, his fingers mastered the piano keys, and after we married, he bought himself a nice big gleaming instrument. He preferred the loud, romantic works, especially by Wagner. He looked strange when he played, he made terrible faces, he closed his eyes and threw back his head, and his torso swayed in rhythm. I did not like to watch him, but I liked to close my eyes and listen.

By the time she was just eight years old, Renate was playing the very same pieces. Even I could tell that she played them better. She had started taking lessons but she didn't have to work at it, her hands made sense of the keyboard as easily as if they were petting a bunny rabbit or playing with a doll. She had, said the teacher, "piano hands"—Carl's hands.

Of course I was enchanted by her. But I did not ever let her see that. It is bad for children to be admired. It makes them think too highly of themselves, and that undermines their character. So I supported Carl in his endeavor to show our disapproval. And when I took her little hands in mine and noted how strong they were, how agile, how unlike mine, I was secretly thrilled and I thought, She will become a surgeon like her father. And then I sighed and said, "Why are your hands *always* dirty?"

Carl and I worked hard to mold our offspring. We pressed her with an iron routine. We were early to bed and early to rise; at five o'clock we were saying our rosaries, then we had our baths and our humble breakfast, the fried egg quivering on its last bed of buttered toast, Carl's chauffeur already standing in regalia before the back door of the spit-polished car at six-thirty. He returned for me and Renate, dropping her off at school, and bringing me to the clinic in time for my shift, assisting Carl. The first operation was at 8:00 a.m.

Carl was happiest in the operating room. He believed in old-fashioned handiwork. But innovation delighted him. He fell in love with the X-ray machine. He never allowed anyone else to handle it, because he felt others did not have the sensibility to understand the new instrument, they treated it fearfully or arrogantly, they never held the plate steadily enough. He trusted only himself to take X-rays, clutching the plate, crooking his thumb over the edge, so that each picture bore an X-ray of his powerful digit, and he never tired of seeing that. God does not like vanity in men! Cancer grew on the X-rayed thumb, traveled up his arm, and, unknown to us, in trace amounts, down to his testes.

His colleagues advised him to have his entire hand removed. He considered it and concluded that he would rather die. He settled on losing his thumb. That was not all that he lost. After several years of trying for another child, I advised him to look at his little men under the microscope. I sat at home and waited for this court to clarify once and for all the fault question. He returned home with an expression that I could not fathom, his features and his posture stiff, a kind of rigor. Still standing in the entry hall, he stated, "We are monocarps," his voice already full of a bitter sap.

It was the only time he ever used a word I didn't know, usually he was cautious not to offend me. I understood what he meant anyway: no more children. A certain chore removed from our routine. Which continued at noon with lunch—we came home for that.

The table was set for three, with napkin rings and silverware holders. We sat down shortly before one o'clock. Renate said prayers. We waited in hushed silence. The clock ticked. As the big hand swept finally over the twelve, footsteps drowned out the clock. The cook entered pushing a trolley. The high point of the day began with soup, steaming thick meat and potato stews in the winter, delicate broths in the spring and fall, iced soups in the summer. The tension did not diminish. Many courses followed. I will not itemize them, because even now, the memory stirs up my longing to sit down one more time at that heavenly table. Carl objected to my pleasure. He tried to distract me, stirring up a discussion about that morning's adventures at the clinic. The spoon was scarcely in my mouth, then he was asking me a question, my impressions of a patient, or a certain decision taken. I always felt crestfallen when lunch was over.

Immediately, Carl returned to the hospital, where he took care of his postoperative patients and his diagnostics. I admit that I often amused myself in the afternoon. I tossed balls to the dogs in the yard, and Renate and I had, well, we had a good time. I taught her important skills for getting along in life: for instance, how to look extremely stupid. If you are not dumb, then this requires both inventiveness and practice. Crossing your eyes very slightly, so that it is barely noticeable, is an effective tool. I also pointed out techniques to establish hierarchy, such as directing a stare at an annoying person's midriff, which they find very disconcerting. Most important, I showed her how to remain absolutely serious when your mood is most frivolous. You have to relax your face entirely, starting with your mouth, working upward, just . . . relax. This expresses decorum. It's funny how your mood quickly obeys your face. After practicing this, we enjoyed laughing ourselves nearly to death, so that in order to stabilize my blood pressure, we had to eat cookies in my room.

The cookies. I was growing fatter. I know that my daughter felt ashamed of me. I watched her from my window as she squatted in the garden to poke a slug with a twig. She was mumbling some-thing. I opened the window to overhear her. She had named the slug "Mama." I paid her back. It was New Year's Eve. The Christmas tree stood in the corner of the living room. I realized we were alone, Carl had gone upstairs. I let my head droop, my mouth open, my eyes lolled. I looked like I had gone mad. "Mama," she whispered, the words now full of fear and respect. "Mama, what's the matter?" I said nothing. She began to whimper. "Please, Mama."

I replied, "I've turned into a slug."

She stared. Then: crybaby. I hugged her. I forgave her. After all, she was right, I was fat. But the fatter a face, the prettier it is. Faces matter more than figures, in my opinion.

But where was I? My daily life. After lunch.

I saw to the household, which means I managed the servants. I also managed our relatives; I wrote and received letters. If I had nothing else to do, I went to visit Helga.

Helga Weltecke was my assistant nurse at the hospital, and her husband, Dr. Joseph Weltecke, was the hospital's second surgeon, so we had a lot in common. The Welteckes could be pleased that they were on such good terms with their superiors. They were cheerfully churchy, the way I liked it, and we always went to mass together. Dr. Weltecke and Dr. Rother shared a love of good cigars and stamp collecting, while Helga and I had in common a keen in-terest in fruit spirits. We experimented making our own, from large vats of fruit we kept in her basement. After they had fermented for a year, we would assign them either to silver flasks that could be kept in one's pocket during walks, or to pretty glass decanters that could be kept on one's dressing table. We felt that raspberry spirits in particular established, with just one nip, a special link to God.

I returned home in the late afternoons to be there when Carl swung open the door at four o'clock. He did not remove his coat, but gave a long, low whistle, which summoned the dogs to his feet. Rain or shine, he turned around and went back out with them for a brisk walk. He was a big, vigorous man. The opening door, the whistle, the excited yipping of the dogs, the closing door, summoned me to my window to watch him stride down the road toward the little woods in Leobschütz. When he returned, sweating and happy, we had a nap together. This was Renate's time at the piano, and we woke up listening to her play. Meanwhile the Help had prepared coffee, and Carl soon retired to the den to read or work on his stamp collection, and for one hour every evening, before dinner, he too practiced the piano. Dinner was at nineteen hours, a light meal hardly worth recounting, Schnittchen of thinly sliced moist black bread, with thick sweet butter, cervelat wurst or hard cheese, followed by a slab of chocolate and perhaps a swallow of fruit spirits, after which the evening prayers were a deeply felt but quick formality before we slipped into bed, always by nine o'clock.

On Sundays, Carl worked only in emergencies. Then we got up recklessly late, whenever we felt like it, but in time for mass, which we attended without even so much as a drop of coffee. We enjoyed the hunger pangs knowing they were for our Lord, and by choice; the big meals afterward tasted all the better for it. We often broke our fast at the town restaurant, in the company of the Welteckes and their four well-disciplined little boys. Sunday afternoons were reserved for excursions with Renate, either in the form of a long walk or a drive to a nearby sight, and in the evening we invariably had dinner with some members of Carl's family, the Rothers of Leobschütz.

The Rothers were not like the Gierlichs. The Rothers were slow-witted, easygoing little people who had never left their tiny spot on the map and yet smiled upon me, the Christian newcomer, and upon the rest of the universe. They did not even think poorly of Jacob, the family thief—he merely puzzled them. In truth, they were so good that they could not identify bad. Take Carl's sister Else. She looked like a soft, beautiful milk cow, with mellow brown eyes and a lustrous black mane that was hidden by her lustrous black wig, heavens she was pretty, she was the town beauty until I came along. She never had an unkind word to say about anyone, she just gave and gave of herself all day long, and I often felt ashamed in her presence; she would have effortlessly made an Ideal Christian.

The Rothers lavished attention on each other, and on Renate. My daughter had twelve aunts and uncles, a granny, and twenty-one cousins who called her one of their own. Of course this planted a big question mark into Renate's brain about her position in the world. Did she belong to their end of society, with the small-town Jewish shopkeepers, or ours? Even worse, by hiring Liesel, I had invited the lowest of the low into Renate's heart.

Liesel was sixteen years old when Renate was born. She had already been working for me long enough to trust her with the silverware. She came from Lower Silesia, her German was infested with Polish syntax and vocabulary, and she had a stutter that tore her speech into a hee-haw. I did not think, when I hired her, that I would be listening to her speak much. Apart from her stutter, she made a nice clean impression. She owned two identical pale blue cotton dresses with white belts and round white collars, which she pampered, mending and starching them, covering them with an apron, so they never wore out. In cold weather, she added a white woolen jacket and woolen stockings. I accepted these outfits instead of a uniform. She kept her coarse brown hair up in a tight bun and was passably pretty but for a harelip that had been poorly sewn. Her eyebrows were bushy and obscured her eyes, her features stayed put, they did not register her feelings. I never saw her face look happy or sad. Her posture did the talking for her. In church, she closed her eyes to pray, and held her hands to her nose like a little girl. I believed that most of her emotions were spent in her relationship with God. Although she was tiny, she was very strong. She loved work, couldn't get enough of it. After working her ten-hour shift, when normal domestics want to have dinner or go to bed, she asked if she could clean the basement or polish the candlesticks. And she never spoke about money, never asked for a raise. She did not have that social resentment common to her class—her people were social democrats, but thank heavens, she had no desire for equality. "Order rules here," she liked to say. *Hier herrscht Ordnung.* Later, I learned that her *Ordnung* was not a simple master.

I had Anna, a trained nanny, looking after Renate when she was born. She was very efficient and the baby always looked starched and ironed. One day, after my afternoon visit with my child, I handed the baby back to Anna. When Renate felt those trained hands close on her, she began to scream. I didn't know much about babies but I gave the nanny a week's wages and asked her to pack her bags. I had the entire afternoon left to find a substitute. The town was brimming with unemployed servants. I sat in the nanny's chair in the nursery and cuddled the baby, who lay in my arms unresponsively. Liesel had appeared briefly in the doorway as I was firing the nanny, and she gave a big gasp of irritation. Then I could hear her footsteps in the attic, where she was packing mothballs into the trunks of summer clothing. Her feet rapped angrily on the floorboards. A few minutes later she appeared again; she strode right up to me (I had not invited her in. The nerve!) and stuttered, "Frau Doktor Rother cannot just fire Anna for no reason. A baby will cry about being picked up, it has nothing to do with *who* is picking her up." Such a long sentence cost her much effort.

She was making my employment practices her business. Rage planted her right there, in her white and blue uniform, her hands on her hips in the manner of a sheriff, and repeated, "How can Frau Docktor Rother blame Anna for the baby crying? They always cry!" Well, she had a point. At once, I stood up and shoved Renate at Liesel's apron. She had rolled her sweater sleeves up and was sweating slightly. I could see the muscles tense in her short white forearms as they moved forward reflexively to accept the burden. The baby lay in this unwilling, rebellious cradle and gazed in silence upward, toward Liesel's limp eyes, the strands of black mule hairs on her forehead, the black eyebrows, and the gash of her cleft lip. I watched my infant, lying calmly, studying this new physiognomy. And then, for the first time in her life, Renate smiled.

From then on, Liesel took sole care of our daughter. She also cooked and sewed for her, and of course when the child was sleeping, she helped the other servants with their chores, and also did some of the cooking. Our household soon depended entirely on her and I discouraged her from visiting her family. Liesel was blessed. She didn't have a husband, she didn't have children. Once, when she was about twenty-one, she had gotten it into her head to marry Josef, our chauffeur. I had seen that coming. I was prepared. I simply forbade it.

I had seen Josef visit the kitchen once too often. I began referring to him as a hunchback. I rammed that nickname into circulation. Hunchbacked Josef. He didn't really have a hunchback, but he would one day, you could tell, he was very tall and humble by nature, so he bent down when he spoke to people and one could see plainly that in another few decades, he would be permanently bent.

"Liesel, it is out of the question. Not to such an ugly hunchback," I said. "You are giving your life away. I cannot stand for that."

"He's a good man," she said. "He works hard."

"Work? He has fun. Every young man wants to drive a nice big car. And he is sensible, I have to hand him that. Because he wants a wife like you. But it's out of the question. Renate can't make do without you. She is only five!"

She told Josef she didn't want to get married, and that was that. He was so disappointed that he quit our services. Which was fine. Liesel stayed. Chauffeurs are easy to come by. I saw to it that we never hired any single men.

I know horror stories about maids running off to marry. The

Keils, for instance. They had a nanny named Fraulein Strecker for their child; she stayed on after he was grown up, and took care of the house along with the maid. Her butter cookies were pure poetry, and her sewing legendary. Fraulein Strecker lived in a third-floor room, with a pretty bed, and its own sink so she didn't have to use the bathtub to wash. When she was sixty, Herr Keil was late for a luncheon at home with a colleague of his, a very rich but lonely banker, and Fraulein Strecker brought him something to drink and a newspaper to read. Somehow, this very fine gentleman fell in love with the old maid. He married her right under the nose of the Keils, and she spent the rest of her life as Frau Doktor Edelmann, in her own villa that was larger than the Keil villa, had a much larger garden, and more servants. She still used to bake cookies and send them over to the Keils, and when someone's figure changed, she insisted they bring their wardrobe over and she would adjust it. But this was a shock to the entire community.

Carl warned me that Liesel posed a different kind of danger. He felt that I was too dependent on her and she would take advantage of that. She would take charge.

"You have to watch that Liesel," Carl warned. "She is going to run the family someday. If you don't watch out."

"Her behavior is impeccable," I said. "She never stops working. And Renate is clean and well fed, and seems happy with her. But the child must never speak Silesian. It makes me feel ill."

The child grew and learned to speak Liesel's Silesian fluently. In that ugly dialect, one "does" a lot—"I do take a walk, I do clean now"—and it just will not do. But Renate spoke perfect High German with me, so I could not complain. She was a social chameleon. She could chat with our company at home like a little lady. Then she went into the kitchen and wrapped herself around Liesel When she skinned her knee, she appealed to Liesel, even though I was the trained nurse. If she was sad, she crawled into Liesel's lap.

But she did not cry there. She did not cry anywhere. Even as a toddler, she rarely shed a tear, and she was fearless, which is a lack. Because she was also, clearly, lacking any fear of God. This was not apparent to others. In school, she blended in by keeping her personality under wraps. Her luminous dark eyes fooled even the drama teacher; each year in the Christmas pageant, she played her namesake, Maria.

I bit my tongue, hoping she would grow into the role. After three years, I lost hope. "If they only knew what you are really like!" I told Renate.

"Not even God knows!" she said.

"You be quiet!" I snapped.

During that pageant, she cast her eyes up to heaven with shattering intensity, her hands clasped to her chest. But as she looked down again, her gaze sought mine, and fleetingly, she winked. Laughter boiled up in me. My face refused to relax into an earnest expression; I buried it in my hands. I begged the Lord to make me sad or serious. He did not hear my prayers. I managed to have a huge laugh burst into my palms where it sounded like coughing. My eyes were red. Carl tapped me lovingly on the back.

The teacher and the audience never suspected the real drama taking place. I reprimanded Renate, of course. "You put me on the spot!" I told her. "How can you be so ruthless!" She apologized, a rare occurrence. I suggested she see our confessor. But my daughter did not turn to others for help. She did not need it.

She took after Carl in all matters requiring ability, even excelling in sports—she had inherited his broad shoulders and coordination and also his spirit of competitiveness. She loved a good match. And like Carl, she was not only musical but also clever. She skipped the first grade, and then the fourth, she was already in the upper grade of school, with two more to go before her *Abitur* when she was fourteen; it was 1935. The bill had come. I had to pay the price for my stubbornness and folly.

❧

WHEN I LOOK BACK at those childhood years of Renate's life, I see no hint at all of my granddaughter, Irene. Of course one reflects upon the future. Someday soon, Carl would become a professor somewhere in the Rhineland, preferably Koblenz, but I wouldn't mind Cologne either, and we would move there. I always knew, just knew, that someday I would have a good relationship with my brother Otto, he would forgive me for marrying Carl, see my point, even apologize to me. His children would be close cousins to Renate. They would go to university together, attend balls, marry one another's friends. My daughter would marry a good Catholic, perhaps a doctor, or a lawyer like Otto, and have several children. They would live nearby. I would have a granddaughter named, if I had my way, and I would have my way, Elisabeth, after me. And my granddaughter would take after me, with small, dainty features. I knew too that I would not grow to be terribly old, perhaps just under fifty. I gave myself until 1945. One can sense one's fate, and mine was a grave illness at a relatively young age, leaving my husband and daughter and grandchildren to grieve together for many decades. Otto would grieve too.

Otto was enjoying the fruits of his good character in Koblenz. He was a prosecutor. I sometimes even read his name in the newspaper. He was fabulous at his profession, which required a rock-solid certainty about what was right and wrong. My older sister Maria had become a nun and gone to South America to live in a convent dedicated to saving the souls of the Indios. She had outdone me on the adventure scale—so it seemed then. Little Heinrich was still the family problem, he had slithered down into the working class, as an electrician in a small company. He and Otto both had wives, and children that I hardly knew, because they never visited us. Well, we lived too far away. No one in his right mind voluntarily visited Upper Silesia. Only my mother, now a widow, came. My father's final illness had been a strain, he was weak and had given in to his pain, he had moaned loudly and grown childishly demanding. She had managed him like an infant, and when he was finally no more she wore her black clothing regally but her gait was noticeably lighter and her gaze became clear and steady again. She had learned to treasure Carl, and she got busy teaching Renate how to be imposing.

Alas, her lessons were wasted on my child. In her social style Renate took after the Rother women, who only entered a room if they were carrying something to feed those within. Their modesty was a chronic illness. Renate had a particular dire form of this, because it was all surface, which covered up impetuousness and rebelliousness and also superiority of the worst sort. But when she was thirteen, none of this was obvious to others. My girlfriend Helga Weltecke once said about Renate, "That daughter of yours is such a lucky girl. Carl and you are responsible for her accomplishments. Your genes and your upbringing are just exemplary."

"Helga, you have four lucky boys. Just exactly what I wanted to have. Blond boys," I sighed. And then we fell into each other's arms and, having flattered the other, we laughed until the buttons on our skirts popped and Liesel had to be called to sew them back on. Helga was not as pretty as I was, she was very pale, with one deep wrinkle in her forehead running parallel to the ground. Beneath it twinkled small, mirthful eyes and a pretty nose, but her blond curls had melted away under the onslaught of multiple pregnancies, until they were no more than mournful wisps she hid with little hats. Her body was as bony as a fish. But it was not my concern. I was delighted to have her in Leobschütz. After all, she was urbane, she came from a good family, her father worked for Siemens in Berlin, she had grown up in Lichterfelde, she felt comfortable only in large-enough houses with interesting gardens and hurrying servants, she loved dogs as I did, and she had studied nursing, married a doctor, and of course she was Catholic. She hated sex even more than I did, because she had to endure it for much longer, years and years. I could always see the torment in her posture the day after she had given herself to her husband, the way she placed her feet carefully, along a circumference of disgust. He was a small man, with round shoulders and very smooth cheeks, but she said he enjoyed drawing out the procedure. Once, she admitted to me that he had a proclivity for taking the strangest positions, forcing her to sit on his creature, for instance, while he was lying comfortably on his back, and rocking her back and forth there, as if she were a child on a hobbyhorse. After she told me this, I could not look at him for several weeks of Sunday lunches. He was a competent surgeon, but he suddenly appalled me. But then, mercifully, I forgot about it. After all, what she allowed him to do with her body was none of my business even if she was my dearest friend.

I have tried to portray our family life, in all its colors. There were few dark spots. In retrospect, and this is something I am in a position to judge, it was as close to paradise as one can get.

❧

IT WAS HELGA who broke the news to me. "They have passed a law," she said. She had dropped over one autumn afternoon.

Liesel overheard and began her dance of anger, her feet pounding the floor. She became so loud that I had to excuse myself, go into the kitchen, and say, "Liesel, you will please behave yourself."

"Good heavens," I said, returning to the living room. "I don't know what she is so worked up about. She tyrannizes me, I tell you. So. What law?"

It turned out that the government had passed a law forbidding my marriage to Carl.

It was too late, of course. What was done was done. They weren't going to undo marriages. But they were going to make life difficult for Carl. He was, regardless of his faith, not noble of race. All I had to do was look around into the forty or so related faces in town, and know that.

And Helga said, "You should divorce him."

👑

BUT OF COURSE divorce was out of the question. Divorce is forbidden by the Church anyway. Besides, my dear husband! With the brooding black-eyed gaze that could easily fluster me, and the big nose! Through his nostrils, I tried to view his brain, to figure out what he was thinking. I never could. He was a mystery to me always. As was his cleanliness. He had no body smell at all, just a slight waft of eau de cologne. At the clinic he smelled of disinfectant, of course. Even when we were intimate, I could smell only myself, a stench that didn't trouble him, or he didn't complain in order to spare my feelings. We did not discuss politics at all. We waited for this tempest to blow over. Jews were just not popular at the moment. They never had been socially. And now one was trying to formalize that. It was inevitable.

A few weeks later, in October, my mother-in-law burst into our house just before lunch, panting with exhaustion or agitation. First things first, I had an additional place set for her at the table. She protested that she could not possibly eat, so I placed her on my settee. It was covered with yellow leaves on a beige and dark brown background; I couldn't help noticing how with her black dress she fitted into the pattern. She fussed briefly with her white bun while trying to catch her breath. When Renate appeared in the doorway, the old woman stared at her, and burst into tears. Carl knelt down at her side, like a small boy, and held on to her knees. His hands were trembling. I told Renate nicely to go to her room.

It turned out that city officials had arrested all the men in the family over sixteen, and taken them away. No one knew where. Rumors abounded. She wished Carl would find out. He should call up and ask. He had protection, he was head of the clinic. Carl said nothing. He remained on his knees next to her and I noticed his hands still trembling. It shocked me. I collected myself. I told them a remedy could be found. After all, my brother Otto was a high-ranking Party member now. And my other brother, little Heinrich, always a loser, was now a winner. He had joined the Party, where no one cared about his lack of an academic pedigree, and he soon had a desk job with the SS. My two brothers would never tolerate anyone messing for long with Carl.

I was not interested in politics. I didn't listen to the radio. I didn't like our Uncle Adolf. I didn't want to hear his voice. When we turned on the radio and he was giving a speech, I liked to say, "There he goes again, screeching like a middle-aged woman going through the changes!" Just a day earlier, I had said this while Liesel was serving coffee, and she had stopped pouring and said, "Frau Doktor Rother does not screech like that," her way of reminding me that I was a middle-aged lady myself. I slapped her verbally, hard and quick. "Liesel, your opinion about me is of no interest." Now all the light, silly slights of the past years melted together into a ton of certainty: I was being humiliated in the worst possible fashion; the government was embarrassing my husband. My background rose to the occasion. I said, "Excuse me, Carl, this is a very simple matter for *me* to take care of. You stay here and rest with our mother. And keep Renate *inside*. No visits today. I am going out. If necessary, I will ring Otto or Heinrich."

And with Liesel's assistance, for the maid gave me to understand that I was doing just exactly the right thing and had already fetched my coat and hat and scarf and was waiting for me in the foyer, I hurried out into the cold afternoon. I did not even have time to reprimand her for rising above her station and implying to me her opinion.

MY IMPOSSIBLE GRANDDAUGHTER could never understand any of this. It is beyond someone who has been so spoiled by circumstance—a mother who idolized her, a father everyone looked up to in society even though he was Jewish and also had the worst manners, a childhood that was marred by the mistakes Renate made. First my daughter had repeated my own, marrying a Jew, and then she had added more mistakes, most glaring of all marrying a second Jew, and then, as if that wasn't enough, she married a third Jew. But more, much more, about this later.

Where was I? My appearance. I was a pretty woman nearing the end of my forties. I dressed well, I was well kempt, I had that thick blond hair, blue eyes, and above all, I had class. I walked into the police station in Leobschütz and the policeman on duty sat up, and one hand slipped down to check furtively the status of his trouser buttons. Closed. "Yes, *Gnädige Frau?*"

A squeaky-clean police station. A desk. An officer on duty. The flag behind his desk, the photograph of the Führer. "Sir, I am a German woman. I come from a good family. My brother Otto Gierlich is one of the chief prosecutors of the Rhineland and a member of the NSDAP. I would like to know what you have done with my husband's relatives. The Rothers. They have been arrested. They have done nothing wrong. Speak up, sir. I want an answer At Once." I did not raise my own voice. I allowed it to slide into him unflinching as a steel blade.

The blood burst into his face.

"I have not the slightest idea of what you're talking about, dear lady."

"Then you will have to open a police investigation at once. My family has been kidnapped. Picked up at their houses this morning at 6:00 a.m., forced to march to the train station, and packed into a waiting train. Find out where they are Now."

He marched out of the room.

I took a seat. I did not like to stand for long, it is bad for the varicose veins. And I cannot deny that I was upset and worried. I kept thinking of poor Uncle Simon, with his heart condition, his strapping boys, all in yarmulkes. And Else's husband, Uncle Leon, who was supposed to cut Renate's hair again soon, and his wealth of five sons. And Uncle Jacob, the young thief, finally put in his place.

I heard agitated male voices in a back room, and then footsteps. An SS man. Like one of my brothers. He looked down at me, the tidy garden of medals on his uniform seemed to grow in the lamplight. I arose.

"Dear lady," said the high-ranking gentleman. "Your relatives—"

"They are not my relatives by blood," I interrupted.

"I presume you are the wife of Dr. Carl Rother," continued the official, ignoring my remark. "He was not invited on this excursion, because he took out my wife's ovaries last year, a regrettable necessity, and he did it well. He is much in demand. An excellent surgeon."

"Thank you," I said automatically. Then I caught myself. "Herr Heussler, are you not a Catholic yourself? I know you are not from here, but I have seen you at mass."

He ignored my question. "The town of Leobschütz is in urgent need of having the quarry cleaned out. And some of your other relatives were deemed eminently suitable for such a little task. They are in the able hands of the town garbage unit, under the management of Obersturmführer Wolf. They will be returned to their families as soon as they have finished. Possibly tonight. Otherwise, tomorrow."

"I want to lodge a protest against this form of treatment."

"Perhaps you will wait until their return. I understand that they all went willingly because they were being well paid. Money has a lot of attraction to these people."

❦

IRENE WOULD GROW UP in New York, in a neighborhood of last resort. No one chose to live there, they ended up there. There were no Germans. But Renate found it acceptable. Why did she have to do this to her children? She could have lived with them in spotless Yorkville, where they received their religious training. The Sisters of the Immaculate Conception could not put a dent on Irene's soul, not when she was commuting between their calm sensible world of Belief and that squalid uptown of Jews and mixed-up dark people. Renate promised again and again to move the family downtown. But this was Renate's method, to be as agreeable as Carl's mother Granny Rother was, to say yes, yes, of course, you are So Right. And then do the opposite. Any criticism was met by a big fake smile, or a present—she was always giving presents—and an acknowledgment that she was making a huge mistake, thank you for pointing it out, it would be rectified immediately. But it wasn't. She did what she liked. I found out that after Irene's two-hour blessed sojourn among the nuns, Renate always took her to a Jewish butcher to buy what she referred to as "an antidote"—kosher hot dogs. On their way home, they devoured these raw. As an antidote to what? But more about this later.

Carl's relatives were returned to us after three days. They had had their sidelocks and heads shaved, they had been forced to work in the bitter cold without their overcoats, and they were bruised and scratched from this job. Uncle Simon's Hebrew Bible, which he had stupidly secreted in his trousers, had been spotted, a lump in his pants. The entire company had to stand in a circle and watch while the Holy Book was torn apart, page by page, until it was no more. The worst part: they were made to use a big ditch for their needs. They had to squat in public, in the cold. They were not permitted to wash. They didn't have a change of underwear.

On their return, they did not come to our house for medical treatment, as they ought to have. They were too ashamed because of their bald heads and bare cheeks. The smell was probably appalling. Their women came and told us, weeping, what had happened. I was outraged that they didn't have the strength to get their husbands to wash up and then accompany them the few blocks to our house. What kind of woman cannot move her husband? I took Carl aside that evening and said, "We are leaving Germany. We can't stay. They are not going to make you squat in a public latrine. And you know what? It won't end there. There's worse to come."

He was annoyed. He said, "Be quiet. You are hysterical and not very bright. Don't speak to me about this again. Ever."

I continued anyway, although his judgment about my intelligence had cut me to the quick. "No, Carl. We are leaving. Renate shall not grow up like this."

"It is out of the question. Do not bring it up again."

All evening, Renate kept up a lively monologue about school, grinning to prod us into smiles, and refused to notice that her parents were no longer speaking to each other. Carl's form of prolonged silent rebuke weakened my heart, I began suffering pulmonary congestion, and so after the second day of this, death was looming; I stayed in bed. He joined me there at night, but turned his back to me. I couldn't sleep then, not in the dark, but I dozed all day and refused all meals. Liesel brought me almond butter cookies, and I ate them in bed. On day three of this treatment, I confided in her that 1935 was my final year. She approached Dr. Rother after lunch with the news that his wife was not well. He came up to the bedroom and stared at me lying in bed. I had arranged myself flat on the bed, with my eyes closed and the crucifix between my hands on the cover. I could feel his eyes checking me out. He was a good diagnostician. Suddenly he bent down, took my hand, and kissed it. He said, "Come on, time to get up." And I did. You can imagine how relieved I was that he had forgiven me for trying to bully him.

Carl was allowed to continue his work. He was referred to as an *Ehrenarier*, an honorary Aryan, and he wore a swastika around his upper arm when he operated. He did not complain. I no longer assisted him. My spirits were low. I had no power over him. My best friend Helga no longer visited me, and so, I no longer visited her. No longer, no longer. We saw each other at Sunday mass, my mouth twisted into the smile position, and hers followed suit. I was angry at her. I could not squelch it, no matter how hard I tried. After all, her suggestion was sensible. I was angry at Carl too. So she was doubly right.

Nor did I have any contact with my brothers. They ignored me in my predicament. I also avoided Carl's family because they too angered me. If it hadn't been for them, I wouldn't have been in this mess.

Oh my Father, forgive me, I have been angry.

Why, my child?

Father, just absolve me of my sins and be done with it.

Carl sailed along ignoring all. He attended a conference in Berlin and reported that his friend, a half-Jewish physician, another honorary Aryan, gave a speech at the Medical Congress urging sterilization for mentally ill and handicapped patients. Carl did not feel good about this. He no longer played the piano or took the dogs for a vigorous walk to the square, where he was no longer greeted in the same deferential way; he no longer attended to his stamp collection. After returning from the hospital, he sat down in his den, his body so heavy that the chair creaked through two ceilings to the laundry room, where Liesel heard it and came up a flight of stairs to where I sat, eating cookies in my sitting room. She knocked, entered, looked at me impassively until soon enough the chair creaked again, then she shook her head and left.

But he was busy. He was penning letters to the archbishops and cardinals of the land. He wrote as Dr. Carl Rother, a devout Roman Catholic, urging their intervention against the practice of sterilization. It was clearly against the laws of the Church. Something must be done immediately. The authorities would find out about his letters, of course. They would be annoyed. But I counted on my brother Otto to protect us.

In the meantime, the Welteckes, once so proud of our company, were now openly ashamed of it. I always needed a best friend, and I turned to Carl's sister Else. Her dark hair was turning white, although she was only thirty-five, even her eyebrows were white. She wanted to acquire a white wig to match it, but I forbade that. I confessed to her that I dyed my hair. We talked about cooking and child rearing. We talked about how to clean rugs and walls. I kept my Rhineland personality under wraps, did not strive for a good laugh, or ever dare make fun of others. It was a bit dull. But I didn't have anyone else to talk to. Was I supposed to start chatting with Liesel? One day I told Else about Jesus, and she listened closely and asked me all sorts of questions. I saw that she had talent, that she could be a Believer. At last, we had a topic of conversation that interested us both. I became greatly attached to her. She came to see me every afternoon. Liesel sometimes entered the room with fresh tea, and without asking my permission, she stayed and listened in on our conversations about Jesus and the Holy Mother, and how they could save Else's soul, and about the strength and riches of the Catholic Church.

The Church took its time responding to Carl's appeals. That is, in answer to all his letters, he received just one reply. Cardinal Bertram of Breslau wrote back, the letter signed in his absence by a secretary, saying it was the Church's reluctant opinion that it could not meddle in state affairs. I waited for him to discuss it with me. "To whom exactly do I owe obedience?" Carl burst out one night in bed, in the dark. "To my conscience or to the Church, or to the state?" I realized I did not know. He lay next to me on his back, wide awake, waiting for my answer. Finally, I turned to him and stroked his hair gently. I kept it up, my hands aching, until he fell asleep. Carl went to the clinic in the morning and sterilized another patient. His conscience flogged him. The pain of this took away any fear another man would have felt—he returned in the afternoon and wrote more letters. He knew that they were surely being filed away in a Gestapo office. No more replies came. He obeyed the state. The patients did not know what was happening to them, and if a patient asked, "What is wrong with me, why do I require an operation?" he looked him in the eyes and murmured, "It is a short operation," and no more, because he was not willing to lie.

Our daughter was oblivious. She was having a good time. She had taken a turn for the pretty, her face was rounder now, and it made the hook in her nose less noticeable. Her eyes were also a distraction, not only because they were very large and dark, but because they had an arresting expression. No one would have cast her as the Virgin Mary now, her eyes had a dangerous glint that made it hard to study the rest of her face. Her hair was another distinction, being very thick and auburn. I think that was one of the reasons she had so many friends, but of course she also excelled at school. I found her happy attitude pleasing, and aggravating. On the one hand, I was glad that she did not suffer from her genes; on the other, I would have liked a little commiseration from her. I should add that at this time, however, she was the toast of the town. She had been chosen to play with the town orchestra on New Year's Day, Chopin's piano concerto. She practiced diligently, without ever seeming to strain herself. I don't want to flatter her inordinately, but she was always energetic. Her school friends were proud of the way she played, they sought her company, but I noticed that she preferred the company of her Rother cousins. As she had no siblings, they filled a need, and she was always visiting them. I decided it would be wise to send her away.

I wrote to my brother Heinrich and asked him whether Renate could live with him for a school semester and attend a good Catholic school in Koblenz. He wrote back, a reluctant no. He had a position he could not afford to jeopardize with a racially impure girl in his house. I understood. No use asking Otto. He had just made a name for himself as prosecutor in the Rhineland. He had single-handedly locked up an entire order of monks that ran a hospice for the handicapped. He had proved that they were sexually molesting their charges. I considered boarding schools. I feared Renate would be extremely sad to be away from us, and did not tell her of my research. And I guessed we were heading for the saddest Christmas of my memory.

Liesel left our household. I had fired her. I had fired her because I had to, she wouldn't have left otherwise, she was so stubborn. Aryans were not allowed to work for Jews. I had waited until after dinner the night the law went into effect and I called her to us, into the sitting room. She came in her apron, her hands wet with dishwater. She said, "What may I do for you?" And I pressed an envelope into her wet hand and said, "Liesel, you may pack and leave. You are holding next month's salary in advance."

She sighed but her face remained impassive. Her hands said more. They fell to her sides, and soapy water dripped on my carpet. Suddenly she said very loudly, "I know about the law."

Then she turned around and hee-hawed, "Law!" It took her only a few minutes to pack her modest possessions, and soon, without saying goodbye, she was gone. She had left behind the envelope with her salary, as well as her blue apron, hanging on its nail in the kitchen. I assumed she had gone home to her parents. But someone whispered to me at the market that she was now working as the maid and cook for an elderly Catholic priest in a nearby town. I was extremely jealous. I imagined that Father Hanssler was higher in her opinion than I was. A man of the cloth. I wrote her an unkind letter wishing her well in her new position with a Catholic of such unquestionable faith. She did not reply. She was not good at writing.

On Christmas morning, she knocked on our door. "I have a day off," she said, and stepped inside resolutely. It was her second lie of

the day. Petit Mal Lie. A few hours earlier, she had told her beloved
Father Hanssler that her mother was ill. Renate leaped into her
arms as if she were a toddler, wrapping her legs around Liesel's
waist. She was much taller than Liesel by now, and much heavier.
In truth, Renate had a womanly bosom that I tried not to notice. If
I noticed, that meant others probably did too. It was big and
bouncy, as if stuffed with springs. Anyway, jumping into Liesel's
arms when you are top-heavy is asking for an accident. Liesel staggered, held her briefly before dislodging her and grumbling, "Renate! Don't be so wild!" And then she addressed the happy
assembled: "Excuse me, ladies and gentlemen." She was en route to
the kitchen; she donned her apron, looked about, disapproved. Her
order had been disturbed by a Polish maid who had replaced her.
The *Polka* had shamelessly not shown up for work on Christmas
and I had fallen asleep the night before with my nose in a cookbook, my hands clenched in a prayer for divine help preparing dinner myself.

A few hours later, I followed the siren smells from my settee to
their source, but Liesel blocked my way and cried, "Out of my
kitchen!" I withdrew without protest. She cooked our traditional
dinner: carp, and red beets. Renate was permitted to stay in the
kitchen and help her. The girl was in annoyingly high spirits.

She was fifteen, and the very next day, Christmas Day, she was
going to play her first public concert. She ridiculed my admiration
and concern. She said, "Leobschütz is not Berlin, you know. What
happens here means nothing." For two weeks, she had spent her
afternoons practicing with the town orchestra. I had walked her
there once, but became so nervous on her account that I felt I
might not survive it. "My heart is not strong enough," I warned her.
She replied, "So stay home." Now, the evening before the concert,
I could think of nothing else. She acted as if nothing special was in
store. Before sitting down to our Christmas Eve dinner, she played
carols, and even Liesel sang along in a wobbly soprano. Taking Re-

nate's whispered advice, I invited Liesel to dine with us, but this giddy suggestion injured the festive mood because Carl was taken aback. He stared at his plate to indicate his displeasure. Luckily for me, Liesel refused, never forgetting, as I had, her place. She ate by herself in the kitchen. Renate was too cheerful to sulk. Her energy was already a raging river by then. That night she refused to go to bed early. Much later, she was still scampering around the house playing with the dogs. Carl was working on his stamp collection for the first time in months; he dreamed of completing the German colonies. Renate's joyous footsteps disturbed him. His massive fist pounded the table in the *Herrenzimmer*. He shouted, "A house is not a lawn!" She was afraid of him, and retired to her room.

Carl had drunk a fair amount of red wine that night and insisted on having me. I allowed it. I don't wish to complain. At least he stayed where he was supposed to, not like Helga's horrible husband. I have to say, in the ensuing months I even on occasion encouraged him in this practice because it clearly took his mind off his situation. I liked to see him smile afterward. He always thanked me. That night, he did not thank me, because he fell asleep instantly. I got up in the darkness and washed myself for a long time. We had a big day ahead of us. I hoped our daughter would play to the best of her ability, and not make fools of us. And that was Christmas Eve, 1935.

NO ONE ENJOYED CHRISTMAS more than Carl. The birth of our Savior, that really meant something to him, because his love for Him was new, and all the more intense for it. I confess to the sin of envy—I was envious of Maria because she had the good fortune to have a virgin birth. Now I know the truth, and can assuage any doubts—yes, virgin birth. It is really true. Which means that coming through, baby Jesus deflowered his mother. I often mulled this technicality, but I never discussed it with Carl, because I didn't want to dampen his pleasure in his Belief.

Christmas morning was bright and clear. I recall waking up to the sound of Renate practicing one last time. The concert was at 11:00 a.m. We were going to go to mass first. Liesel was already up and cooking, having judged that Renate must eat a good breakfast instead of fasting, because the concert was more important than Communion. Liesel was so cocksure of this dubious decision that I did not question it. She said she was not coming to the concert, she didn't understand anything about music and it was a waste of a good ticket. As always she would come with us to church, but then come straight home again afterward. We sat one pew behind the Welteckes at mass and I hazarded to lean forward and ask Helga whether they were attending Renate's recital. Briefly, she turned just her head around to me, her torso facing ahead, smiled, and said, of course. I have that smile in my memory like a snapshot.

Later, much later, both Carl and Renate always refused to let me mention the following incident. If I brought it up somehow, they would both raise their voices, calling me unbearably silly to fuss about a triviality, it had meant nothing. But I will not let them prevent me now from recounting what happened.

Renate was in merry spirits after mass as we directly hurried to the town hall, while I was ill with worry. The long walk there further reduced my patience. You need patience to breathe properly. I began to pant. Now the Silesian air was so bitter cold, I feared that I was going to catch my death inhaling such a lot of it. I told Carl, "I will be dead by New Year's Eve, you'll see." Nobody responded to this so I added, "The year 1936 is my death year. I have the intuition." Still, they ignored me. I grew so agitated at their hardheartedness that I slipped on some ice. A painful fall ensued. I knocked my jaw, and my teeth ached. Carl and Renate had to pick me up. Renate began laughing at me. "Mama," she said, "when I

look down at you like this you look like a pug dog, a Mops, to me."
She danced ahead, giggling. "She fell and broke her chops, our
Mops!" She was already out of sight. When we finally reached the
town square, she was standing in front of the hall.

The hall was closed. The concert had been canceled. She did
have a strange look on her face. I can reconstruct it.

Her eyes were squinting. Her mouth was pursed in a stiff smile.
A smile. I thought that her lips looked almost negroid, in that position, and nearly said so. Her cheeks were bright red, either from
the cold or because she was blushing. She stood staring at the program affixed to the concert hall. Someone had crossed out the
program and written in big black ink, "*Jüdin.*" Jewess.

So we all turned around without saying a single word, Renate
skipping—skipping merrily!—ahead of us, all the way home, where
Liesel received us in a rage. She had overheard the Welteckes
speaking about the cancellation on their way out of church. I asked
her to keep her thoughts to herself, they were of no interest and
most certainly of no consequence. I could hear her fuming in the
kitchen about the Nazis. The *z* in Nazi produced a major blockage
in her mouth, it took her several tries to get beyond the first syllable. Then she demanded that Renate play the recital for her, she
had wanted to hear it. She brought in her kitchen stepladder, set it
down in a corner, removed her apron, and listened to the entire
piece with us. Piano concertos don't sound as good without other
instruments, I find, but she played it with verve, loudly singing
the orchestra part. Afterward, we clapped, although it is a stupid
way of bestowing approval. She bowed deeply and then she said, "I
am so glad it was canceled. You didn't even notice all my mistakes,
did you?"

Carl said, "I did. Glaring mistakes. It's a good thing you didn't
play in public, you're right." I was glad he said so. We didn't want
all that applause going to her head.

Renate's mouth suddenly twisted, and she looked as if she might break into tears. Immediately, Liesel stood up from her kitchen stool in the corner and said very loudly, "Renate, you played very well, as well as anyone has ever played this . . . this song . . . this piece . . ." Carl and I stared and prepared our rebuttals. And Liesel trumpeted, "The Christ child loves you." She was sly. That shut us up.

"Carl," I started up again that night, in bed. "They won't let your daughter live a normal life, you know. We must pack and leave."

Carl was waiting. "'Normal' is not playing concerts," he snarled. "I made a mistake permitting it in the first place. What's a normal life in your eyes, I wonder? She should live an orderly life, and then she will not be disappointed by something like this. Enough said. We need an ordered life. No more concerts." I didn't like it when he committed the sin of anger, and I dropped the subject. I would not raise it again for a long time.

CARL WAS RIGHT, of course. Order is something to hold on to, order is like a life vest for a drowning person. My granddaughter, Irene, was raised without it. The only order provided was by the maids we arranged. How can you expect a maid to stay in a household where there is not even a semblance of order? Worse, where they find the arrangement bizarre, distasteful. No one is ever home, the mother, Renate—"What kind of mother!" they cry—cuts up dead people for a living and the father, Dische, is a crazy genius, horrible. Conducting experiments on himself to prove that there were elements in food one needed, he had eliminated certain foods systematically from his diet, taking notes, destroying his gut. The maids knew what counted, namely that he had a problem with his digestion and that he was always on the toilet; the genius is on the toilet. And

when he was off the toilet, he twiddled a plastic spoon while con-
juring up chemical reactions, and didn't notice human responses of
any kind. Dische didn't deserve to be called father, he spent his afternoons twiddling his plastic spoons, which had to have a certain
weight and cheap consistency or his thumbs would not twiddle
right, and then he couldn't think, and thinking was his sport, so he
twiddled all day, pacing the apartment or visiting the toilet, but
then at night—the nights—they were worse, because the mother/
wife slept on the living room couch, while her husband slept (his
thumbs finally at rest) in the *dining* room! The maid, angel of order,
had her own room. The grandmother, that's me, she saw to it that
this room was furnished, it was a real room. Dische kept his clothing in the hall closet. His bed stood next to the dining room table.
The maid shuddered and made it up before she did another thing in
the mornings. Renate put her own linen away, the maid did not
have to deal with it. Her couch was not even a pullout sofa, but a
small, hard, cheap sofa without cushions. She came home late at
night, put a sheet down, went to sleep. The household had no
knickknacks, because no one had any sense for them. The angels of
order all deserted as soon as they could find a better job.

Renate and Dische had moved to Washington Heights, where
no one else in their right mind wanted to live so it was affordable,
when she was bursting with child. She didn't prepare in any way for
the newcomer. He just popped in on her. Naming him Little Carl
after his grandfather did not alter the fact that he was pure Dische.
As much as I had longed for a male grandson, I was deeply disappointed. He was ugly, thin and dark, just like his father. I said, "Renate, he looks like a monkey!" Renate hired a pretty gorilla to look
after him, a Colored woman named Hazel, and went right back to
work. She didn't consider that a Negro cannot speak German, and
could not communicate with this child. Nor that a woman so pretty
is bound to be noticed by men. Hazel loved Little Carl, though. I
have to credit her with that. And the boy loved her. He had Re-

nate's huge brown eyes. He had so little else to go with it, his face was just eyes. One day, though, I heard that Hazel was so pretty that she was modeling her breasts for a girlie magazine and I came right over and fired her.

That was in 1950. Liesel came to the rescue. She did have a way of doing that. But I have jumped way ahead.

Without Liesel, I would not have survived the year 1936. God was testing me severely. On New Year's Day, Liesel dropped by again briefly and I invited her into the salon to drink a cup of tea with me. It was an honor, but she refused it. She stood in the hallway without surrendering her coat, and tried to tell me something. "Renate—" she said. Her stutter lamed her. Finally she managed the words "Renate must leave." And then she turned around and left, back to Father Hanssler. I don't like to admit it, but Liesel's intrusion gave me the strength to act. Soon afterward, I wrote some letters, made some telephone calls, and then I packed Renate's bag. She and I said goodbye to her father and boarded a train to Munich. We told no one where we were going. It was one of the happiest, saddest journeys of my life. Renate and I had a lovely first-class compartment, and excellent meals, and each kilometer farther from Upper Silesia seemed a plus, not a minus, a kilometer between the ugly times in Leobschütz and the cheerful times ahead in Bavaria. A convent school there, not yet informed of her background, had agreed to take her as a live-in pupil.

When we arrived, I took the mother superior aside, and I told her the ins and outs of our little predicament. I was very upper class with her, I said Mother, a Catholic is a Catholic and therefore you will have no objections. She said of course, a Catholic was a Catholic, and Renate was most welcome. She handed me an application for the Hitler Youth. Renate, she said, could fill that out. I glanced at it. She had to describe the racial background of her family, going back three generations. She would have to lie. "She must not *lie*, Mother," I said. Liesel may lie, she is just the maid, but my daughter may not. "She will simply keep it on her desk, as if she intends to fill it out," decided the mother superior.

Several months later, Renate repaid her for her kindness by passing around obscene drawings in class. The drawings were traveling from hand to hand when an alert nun spotted the hilarity that was out of place in Latin class, and pounced on them. They depicted men at the city swimming pool. She had lavished attention on their hairy legs and that silly bulge in their bathing trunks.

I had to take the train back to Munich, had to pretend not to be incredibly glad to see my daughter after such an interminable time. I was expected to grovel. I did not. I told the mother superior that I appreciated her help with Renate, and, moreover, our God appreciated it. But the child obviously had a talent for drawing, and this talent should be furthered, not discouraged. I promised a handsome donation to the convent. Instead of further chastisement, Renate was ordered to submit her artwork to the university, applying for special permission to enroll in a painting class in the autumn. Then I took Renate aside and told her that I had never been more ashamed of her in my life. I laid it on so thick that she began to cry, and said she hated me. I said, "That's fine." Then she flung her hands around my neck and kissed me, and said, "Oh, Mops, it's not true."

With triumph and a heavy heart, I returned to Leobschütz, to the besieged family Rother and the Silesian gloom. I felt Renate was in the safest hands possible. Little did I know.

THE WOMEN IN OUR FAMILY were always strong, the men weak. My father did what my mother told him, for the most part. When I misbehaved, she told him to beat me. He took me by the scruff of the neck, hauled me into his study, snarled at me that now he was going to teach me a lesson I would barely survive. He undid his belt with such a flourish that the children, pressing their ears against the door, could hear the buckle snapping open, and then he cried, "One!" and lashed the sofa, "Two!" and lashed the sofa. I screamed as the belt crashed into the cushion, and wailed, "I'll be good, but please stop!" Twice usually sufficed. Then he dried my eyes, snapped, "There, there, stop carrying on. I don't like to beat you, you dreadful child," and flung me back out of the room. He stayed behind, sighing loudly for a while, and frequently pouring himself a sherry. He was weak.

My husband was weak too. He never raised his hand against Renate or me. Instead, he sulked. The day grew dark. No affection or cheer could penetrate his despondency. He would not raise his hand, and therefore, he suffered. Weak.

But the weakest man I ever knew was Dische, my first son-in-law. After firmly swearing to thrash his daughter, he needed ten minutes to coax his belt out of his trousers, giving Irene—his son never needed to be punished—ample time to hide in a closet or under a bed, and although he was an acclaimed genius, he did not have the imagination to find her hiding place. I have to credit Renate, she was no slouch in this respect. She took a stethoscope and whacked her misbehaving daughter on the behind with it. Irene had a fighting spirit, she screeched that this was against the Hippocratic oath. At school the next day she tattled to the nurse that she could not sit down, as her mother had beaten her. The headmistress called Renate at the morgue, interrupted her at an autopsy, and demanded that she answer for corporal punishment. I gave my daughter a talking-to. "Renate, can you imagine the impression this made on her teachers? A mother who sleeps on a couch and cuts up dead people and beats her daughter with a stethoscope?" A laugh began rumbling in my chest. Because I could not help myself: I found the picture amusing. So did she. We laughed. But what happened after that was not funny.

I will come to that.

RENATE, AT SIXTEEN and ever afterward, lacked certain built-in inhibitions meant to protect the female of the species from self-destruction. This became obvious at her safe house in Munich. Of course our greatest concern was that someone could figure out her background. Impure of race. Any child who found out would be so shocked as to broadcast the news. Only the headmistress knew the facts, and after she decided to keep Renate, she could not possibly reveal the truth without losing her position. For this reason, Renate had, in contrast to the other students, her own room. She could plausibly explain this as being due to her disorderliness. Within a minute of her putting on a dress, it turned into a bramble of wrinkles; within a day of her entering a room, it lay in shambles. Her hair escaped enclosures, her bed would not stay tucked in. She exuded a mess. Her mind, on the other hand, had a powerful force of order—she had to keep her lies straight. I counted on her natural deviousness to keep her out of trouble at school. I figured she would not spill any beans about herself. Having her own room simply cut down on the temptation for exchanging intimacies.

But it turned out that she was careless beyond my imagination, even though her life was perfectly ordered. She moved in a group of girls, good girls, who were like walls holding her in. Mass in the morning, school until noon, lunch, sports in the afternoon, mass in the evening, dinner, bed. On two afternoons a week, she rode the tram to the art school, where she attended a drawing course. The other students were older than she was. I thought it would be good for her, setting her good examples. And she never revealed anything about herself. So I thought.

Professor Schunter at the academy took a special interest in Renate. He called me on the telephone, at great expense, to tell me that in his opinion, Renate had the temperament and talent to become an artist. I was pleased to hear this, but told him that my daughter might prefer to become a musician. He was very surprised. She had not mentioned to him that she played the piano seriously. I told him that the most important thing was that she complete her studies, get a satisfactory high school degree, and that her art studies were first and foremost a way of disciplining her. He laughed and said, "Yes, yes, a well-rounded education is essential for brilliance in an artist."

"Carl," I said that evening over dinner, "if I am not mistaken, Professor Schunter feels that Renate is a brilliant artist."

He stopped chewing the meat our new Polish cook had prepared to torment us, and his gaze drifted to the window. A few weeks earlier, we had moved to Breslau. I had thought the 7 in the year 1937 would offer us some protection. It had not. There was no point in staying in Leobschütz after Carl had been fired from his job as head of the clinic, and two SS men taken up positions in front of our house, to turn away any Aryan patients. In a small town like Leobschütz, a Jew was noticed. In Breslau, the situation was clearly better. Carl still had a professorship and many patients from the university clinic. And we owned an entire building in a central street. It had ten apartments. When one of the apartments became vacant, we grabbed the opportunity and moved in. It was quite small, just three rooms, so I had most of the furniture in Leobschütz boxed up and placed in storage. It had been my hobby for a few months to invest our savings in real estate, and the building in Breslau had been a good investment. Carl refused to have anything to do with it, he said investments were for Jews, if I wanted to dirty my hands with that kind of business, he would not interfere. I had kept my composure and bought the house, and he had every reason to be glad when we had a pleasant place to go to. The front room became his office, where he saw patients. Of course the new cook was a dud. The news of Renate's success at art school in Munich, which I broadcast on purpose during our evening meal, would be a pleasant distraction. After I told him, I could see him trying to swallow a large wad of half-chewed pork.

I had lost a front tooth crown, made by Professor Waisberg, the finest dentist in Berlin, after biting on a slab of this Polish maid's roast. Her cooking could best be rated with industrial norms. If I dared to complain, Carl became furious—after all, it was because of him that we had lost Liesel. So our meals were never the object of conversation. When the tooth fell ringing down in two pieces into my plate, I did not blame it on the cook but on Professor Waisberg, for using me as a guinea pig for his newfangled procedure. Now, being Jewish, he was unemployed. He had a similarly unemployed colleague in Breslau who fitted me with another one. He was glad to have some business, and I went to see him only at night, at home, so no one could complain about him treating an Aryan patient. "Carl," I repeated, "Professor Schunter thinks Renate is very talented. He used the word brilliant."

We did not have a single artist in the family. So it was all rather unlikely. And Carl was not interested. "Look outside," he said.

It was already dark, at about 7:00 p.m. I could see the two gentlemen at the gate. SS men.

"When I go out, they will arrest me," he said.

At that very moment, having excused herself from dinner at the convent, Renate was meeting Professor Schunter at the gate of her school, slipping out into his waiting arms. He knew everything about her. He knew her inside and out, in his atelier, in his garden, and on this particular evening, in his car. She didn't mind it at all. She liked feeling indispensable. God spared me from learning about these goings-on when I was in a position to do something about it. Because Renate was highly abnormal in this regard; she had no scruples. Her lessons at the university in Munich ended late. But she was always home in time for mass, and Holy Communion. She took the host in her mouth, when her body was besmirched. Sin upon sin. Dare I say—depravity.

I have since had the pleasure of this professor's acquaintance. A man of simplicity, rather short and stout, but handsome, with the big hands that painters inevitably have. He laughed at himself for being a professor but he really *was* one, and he liked my daughter and that was that. He did what the animals did. She was only too happy to oblige him. He bossed her around in his kindly way, and she obeyed him. Draw this. Yes, of course, Professor. Use these colors. Fine. Take off your clothes, I want to paint you. Yes, yes, Professor. I want to—may I? Yes, Peter. He knew the truth about her, and it didn't trouble him an iota. He did not have a healthy sense of convention. After she disappeared, he was sad and worried, and tried hard to find her. Ten years later, when he had only five marks in his pocket, when the university lay in shambles and his patrons were dead or penniless, a one-legged soldier asked him for spare change, and he gave him his entire wealth, the five marks. He thought nothing of his own generosity and God did not reward him on earth for it. He would die shortly afterward, young, in an accident in a vegetable garden, where he was trying to steal some potatoes, and the owner defended them with his secreted pistol. He still lies there, where the killer buried him, now beneath a concrete slab holding the garbage bins serving an institution for unwed mothers.

"The SS are only making sure you don't receive any Aryan patients," I suggested to Carl. "I guess it has come to that here too. Finish your dinner, please. The red cabbage is quite good. She used a lot of apples. And no butter, according to your instructions."

"Those patients were here a while ago, they haven't been back."

The Gestapo newspaper, *Der Stürmer*, had run reports citing the names of Aryan patients who had sought treatment from Dr. Carl Israel Rother at the clinic. The report had worked, no one dared come. When a few showed up at our doorstep, *Der Stürmer* found out and revealed their names. That put an end to such visits too.

"Carl. Eat. I am going to finish everything on my plate. The dumplings are smooth and light. And no butter." He had ruled butter out of our household owing to my girth. "No butter! But delicious."

"The patients here are not the problem," said Carl. "It's the Jewish patient in Leobschütz."

Another reason we had moved to Breslau: a few weeks earlier in Leobschütz, Carl had been ordered to sterilize a young schizophrenic. Before an operation, the surgeon visits the patient. This one was young and strong, a farmer. He clutched Carl's hand and said, "Don't do it. I am not ill. I am Jewish. They say I have too many children. Six already. Don't do it. Remember what you are. You are one of Us."

Carl went ahead with the operation, just as usual. He opened up the abdomen and fiddled around inside, as if he were performing a sterilization. Then he closed the abdomen again. Helga Weltecke was assisting him. She glared at him over her mask, her blue eyes whipping him, but she didn't dare say anything during the operation, because she could have been reprimanded for creating a disturbance. But afterward, in the washup room, she hissed at him, "I saw what you did!"

Or what he didn't do.

She did her duty and told her husband, Dr. Weltecke, Carl's old best friend, who tattled on him. That same day, Dr. Rother lost his job as head of the clinic. And now they had finally come to arrest him. I lost my appetite for the red cabbage.

❦

CARL ALWAYS SAID, "One finishes the food on one's plate." My grandson was compliant. He ate whatever was put in front of him. Irene treated food dished out on her plate as an order, and she refused orders on principle, and would not eat. We tried to break her will. Her cold, uneaten dinner was placed on the floor in a corner. She was made to sit down with me, and not allowed to get up until she had eaten everything. By trial and error, we located a corner in the hallway without any nearby windows she could use for quick disposal, and no furniture within arm's range for food storage. I had found mashed potatoes behind the sofa cushions, carrots wedged between books. In the hallway, the carpeting ended conveniently a meter from the corner, so she could sit on the wooden floor, and if she cried a lot or vomited, this did not bother the carpet. She used to get stomach upsets before she even arrived at our house on Sundays, as a preventative measure. Then she would not have to eat. She was dumb and greedy and easy to trick. I always left candy in the kitchen, and if she stole one, then I knew her stomach was just fine. She knew the candy was a lure, but she couldn't resist it, even though it ruined her excuse not to eat. Because in our house, your plate was piled high with food, and if you didn't finish everything, that was an insult to Jesus and also to Carl, who paid for it all, dirtying his hands handling money, and naturally wanted his family to value it.

On that night in Breslau, I made Carl get up from the table with its view of the courtyard and the gentlemen waiting for him there. I tongue-lashed him into the bedroom. He sat down at the end of the bed, looking out the window. I drew the curtains and I fetched the large leather suitcase we had taken on many a Sudetenland ski trip, plastered with decals of ski resorts, and laid it on the bed, and said, "Tell me what you want to take." He just hung his head. Weak. I packed his best suit, two middling ones, several pairs of shoes, and underwear. I packed a hatbox with a Stetson hat. I went to get his winter coat from the communal attic where I had stored and locked it. When I came back, the Stetson was back in the closet, the hatbox contained something else, something much heavier. I did not have time to check or object. We were in a hurry. I closed the suit-case. We went out the maid's entrance, down the winding stairs, into the back courtyard. The other tenants were eating dinner. They were good tenants, they paid their rent, which took care of our expenses when Carl was no longer earning anything. What's so bad about investments, Carl? I knew about a back gate, behind some shrubs. We walked quickly but without rushing. We reached the train station, and he boarded the first train heading out, which went to Koblenz. I shoved the money I had saved secretly into his pocket. "I will call Otto to pick you up at the train station tomor-row morning."

I kissed him on the cheek and didn't wait for his train to leave. I rushed home. The two SS men were still standing in front of the door. They finally came upstairs and knocked at 2:00 a.m.

By then I had called my brother Otto and told him I was send-ing him a bottle of really first-class medicinal water from Carlsbad with our childhood friend, she would carry a sign with his name, he should pick it up at the train station. Otto understood me, he said, a present, just what he had always wanted. He was very ironic. He told me that he had just been named to be a judge on the supreme court, he didn't need medicinal water, he was healthy. Furthermore he was too tired to trudge to the station, and it was out of the ques-tion, I shouldn't send him presents. I called my mother. She went to the train station herself at seven in the morning and fetched Carl. Two hours later, the Gestapo knocked on her door. She re-fused to let them come in. No one could pull a class act like she could. She told them they were disturbing a lady, an Aryan lady. And then she added, "By the way, my son-in-law, Dr. Rother, is a gentleman, a good Catholic and a good German, and also an excel-lent physician. He is not here now, but I wish he were, because he could take care of my rheumatism instantly."

The Gestapo apologized.

Instead, they disturbed my evening peace. I was invited to an

interview by my local Gestapo, who did not believe Dr. Rother had
gone to a spa in Carlsbad. I lied, the clouds of sinning with fore-
thought gathered over my head, and I lied again. The clouds dis-
persed. God forgave me. He had no better suggestions. And they
wouldn't even offer me a chair. I had to stand all night. My ankles
billowed. A series of thugs plied me with questions. They ate cake
and drank coffee and smacked their lips and sighed with pleasure,
and didn't offer me any. They had no receptors to identify good
family. Working-class hoodlums. So I didn't bother trying to explain who I was. I was too proud to mention my brother Otto, about
to become a supreme court justice. Or too sensible; Otto might
have told them everything. Finally, at dawn, they all started yawn-
ing and I knew my trials were over. When they released me, I relieved myself in back of the building, squatting between two cars. I
am proud of how I directed my urine onto the foundation of that
building. It was just a drop, I know. But it signified a torrent. Then
I walked directly to the office of the Cardinal of Breslau.

I forced entry, past two assistants and three secretaries, to his private rooms. He hid. Weak. His aide came scurrying. I told the aide
that someone must come to the assistance of an upright Catholic. I
told this little man the whole story, reminding him about the letters
concerning the unquestionably immoral practice of sterilization,
which the important man, the cardinal, alas, had decided not to oppose. I left out the detail that Carl was born a Jew. I asked for a glass
of water. Someone brought coffee. Finally the cardinal himself appeared, dressed modestly in white, and shook my hand, and offered
to help. While I watched, a telex was sent to New York.

I went home. Two SS men in front of my door. They let me pass.
They scared our Polish cook away. I would have to make do myself.
But at least the Church machinery was working effectively and fast.
After a week, my mother called and said, "Uncle Bertie in Paris has
terrible gout, so I have just sent on your excellent medicinal water
from Carlsbad to him with Louise Mueller, my girlfriend, who is go-

ing there on vacation." So Carl had passed the German border to France. Within a week, he had boarded a vessel to the New World. His case was heavy with the stamp collection he had stuffed in there when I wasn't looking. In his hatbox, he had placed his spiked pickel helmet and the medals for heroism he had won in World War I.

❦

BRESLAU IS ONE OF my favorite cities. I have traveled a great deal, and have probably seen more of the world than I ever wanted to see. I have seen Weehawken in New Jersey, for instance, from every possible angle including the gutter, and Weehawken consisted almost entirely of gutter for a while, at least socially and also morally. I will get to that later. Breslau had lovely plazas, romantic canals, a good university, shops that catered to every need and whim; it was a perfect place for an intelligent woman on her own to enjoy life. I did a lot of shopping. For a while, I bought one pair of white leather gloves a week. When my granddaughter found them she looked at those gloves and said, "Christ!"—she liked to take the name of the Lord in vain—"They are all alike!" But I knew and treasured each glove as an individual, and I could decide which one to wear on the basis of a seam, or the color of the stitching.

I had lots of money to spend that year in Breslau. There seemed no point in keeping it.

And now that Carl was gone, I had Liesel back. She ditched her employer, Father Hanssler, without a backward glance, because minus Carl, we were a racially pure enough household according to the Law, and she could work for us again. She set up shop in our apartment. She cooked and cleaned, she sorted my white leather gloves and my hats, my pocketbooks, my scarves, and I had my settee, with the cookies on the Bunzlau plate. We had butter on the table.

My routine was slightly changed now. Every morning after breakfast, I took a brisk walk over to the Gestapo office and asked them if they wanted to see me today. This spared them the trouble of knocking on my door at unsuitable hours. Usually they just said no, no, that's fine. But every so often they said I had come just in time. Then I would allow them to usher me to a lawyer they kept for this purpose, who looked me deep in the eyes and handed me a sheet of paper to sign. My divorce papers. And I tried to look very normal, very average, I mean: dumb, not clever and upper class in this instance, because it would have been detrimental to my cause, and I just shook my head and said, "No, that's quite impossible. I'm a good Catholic. I don't believe in divorce."

From time to time, probably because he had lots of cases like mine, the Gestapo lawyer forgot how dumb I was and tried to argue with me. He was a little absentminded. He said, "You have a daughter, I see. She will have a much easier time of it if you are divorced."

To which I replied, "Oh no, Renate is a good Catholic too. She does not want me to go to hell!"

And generally they excused me after that, at least for a few weeks. And I went back to my good time in town. I didn't worry about Renate, because she was well hidden in Munich. I had seen to it that no one, not even my relatives, knew exactly where she was. Rother is a rather dull name, common to every religion. Even Upper Silesia had Protestant and Catholic Rothers. No one would ever have known but for that infernal clapping game.

This game was apparently infantile, but in fact, it was a sophisticated, surefire way of finding out the truth. The Gestapo should have thought of using it. The girls stood in a circle around one girl, and clapped their hands, and fired questions at her. One, two, clap, clap, and then a question. Easy questions, faster and faster, until they hit the victim with a hard embarrassing one, like Who do you like best? or Who do you hate most? or What man have you loved?

This simple procedure always elicited honest answers, or pained and stuttering and tearful lies. Thus it was a popular pastime. But in Renate's case, it was just a routine question that threw her into disrepute. To warm her up, they asked her the name of her dog, the number of her siblings, and finally, how many generations of her family were racially pure.

The girl asking this meant no harm, expected no surprise.

And in retrospect, I would have expected a better performance from my devious daughter. But in this instance, she was utterly shocked into confession and a kind of hysteria not typical for her at all, and she answered with a shout, "None!" no doubt anticipating a cascade of laughter and the continuation of the game. But instead, the clapping lost its rhythm, stopped, and uncertain looks were cast at the poor girl, with her big nose and dark eyes, who hastened to add, "I mean nine, dummies."

But they didn't believe her. They saw her in a different light. And her talents, and her cleverness, and her way of coming late to evening mass because she was hanging out at the university, began to add up.

One evening and a morning passed before she was returned to me by the mother superior, who had no idea of the extent of her sin and still gave her no hope of reprieve. I was delighted to have the girl back, although her mood was recalcitrant and critical and I felt obliged to remind her that I would soon be dead, my heart was weakening, and she would regret her tone of voice to me in 1938, my death year. She did not seem to miss her father an iota, or worry about him. She took everything calmly. It seems I had created a monster of courage. I have to admit that despite my excellent powers of observation, I did not see that she was no longer a girl, but a full-fledged woman. Of course I was not expecting that, as it was frankly inconceivable to me. Even now, when I have the ability to understand all, Renate's behavior as a schoolgirl still takes what is left of my breath away. Anyway, I enrolled her in a local Catholic school without offering any explanation to the nuns, and no questions were asked. Watched by me and Liesel, Renate toed the straight and narrow. Almost instantly, she came into a best friend there, an aristocratic, motherless girl named Eva.

Eva was a little strange. She had grown up on a huge estate in eastern Germany, had known Jews there who seemed to have cornered the market on cleverness. Eva admired cleverness. Therefore, she admired Jews. When she realized how clever Renate was, her heart hopped, and she decided she must be Jewish. She was disappointed to find out that it wasn't quite so bad, just half Jewish. Eva was highly intelligent herself, with a malicious wit that suited us, and a heart of gold. Her mother was dead, so she just attached herself to me. She did not much like what remained of her high-and-mighty family. She started spending as much time with us as she could. We had fun, we laughed about others and played cards at night. I adored her. Sometimes I told Renate that Eva was the daughter I had always wanted to have. She had a tiny nose, and blond hair. She suited me very well. And she was not devious, but discreet.

The year 1938 was in fact strangely happy. We were a household with four women, of which I was the boss, and Liesel was in control. The only male was Mister, the remaining dachshund, and he stayed in his place below. Liesel had more power now because she didn't share it with any other employees. She ruled the two young ladies with her iron fist, and kept the household running. She slept in the maid's room, a cubby at the end of the corridor, and used the guest toilet to take care of her business, and once a week she was allowed to use our bath, because in these new cramped quarters we only had one. This frankly didn't bother me; she kept herself extremely clean, and had never had a man. Her devotion to us was deep and even reckless.

One day, in Breslau, Hitler was having a parade that passed right beneath our house. The girls and I were enjoying coffee and cake after our afternoon naps. Liesel served us. We listened to the thunder of marching feet. By the swell of voices incanting the Führer's name, we followed Hitler's approach as he drove by in an open car. When he was just beneath us, Liesel suddenly put down her tray, rushed to the window, and leaned way over the sill to shriek downward, "Heil Moscow!"

I dragged her back in again. She was lying on the floor, and I stood over her. I must have looked like I was about to beat her, but her face showed no fear. Renate and Eva began cackling so loudly that the walls shook. They infected me. I laughed too. God closed everyone's ears. It was our salvation that no one heard us over the crash of footsteps outside. I told the girls that Someone was holding a protecting Hand over us. To which Liesel said, still on the floor, "I am." She stood up, left the room with an ugly snort.

In June, Eva and Renate took their final *Abitur* examinations. They had a high-ranking Nazi educator in charge of their history oral examinations. The answers he expected supported his thesis of German superiority rather than historical truth. The girls did not know these answers. But by happy coincidence, their history teacher, a nun, was his sister. She knew him well, and was not afraid of him. Positioning herself in the examination room, as was her right as a teacher, she glared at the girls violently, batted her eyelashes thunderously, and guided them surely through all the politically colored questions. And so my two daughters shared the honor of the highest *Abitur* grade achieved that year in the city of Breslau. Eva enrolled in medical school and I encouraged her to move into student housing. I promised Renate she could move there too, in the autumn. In truth, I did not want Eva growing so dependent on us. Sure enough, someone had tattled shortly afterward to the SS paper that Renate was not pure of race, and the dear history teacher's brother, the Nazi educator who had given my daughter such high marks, thus failing a higher obligation, received his just desserts. He lost his position. His sister remained in her teaching post. Renate was not allowed to study. I loved Eva, so I pushed her away because I did not want to drag her down too.

☙☙

"OH, HEAVENS TO BETSY."

This was Carl's favorite expression the first year that he was in America, although he sometimes wondered whether it was "okay" to say that in *all* circles. Perhaps it was crude, he couldn't judge that. The phrase was very fashionable in his rooming house in Weehawken, New Jersey. He never could tell what was slang and what was high English. He showed off his growing vocabulary in his weekly English letter to me. Six times a week, he wrote in German. He told me everything as if we were having a conversation. Or rather, as I later found out, he told me nearly everything.

He lived in a circle of Catholic bachelors. They were proletarians, taxi drivers, factory workers. They were lower than his own family, but they were all churchgoers. His only real friend was Father Joe. Father Joe worked for a mission in New York that helped displaced Catholics all over the world. The archbishop of Breslau had contacted them on behalf of Carl, and the mission had agreed to take care of him when he arrived. Father Joe was put in charge of the case. He had studied theology at a seminar, and could speak with some knowledge and lots of passion about the Scriptures. He had greeted Carl at New York Harbor, brought him to his new lodgings, and once a week, he gave him a check. Once a week, when he brought that check, he took Carl out for dinner too. They ate hamburgers and hot dogs, and Father Joe warned Carl to keep his left hand in his lap, in the American manner, instead of next to his plate in the German manner. Father Joe sometimes splurged and took him to an Italian locale that had just opened in Fort Lee, where a lot of wealthy Catholics apparently lived, and they had spaghetti. Carl observed that Fort Lee seemed a good neighborhood for a private practice, and Father Joe, who was of Irish descent, said rather bitterly that they wouldn't accept a German doctor there, or an Irish priest for that matter. Father Joe was a red-haired, pale-faced Irishman. He enjoyed Carl's company; he was flattered to have a friend who was a real doctor, a surgeon, even if he was no longer one, now he was just a refugee.

Father Joe had arranged for Carl to take his medical board examinations two days after he arrived in New York, still dazed from his travels. He had practiced his schoolboy English on the boat and knew just enough to feel elated when he managed to discuss the weather with a stranger. Still, he had scraped by in nearly all subjects on the examinations. But he had failed pathology, the study of the dead. It had never appealed to him. Given his dismal results, the board ruled that Professor Dr. Rother, fifty-six years old and used to being in charge, must repeat his last year of medical school and then take the examinations again, and hopefully qualify this time. He had to prove he could keep up in the United States, where medicine was considered, by the Americans, to be so much more sophisticated. The only medical school that would take Carl on such short notice, and at his advanced age, was a small Catholic medical institution in New Jersey. Thus begun Carl Rother's long ties to the Garden State. My husband had not asked himself *whether* his social decline would end after his boat reached the Statue of Liberty, but rather *when* it would end. He had enjoyed nearly fifteen years of unencumbered life as someone somehow Better. Then he was hurled down. He strove for his well-earned place in society the way an ill person fights for a return to good health. But fate did not simply ignore his strivings, it pummeled him.

The truth is, Carl's situation was perfectly commonplace. Youthful hard work, talent, or plain luck raises many men high. Most become immodest, accepting their status without questioning it. And then, when they reach middle age, it often happens that fate simply tires of them, or they make a series of mistakes for which they have themselves to blame, for their pride, or lack of judgment, or vanity catches up with them, and they start slowly to sink back down where they ought to be. But I have noticed that once a man has lost his position, he will never regain it, just as a woman cannot regain her youthful beauty.

Still, he fought on for his pride. He dressed smartly, never in shirtsleeves even in sweltering weather. He took the bus, an oven on wheels, to school every morning. He sat in lectures with juveniles, most of them taking an extra summer semester to make up for bad grades during the school year. He ate a bologna sandwich for lunch, attended more lectures, and took the bus back to the rooming house, where he ate a big meal of toast and margarine and sometimes a beer, sitting with the others in his full regalia—dark suit and tie, dress shoes—at the Formica kitchen table. The kitchen, he wrote ironically, was quite luxurious, it had an icebox. "Hey, Doc, whyncha take off your jacket at least? You're home now," they joshed him. He smiled but did not respond to personal talk, in order to discourage questions. His tailored suit hung off his bony frame, as if he had bought it off the rack several sizes too large. He listened to them complain about their jobs and talk endlessly about money, which made him flinch at first, it was so vulgar, but then he got used to it. And if they had health problems, he offered them advice. Soon the whole neighborhood knew about the Doc at the rooming house who kept his tool kit under his bed and would sew you up if you got hurt, and knew a thing or two about bellyaches. They consulted him, and he treated them all, with pleasure, because he was good at it. Soon an evening didn't go by, and often not a night, when his help was not solicited, and he began to feel better about life.

In the evenings, he sat in his cubicle, perched on the edge of his single bed, the mattress full of ruts and potholes, and wrote to me. On Sundays mornings, he attended mass with his friends from the rooming house at the Church of the Redemption, a squat brick church just a few blocks down the main road. Afterward, he mingled with the parish over coffee and cake in the church common room. He was repelled by their appearance—they were poorly dressed, the women in hysterically bright colors, their jewelry jangling loudly like a herd of Bavarian goats, while the men wore identical badly cut suits. But the locals were all very kind and also curious. They peppered him with questions that he never answered, but this did not discourage or irritate them. Soon everyone knew Dr. Rother by name, and looked for him. They recognized that he was rather old to be all alone in a new country.

The autumn semester began. His English was gradually improving. His suit started sitting properly again as he began to gain back some of the weight he had lost. He kept his hair cut very short and his mustache trimmed to a gray bar beneath his nose. He would not cut this, even after a bunch of medical school boys approached him having lunch on a park bench and asked him whether he was Hitler come over for a visit. He had worn that mustache long before there ever was a Hitler, he told those boys swaggering around him, when he was a medical doctor saving the lives of boys just like them on the Front. He bragged to me how this had made them "shut up."

Father Joe began discussing which position Carl would take when he had passed his medical boards. Soon it was decided that Saint Mary's in Weehawken, a small hospital in need of a surgeon, would be just right. Carl was invited for a visit and he was impressed. It was much like the hospital in Leobschütz, very clean, and staffed by honorable-looking nuns. Crucifixes hung over every bed and in the operating room. He turned to Father Joe and made a joke: "I prefer to operate under the Holy Cross rather than under the hakenkreuz." Father Joe thought this was incredibly funny and deep, and shared it with his colleagues in Manhattan at the Mission to Save the Catholic Refugees. He took Carl out for an expensive steak dinner and told him that someday, he expected to be repaid in kind. Carl swore that it would be his first investment of money when he started his job—a steak dinner for Father Joe.

In the meantime, Carl was feeling so certain about the future that he wrote a letter ordering the furniture in storage in Breslau to be packed and sent to New Jersey, where he organized a warehouse to keep it. Something prompted him not to tell Father Joe about this. Perhaps it was a wish to keep just one corner of his material concerns to himself. After all, Father Joe had access to all of his finances. Without that weekly check, Carl would have gone hungry.

The medical board exams took place just before Christmas. The rooming house was empty, the other residents had gone somewhere they called home. The Church of the Redemption encouraged their parishioners to invite the lonely to dinner over the holidays, and Carl received a dozen invitations. He bought himself an appointment book. In Germany he had a heavy leather-bound book for this; in Weehawken a palm-size leaflet sufficed. He kept this and his few books under his pillow, which propped the worn-out cushion up a little. He acquired stationery, with a motif of Baby Jesus in the crèche at the top, to answer letters. Each act of accepting an invitation was a stepping-stone upward, and he accepted them all, taking pleasure assigning each evening to another set of "friends" from church. He received several letters from Leobschütz, from his brothers and sisters, wishing him a happy Hanukkah. His mother did not write. I know he was very sad then, but he fought back, reminding them on his new stationery that it was Christmas he celebrated now, and begging them to kiss Mother for him. And then he prayed to Jesus to give him some grounds for cheerfulness. Jesus made an exception, and heard his prayers in the most stupid way, in my opinion.

Only one person had invited him for Christmas Eve dinner, a widow named Margie who had drawn everyone's attention at one church gathering with her remark, garnished with a giggle, that she had "a lot of money in my pocket, and a lot of unhappiness in my heart." Her husband had died tragically a while ago, leaving her alone in a brick row house in Fort Lee, and even though she was not Italian, she liked it there fine. She offered to fetch Carl from his rooming house, but on the way, she stopped and picked up any hoboes willing to climb in. By the time she arrived for Carl, her Cadillac was stuffed with hoboes, but she had saved the place in the front seat for him. She said she was all cooked out; she had spent days preparing a feast.

She seated Carl at the head of the table, and she sat opposite him, the hoboes like their children around them. A Christmas tree in the corner sparkled with electric candles. The hoboes behaved themselves, knocking back the beer and milk and water she served as cocktails before dinner. She served dinner herself, without embarrassment, explaining that she always gave the maid a day off for Christmas. Carl and she compared employment practices in the New World and the old one, while she loaded the plates with "home cooking" and forbade anyone to start eating—the hoboes were toying with their forks and shooting each other glances. She asked Carl to say grace. This made the hoboes even more restless, but she called them to order in a nice but decided way. They put down their forks and bowed their heads, while Carl spoke slowly and clearly, his eyes closed.

And so Margie entered my life on Christmas Eve, while we ladies back in Breslau handed the serving dishes back and forth, our lips shining with gravy. And I missed him very badly, and assumed he missed me just exactly as much. He wrote the next day that he had experienced a real American Christmas. He didn't report what he saw in his hostess, he left that part of his letter blank, but he described her. She was slim, dressed in a pink woolen dress. Her ankles were slender, her feet small, in shiny patent leather pumps. Her hair was very blond and puffy, in an American style, and she wore too much makeup for him to tell the quality of her skin, but she looked healthy. He figured her to be in her early fifties. She did not overeat, but she took her water glass from the kitchen rather than serving herself at the table, and he guessed she was drinking something else. But she did not have any broken veins on her face, so perhaps he was mistaken. It was one of the nicest Christmases, he wrote, that he had had in a long time. That's what I got for missing him.

The end of the holidays was marked by the news that he had failed his medical boards in pathology again. This information made my scalp crawl. It was just a minor setback, he wrote to me. It would make the first half of 1938 not exactly as he had envisioned. Father Joe took the bad news very personally, and said that Saint Mary's Hospital could not wait much longer for a new surgeon. After several critical meetings with the director of the hospital, it was agreed to pay for one more semester of study at the university, and if he didn't pass his exam then, well then Saint Mary's would have to hire someone else. At least once a visit, Father Joe referred to Carl's failed exams, and hoped that Carl was working hard enough. He said he was interested in having his steak dinner soon. He was taking Carl for soup now, instead of a sit-down meal, or they went to a hot dog stand. After a while, he didn't bother with that either, merely dropping off his check and speeding away, leaving in his wake a few bitter words of encouragement.

Unbeknownst to me, Margie took over the task of admiring and helping Carl when Father Joe grew distant. She proclaimed his English absolutely charming but alas to blame for his poor performance on the boards. He should concentrate on improving it. Once a week, she picked him up at the rooming house and brought him back to her row house, where a banquet waited. Her maid was good at roast chicken and broiled potatoes, but she was sent home before Carl came, he never laid eyes on her, and he sometimes wondered if she existed. Margie said she liked to serve her guests personally. She quizzed him on his vocabulary over dinner, and lauded him for every improvement. When he got something right, she would cry, "Heavens to Betsy, you're a fast learner!" That's where he picked up that ridiculous phrase, not in the rooming house.

He described these dinners in his letters, as an example of American kindness that he was forced to endure. Time, he wrote, was passing very quickly now and he knew he would see us soon. He was certain that he could pass the examinations easily this time. April was gorgeous. He tried not to think about the spring in Silesia, which was more modest perhaps but also very sweet. He wished we were there to see all the flowers. When Margie discovered his enthusiasm for nature, she began taking him on long walks along the Hudson. He told her about me and his daughter. He tried, I imagine, not to notice how attractive Margie was. He asked about her husband. Margie wore a clunker of a diamond on her hand, which she said was her engagement ring. She no longer had a wedding ring. She had lost so much weight after her Hal had died some years earlier (sorrow had ruined her appetite) that the gold band had slipped off somewhere, possibly dancing one night at a club, which she had done in an effort to revive her spirits the summer he passed on, but most likely while swimming in the Hudson on a hot day. It was hopeless looking for that ring, she imagined it buried deep in the slimy bottom. Carl told her she should take him to the spot on the river where she had last worn it, he would dive for it, retrieve it, she must have it back.

In the meantime, our furniture had arrived in New Jersey and was waiting in storage for a new home, in spacious quarters. Carl had to spend nearly one-fourth of his weekly check to pay for this, and he would have had to leave the margarine out of his diet had it not been for Margie, who always provided him with a few staple items packed discreetly in a paper bag, to take home after his visit.

In May, Carl took the medical boards again, and this time he passed them. When he received the news, he couldn't get the smile off his face, waiting for Father Joe to come and find out. When he heard Father Joe's steps on the landing, Carl rushed out the door to meet him. It was a bright, clear warm day. The sky was deep blue. But Father Joe's face was set in an expression that did not invite the warm embrace Carl had planned for him, so instead he cried, "I have something wonderful to tell you finally!"

Father Joe stood on the staircase, looking up, not climbing the last few steps, and said, "We have to talk, Carl. Why don't you come down and we'll go for a little drive."

Without speaking much, he drove to the Catholic mission in Manhattan, and invited him upstairs to the office. There, two other priests were waiting. They had found out about our furniture in storage. There was enough furniture to fill three houses. They had read the itemization list. They had paid Carl a total of $245 for the year he had been there, and he could simply have sold his furniture for the same amount. He had deceived them.

But the matter could be resolved. Carl would sell the furniture and pay the Church back every penny he had taken from them.

Carl agreed, but he was lying. He would not dream of selling his furniture. He was probably more bewildered than he had ever been in his entire life. When Father Joe took him downstairs again to drive him home to Weehawken, Carl said, "You know, Father Joe, this furniture actually belongs to my wife's family. It is not really mine. And I don't know how I can sell it without asking her first."

And Father Joe's face twisted up in disappointment and he said, "Carl, you are just a common thief."

As the word "thief" came out of his mouth, Carl's fist took over the situation. It traveled at a clip, right into the offending place, taking down several teeth.

I had no idea of any of this at the time, of course. I didn't picture Father Joe lying bleeding on the sidewalk. Carl, the doctor, bent down to help him, without apologizing. But Father Joe shouted at him to keep his filthy hands to himself. Within seconds, priests came running from the office. They ignored Carl and busied themselves with Father Joe, unaware of the fracas. They sat him upright, and he pushed them away slightly and addressed Carl, blood welling out between his broken front teeth, his voice clear as a church bell: "You have no job. You have nothing. Get out of here."

I didn't know any of this.

INFORMED ONLY THAT CARL had passed his medical boards, I applied for our exit visas. Then my interviews with the Gestapo began to take on new intensity. I rarely saw the same face twice, as if they wanted to impress upon me how many of them there were, how many against just one. They were aggressive or resigned or regretful, but always stubborn. I would divorce Carl Israel Rother and lead a normal life. For once, my good family ties were working against me because the newly appointed supreme court judge, Dr. Otto Gierlich, apparently felt embarrassed that a close relative of his planned to desert the motherland, and he had passed on orders that I should be kept at home.

Then I received the letter from Carl that his job at the Catholic hospital had fallen through, that he was without any means whatsoever and had borrowed money from a couple he had met at the church. I knew he was lying. Surely, I thought, he had borrowed from that merry widow! I grew angry. Without knowing any details, I suspected he had wasted his time and was just amusing himself.

I withdrew our applications for exit visas. I told Renate that her father was in trouble over in the United States, and before she could say peep, I had dispatched her with my little sister Clemie on a cruise to Norway. Clemie had made a success of her life as a Virgin. Despite multiple attacks on her unmarried status, she had stayed single and was immensely proud of it. She often recounted, shuddering, the attempts on her virginity by a stray man down at the Rhine, where she was taking a walk on a pretty spring Sunday. He had chatted her up with a nice smile, and then suddenly squeezed her bosom. Then he ran away. It had been a very close call. Tante Clemie worked at the International Red Cross as a secretary; she was married to this organization. She disliked the Nazis, she loved Carl, she was appalled that our brothers had joined the Party, and she refused to speak to them. She hardly ever had any fun, so I was pleased to invite her on this first-class boat ride up the Norwegian fjords. Alas, she had a dreadful time. She reported that Renate was not the slightest bit impressed by her parents' dreadful situation, separated now for good on account of her dearly beloved father having blown his opportunity in the New World and languishing in such poverty that he could hardly buy himself an egg. Within minutes of boarding the ship, Renate cut loose. Instead of sitting solemnly with Tante Clemie and shaking her head about the Situation, she was off gallivanting with the Norwegian sailors. Tante Clemie was hard-pressed to see her even in passing, until the late evening, when she tumbled back into the cabin with a look of bliss exhausted. Clemie sent two telegrams. The first one read RENATE IMPOSSIBLE. RETURNING HOME. The second read RENATE STILL IMPOSSIBLE. RETURNING HOME but she stuck out the trip, which was only ten days.

Pushing through our front door, Renate radiated health and happiness, and before I could reprimand her, she threw herself into my arms and said, "I had *such* a good time!" Although I classified this incident as Bad Behavior, and frequently referred to it, I did not scold her. Sin of omission. I was glad that she had enjoyed herself, and I did not entirely believe Tante Clemie's suspicions, because I didn't know my daughter well enough. She had disarmed me with a single confidence—she told me she had an admirer, whom she quite liked too. He had been on the boat with his parents. His name was Paul. He sounded like an eligible young man, the son of an old family in Bremen. He had thick blond hair, a nice sporty figure, and he was cultivated, he played the piano. His uncle was a professor at the finest music academy in Berlin, a pianist too; indeed, he was the head of the department, I recognized his name from the papers. Paul had enrolled in this academy and was moving to Berlin in the autumn. He would be living with his uncle. And oh, the family was Catholic. I thought Paul and Renate would make a very nice match.

Carl still wrote to me every day, reporting his travails in the New World. He was being blackballed by every Catholic hospital because of the furniture. His only hope was to apply to a university clinic, or open a private practice. He decided on the latter. With the money he had borrowed from his new friends, he was going to open an office in Weehawken, right under the nose of Saint Mary's Hospital. The Church was also suing him for the money they had lent him, but he was going to fight back. I found his news depressing, and I answered him in short messages. I was undecided about what to do.

There was other mail.

Paul wrote to Renate. She showed me the letter. It was the passionate, reckless letter of a young man in love for the first time. He wrote that he was determined to marry her despite the opposition of his family. He explained that his mother was railing against the match, calling her a pretty vixen. Paul wrote, "Their real concern is that you are a J but this does not trouble me in the slightest. We will be happy anyway." Toward the end of his letter, he wrote that his uncle, the Berlin professor, was not to be told about her being a J, because he was in the Party, and he would probably refuse to have his nephew come to the academy under those circumstances. He enclosed a picture they had taken together, the two standing next to each other, looking at each other, obviously liking what they saw. Renate had her braids wrapped around her head. She looked like the perfect German girl to me.

I was much, much angrier than Renate was. I told her to write him back that she was a K not a J, and didn't he know how to spell? "What are you getting so heated up about?" Renate asked me, so that I heated up even more. "Don't you be rude to me!" I said, despairing of her character, her utter lack of respect for me. She wrote Paul back, telling him that she had changed her mind, and she wasn't interested in getting married anyway, because she was leaving for the United States. She showed me this letter, and I read it and did not know what to think or say, so I kissed her and made no comment. She did not open his subsequent letters, begging her to reconsider, something I knew because I fished them out of the garbage and opened them. I also found a letter from her old friend Susanne, in Munich, asking her not to write anymore, "because it can get me in trouble," and a crumpled-up note she had written to herself, with a prayer. It read, "Mother of God, Please guide me. I am Your child. I need Your help. I have lost Paul, Maria, Sister Bertha, and now Susanne." I applied for our exit visas once again. My chosen daughter Eva learned about our efforts and begged once again to be taken along to America.

DOCTOR OF JURISPRUDENCE Otto Gierlich had always had stomach problems. But this was worse. He had just recently received the news of his appointment to the supreme court of the land, the highest honor accorded a lawyer. He knew this was a reward for loyal service. He had put an irritant out of commission, the group of friars who had steadily agitated against the ruling party. The charge of homosexuality had been his idea, and it had been easy to prove—in his eyes, the Church was loaded with pederasts and perverts, and even if it wasn't true on an individual basis, it was always true in general, and therefore he felt no qualms, the whole pack of them were now in a concentration camp where they belonged.

He could not hold down food.

After a few days of this, his handsome face looked pinched, his blue eyes grew larger, but he still did not see what was coming. His wife had gone to live with her parents, taking the children, officially because they needed her more than he did. When a friend called her and told her that Otto could not manage on his own, she must have felt badly, because she called him for the first time in months and expressed concern. She insisted he consult a doctor. He listened briefly without responding, and finally remarked that his health was none of her business. He hung up his phone. The doctor saw him after hours, did not allow him to languish in his waiting room, because Dr. Gierlich was so busy, so important. He recognized the gravity of the ailment and made a few phone calls. A specialist assigned the unwilling patient to a hospital bed with such speed and determination that he could not protest.

His body had always been an opponent. He had wanted to be a pilot, and he had lost his foot in an accident when he was ten. A threshing machine had run over it, and cut it right off. The two of us were playing at a neighboring farm. I was just his little sister. I had caught the foot in my hand and screamed, and he had grabbed it back, and told me not to be such a ninny. He was clutching his own foot, his blood was splashing everything, and then he fell asleep. I had run, run for help. When he woke up, in the hospital, our father was bending over his bed. Otto pushed him away and said, "Now I can no longer be a pilot." His body's fallibility had gotten in the way of his wishes again and again. When he was a teenager, a priest at school had taken charge of it. He had shown him tricks that a boy's body could play, and he had thereby locked up Otto's feelings, so that he stopped caring for me, his favorite sister. Our mother had found the evidence, love letters in his pockets. She had shown them to me, to no one else. We were the strong ones in the family. We looked at each other, and never spoke about it. And now Otto was locked up in a hospital bed.

The pain was unbearable.

I called from Breslau and said I would visit him, but he told me he did not wish to see anybody.

A day later, I arrived with Renate. He did not hide his sentiments—for an instant, he stared at her, showing his revulsion that she was seventeen, full of female juices, with an enormous hook nose and dark eyes.

After that, he refused to open his eyes as long as she was in the room. I sent her out with an excuse: "Please go and buy some mineral water." His eyes opened. His gaze met mine. Anger. Our sister Clemie arrived, toting flowers and a huge handbag. He played dead again. He stayed that way, although he felt us there, messing around in his room, putting flowers into vases. Clemie removed something from her bag, eyed me, and we hung it up on the wall across from his bed. He heard Renate return, carrying clanking bottles. Finally, to his great relief, his colleagues from the supreme court arrived, and the womenfolk had to make way for such important visitors. We kissed him on the forehead, one after the other, three kisses, which he pretended not to feel, and then we left. Thereafter he could devote himself to his colleagues. He enjoyed their visit, accepted their praise of the beautiful flowers on his night table, drank the water Renate had brought, and forgot his pain. When they too left, he was exhausted and fell asleep. Much later, when he woke up, he saw what we had done. We had hung a crucifix opposite his bed, where he could see it when he opened his eyes, but where visitors wouldn't notice it. He did not dare point it out to the nurses, and so it remained.

I was back in Breslau, but Clemie lived nearby. By the time she finally returned to visit him, he was already raving. She reported how he stared at the crucifix, wild-eyed, and his lips moved. She said he was excusing himself to the Lord for his evildoing.

It became the official family version of his death—he was begging for forgiveness as he passed into a better world. I chose to believe this then, and it has turned out to be true.

🌿

THAT YEAR THE CHRISTMAS SEASON began—with the *Kristall-
nacht.* I ordered everyone into bed when the festivities began—
with a cymbal crash of Jewish shopwindows on our street being
smashed. I told Renate, "You go to sleep now," and then to my an-
noyance, she did, she went right to bed and fell asleep instantly. I
wandered around the house, listening to the racket of the German
soul rising up, and I knew I could not influence it. That form of
helplessness certainly cut into my ability to sleep. I lay down fully
clothed and stuck my fingers in my ears. But then I felt the pressure
building in my brain, forcing my eyes out of their sockets. Soon, the
blood vessels would burst in my brain. I stood up to check my vanity mirror, and saw that my face looked normal, death was being
stealthy. As a matter of fact, I did not like what I saw. My eyes
looked smaller, less spectacular than in my youth. But they would
be closed soon, their beauty obscured forever. My pale skin had not
a single crease, although I was forty-five years old. My final night. I
imagined Renate finding me, in a tranquil, permanent sleep, on top
of my bed, rosary in hand—but where was my rosary? Loud singing
on the street, bursts of noise, shattering glass, screams, it was quite
a party. I found my rosary just where I had left it, on my vanity
table. It did not belong there. I had certainly been distracted in the
morning, had a premonition about bad things happening. The murder in Paris of a Nazi official by a crazed Communist Jew was death
stirring up more death. Fully clothed, I assumed the "dead saint"
position on my bed. My hair was tidy, my fingernails impeccable. I
looked forward to waking up in heaven. Renate was punching my
shoulder. It was already nine o'clock. Sunshine. A lovely day. She
had been outside. She was very excited, she told me to get up and

take a walk with her, the streets were quiet now but full of glass confetti. Liesel was beside herself because of the mess. She volunteered to take the train to Leobschütz to see after Carl's family.

I should have gone myself. Sin of sloth, possibly pride. Very likely pride. It is hard to fathom one's own depths. In any case, I did not want to go. I could not bear the idea of boarding a train, and then slinking around Leobschütz where I had once held court. I thanked Liesel, although Carl would have disapproved of that, one does not thank the help. I thanked her with all my heart. A long day of waiting began.

For hours, I sat in the window and watched for Liesel's small, resolute person stomping up the sidewalk, bearing good news. I sat all day while Renate explored the destruction outside, seemingly charmed by it. She had a healthy appetite for lunch, and then dinner. Still no Liesel. We had to prepare something ourselves. Renate and I set the table with bread and butter, it was simplest. I told Renate the bad news, that my blood pressure was high, I would probably not last the night, and hearing this she retired to bed, going straight to sleep. I was still sitting in the window at midnight, the window open a crack, so that I would hear Liesel's footsteps when it was too dark to see her. They were recognizable: the sharp, quick steps of a small, determined person. They arrived just before dawn. Her bun had unraveled, and she had just noticed it in the hall mirror. She said, "Just one minute," in a bullying voice, and kept me waiting, going to her room to comb her hair and make herself presentable before giving me the news. By then, I suspected it. The Rother men had been arrested. They had been taken away on a train. Granny Rother had gone to bed, and not gotten up again. The remaining women had no more energy than she. They just sat there moaning. Liesel had gone from house to house, cooked for the children, and forced everyone to eat. On her rounds, she had seen the Welteckes, the entire family, dressed in their Sunday best, standing on a street corner across from the smoldering ruins of the little synagogue. The parents were pointing and explaining something to their little boys.

The next morning, I had another appointment with the Gestapo. This belonged to my routine and, again, involved a lot of waiting. I saw this as my quiet time with God. I arrived, took a seat in the hallway, and began a Long Conversation with Him. I often thought He was in cahoots with the Gestapo. He had my undivided attention in their offices, and He apparently valued that. My waiting took much longer than my interviews, which consisted of someone urging me, a proper German woman, to withdraw my application for an exit visa and to divorce my husband. I replied that I would not, and asked when I could expect to have my visas, and they said they were being processed. I always thanked them for their "help." This seemed to make them nervous. I liked saying it. I waited for that moment when I could say "your help" and observe their squirming.

Soon we had word from two of Carl's brothers. They were in a kind of prison camp near Berlin, and if a family member would come for them, they would be released. The younger Rothers were being "employed" at a munitions factory, but the oldsters were being released. I persuaded their wives that this was a job for a young, strong woman, and I sent Renate to fetch them. This would keep her busy, and a trip to the capital is always an adventure. Besides, she was hard as nails.

❧

LITTLE EVA, my chosen daughter, wanted to leave Germany too. She hated the Nazis and she loved us, and she demanded to leave with us. I said no. She did not have to go, she had everything Renate didn't have, she was blond and blue-eyed, she could study and marry a German, even an aristocrat, and have a good life in her own *Heimat*. I sinned. Sin of knowing better and being stupid and hurting that sweet, courageous girl. One day, she bolted to England.

She planned to learn English there. Then she could come to America too. In London, she found work as an au pair. She looked after a brat, and was treated with condescension because no one knew her aristocratic background. She would never have told them. From afar, she begged me to reconsider. Lovely child! She could help us with English, she was speaking it fluently now. Foolish child! Her letters were smudged with tears. We had no patience for her. What was there to cry about? We sealed ourselves off emotionally, a family of three cheerful women in hostile surroundings.

👑

THE TWO ROTHER BROTHERS, Uncle Leon and Uncle Simon, were scheduled for release from a county prison in the afternoon. They had not been charged with any crime. Before they left, several soldiers brought them to the long ditch outside that was used as the prison latrine. It had a concrete shelf, where the prisoners sat to relieve themselves. The soldiers told the Rothers to get down on their hands and knees, and crawl the length of the latrine. They did not argue. When they reached the far end, they were ordered to submerge their faces in the latrine for three seconds, so they did that too. The soldiers had already seen dozens of prisoners perform this feat, but they never tired of it, each time they laughed anew. The two uncles stumbled into freedom, where their young niece Renate was waiting for them with winter coats and a thermos of water. Her face registered no revulsion. She kissed them on the cheeks, and then rubbed her mouth quickly with her sleeve. They were too weak to walk, however. They were sick to their stomachs and the diarrhea ran out of their behinds. They crept along (weak, weakness personified) until a young priest waiting outside the compound gates approached them. Renate did not note his name but I would like to remind everyone of him. He was waiting on that winter street corner for the express purpose of helping strangers released from the camp. He led them along a side street to a nearby building, which proved to be a seminary. Inside, the priests had food and hot water for washing. For anyone who ever doubted man's superiority to animals—what animal would think ahead, and risk his own neck, to give a Jew a shower? Uncle Leon collapsed in the hot water, and the priests put him to bed in their infirmary. They would place a phone call to Breslau when he was well enough to travel. These priests were very kind, although, as it turned out, they were Protestant.

Renate continued with the now-cleaned-up Uncle Simon, who had been generously outfitted with the robes of an Anglican priest, which peeped out from beneath the winter coat. The priests had provided some old shoes that were much too big. He shuffled in them. She told him he looked handsome in this getup, but he said he was ashamed to wear it. She said, "You don't know what looks good on you." His hooded eyes squinted out unhappily over his beak nose, and he said nothing. "You were always my funny uncle," she said. "Please let's have a laugh." She bought him an apple, which he ate, and kept down. He refused to tell her what happened, because someone might overhear. He held her hand. His hand was gnarled and cold, hers was soft and hot. They took the tram back to Berlin, and then to the Anhalterbahnhof, where they boarded a train east. He refused to tell jokes. He was running a high fever, his hands were icy, but his eyes were on fire, and everyone was afraid of the contagion, so they had the compartment entirely to themselves. Renate kept feeding him water from the thermos. They arrived in Breslau late at night. Liesel and I were waiting at the train station. We helped him walk to our home, nearly carrying him. His hands were hot now. At home, we put him to bed. He died during the night. His brother had died a few hours earlier in a seminary sickbed.

That night we smeared a quarter pound of butter on our bread, I called it Grief butter, and only Liesel did not think it was funny.

Life for the Rothers in Leobschütz did not suffer any more changes. I stopped spending money frivolously and sent it to the Rother widows, now deprived entirely of any income. Their sons could not help them, forced labor was not a high-earning profession, and they were not allowed to visit. Jacob, the youngest Rother, the thief, who had disappeared from Leobschütz after his nerve-racking experience working without pay in the stone quarry, had traveled all the way to Australia. He wrote, offering visas and lodgings to any family member willing to undertake the journey. He bragged that he had a photography studio in Melbourne, and could find everyone work. But no one trusted him, and no one wanted to live that far away from home.

❦

TIME TO GO. This is how to pack when two men with loaded guns are watching you.

Bribes are useless. The SS men would not accept a glass of expensive juice. It was May. Warm enough for Renate to wear a short-sleeved dress. She had grown quite plump over the past year because she was no longer playing any sports. Her arms were fleshy. "Show your arms," I had said. I had told Liesel to wear a short-sleeved dress as well, although she did not look particularly attractive, she looked like a madwoman. Her brown hair was going gray, it stuck out like loose wiring over her forehead. Her eyes were raging and her feet sounded like fists thumping on a table. She could not keep her mouth shut. She would say, "You gentlemen are *in my way*, please *move*," and then she would bump against them with her arms full of clothing, in order to brush them back a little. Because beneath the clothing, clutched in her hand, was a Leica, or a ring, or a watch or a wad of cash. The suitcases lay open on the bed, for the gentlemen to watch the packing, to ensure that nothing went in those cases but clothing. Liesel had worked hard, sewing small diamonds I had acquired for the purpose under the large buttons of winter coats.

Jewelry is either a seal of belonging, or insurance. You do not sell it just because you need money to buy some luxury item, or because your bank account should stay above a certain amount. You sell it when you need food on the table, and all other ways of acquiring it have been exhausted, and there is not a groschen left, and your children are starting to eat grass. Then, then you may consider selling jewelry. Irene doesn't understand that. She handles it . . . casually. Even now, when nothing is supposed to annoy me, when I am beyond anger, the thought enrages me. I risked my life, and Liesel's life and my daughter's life, for that jewelry, we plotted how to pack it, we dreamed about it. And did we succeed in rescuing it? No. Why? Well, because of Irene. She sold it. More about this later. Much more. I am not there yet.

Before we even got started packing, though, we had to stack what we were going to pack. The gentlemen had checked this too, checked every morsel of clothing, even the girdles and the brassieres. They paid particular attention to Renate's underwear of course. They examined every seam. I rolled my eyes at Renate. I found it a good sign. They were paying attention to minor matters. It would not be hard to distract them. How good that I had decided earlier that the blue silk dress would be ideal.

"It's a little tight on me now," Renate had said.

"Perfect."

I wore a dirndl. I wanted them to see who they were dealing with: German Woman. I wove my hair in the traditional style in two braids about my head. And finally I assumed a dumb, sad look. Poor German woman. But it was not necessary. They only had eyes for Renate, because she was young, and then for Liesel, because they sensed her hatred and needed no evidence to identify her as an Enemy.

When the stacked clothing had been checked, carried to the

suitcase, and the suitcase had been filled to the brim, I gave Renate a look. She leaned over right in front of our two SS gentlemen so that the dress nearly ripped along her backside, and then I said, "Can we close the cases now?"

"Yes, of course."

Liesel and I closed them up, and they taped them shut, and stamped them, to show they had been thoroughly searched. Renate smiled and asked if they would like something to drink now. Since they were all finished, they agreed. I rushed to get five glasses and the bottle of pear nectar I had been saving for a special occasion. We drank up solemnly. Liesel did not drink. She would not drink with SS men. Then they hauled the suitcases downstairs, to their waiting car. We were being assisted out of the country.

A day later we boarded ship in Hamburg. Liesel brought us along the dock all the way to the gangway. At the very last moment, she handed me a slender glass bottle of raspberry spirits, which I had made myself from our garden in Leobschütz, after Helga and I had stopped speaking to each other. I clutched it to my breast. "Frau Doktor Rother will not drink that now. She will save that for a special occasion," Liesel commanded. She was hardly stuttering. When I looked at her a little mournfully, perhaps, aware that I might never see her again, she said, "Frau Doktor Rother should stop frowning, she will get wrinkles." This made Renate laugh, and ask boldly, "Frau Doktor Rother is thinking, Why should we say goodbye to you when you are coming to New York soon?"

"How can I come to New York?" Liesel demanded. "I am going to go back to Father Hanssler now, I am staying right here, he needs me just as much as you ever did. Now you better hurry. Get on the boat. It looks huge. I will never set foot on such a thing. I hope it stays above water all the way." She shuddered. She didn't even kiss Renate goodbye.

Instead, she waved her hand dismissively, turned her back, and began walking away briskly. We began climbing up the stairs, but when I looked back once, I saw that she had not gone far, she was standing on the dock, holding a handkerchief to her eyes.

NEW YORK: when we arrived the sky was deep blue, the sun poured blinding light into the river, I had to squint and I probably developed many new wrinkles. I could not afford to look away. Arriving was like walking up the aisle to get married to a man you had never seen before.

Renate took it lightly. She devoured her grand American breakfast, with eggs and bacon. I could not eat a thing. "I will die of starvation before the year is out," I told her. "New York will be my gravestone." But this news did not dent Renate's enthusiasm for food. The captain announced that in a few minutes we would see land. Renate and I were late. We joined the crowd on the first-class deck. Many were traveling like us, in first class, with just two dollars in their pockets. I would have preferred to make myself comfortable on a deck chair, and watch people's backs, and not have to squint, but Renate took my hand and forced me to follow her, squeezing unbecomingly between people to get to the railing. She forced me. Normally I would not have let my child force me to do anything. But under the circumstances, I did, and this became meaningful, that upon arriving in America she bullied me.

We leaned over the railing as the boat approached three slips of land that lay, in a symbolic orbit, around the Statue of Liberty. The boat pointed its nose to the middle strip, the one so loaded with buildings it looked as if it might sink. A woman standing next to Renate burst into tears and wailed loudly. "Bronx," she cried, and pointed to the far right-hand shore, which was pebbled with little houses. "That's our new home, Bronx." Renate snapped at her, "That's Brooklyn." She had studied the map.

And she told me, "Before you get excited, Mops, that over there is New Jersey. We're not going there. That's Hoboken, it's ugly, and Weehawken is even worse. Where we land is midtown, and that's where we want to live. Although I would like to go to Columbia University, which is uptown a little ways."

"Uptown, what does it mean?" I asked. This is a perfectly normal question.

"Uptown—you don't know what uptown means?" She laughed at me. "Mops, uptown is to the *north*. Obviously."

"How will we ever find your father in this crowd—" I was worried.

"He will whistle for us, the way he whistled for the dogs. And then we will find him, I bet. You'll see."

She was entirely calm.

But I was no longer watching her as we continued steadily up the radiant river. With the blessing of the Statue, we passed along the jammed isles in a sudden shower of mist. It was a slow approach after the years of preparation, the water lapping hard against the boat like footsteps in a cathedral, the gulls cheering and the ropes whistling and finally the resolute ringing of the ramps let out on the landing.

Part
Two

ne of the critical junctures where Irene came off the track of goodness lies way before her birth, which does slightly exonerate her. Immigration is an experience that she can never have, and as soon as she realized that have-not state, it galled her into making the most horrifying mistakes. I can compare it with being the only person in a large clan who did not get married, or could not have a child, and she feels her life blighted by this omission.

It all goes back to our precarious union with America. For Renate, it was love at first sight. I was skeptical, because I had some sense. She was dizzy for it: you should have seen that girl walk, as if with each step her foot was smooching the sidewalk. When the street got excited by the sun and began emanating powerful odors, she gasped at the thrill, while I had a more normal response—I nearly gagged. She was undeterred. When asked by a sailor loitering at a red light, "Hey, sweetie, where do you come from?"—a question that did not include us, although we were standing right next to her—she obliterated us from the picture too and replied casually, "I live in New York City." There she was, right off the boat, and she nearly strangled on her own tongue it was so coated with pride. The fall was right around the corner, but she didn't realize it yet.

Now, just who in her right mind would like to experience such a long, drawn-out fall? My granddaughter, Irene. Who I happen to know is sound of mind, although others have often questioned it. Irene envied us our misery just because she was not privy to it, and she pestered us for details the way other children want to know about your wedding day. Luckily for her, I liked to tell stories, so I gave in to her pleas, and I always particularly enjoyed recounting the horror story of our arrival in New York Harbor.

I never hid the fact—America was my second choice. Or even my third choice. My favorite place where I have lived was the Front. I had announced my intentions of going there in 1917. I packed my trunks and hatboxes. The maid had called me from my room before dinner, telling me I was expected in the lounge. When I entered, my father invited me to sit down on the couch where he had not beaten me as a girl, thereby appealing to me to pay him back for his conspiratorial kindness, an old debt. My mother wept silently in that way of hers that I admired, making sure her face did not alter its contours—she must have practiced in front of a mirror. The Front was not suitable for a woman, they said, certainly not a young woman, especially not a headstrong, careless young woman. I unpacked the trunks and hatboxes, packed a small bag with a change of clothes, and slipped out the back door. My parents were not the only authority I disobeyed. I have noticed that you feel most alive when you are risking your life, and I risked it in my twenties knowing that God would not allow anything to happen to me—sin of arrogance, but He let it slide.

One spring night at the Front, a Russian soldier slipped into our medical compound. He lay by the bushes, near the entrance gate, too weak to move. I had gone for an evening stroll, and I stumbled over him. Someone else would have found him before too long. His stench gave him away—no German smells like that. I knew he must be very ill. And I knew he would be shot if I told anyone. I moved him slowly, dragging him along on the ground by his jacket, stopping when I heard someone coming. I managed to negotiate him into the back entrance of the infirmary, where I hauled him to his feet. He proved to be rather small and square, and I could force him to climb the one flight to my room. I positioned him so that when he collapsed he would fall into my bed. It was the first time I allowed a man in there. I checked him out. He had black bruises all over, and fist-size glands in his neck. Bubonic plague. I stripped him and sponged him off. I combed his hair. I talked to him. I prayed for him. After a few hours, he died. He died in a civilized manner I believed God chose for him. It was dawn. I called the attending physician. They cleared out the infirmary to disinfect it.

The director ordered me to his office. Dr. Rother was there too, but I didn't know him then. I noticed that he had the same black hair and black eyes as the dead Russian, but both his hair and his eyes gleamed, and instead of a boy's straggly beard he had a mustache with edges straight as a ruler. The director told me that he wanted to fire me, but Dr. Rother had intervened on my behalf, explaining that by helping the Russian I was following the orders of Hippocrates. The director owned that he found this in all honesty to be a highly confusing argument, since I had endangered the welfare of the entire hospital. I was, he predicted, highly contagious and must be examined and treated, which only Dr. Rother was willing to do. The director kept his distance from me. Dr. Rother did not. He brought me to his office, and ran his beautiful long fingers over my neck and declared me tip-top. He was not the only admirer I had. My stay at the Front was the happiest time of my life: I was beautiful, the object of intense worship, and permitted to sleep alone. Of course I always dreamed of going back there, even in 1937 it crossed my mind to take up a career again in some military hospital, although by then the only Front was in our own home, and it was not cowardice but reason that told me to flee.

My second choice was Brazil, where my oldest sister Maria was the mother superior of a rural convent. She wanted to take us in. Portuguese would have been easier to spell. Poor spelling is unforgivable, and I had a glimpse of the future: struggling with a heavy slab of an English dictionary, trekking back through my letter to a friend, checking each step. Carl and Renate were swarthy enough to pass as locals in Brazil and the Church powerful enough to look out for us.

But back in Germany, the Catholic Church had also sprung into action. After I had shamed Cardinal Bertram of Breslau into a fit of sympathy for the good Catholic doctor's plight, he had contacted a German underling of his in New York, and before our imagination could take us much farther, the Church in America was stretching out a welcoming hand: a nice home in New York when he arrived, English lessons, and help with his professional accreditation. Hiding like a criminal at my mother's house in Koblenz, Carl had no choice but to accept this offer and go to New York. How was I to know that as we disembarked ourselves nearly two years later, in the very act of setting our feet down, we were allowing fate to admit Dische to the family, with all his unsavory genes, that would bring about this most peculiar granddaughter? A girl who would someday feast mentally on my impressions of the jostling crowd, the fear we felt when we could not find Carl, the relief when we heard the warbling whistle he used to summon the dogs. We followed it. Strange men held aloft bouquets of flowers. I looked forward to Carl's bouquet. I wondered whether it would be better than other bouquets, and prepared myself to praise the New World blossoms. It would certainly help us find our first words. I practiced, "What beautiful flowers you have brought!" The whistle had not abated, and we pushed on toward it.

Finally, we saw him, wedged in on all sides by excited strangers. He stood in an aura of solitude, a smaller older man, with white hair, and a white mustache, and a handsome suit that was more familiar to me than his face. I could not look at that face, because the expression, when he finally located us, frightened me—it broadcast an emotion I did not recognize. He was not holding a bouquet at all, but a brown paper bag. His leather suitcase, with the stickers from ski resorts, the one I had packed for him a year and a half ago, stood at his side. He placed the paper bag down on the suitcase when he saw us, but it wobbled and began to fall, so he picked it up again, and when we were at last within reach, instead of hugging or kissing us, he reached into the bag and pulled out grapefruits. He handed us each one ungainly yellow grapefruit, his face turned bright red now. Suddenly tears began to spill down his cheeks. He was crying, openly, in front of Renate. His lips under his mustache turned downward unattractively. He sobbed. Dare I say it—weak! We just stood there. We hadn't come all this way to comfort him.

It turned out we had nowhere to go. He had been asked to leave the rooming house for men when he explained that his wife and child were coming. The scepter of family power, which Renate had torn out of my hand on the ship, was returned to me again. "First we will find a place to stay," I commanded.

We grasped our suitcases and heaved them along into this great unknown. Their heaviness had been a source of reassurance to us. Our possessions. Now they became a curse. The grapefruits were the last straw. But we saved them to eat later, impossible to abandon them. Carl directed us uphill from the terminal—"Uptown" said Renate. I blessed our Führer for allowing us to take only one suitcase apiece. And in this heat—we might have just arrived in the tropics. Were we perhaps in Africa, after all? Negroes everywhere. They trotted along or lazed about, looking respectable but strange. When you have a dark spot on your skin, you find soap and water, you don't dillydally, you scrub it off. They can't. That's the way I feel. I subsequently read a lot about the subject in magazines, and learned that I am a racist. Well, I don't think I am. Because I don't feel superior to Negroes. All men are the same in God's eyes, even Russians. And when I think about it, the color brown is much nicer than the color pink. I just could never get used to the way it looked, that's all. But here, on that first avenue we ever saw, I wasn't inclined to be charitable. Besides, they were clearly better off than we were. Because this was their home. And we had no home. As we stumbled along like plow horses under the lash of our fear, I muttered, "We have no money. We don't know anyone. I cannot even speak to anyone." But Renate looked at me, full of sudden rage, and ordered, "Sssssh, Mops." We reached the red light, and could not move, pinned to the corner by the law and the heat, and I said, "The purse holding my vocabulary is nearly empty. And yours is not much fuller! You do realize that if this, this relationship fails, we have no familiar place to return to." She said, "Mops. Please. Speak English. We've arrived, in case you hadn't noticed."

The gutters were gullies filled with drifting garbage that spilled over onto the sidewalks; you had to wade through it. I had never seen so much dirt in my entire life, not even on the Front, when we were stationed in some French town where no one ever washed. Maybe the French don't wash, but at least they keep their streets clean. I wasn't going to survive America more than a day; I would die shortly after arrival. After I had suffered heat prostration, heart failure, and stroke, we finally reached a cleaner area, with streets of small houses that I learned were called brownstones. Some had signs in their windows reading ROOMS FOR RENT.

Carl asked us if we might wait at the foot of the stairs. He did not tell us to wait, he asked us. He was hesitating all over the place. He was wearing his winter coat, in the middle of summer. This may sound unreasonable, but he would have felt just as hot carrying it. He hiked up the stairs, and his good thumb rang the bell. The door opened briefly, and then it closed again. He said nothing, turned around, trudged back down the stairs. He said, "They don't take Jews." Renate deciphered the smaller sign, perched in the window.

NO NEGROES. NO JEWS.

"Carl and Renate, you let me try it," I ordered.

This time, they waited at the foot of the stairs while I marched up to the door. I put myself into character. I recalled booking a room in Oberammergau in 1937, when Carl and I attended the Easter pageant for the last time. How had I spoken to the concierge? Like this: air of upper class, wealth, and family name. I pretended I was in Oberammergau again. I rang the bell.

A woman opened the door. "I am Catholic lady, I need a room," I said loudly. Every word was perfectly correct English.

Her gaze swerved down to the foot of the stairs, at the anxious faces of my family looking up. "I don't take refugees," she said, drawing out the word, refugeeeeee. "No. No way. " And she closed the door.

I made Carl and Renate hide around the corner, and repeated my plea farther down the street. The landlady looked me up and down, and said, "Sorry." I understood. No one likes to have a beautiful single woman in a rooming house.

Then I told Carl and Renate to stand at the foot of the stairs, but look away, keeping their profiles hidden. "Let them see the back of your heads. It will do," I commanded.

Success. We got a room with a double bed and a camping cot. There was a sink, and a small closet. I hung up Carl's suits and four of our dresses, two per lady. The suitcases took up what remained of the floor space. The window shade had been drawn against the sun. Our new home. I was so relieved to have a bed to sleep in that I declared it delightful; Renate one-upped me by saying she would like to grow old right in this cot, and even Carl was forced to admit that having us there made it paradise. As it grew dark, we opened the window shade, and the heat washed in. We settled down into our beds, pulled the sheets up to our shoulders, and listened to New York: fragments of conversations that did not concern us, cars swooping past on their way somewhere, and, in between, the faint rustling of a tree. As it cooled, the sweet, familiar smell of wet foliage filled the room.

IN THE NIGHT I heard the following German dialogue through the wall.

"No, please . . ."

"Why not?"

"We're not alone."

"She's sound asleep."

"I'm too old for this."

"Dearest. Please. I am made of flesh and blood."

"So am I. And I can't bear it. I will be sick."

"I'll clean it up."

"Hail Mary full of grace . . ."

"See. How easy it is . . . And you're not sick. Just relax. I'll be quick."

I had a kindred spirit on the other side of the wall. I decided to find her first thing in the morning.

I stopped in to see the landlady and asked to meet our neighbors but she said we had only one, an old man with palsy, she took care of him. "Are you sure he's not German?" I asked.

So I had dreamed it.

"I may be losing my mind," I said at breakfast. The rooming house provided gray porridge and brown water, which the landlady referred to casually as coffee.

"Why, Mops?"

"Because of the heat, or the journey, I don't know."

"I mean, what are the symptoms?"

"Never mind. I feel better now."

That was the last time.

FOURTH OF JULY. Our first Independence Day! An important
event for us now. We went to see the parade. We walked through
the park, and as we approached Fifth Avenue, fate honored us,
prodded a family into leaving their park bench just as we passed by.
So the bench was ours. We left Renate on her own for five minutes.
A man approached her. Instantly, she started to flirt.

She was weak in this respect—easily flattered by male attention.

Things were looking up for us. We were going to start work in
one week at a summer camp for small children. Carl had been appointed camp physician, I was his nurse, and Renate would be a
counselor. We were going to have a free vacation. We would make
photos of ourselves in rowboats on the water. I would look very fat
in an American bathing suit, they are poorly cut for a large bosom,
everything falls out. Carl would smile into the camera, with the
mosquitoes hovering in a cloud in the background. One gets used
to the jungle. The camp sent us money to cover our bus trip. We
were learning the ways of the land, we bought a family ticket instead of three separate tickets, and saved three dollars. We were
spending it cautiously. Carl was not stingy. He knew the value of
money: money is there to spend, not to save. Jews save. That is
their disease. Let us buy ice cream. We left Renate holding our park
bench, and went to make the selection. There were many kinds. I
preferred something simple, not too expensive, a cup made of bis-
cuit with a dollop of ice cream inside. I chose chocolate for us girls,
Carl chose vanilla. Renate was waiting on the park bench. Out of
the blue—out of the red, white, and blue, for the sky was filled with
flags—an American boy sat down next to her, he showed all of his
teeth smiling, and started chatting with her. Yakety-yak. She was
smiling back at him, her teeth were not so white as his, and I always
told her, don't open your mouth so wide when you smile, but her
heart was so joyful that she forgot her teeth and her smile took up
half her face. He told her about his college, he was a college boy. A
college boy was speaking to her, smiling at her. She told him she

was "originally" from Germany and that she would start college in the fall. She did not tell him that her plans to attend Columbia University had proved silly, because the Americans did not recognize the merit of an *Abitur*—in particular, not of the highest grade *Abitur* given in a big city—and the only place charitable enough to take her at all was the College of the Helpers of the Holy Souls in a small town in Pennsylvania. The college offered mostly homemaking and home economics, with beginning to advanced courses. But it also boasted a science program. An alumnus had organized a special scholarship for Catholic refugees, a present from heaven that Father Joe, in his ineffable goodness, had arranged for Renate and, after his falling out with Carl, had plumb forgotten to unarrange. So she was heading out to western Pennsylvania on the third of September. It was a good school because it was strict, and she could go to mass every morning. She told the boy the name of the college, but he did not recognize anything but Pennsylvania, he knew that; he said, "Well, lucky you. It's really nice there." Her thoughts were racing ahead, perhaps he would become a friend? Perhaps he would visit her there? Perhaps fate had arranged this chance meeting? She noticed that his feet were fidgety and she concluded he was excited about their meeting. She even saw that his feet, in their restlessness, were pushing around a small package under the park bench. She noticed but did not stop to reflect about this. He was telling her about Trinity College, in Hartford. Suddenly he jumped up. He said, "It was nice, real nice, meeting you, I got to run, meet this friend. I'll try to come back in a few minutes." He dashed off. She was puzzled and disappointed, but still hopeful. He had blond hair.

As we came around the bend in the park road, I saw her sitting on the bench, her round red cheeks, her eyes squinting into the distance, her thick brown braids, her ample bosom. My daughter. These sentimental thoughts were punctuated by the loud crack of an explosion. I watched her lift up off the park bench, stumble, and fall forward. Everyone was staring. They are staring at her because she is a foreigner, I thought, and wondered what she was doing. She was trying to stand up again, pulling down her skirts and holding her thigh at the same time. Blood gushed between her fingers. We ran toward her, carefully, afraid of spilling our ice cream.

Bystanders surrounded us. They poked at the ground. It was a powerful firecracker, a firecracker under the park bench. The boy must have placed it there. "What do you expect?" someone grumbled. "Today is for Americans." We were so embarrassed. Carl pressed Renate's wound with the ice-cream napkin and stanched the bleeding a little. We told everyone that our daughter was just fine. We left hurriedly. We walked across the park, toward Fifth Avenue, where Carl knew of a hospital. The parade was in force, and very loud. Every nationality had its own brigade. As we approached them, a coincidence occurred: the German contingent passed by. The marchers were dressed in brown. They waved a familiar red flag, and wore familiar armbands. Swastikas. Carl looked at his feet. I did not look away. I glared at them: a real German lady looking disgusted. But they didn't notice. We continued up the avenue, Renate walking very calmly, completely indifferent to the parade. I thought to myself, She doesn't see what she doesn't want to see.

A Chinese doctor sewed her up. He said, "Happy Independence Day."

The ice cream was gone. Somehow, we had dropped it. This seemed a bigger loss at the time than it perhaps was. At the time, it seemed worse than losing all my furniture and relatives.

WE MET MARGIE.

She invited us to dinner at her house in Fort Lee. I thought she was very ugly. Her hairdo was ludicrous, and she had on a tight shirt and skirt, in pink, and perilous white high heels that took real valor to wear, because if she stumbled it would be a long fall. Her varicose veins would be bursting. She was most welcoming. She squeezed my hand and said, "Aw shucks, I am so happy to meet you." She couldn't help herself, she had to embrace me. Her diamond ring scratched my arm. "So this is Mops!" she said. When she let me go again, I gave Carl my severest look, expressing my disgust that he had told this stranger my nickname.

I didn't notice much about her house, because I didn't want to. We were ushered directly into the dining room. She had a banquet table, even though she lived alone. Ten chairs stood around it, all covered in the same baby blue. Matching curtains. Matching table-cloth. On the wall, a painting of the Madonna wearing a matching veil. "This blue is so restful to the eyes," I said generously. The table was set with roast meat and potatoes and a pitcher of fresh milk. She drank only water, disappearing occasionally into the kitchen to refill her glass. I had my immediate suspicions about that but said nothing. It was much too hot in the room to eat. My face was wet with sweat. Renate betrayed me and allowed our host to load her plate. I was on my own with my pride. I explained that I had a bad stomach, and she obliged me with only tiny helpings of food. I drank several glasses of milk to still my appetite. Margie had ugly dishware, very heavy and plain white. The milk in America tasted chalky. We kept our left hands in our laps in the American manner.

We chatted about Germany. Margie was not well informed, but she knew that Hitler was bad. "After all," she said, "he drove out a good Catholic like Carl." We nodded in agreement. How true.

"What is it about the Jews," she asked, "that makes Hitler dis-like them so much? Are they different in Germany?"

We did not nod. Finally Carl said, "The Jews are getting what they deserve." No one added anything to this. I admired him for his convictions. They were firmer than mine. Still, I hoped he would not elaborate. He went on, "Their attitude toward money is the problem. They are greedy."

"Are they really?" she said, appearing to be shocked. "Well, here they're not." She passed the meat—in order to change the conversation, I thought. Maybe she had Jewish blood. Or the subject bored her. It never occurred to me that she might have suspected the truth. While Renate ate and ate, Margie and Carl began a rapid-fire conversation about the advantages of life in Fort Lee. He seemed very informed. He knew about the chocolate cake at Fort Lee's new bakery, and the kind of soup they served at the diner. I admit I resisted all efforts to talk. The summer camp, it turned out, had been her idea, her initiative, and it was her cousin who ran it. What could I do but thank her modestly for all of her efforts on our behalf? On the bus ride home, I said nothing. We drove along the west banks of the Hudson, on the Jersey side. We peered across the river and saw an extraordinary tableau: the setting sun lit up the windows of Manhattan, as if fires were raging in the houses. Sin of envy, sin of jealousy, sin of mistrust. I called myself to order. I declared that I thought Margie the nicest woman I had possibly ever met and that God must have sent her to us. Carl said, "I knew you would like her." But she wasn't going to be my friend, and he did not force me to her house again. We left shortly afterward for our camp job. It was just as nice as we had hoped. Renate spent most of her time with small girls who never questioned her accent. She learned to say, "I had a ball," and she did. There were no young men to distract her and she gained ten pounds in a few weeks. They suited her.

After summer camp, we moved to a more spacious rooming house in northern Manhattan, where no one questioned whether we were Jewish or not, because they assumed we were, everyone there being Jewish. I did not enjoy living in such a neighborhood, but in fact, most people were rather nice and they would all speak German. One saw a lot of Negroes, going to and fro. It is impolite to stare at people. We all committed the sin of impoliteness until we had eventually seen our fill and grown used to those dark faces. The War began in Europe.

We bought a Kodak. We bought an Automobile. Our Automobile was a black Buick, only a few years old. We were Buick types: respectable, solid citizens. We drove Renate to college in Pennsylvania and took pictures of the scenery along the way. The school was civilized, with nuns teaching, and not a man in sight. The girls looked as manicured as the college lawns. They went to church every day, or they wouldn't have wanted to attend this college. Renate would have loads of friends.

We improved our lot. We left the rooming house and moved to an apartment in Weehawken, one door down from a grocery store, one block from the Catholic Church, two blocks from Carl's new office. You can't get more central than that. Now we had our own kitchen, own icebox, own bathroom, and I decorated feverishly, with Renate's help. It turned out that she was handy, she could drive a nail straight and true, and figure out electrical switches. After she left for college, we had to make do on our own. We spent two days without lights waiting for her to visit and show us contemptuously how to pop in a new fuse.

Even without her, we were a family. I learned to cook. I made sandwiches. I liked baloney and Swiss cheese with mustard. We bought a new gadget, a toaster. We toasted. We started buying butter, as soon as we could afford it. I heard that in Germany they were rationing butter. We had as much of it as we could afford. I gained weight. We took our bed out of storage, and a few items of furniture. I bought an autumn suit, in dark brown, with a little red ribbon at the neck, and passed out flyers door to door announcing that a German doctor had opened a practice in the area. A few people came. Carl had a wonderful manner, he observed his patients and knew what the matter was before they had a chance to complain. They told their friends. Very soon, he had a lot of patients. I worked as his nurse, and in the evenings, I cleaned the office. I learned to get down on my hands and knees and scrub the floor. When he saw me in this position, he never failed to reach out, lift me to my feet, and kiss my wet hand. "Lady von Weehawken," he said. "I am grateful to you." Then he let me get down on my hands and knees again. Sometimes Margie dropped by, and I was extremely friendly to her. Carl admitted that Margie had lent him the money to open his office. I did not reprimand him. She made no mention of it, and he was paying his debt off every month. Every night I wrote Renate a letter admonishing her about her weaknesses and warning her to work hard. Every night she wrote me a letter about her friends and listing her activities. Every night, Carl smoked a Cuban cigar.

👑

THE NICE CHURCHY GIRLS at the convent college knew that the German girl's hair was one of her Good Features, being thick and auburn and wavy. But she didn't *do* anything with it. She just wore it in braids, like a dumb Girl Scout. Her eyes were a Good Feature, large, with thick eyelashes, but she didn't accent them, she didn't have a clue about makeup. Her skin was incredible, clear and smooth. But after that, after the unfashionable hair and the big eyes and good skin, it was all Bad Features, and someone should tell her so, but no one bothered. Her figure was coarse, very strong, she looked as if she could play football. Her shoulders were much too broad. She could have dressed better, no matter how impoverished she was. She had ugly German dresses, with puffed-up sleeves and something that looked like an apron. She strode around in tie shoes instead of pumps. She wore kneesocks with her dresses! Furthermore, she had a thick German accent. Worst of all, she was clever. Someone heard her play the piano, and reported that she played well—really fast. And Sister Audrey gave her an A on her first chemistry test. Of course that didn't require much English.

Her roommate told everyone that Renate had confided something incredible to her: since the War began, the German girl had the status of an "enemy alien." She had to report to the police in New York every two months. Universally, the girls referred to Renate as "the Alien." They doubted that she believed in God. She did not close her eyes to pray. If you caught her eye while she was praying, she smiled. Proof.

Renate accepted their palpable scorn. When she sat down at a table for lunch, everyone fell silent. Invariably, some girls stood up, made hurried excuses, and moved to another table. But she pretended not to notice. She wrote her parents a letter every evening describing her day in detail, and exclaiming that she was so extremely happy. She did not know about the nickname.

If I had been in that situation I would have made sure all the girls knew that I came from a fine family, that I was a fantastic piano player, that I could draw and think better than anyone else there. I would have felt contempt for them, and they would have respected me. But Renate felt no contempt and no superiority. She was always committing the infernal sin of being overly modest.

She had been at the school for three months. It was autumn. Her roommate Stella was going for a walk with two other girls. Renate asked if she could come. They said, Oh, it's only a short walk, we'll be right back. She said, Fine, I'll come. They told her they planned to cross into the neighboring grounds, which was probably illegal, and a girl with her status (hint about "enemy alien") should not risk it, but she waved her hand, said, Aw, that's okay, she'd risk it. She went along.

Now they were forced to jump over a wall, which they had in fact had no intention of doing, and going into the neighboring grounds. They were moving along a wide path through the woods, rather scared, when suddenly they heard barking. The barking drew closer. The girls, with Renate trailing, turned back, and hurried toward the wall. Before they had gone more than a few yards, two boxers burst into view from the side, snarling and snapping at them. The girls ran. They scurried. But they could not outrun the dogs. The dogs surrounded the girls, snarling at them. The girls huddled, and prayed, and covered their faces. Coming up from behind, Renate walked quietly until she was a few yards from the dogs and whistled at them. Abruptly, they turned toward her, and their barking ceased. The girls unwound slowly, and peeked. They saw Renate standing there, stock-still, her arms akimbo, staring at the dogs. The dogs looked down, and then turned away, as if they were ashamed. They began to whine. They sidled over to Renate. They lay down, rolled over. Renate bent down to the dogs now lying on their backs in front of her. She scratched their stomachs and murmured to them, "Now, darlings, whatever did you have in mind trying to frighten us like that?"

The girls knew that Renate had saved their lives.

She had the ability to Calm Savage Dogs. She may be a Saint among us.

On the way home, they jostled for a place next to her elbow. Timidly, they asked her, "How did you do it?"

For once, Renate was smart. She assured them that she could talk to all animals. She did not tell them that she grew up with a boxer, and that she knew the creatures intimately. From then on, she had admirers. Her company was sought after, and when the girls watched her praying in church, and she smiled at them over her hands, they smiled back and felt flattered.

After this episode, she wrote us less often, so I chastised her about her lack of gratitude to us.

✠

OUR FIRST YEAR IN AMERICA PASSED QUICKLY, and on its heels, another year. Germany was at war and I was not at the Front. Carl said, "We are too busy to think about it." At night, I could think of nothing else but my family and Carl's family. All the Rother men had been dispatched all over the Reich to work in various factories, and they were no longer allowed to go home. Their women remained alone at home. I prayed for them. I prayed so hard that I could not sleep. Carl slept easily. He gave me Valium. I fell asleep mid-prayer. I liked it, and began taking it every night. In 1941, we received a letter from Carl's sister Else that began, "Imagine my luck." A good beginning. I read it aloud to Carl over dinner.

"'On Nov. 16th, the church is having a confirmation for new converts, and I will be one of them!' Carl! Isn't that amazing? I always knew Else was a true Catholic."

I had noticed her interest in Jesus earlier and never tired of talking about Him. I had converted first Carl, then her. I wondered if my sister in her Brazilian convent had ever converted two people. If she had, they were both Indians, and it doesn't really count. I pictured beautiful Else kneeling. Was she still wearing that absurd black wig? She no longer needed it, as a Christian. Her upper lip had a fan of wrinkles in it. I imagined them spreading slightly as she prayed. Then I continued reading her letter. "Last week, Liesel visited me and brought me a present—a book about the wonders of baptism. I can no longer live without Jesus, and my new religion. Because Jesus is making it easier to endure the separation from my children."

Her eldest son, thanks to the power of her continuous prayer, had been given permission to visit her in Leobschütz in December. Scarcely had she started believing in Jesus than he had received all sorts of privileges.

Of course Else's lightning conversion was also Liesel's doing. Liesel's employer, Father Hanssler, was permitting Else to take the Sacrament after just three months of lessons. Other converts require three years of hard training. Else wrote that "Father Hannsler is speeding things up because he knows that my love of Jesus is so intense." And then she added, "Isn't that the greatest luck of all?"

I told Carl, "I will write to her—her conversion is hardly a matter of luck, but of talent. Not all people have the talent to believe in God."

I can just hear Irene scoffing. She considers the love of God simpleminded, somehow. Let me ascend to the pulpit for a moment and address her: Irene, you yourself love music. Is the love of music understandable? Not really, is it? Yet it pleases you, even fills you with feelings of respect and wonder not unlike love. But, although it pleases you, it does not please others. Some people take no pleasure in music whatsoever, and yet they don't sneer at you. And when you, Irene, find someone who shares your love of music, you feel understood and thrilled—and haven't you already done that to exhaustion? Enough pulpit.

I put down my magnifying glass, and Else's letter, and told Carl that we should bring out champagne. If only we had some. Instead of drinking champagne, Carl and I prayed at the kitchen table. We thanked our Savior for taking such good care of Else, and we trusted that He was also taking care of the other Rothers.

God was helping me too, helping me in His way to accept that I wouldn't see my mother again, and never receive another stern letter from her. She was no more. God allotted me no free time to think about her. My little sister Clemie was kind enough to send me the simple glass rosary Mama had been holding when she died. I planned to hold it when I reached that point, and for a while I kept it handy, in the kitchen cupboard. When it became plain I wouldn't need it there, I moved it to my night table, for sudden necessity at night, and then I forgot about it because I had no energy to wonder when I was going to die, or to fret about Mama being so permanently out of reach.

Another few months passed. The conversations with Else and the others in our family had stopped. We wrote and wrote, as if we were calling into the night. We received no replies. Such dreadful behavior, I scolded. I sent some telegrams. They were not answered. The war spread everywhere. And then I knew that they would write if they could, and I confessed: Sin of Asking Too Much. I wondered aloud whether the United States should enter the war, and Carl said, "It is none of our business. We are not American citizens."

"Carl, let us buy the paper today," I pleaded with him on December 7, 1941. He did not reply, but his look was a door slamming in my face. At home, I switched on the radio loudly. Our president was speaking. Our nation was under attack. We sat in our kitchen and ate our cheese sandwiches and listened together. "Now we must fight back," Carl said suddenly. He banged his fist on the table and announced, "I will volunteer for the American army, they need medics," and then he added angrily, "even a second-rate one like me." I snapped at him, "You will volunteer over my dead body," which is a very nice way of putting things, because we say that in German too. And he was quiet, I could see the bitterness ebbing, and he said, "Well, really, I have fought enough, I will stay put now."

Then he complimented me on my good English, but warned me against the dangers of slang. When I told him I was going to concentrate on English instead of worrying about the news, he beamed at me. Then he stood up from his end of the table, took one short step to reach my end, bowed before me, and said, "Nothing can keep you down. Soon you will be the Empress of Weehawken."

An empress must be able to communicate her wishes. I worked hard at English. I bought myself detective stories and firmly resolved never, ever to read anything in German again. Carl and I kept ten-hour-a-day office hours in Weehawken. We bought a cocktail set, with a mixer, and learned to make drinks. I waited for the perfect moment to break out the raspberry spirits from Leobschütz. Perhaps when Renate got married.

***

"DO YOU PLEDGE ALLEGIANCE to the flag?"

"I do."

Renate did too. But she did it in a manner that suggested she found it slightly embarrassing. All the more pride did I show when pledging. I spoke loudly, clearly, and I had learned the entire text by heart—meaning in this case exactly what it says. I knew I was making a fool of myself, but I was willing to. Becoming an American citizen meant so much to me. I bought a dress for the occasion, it was sky blue, with a red ribbon at the neck. I wore my best jewelry— the ring with the Lassaulx family crest, the gold necklace from my great-grandmother, and I carried my mother's rosary. And I put my hand over the left side of my chest, the way you were supposed to, although I knew that the heart lies in the middle of the chest. Renate had to read the text off the little card and I could tell from her demeanor that she found me embarrassing too. The others in the room all looked at me as if I were doing something silly. I plowed ahead. And Carl raised his voice, to show his support for my endeavor. The bureaucrat administering the oath said afterward that such open love for his own homeland had made his day. He had tears in his eyes. He would tell his wife at dinner.

Later, that pledge became one of the many bones of contention with my granddaughter. Her father, Dische, scorned the flag, and felt that patriotism was for the hoi polloi. Renate was too modest about her own opinions to oppose him. When Irene went to summer camp, the children got out of beds, raised the flag, and pledged allegiance to it first thing. I liked that. Irene watched the flag rise up along the pole, like a giant pillowcase, while the pledge was intoned. She aligned herself with Dische and refused to open her mouth.

Her attitude galled us. We took up the issue often. At dinner. "You owe allegiance to your country, Irene, even if you cannot fight for it, the way Little Carl can, and must, when he grows up." Dische was sitting there, the family oldster, without any aptitude for sports, all brain and stomach, eyeing the sauerbraten and dumplings, eager for portion number three. He piped up, "Little Carl shouldn't have to fight in the army. We'll find an excuse for him. The Jews are too intelligent to give away their lives for no good reason. Jewish mothers used to brag about their sons sneaking away from a battleground." He reached for the meat. Our grandson was Dische's spitting image and, at that moment, mortified about any similarity. Irene was snickering again. She thought her father was funny. She thought everything was funny. I weighed in to save the situation. "Not all Jews were cowards," I said, eyeing Carl, reminding him, propping up his self-esteem. "Some Jews were more courageous than any German."

Dische didn't recognize the sneers. He was so self-satisfied that he didn't recognize criticism if it was applied too lightly. He kept forgetting that the Nazis hadn't liked him.

His daughter takes after him in that respect: if she has inherited my tendency to laugh when laughter is inappropriate, she has inherited Dische's inability to take correction of any kind. She hates being chided, but in addition, the content of the criticism just washes off her like water off a raccoon; she doesn't even have to shake herself. She likes herself just fine. She carries on with her bad behavior. She told herself, well, it is not in my stars to know the Pledge, just as I cannot spell the simplest words correctly, and she made not the slightest effort to learn it.

But back to our very first Pledge.

After we became American citizens, we bought war bonds. I had lived with America for seven years, but I had no seven-year itch. I loved my country more every day, and I would vote Republican to keep it strong. After acquiring our passports, we had lunch in a restaurant where they served ice-cream sandwiches in the shape of battleships, with American flags on the mast. I had two.

The War in Europe ended one day later. The Nazis had lost their jobs. We would go back and visit as tourists, as soon as we could afford the passage.

STILL NO NEWS FROM OUR FAMILY. Our own metal mailbox with
the daisy-shaped holes, positioned anonymously among a dozen
identical metal boxes at the entrance to our windowless hallway,
became the receptacle of my entire social life. There lay the letters
from Renate. And there did not lie the letters from anyone else.
Coming from work, we passed through the front hall. I slowed
down, my eye greedily fixed on our mailbox. Carl pulled ahead of
me, made a demonstration of starting up the stairway alone, while
I fumbled open the box and grabbed what lay inside, usually no
more than bills. He did not wish to hear any news about what he
called the "past," to which he evidently assigned his family. Only
once did he mention the mail, when we were approaching the hallway; his big hand swept up and pointed ahead to the mailboxes,
and he remarked bitterly, "They have the charm of little coffins." I
bit back the reply that this very possibly described the whereabouts
of his loved ones.

At this time, I had secretly taken to reading the Jewish newspaper *Der Aufbau*. I knew Carl would be extremely angry. Why read
a foreign newspaper when we were Americans now, and weren't we
Catholics? I had taken the bus to Manhattan to buy some German
groceries—gherkins, herring in cream sauce, which he could not help
liking—when I noticed the paper. I did not read it in public, for fear
of being addressed by some tiresomely friendly person and having to
explain that I was not Jewish at all, but I happened to find the reading material interesting nevertheless. I had discovered Heinz baked
beans on those pages, kosher but tasty. They came in glass jars, and
the inside of the cap, if you put your nose right up to it, smelled like
pork. It was some kind of trick. I believe this was used by the Jewish
manufacturer to attract his own pork-starved people, and that trick
is as much proof as one needs about the ingenuity of the race.

Aufbau was also almost entirely in German, a great relief for me to read. It had interesting articles about what was going on in Europe, but it also featured an exhaustive column of petitioners seeking information about lost family members. I hid the *Aufbau* in my purse, and read it on the toilet, or alternatively, when Carl was on the toilet. I studied those search ads and had an idea. They cost one dollar for a simple ad. A more deserving large-print ad cost $4.50. I took the cheap one: "Looking for relatives of Dr. Carl Rother of Leobschütz." I received no response. I placed another ad. Months passed. We bought a vacuum cleaner that was the very best and most expensive on the market. It was pale green, the size and shape of a dachshund, and it rolled obediently on the floor behind me.

One winter evening when we returned from work and stopped at the letter boxes, I could see through the daisy slit that a foreign letter lay inside. Light blue. It bore one of the new German stamps. It turned out to be from Dr. Weltecke, Carl's assistant in Leobschütz, husband of my best friend Helga, who had turned us over to the Gestapo. It was addressed to Carl alone, but naturally I did not give it to him. Instead, I carried it around with me for a few days, and finally opened it in my "library," the bathroom.

It began:

> *Dear Carl.*
>
> *It has always been a puzzle to me why our friendship fell apart, for no reason that I could then discern. In any case, I imagine you have been wondering how the Welteckes fared since you, lucky man, left the motherland. For I must praise you for your wise decision to go before the War broke out and shattered our lives. You cannot imagine the misery you escaped.*

The letter continued in this vein for five tightly spaced pages in the doctor's immaculate handwriting. It itemized each and every shortage, from butter to paper to pride. And it ended with a request to send the family money. Instructions on how this could be accomplished with the help of the military government, along with an address, and the most sentimental regards.

I did not think hard. I passed the letter between my legs into the toilet bowl.

A few days later, another letter came. The postal service in Germany was clearly up and running again. This one was labeled from my sister Clemie. I followed Carl upstairs, my heart so agitated that I could barely mount the steps.

It was good news. The family was alive. Everyone was healthy. Clemie was living at home, but the military government had packed our Rhineland villa with two sprawling families from the East, and it was impossible to bear. She had to cede the best floor to them, and was forced to move into the smaller third floor herself. All the family friends had survived too. Shortage of food, shortage of medicine. I squinted through my magnifying glass to read the letter aloud to Carl over dinner, after he had finished his sandwich and baked beans, and he listened to the entire thing without saying anything; then he kind of grunted and asked for dessert. I brought the applesauce. "Now my family is accounted for," I said. "I am so truly happy. Only one thing is missing from my happiness. I want to find your family too, and we can have this pleasure of reading their letters together." And very quickly, to get it out, I hazarded to say I had put an ad in the paper looking for the Rothers.

He stood up from the table awkwardly, as if he had forgotten the exact mechanism of standing up and pushing away from a chair, and he bumped his way out of the kitchen. His speed increased in the narrow corridor; then he came to a halt, as if sizing up his opponent—me, I had not moved—and estimating his own forces, and from then on he proceeded methodically, opening the front door just enough to squeeze by, and pulling it shut gently behind himself. His footsteps were inaudible on the stairs; he must have been tiptoeing. He had not put on his coat.

I stayed seated in the warm kitchen, stretching to turn on the radio. This was usually Carl's task, because he liked to decide what to listen to, so the radio stood next to his side of the table. "Seasonably cold," said the commentator. I glanced at the window. The streetlight looked like a weak sun in an unknown, hostile galaxy. The snow began. I knew the streets had a gleaming black sheet of ice, and he would be fighting for his balance. I was overcome with pity and contempt.

Perhaps middle-aged women are given to hysteria, and to talking too much. But once a man reaches sixty, the memory of his heyday swells into an all-consuming desire to have it back, and even the loss of his parents hurts him mostly as a sign of his own failing. He wants youth with all of its trimmings, including robust parents, and a young wife, and his children small and impressionable. His bossiness and contempt for the opposite sex in his own age-group grows. His agitation is chronic. Only the sight of youthful flesh will calm him down. And so it happened that Carl, taking refuge from the snow and from the heavy cover of rage at me that blanketed and muffled his sorrow when he thought of his family, sat down in a diner and was served by a young waitress. She looked at him, and recognized the tension in him, and assumed he was, like her own father, like all elderly men she knew, miserable. Women, she knew, are made buoyant by their own realism; they are held up by their sense of the inevitable, and cannot descend to such depths of despair. When she recognized his longing, she felt touched.

I know all this now. I didn't know it then. If I had, Irene's biography would have turned out very differently. She would have grown up without Carl. But now I am in a position to forgive him. Her name was Hannah. She sat down with him and she took his hand, and she addressed him very forthrightly. "You are cold and hungry, aren't you?" The back of her hand was a smooth caramel he wanted to lick. A warmth and happiness erupted in him that he had not known in decades, perhaps ever. Because when he was young, he had not worshipped youth. Suddenly he was aware of how much it meant to him. He put his head down and blinked the tears from his eyes. They trickled down his nose.

She withdrew her hand. "How about some chicken soup?" she asked. "It's kosher, just like your ma made you."

He stayed sitting there long after the soup was gone. She brought him some coffee on the house. And he drank it, and didn't get up to leave. She brought him a piece of apple pie that was sweet and sticky and vulgar—revolting, in short. But he ate it with delight because it had been sliced and dished out by her hand. Closing time came, and she came to his table and told him it was time to go. He looked up at her through his thick glasses, his eyes begging. She was lonely. Her husband and brothers were in the navy. Her parents were in Florida. She took him upstairs, to her little room, and she allowed him to sleep there with her, in her marital bed. She thought he might keep his shirt on during the proceedings, to shield her from the sight of his old belly, but he was so keen on the game of pretend that he removed it, and fancied himself a young lover. She amused herself pretending she was with President Roosevelt, a fantasy she had. In the morning, he woke up early, as always. She was sleeping soundly next to him. He slipped on his clothes, left her a ten-dollar bill on the pillow, and he came home to me. I had the wisdom not to ask him where he had been. I guessed he had gone to the YMCA farther up the road.

ON ASH WEDNESDAY IN 1946, we closed the office early and went home to prepare for late afternoon mass. We were fasting in memory of our Savior's suffering. We would have a light meal in the evening. I felt dizzy and uneasy and looked forward to sitting down in the quiet candlelit church. As we were leaving—feeling very the

German Doctor and His Wife in our black finery, our steps echoing on the steep wooden staircase—a door on the second landing swung open and a neighbor I had never seen before screeched into our faces, "Your mail in our mailbox today!" and stuffed a letter into my gloved hand.

I was wearing white leather gloves. Perhaps I should have gone out of my way to acquire black ones? I had thought about it. But I owned at least two dozen pairs of white ones, and parsimony sentenced me to wearing them until they wore out. The letter was an aerogram, a one-ton feather, from Australia. Perhaps it would contain the news we had been waiting for. I did not recognize the handwriting. There was no return address. I slipped the letter into my spring coat pocket and we continued our short stroll to church. The trees were still bare, but the weather was fine. Carl was mute. We took our places. I prayed: Please, let it be good news. Please, Almighty God, let me have good news. Sin of asking too much.

By the confiteor, I could not wait. Carl prayed with his eyes closed. I took the letter out of my pocket and held it in my lap, gradually working it open. Typed letter. Easy to read in the church dusk when your life depends on it.

Signed: "Your Jacob." Carl's youngest brother, who had put him to such shame. Since Jacob had signed, then at least he was alive: thrilling news in itself.

"Dear Rothers," his letter began. "I cannot wait any longer. I am forced to pass on the news." He had investigated, there were institutions that were most helpful, and he had discovered, one by one, the whereabouts of the rest of the family. He wrote simply: "Everyone is dead." Jacob's one short paragraph of what you might call bad news was balanced by another ten paragraphs of good news, about his wonderful new life in Australia as an honest citizen, with a photo studio, a nearby beach, and good friends. He planned to buy a car. Unlike the Welteckes and my sister Clemie, Jacob did not complain about his lot, but seemed to take only pleasure in it. The letter closed with an apology "for typing this news, but I am unable to write you by hand when my fingers are shaking too much to hold a pen." He said he planned to visit us as soon as he could, we were his last relations. I opened my pocketbook, but instead of dropping the letter inside, I let the rosary fall, and the letter stayed in my hand.

It was time for the ashes. I followed Carl to the altar. We knelt before the priest to receive the ashen cross. When his hand descended and brushed my forehead, it seemed a gesture of tenderness and comfort. I was fat, my patellas groaned under the burden, and one day of fasting had weakened me. I was fat because I could eat every day. But the Rothers would never eat again. Had they suffered? My thoughts latched onto the picture of Else biting into a bratwurst on a day trip to the Sudetenland, her teeth slowly pressing through the skin, the squirt of juice landing on her chin. None of us had the heart to tell her, so she wore the brown stain all day. This image of Else began aching intolerably in my memory. Her conversion had apparently not meant a damn thing to her Savior.

The priest was not satisfied with the cross he had marked on my forehead. He pressed harder this time, ignoring the waterfalls cascading beneath. Carl glanced at me with admiration. What deep religious feeling, he must have thought. But then he realized that I was moved by something else, and he panicked. "Mops, what's the matter?" he hissed. I fell over onto my face and lay stretched out on the stone, wondering why churches are so cold. Hands tugged at me. I knew I was dying, and that I was clasping Jacob's letter instead of my mother's rosary. At the moment, it did not seem wrong.

AFTER FORTY, if you wake up without feeling any pain, then you're probably dead. My knees hurt. My face felt bruised. Alive. I heard Carl nearby, he was dressing for work. When he noticed that I had woken up, he came over, smelling of eau de cologne, and gave me a concerned peck on the forehead. "What is going on?" I asked. He explained that I had fainted in church, he had somehow hauled me to the car, where he always kept his emergency medical kit, and had given me an injection of a tranquilizer. It was his diagnosis that I was having an anxiety attack. He had driven home and hauled me up two flights of stairs. Mindful of my dignity, he had not slung me over his shoulder but carried me in his arms. His back ached, he said with a smile. He did not mention a letter pulled from my hand.

I found it in the trash, dropped carelessly on top. He must have looked at it. I did not ask.

I wrote back, secretly. I engineered to have that mailbox key on my key chain, and if Carl and I returned home together, then I marched him by the mailboxes without giving them a glance. As soon as he was washing his hands, I rushed downstairs and picked up the mail. I had to be quick. It was good exercise. My knees grew stronger. For a long time, though, I had no overseas mail.

After one year, the Welteckes wrote again, assuming that their first letter had gone astray. This time Helga added a long paragraph about her poor boys, and what luck Renate had in comparison. The letter closed with a plea for a care package.

A few similar letters trickled in. Trickle turned to torrent by 1947 and through 1948. Letters burst out of the mailbox. People we had barely known, or known well, who had felt obliged to turn their backs on us in our predicament, or like the Welteckes added to our misery, people whose names were strange to us, but who had been recommended by so-and-so, wrote from Germany. Our address was being circulated. All the letters were extraordinarily alike. They were all long. And they all began the same way, by congratulating us on our incredible good fortune that we had left Germany before the "bad times" began. The bulk of each letter was a list of all that had been lost, and the ending, always, a request for a care package.

I sent a package to everyone who asked. I sent the medium ex-

pensive kind, with the coffee and the nylons but without the can-
died nuts. They cost several days' income each. I did not care. But
I did not write back. And when they thanked me, and asked for another, I sent another. Two per beggar. The Welteckes wrote asking
for a character reference for Dr. Weltecke, that he had been helpful
to Dr. Rother. It had to be notarized. I sent it off, notarized, as a
one-sentence note. But I did not write a personal letter. Turning
the other cheek has its limits.

Not everyone wrote, of course. Eva, my chosen daughter, did
not. She had moved to America after the war, married a Jewish
doctor, but did not try to find us. We had hurt her too much. Paul,
who had loved Renate even though she was a J, did not write either. After Renate left Germany, Paul had joined the Party and
risen quickly in the ranks, on the basis of his virulent anti-Semitism
and party loyalty. It does not matter a damn what became of him.

❦

RENATE HAD A PLAN that made no sense. She wanted to study medicine at Columbia University. She was a snob about the wrong
things. We said she should concentrate on finding an American
husband from an upright Catholic family, and attend any old
school. But she was determined. She applied. She discovered that
her brilliant *Abitur* meant nothing, and her straight A's from a little
Catholic college in Pennsylvania did not inspire confidence. Columbia University didn't even grant her an interview. In fact, no
medical school would have her. So she studied what she considered
the next best thing, biochemistry, at a Catholic graduate school in
Cincinnati that was willing to take her. Biochemistry came close to
medicine. She told us that it was a way of solving the mystery of disease, of natural death. Carl and I thought her claim a bit arrogantly
put, but we did not point that out.

She was thinner now. She wore her hair short, curling it with an
iron. She wore American clothes, skirts and jackets. Her face had

the Virgin Mary look again, with her high cheekbones, pale satin skin, and those huge dark eyes. But her smile wrecked this good impression; her smile was too wide, and too fake. She did not take admirers for granted anymore, the way she had, strangely, in Germany. In America, she was at even more of a social disadvantage than she had been in Germany. When someone, anyone, paid attention, she felt improved and hopeful. She allowed one young man to take snapshots of her in a two-piece bathing suit. She posed on the beach, her head tossed back, her gaze coy, in the manner of a model. She must have thought the picture would amuse me, because she showed it to me. But I didn't like it. I complimented her, though; it was nice to see that she had, at last, a waistline. We were pleased to hear that the boy was Catholic. But she did not mention him again.

We had a telephone.

One day, the phone rang. It was Renate. She had come secretly from Cincinnati to New York by bus, and was coming to visit us.

She had news.

She had written Columbia University another letter, and the head of the Department of Biochemistry had suggested that she come see him. Paul Thatcher Clark. She pronounced his name as if it were a precious stone. I was mollified to learn that he was not Jewish, and had a German mother. She had impressed him, obviously. Renate said he liked refugees, any and all of them, so he liked her too. Sin of infernal modesty. He had agreed to give her a chance. He would see to it that she could enroll in a course in something called organic chemistry, a subject deemed grueling and dull by all students, and if she got an A—an almost impossible feat—then he would take her as his own doctoral student.

She had made her plans without consulting us, which was a shock. But after the initial anger wore off, after about a month of grumbling, we were pleased—she was moving back to New York.

SHE WAS STUBBORN. She was ungrateful. She was selfish. She didn't
come to see us often. A son would have treated me better, would
have been more attached to me. She claimed to be busy. With
what? She was studying. She lived in Harlem with another girl, and
studied organic chemistry. She hated the subject. She forced herself
to learn it. She did nothing else for six months. She got a B. Clark
took her anyway. He said he could understand her aversion to the
subject, at least she had proved that she was made of flesh and
blood. Rare display of pride—she never told anyone about that B.

As if she didn't have enough to do, she started taking piano lessons again. A one-armed pianist, Paul Wittgenstein, who taught at
Columbia, had accepted her as a student. She reported that she was
studying the Chopin piano concerto with him, her tone so enthusiastic as to disrupt the scolding forming on our lips. We managed
one sentence: "Make up your mind, Renate, music or science." She
said we were right, and she would drop the music lessons, but of
course she didn't. She did as she pleased and had no time for us.

We bought a house.

Margie had hit upon the opportunity: she kept her ear to the
ground and heard the noise of a new development going up in Weehawken. An old forest ran along the rocky cliffs that line the Hudson on the New Jersey side. A developer was building brick houses
in this forest. Someday, the developer promised, he would construct
a thundering thruway connecting his development to the new Lincoln Tunnel. This would make the development a suburb of Manhattan. Margie said one had to have some courage and imagination
to buy there. Carl said he adored having nature at his doorstep, the
woods were lovely, dark and deep. The developer threw in sidewalks and a cement road. Each house had three bedrooms and two

bathrooms. There was even a maid's toilet downstairs, next to the kitchen. Margie plucked up her courage, bought a house, and, with a little help from her, we bought the next-door house. So we became neighbors. I had grown used to her, to the big diamond biting my hand when she clutched me. I was sure she was an alcoholic, but when I suggested this to Carl, he committed the sin of anger and rebuked me. He told me to mind my own business.

Finally, after nearly ten years apart, we were reunited with all of our furniture.

The house had low ceilings, so that I commented to Carl, "This is more suited to a dachshund." The parlor was small compared even to the maid's quarters in Leobschütz. "Carl," I cried in despair, looking at the stately Biedermeier desks and wardrobes, "nothing fits!" But when forced, much did fit. The attic and basement were fully furnished. I unpacked the loden, the white leather gloves, the hats, the dirndls. I unpacked the Hummel figurines, the Rosenthal cup collection, the teapots. I unpacked our wineglasses, and served grape juice in them for dinner. When I complained about missing wine, Carl took it personally. He said, "I am doing what I can for you. I cannot start a wine import business." I hastened to assure him that I was only trying to keep myself from drinking the little bottle of raspberry spirits Liesel had given me on the boat. We were keeping it for a special occasion. I was testing my willpower daily not to guzzle it down; he should congratulate me. He said, "I congratulate you," and looked disgusted.

The house was neat and tidy, every inch contained something, we could hardly move. We unpacked our books. Carl set up his stamp collection in the den. We unpacked the prayer stand, and hung up crucifixes in every room. We bought a better radio.

We had a little lawn in the backyard, so we saved and bought a lawn mower, and I learned to use it. We saved, and spent. We bought a beautiful reclining lawn chair of shiny aluminum, with dark green rubber cushions. I hired a maid, an elderly Colored woman. I would have preferred a white person, but they were too expensive. I could not judge how clean she was, because her skin color confused me, but she was immaculately polite and respectful, and never ever attempted to take control of my house, the way Liesel had done. Carl warned me not to socialize with her, but I have to admit, my first inklings about the rest of America came from the well-traveled maid, in furtive kitchen conversations when Carl was on the toilet.

On Sundays, Renate came to visit. She was not talkative. It could not escape my alert notice—she looked happy and distracted, as if her thoughts were tangled up in the details of something enjoyable. I suspected she was hiding something from me. Now I know what it was. A Philippine doctor. Married. Fifteen years her senior. He had been drafted into the American army when the Japanese invaded the Philippines, and been wounded in combat. So fate dragged him to New York. Now fully recovered, he had no idea what had become of his wife and seven children. He had received no word from them for more than two years. He assumed they were dead.

Renate consoled him. He was a short, slight, yellowish fellow, and even now, I shudder at the thought of her giving herself to him. He had a nerve: he said he was in love with her. When the war in the Far East ended in 1945, he returned to the Philippines to take up a big position—he became Minister of Health in the new government. He made Renate promise to move there and marry him, as soon as he got settled. I had no idea what was brewing. Then he wrote her. His family had gone into hiding on a rural rice farm. His wife had seen his name in the papers, and come looking for him. His seven children were thriving. That was the last Renate heard from him.

I suspected something was amiss, because she looked less happy all of a sudden, deflated somehow, and came to see us more often, sometimes two, three times a week. She amused us with stories about the other scientists, who appeared to be, without exception, the greatest "oddballs." She claimed that they were very grand authorities but I discouraged her from trying to explain their expertise to us. She would nonchalantly use enormous words that ended in "acid" or "protein" and I told her, "Renate, stop talking gibberish please." She had a little triumph when Carl did not understand "something as simple as a complex carbohydrate." That angered him, but she kissed him and apologized for being silly, so he let it slide.

After a while, she stopped coming again. I wrote letters across the Hudson, reprimanding her. Every evening I got down on my knees on my prayer stool and prayed that she would find a handsome American man, perhaps but not necessarily with a little money but at least from a prosperous family, and that their children would be our anchors in the New World. God did not hear my prayers.

It's a mystery that I cannot explain, even from my special vantage point: why God singled me out practically to drown in Jewry. I mean, a reasonable person would expect Him to prefer Catholic grandchildren, would expect a little cooperation in making life more conducive to serving Him!

Renate began a secret life with Dische.

She mentioned him just once. She said she had an interesting friend, who was twenty-five years older than she, just a few years my junior. That was all she told us, just "an interesting friend." I think she said, "I had coleslaw yesterday, do you know what that is? Someone advised me to try it. An interesting dish. By the way, his name is Dische." We were eating sandwiches for dinner. I put my sandwich down carefully, so as not to allow the pickles that were stuffed inside to escape, which is their tendency, unless you use pickle spears, but spears were only available in kosher, anyway. I lowered the sandwich, and then placed it, using both hands, on the plate. I leaned forward to Renate, who was just taking an enthusiastic bite from her sandwich, and I said, "He sounds horrible."

I peered at her for a while, to make my point, starving myself for several minutes. Then I resumed eating. She was nonchalant. She ate for a while and then she said, "Oh yes, he really *is* horrible. You should see his table manners."

I looked at Carl, he looked at me.

"Don't you have any other friends?" Carl asked.

"Lots of them," she said. "He just stands out because he's so peculiar. Only reason I mentioned him."

"How else is he peculiar?" I asked.

"He's brilliant, but so are his friends," said Renate. "He is famous in his field, everyone says he will get a Nobel Prize, but so will all of his friends. He is just even more peculiar . . . well, for instance, he cannot think sitting down. He does not keep a chair at his desk. He paces all day long. He goes up and down the corridors. When you want to talk to him, you have to walk with him. But when you stop talking to him, and drop behind, he doesn't notice. He keeps going. And he does not use a pen and paper for his calculations. He calculates everything in his head, and then he passes by his desk, and rummages through everything, hurling it aside looking for a pen. When he finally finds one, he jots down his results on any scrap of paper. And then he loses that. But he remembers the number, so it doesn't matter. Oh, but he can't calculate without twiddling a stick behind his back. And this stick must have the perfect weight and size, or it doesn't twiddle correctly, and then he can't think. Mostly, he uses spoons."

"I wonder that you can be friends with a man like that, who has only one thing on his mind, and that involves a matter your parents cannot understand," said Carl.

"Oh no," Renate said brightly. "He knows such a lot about literature, and history, in fact he speaks eight languages fluently, and he talks to himself in all of them. He reads ancient Greek for amusement. He doesn't sit down to read either, he lies down. He sits down to eat. His table manners are beyond belief. I hate to think of him at the gala dinner in Stockholm when he gets the Nobel Prize. You would hate him, definitely. These sandwiches are so delicious. You must try coleslaw. I am going to go back to the lab now."

She was always in the lab, or in the practice room playing the piano. She did not like going home. She went home just to sleep. Her room did not have a bed, it had only a sofa. She said she had the choice between a sofa, where she could receive friends, and a bed, where she couldn't. So she had a sofa, and she slept on that.

Dische, it transpired, only had a sofa too. They had that in common. But I didn't know that yet.

I told her, "Renate, come home to us and sleep in a proper bed, after having a proper meal."

Carl said, "You are such a disappointment. Living like a vagabond. You have a home, you can live there. I have slaved away to make you a home, and you don't want it. You just spit in my face, don't you."

"She didn't like to hear that. Because it's the truth," he said to me later, after she had rushed out the door, possibly crying but probably not, and I knew we would not see her for a while. We didn't.

We had to visit her. I wrote to her and begged her to be reasonable, she was breaking her father's heart, she should come and apologize to him. She wrote back that she was going to Europe to a scientific meeting. We drove our Buick to Manhattan and met her in a Nedicks, apparently Dische's favorite restaurant. We thought it very cheap. We had coleslaw. She insisted on paying, which offended Carl. He could hardly speak he was so angry. She just ignored her father. She was full of happiness. She said she had been invited to the meeting, her trip was paid for. She was earning some money as a research assistant, and also teaching an undergraduate course at Columbia. She bragged about the money she was earning, and it offended Carl, but she just plowed ahead. And was there anything she could bring us back from England?

Margie dropped by often. I would hear the slam of her back door and watch her skip down her back stairwell. If she walked slowly, then she was heading for her car in the garage. If she danced down the stairs, she was coming over to us. No fence separated our properties in the back. She stepped right on our back lawn in her high-heeled pumps, and instead of sinking in, she rocketed over. She usually came on weekends, when Carl would be home. She watched for the car. Once, on a Sunday, I dropped Carl off at his office, where he wanted to go through his paperwork. I drove home alone, and she must have missed the moment I got out of the car. But she saw the Buick in the driveway. She came right over. Stuck with me alone at home, she declared it was a wonderful opportunity for some girl talk. She made me pour her some grape juice, sat herself down daintily in our gleaming Biedermeier chairs, and before I could stop her, she was giving me advice about Renate. Renate was a wise girl, she would pick the husband that was best for her. Then we could finally break out the raspberry spirits, which she was eager to try. She, Margie, had made a very wise choice in a husband, but he had died young, before they could have children. After that she had never wanted another man. She would not betray him. She started to cry and I gave her my own handkerchief, with my family initials embroidered on it. But my heart was hardened against her because she was giving me advice about Renate and had no children herself, therefore no experience, and worse, Carl had told her about the spirits, which meant he was confiding in her in the worst possible way.

These were hard times for me, with Renate going so far away, even if it was just for a month. And Carl confiding in the neighbor.

I asked him when he had seen her on his own. He told me she had been ill, had come to his office to consult him, and insisted on being given a proper bill. She had not wanted to impose on his free time at home.

I had to respect that. But I decided to put up a backyard fence. In order to put up a fence, I had to buy a dog. I bought a wirehaired dachshund, a tiny burly puppy, which I named Faithful.

Faithful took my side on every issue. He proved to be an alpha dog, who questioned every male including Carl. At night, he lay next to my side of the bed and growled each time Carl turned over. He followed me around the house, casting adoring gazes in my direction. Veneration of the Virgin, Carl said. Faithful trembled when I petted him. However, he had a dark side to him. When we went out, the gentleman in him disappeared. He crawled along, dragging me until he found a place on the sidewalk that apparently tantalized him, for long minutes he licked the spot, worshipping the scent left there, and only a sharp kick in the ribs could move him along. As he grew older, this got worse. He began wriggling underneath the fence and disappearing for hours at a time. We bought a more stable fence. I made sure it was higher too.

The first fence made it difficult for Margie just to drop over through the backyard. Now she had to go out her front door and, in front of all the neighbors, trudge along the sidewalk, and then proceed like the mailman to our door. Her visits nearly stopped. The second fence made it impossible for her even to look over into our yard. I did not miss her.

In the meantime, Renate had set sail for England. Little did I know that she was accompanying Dische, that everyone thought of them as a couple. In his circles, people did not necessarily get married just because they took a trip together. They spent a month together, and when she returned she knew as well as before she had left that Dische was not for her. Still, she could not resist him. Once a week, she descended to the depths of his home to visit him. This apartment must be described in all of its horrible details.

Dische, Renate bragged, slept on a sofa too, but he kept his sofa in his kitchen. I can hardly bear to think of it even now—he slept in the kitchen. He had his desk in the bedroom, where normal people would have kept a bed, and it wasn't a desk, it was a camping table, and he didn't sit down at it anyway, he used it as a depository for papers. He ate cheese and bread without butter or he went to the Horn & Hardart Automat. The apartment had no normal knickknacks, just books and papers. Renate was impressed by his concentration. She described going to see him, how he was lying on the sofa, reading a play in Greek. He asked her to wait a minute while he finished a passage. He lay back down and read for two more hours, laughing loudly. He had completely forgotten she was there. For a while, she waited in the doorway, watching him. Later, she found a book in one of the languages she knew, and she sat down on the floor in the kitchen, smoothing down her skirts, and tried to be half as engrossed as he was. He finished with his book. Clearly, he had forgotten that she had even come, and he didn't notice her sitting there. She kept silent, watching him. He put on his hat and coat, and walked out the door. She ran after him. They had a good Horn & Hardart meal. She thought him delightful.

Even in the ways that Dische might have appealed to my sensibility, I found him repellent. It turns out, for instance, that Dische was chaster than she. But this was because he was such a coward. He had a phobia of diseases, and he was terrified of catching syphilis. The nerve of that horrible little frightened man, wishing to live forever, and dreading the touch of my daughter. To think he could catch syphilis from her! Wasn't there something particularly awful she could catch from him—and eventually *did*?

He had decided as a young man that he would never get married. Decades into this decision, he spoke with fresh contempt of the girls who wanted to marry him. One other attribute worth mentioning in this context—this Jewish man disliked Jewish women. He found dark-haired, small-boned Semitic women gross. He liked blond or brunette women with good German blood. And he particularly liked God-fearing Christians. He actually preferred religious women. He had apparently run through a whole family of happily married Polish Catholic sisters with a weakness for intelligence, forcing them into mortal sins, one after the other.

So he particularly liked Renate because he saw in her a Catholic German girl. Finally a man who saw her for who she was. He liked her broad shoulders and her red cheeks and her very Aryan way of never complaining. He did the unspeakable with her, and then sent her away deep in the night because he couldn't sleep when someone was in his bed. Besides, there was no room on his sofa. And of course she didn't complain. She took the subway uptown to her sofa. During the day, they met in the laboratory, but he was not romantic, he did not waste a lot of thought on a woman. When she wanted to speak to him, she had to find him pacing the corridors, he did not even slow down for her. She had to walk next to him. Conversation was of short duration.

"Do you want to have dinner tonight?"

"Yes."

One day she went out to dinner with his colleague. He was a tall, handsome young man. He would have been just the ticket. He was normal. He was not some kind of idiotic genius. Somehow, Dische found out. Or he had instincts after all, buried deep in his brain somewhere, or his big nose smelled another man on her skin. And he was shocked.

After that, he wanted badly to marry her, to have her in any shape or form, she could even spend the night on his sofa with him, anything.

She agreed to go to England with him.

He was invited, not she. He took her along as his fiancée. A minor role. He introduced her to many fine scientists. She wrote long letters home bragging about that. Even without suspecting her minor role, we didn't approve of her tone. We wanted to pick her up at New York Harbor when she returned, but she was evasive, and couldn't tell us exactly which boat she was taking. She told us she would arrive on the *Queen Mary* on a day in June, and she arrived in the United States one day earlier, surprising us at dinner. She claimed it was all an error. She could have sent a telegram from the ship, of course. We knew she was up to no good. We could not imagine the degree of duplicity.

She brushed off our suspicions and proclaimed herself overjoyed to be back in America. She said she had not felt the slightest temptation to visit the Continent. This too was a lie. She had gone to Paris with Dische, and in her unmarried state shared a hotel room with him (twin beds) because he was too stingy to pay for two rooms. She had allowed him to drag her deep into the swamp of venereal sin and bohemian life.

We knew only a quarter of it, were appalled and could do nothing. Our only daughter: lying to us about when her boat returned. Certainly because of a man. We suspected Dische. But it could be anyone. The world was chock-full of Wrong Husbands. A woman without normal inhibitions would run a gauntlet among them. Often, I consulted my mother. I asked her advice. I clutched her rosary and hoped for solid help, a sudden change in behavior. My mother did not stir. In fact, since it is a useless endeavor, as we have seen, trying to get help from God, why should one have more success getting help from someone who has passed to the beyond? Because no matter how much they loved someone on Earth, they don't want to be bothered by anything material. The Buddhists are right on that one. A dead person becomes a memory. He becomes many memories.

I am just now watching Dr. Thacker trying to perform an autopsy on a small baby. A difficult case: the child died of congenital heart disease. It is 2001. Renate has become an expert on this illness but she is not there to help anymore. Dr. Thacker is sad, and his hand trembles. His colleague notices and advises him, "Just pretend Renate is standing right behind you, discuss your findings with her." And Dr. Thacker nods gratefully, his hands are steady, Renate is with him, he can work again. However, if his hand slips, Renate will not guide it back into place. Memories can speak, but they cannot move mountains. But I have jumped ahead again.

The 1940s reached a great climax on New Year's Eve 1949. Renate had come to spend the evening with us, but then claimed fatigue and an ongoing experiment back at the laboratory that she urgently had to finish, so she would have to stay at the university for the night. She promised to come again the next day. The decade was not yet over when Dische, who liked to party privately on his kitchen sofa, put his poison into our daughter.

She realized soon enough.

She was enterprising. She procured sulfur mustard from the military laboratory. She calculated like a pharmacist, measured grams per liter, and dusted the powder into a tub of hot water. She made a brew of liquid mustard gas. She sat down in the tub, and expected contractions to begin at once. Sin of attempted murder. She had fallen so low. The mustard scalded her skin. She began to cough. She was in agony, but she was not someone to complain. She stayed seated in the brine till it cooled, and the mustard settled in sludge at the bottom of the tub. And then she called Dische, and asked him to meet her at their favorite Horn & Hardart for dinner. She was short of breath and queasy, but she rushed downtown from 168th Street to 42nd Street. When she arrived, and she still had no sign of bleeding, she resigned herself. He was late, he was hungry. He heard her coughing when he came in, so he did not kiss her, because she might be infectious. She reassured him that she had been exposed to something caustic at the lab. He did not ask particulars. He was delighted by the meat loaf. Over black coffee and cupcakes, he began paying more attention to her. She told him she would marry him.

A few days later, she came to see us. It was an ice-cold day in February and she looked tired and miserable. Carl said he thought she was coming down with something. She said no, she felt great. She was not as chipper as usual, though. She made an effort to tell us about her work, her doctoral dissertation, her colleagues. We had lunch. The news came out of her mouth sideways. "Can you imagine, that funny scientist Dr. Dische wants to marry me," she said.

"He's Jewish, isn't he?" I asked. "And much older than you?"

She nodded brightly. "He is Jewish but he likes Catholicism. He knows more about it than I do."

We looked perplexed and she went on. "It's tempting, actually. He is never boring. He's very smart." She was nearly stammering. "He doesn't really look Jewish, you know. He could be Italian, or Greek."

Her father said nothing. I said, "Renate, don't start this foolish sort of talk that deeply offends your father. We are Catholic in this family. Don't you see what you are doing to us?"

And then she took a gulp of air and said, "Well, I have married him. Yesterday. I am Mrs. Dische now."

Carl's response began as a very low growl that slowly gathered strength. "You have undone everything I tried to do!" he roared. His large fist went crashing down on the table. "Get out of my house, and never, ever come back. You are no longer my daughter. I don't want to see you again."

She left.

We did not see her again for a very long time.

RENATE WAS ISOLATING DNA, and experimenting with it. She needed a few more hours to perform some more measurements. The baby was overdue by two weeks. She was glad when she realized she was going into labor. But she wanted to finish up her work. When a labor pain came, she sat down in a chair. When it had passed, she went straight back to her test tubes. She needed to look up data. When the pains were coming every five minutes and she was still not finished with her experiment, she had an idea. She packed the three reference books she needed to consult for data, and her purse, and headed toward the elevator. She was waiting for the elevator when Dr. Chargaff came by. A gentleman of the old school, unlike many of the other scientists, he noticed when a highly pregnant woman was carrying heavy books, and he offered to help her. She declined, saying No, it was no problem, she preferred to manage on her own. But where are you going with them? he asked, and she replied gently, The delivery room.

He took the books, and accompanied her.

Then he hurried back to tell her husband. He liked Dr. Dische because he too was not a dumb American, he too was Viennese, and because he too had read some books that had nothing to do with science. Dr. Chargaff was a real Renaissance man, and that was the norm for Viennese scientists. In the New World, it was uncommon. Dr. Chargaff considered Dr. Dische congenial, but he was a little resentful because he felt Dr. Dische was unfairly hogging the eccentricity limelight. In truth, no one considered Chargaff eccentric, because his manners were impeccable. As he entered Dr. Dische's lab, he heard his rough, loud voice assuring Dr. Clark that Renate would soon be finished with his experiment. Dr. Chargaff protested. "She cannot possibly finish it. Dr. Dische, your wife is in labor. I just brought her to the delivery room." The happy father turned to Dr. Clark. "Don't worry," he said. "She will finish it anyway. You'll see. Pregnancy is not an illness."

And she did. The delivery was slow and difficult. She had time between labor pains to return and finish her work. Then she had a cesarean section. She did not require pain medication after the operation. She frightened the nurses half to death with her attitude. When they asked, "Does it hurt?" She replied, "Oh, it's nothing." She was very pale. They infused her with a little pain medication, just to be on the safe side, without asking her. Then the color returned to her cheeks.

The other biochemists all trekked down to obstetrics and looked at the baby behind a glass window. They thought it very funny that old Dische had just made his first child at fifty-five years. They didn't envy him, and they figured correctly that he would hardly notice any difference in his life. It was Friday the thirteenth. The high-and-mighty professors did not believe in bad omens.

DISCHE CALLED AND TOLD US we had a grandson. Although he had been born on a thirteenth, this was no cause for alarm. To the contrary. He himself had arrived in New York Harbor on a thirteenth. And of course I had to interject that I too had been born on a Monday the thirteenth. "We are turning the thirteenth into a good luck day!" Dische crowed, using the first person plural with utter ease. In other words, he was not afraid to talk to us. He seemed to think it was the most natural thing in the world that we would be angry and then no longer angry. They had named the child after Carl. It was diabolic. Of course we went to the hospital to see her and the new baby, not the new father. The husband was not there anyway. He did not hang around, apparently. I brought a splendid present to show our acceptance of the new family—my set of the von Lassaulx silverware. Carl held flowers. Renate greeted us warmly, none of us cried. Great emotion could not really come up when one saw Little Carl.

He had Carl's large black eyes but the resemblance stopped there. He was a Dische, through and through—tiny, Semitic, unmanly, and soon, as we were to discover, cerebral. How could it be otherwise? Because:

In 1865, in a Polish shtetl, Jacob Dische and Cywie Wittmajer begat Simon Izak Dische, while in 1875 Chaja Rosmarin and Jakob Reich begat Serafine Reich; and in 1895, in the Austro-Hungarian city of Lemberg, Serafine Reich and Simon Izak Dische begat Zacharyasz. And Zacharyasz, called Dische, ate with his mouth open. He talked with his hands, he talked openly about money, he talked about money with his mouth full, and the shtetl lived inside him. He was proud of it. He bragged that his uncle had been founder and head of the Zionist Party in the Polish Sejm. Carl would have concealed that embarrassing information. Nor would Carl have blathered on and on that his own parents were eccentric and brilliant, which they weren't, because the Rothers were lovely people. But Dische thought it was a sign of distinction that his father, Simon, failed to recognize his mother, Serafine, passing on the street, tipped his hat to her, kept going. He was a banker. Money in his veins. Dische found that a merit. He proclaimed it a virtue that his mother had had no time for her children because she was always reading. Serafine was a bookworm instead of a proper mother. They were all dead, anyway, so at least we didn't have to hobnob with them. That was one little thing Dische didn't brag about, didn't even mention how they died, which I could figure out easily enough, however. We felt he should appreciate our tolerance about his shabby background, our accepting him into the family. He had run off with the prize, our incredible daughter. Dische did not seem to realize what a trophy she was. He loved to talk about her beauty, but he never mentioned her gifts; he did not even appreciate Renate's piano playing because his sister had been a musical wunderkind in Vienna, Dische implied she had been better than Renate, in fact no comparison, she had studied with Max Reger and given concerts all over Europe. We shut our ears to these tales. When I found out that he did not give her jewelry either, the way a proper husband ought, that he never gave her a thing, I hit on a plan.

I remembered Renate's Christmas wish, year after year as a child, for a pearl necklace. I was not fond of pearls, I found them too pale, so she wanted them, to set herself apart from me. She was doing that in enough ways already. Nevertheless, I went shopping. I spoke to Carl. And then, Carl made a big fuss about presenting our daughter with two huge beautiful pearls, strung on an otherwise empty chain. I told Dische that I wanted to see two matching pearls on the band every year, they could be purchased at Christie's, and she could wear the necklace for their tenth wedding anniversary. He had no alternative but to say yes, and even thank us for the idea and the start-up pearls. He would have to save money for them.

Now that we are reunited, Carl proclaimed, we are opening our doors to you. But the Disches were busy with their bubbling test tubes. They worked seven days a week. Once a week, they came over for Sunday cocktails. Renate had not been lying about one thing—Dische respected churchgoing. He inquired about the priest, and about our habits, and volunteered information about his own religion without our asking. We rolled our eyes when he was onto that subject. He did not notice. He said he looked forward to our Sunday cocktails all week. He "tucked in." He liked a Tom Collins. We served crackers, he liked crackers, even after he figured out that they must be high in something he called saturated fats.

At our urging, Renate started leaving the baby with us occasionally. The family had moved to the northernmost neighborhood of New York, that Jewish shtetl where we had been forced to live after our arrival from Germany, but had fled at the first opportunity. They could have lived elsewhere, but the neighborhood was cheap, and Dische liked cheap. As might be expected, they had a strange home. Dische had already set up his sofa in the dining room, since it didn't fit into their kitchen, and Renate had set up her sofa in the living room. The baby had the only bedroom. Renate had no aptitude for the Help. After the fiasco with the nude-model maid, I went over to Yorkville in New York and looked for a nanny with German values. Within a few minutes of asking around there, I found Gertrude. She came straight out of German poverty, she had no manners and no decent clothes, but the emptiness of her pockets was balanced by the size of her dreams. She followed me right home to the Dische residence. I did not warn her about Dische or the setup, and I admonished her to be grateful for a chance to make good in the New World; after all, she was there illegally. I used the word "illegally" three or four times, to make sure she knew that I knew, so she would behave herself. But she was not a Liesel. She kept order but she was mutinous. She ironed Renate's only party dress into fiery oblivion, and hung the charred remains back in her closet.

She couldn't stand what she called "gypsy life," the "man" asleep in the dining room. When she spoke about "him," she winced. She came to see me, complaining that he was such a typical Jew. I couldn't exactly contradict her. Then she said that the Dische baby was a typical Jewish baby, and he screamed all the time and her nerves were shredded, and the Hudson River was the right place for him, just to shut him up. I waited till she had finished the sentence before I fired her. And then I acquired the perfect nanny.

A half year after Little Carl was born, Liesel boarded a ship to the United States. She was nearly fifty years old, and she could not understand a word of English. We gave her the guest room, with its small bed, and set up a table for her sewing machine. She had brought her crucifixes with her, and before retiring for her first night at her new home, she hung them up. She also made me take her shopping, straightened out the kitchen, complaining about my order, and prepared a light meal of *Rinderroulade* with red cabbage and apples, and dumplings, which took her three hours to make, from raw potatoes. Renate rushed over after work to see her and show her the baby. Liesel took the baby in her arms and did not mind one iota that it was almost freakishly frail, with dark olive skin. I have never seen Liesel smile like that before. I think it almost tore her harelip in two.

"She is going to bully you," warned Carl.

"From now on, we will have real meals again," I said. "She only needs to learn English. I will find a school for her."

"She does not need to speak English. She doesn't need to speak to anyone but us."

Our routine changed now. Every day I drove Carl to his office, and then I drove to Manhattan, picked up the baby, and brought him home to Weehawken. After a while, it seemed silly to return him to Manhattan, to that sordid apartment with his frantically busy parents, so I just didn't bring him home. He began staying with us for the week, and only on weekends, when Liesel had English lessons, would Renate take him home.

I grew fond of the little thing. He was, after all, a boy. I thought if we raised him right, he might outgrow his genes. If he did a lot of exercise, he would grow strong despite his constitution. He could play tennis. And we would ingrain in him certain values that his mother was utterly lacking. We started early. We ignored the warning signs that began at ten months, when he began to talk. It was much too early, we should have known. At a year, he was putting together two-word sentences, at eighteen months he could identify automobiles by their make. He went up and down the street, a shred of a child, identifying cars, and people stopped to stare. We found this amusing only after we taught him that the name for a Cadillac was "jalopy." There was another slight complication at this time; his sister, Irene, was born. When we visited Renate in the hospital she had only one thing to say, to express her gratitude for the attention we were lavishing on her son—"You're not going to have this one too."

♕

RENATE HAD SCHEDULED HER SECOND CESAREAN for a midwinter day that was Dische's birthday. A birthday present of grand proportions, if you ask me. We suggested that she could choose instead Liesel's birthday, which was a week earlier, but she didn't see the irony in our remark and just answered that she had already honored Liesel's birthday—on that date she had eloped with Dische. Her plans were for naught. The baby, Irene, demonstrated straightaway that it had a will of its own. Irene added yet another thirteenth to the family calendar, arriving on a Wednesday. Wednesday's child is full of woe.

The birth was marked by several peculiarities. The first one: the father did not come to see his new child. Once again, the entire department of biochemistry, minus only the father, tramped down to obstetrics to see the newborn. Crowding around the plate-glass window to inspect the goods, several made the following identical remark: "Too bad about its nose."

But the mother did not mind, not about the absent father or the nose. Renate was not like most mothers. She didn't want a son, the way I had. She wanted a daughter. She had always wanted just a daughter. Now she took the child in her arms and murmured to it, "Here comes an ally."

A few minutes later, this ally began to scream. And that was the second peculiarity. The baby was hungry—greedy—and did not intend to wait for its regular bottle, administered every four hours. It grew angrier and angrier when it didn't get served. It turned blue, its eyes rolled, its limbs jerked. A seizure. A nurse swooped in to take the baby away. She was old and experienced, and when she returned an hour later, she remarked to the proud new mother, "Mark my words, this one will give you trouble."

Renate saw things otherwise. The ally would assist her in giving the rest of the family trouble. Dische did not come to see the baby for five days. He did not believe the child was his. He suspected Renate of betraying him. Renate had not betrayed him yet. She objected to the fact that Dische did not bring flowers the way other fathers did; all he brought were unfair accusations.

Later, Renate defined the birth of her daughter as the moment that she stopped loving Dische.

❦

THE NEW BABY was solid and blond. She had a huge doughy nose, and although her eyes were mercifully blue, one eye was large and round, while the other was narrow. A shame for a girl, looking like that. The boy's frailty would have looked better on the girl. And her robust bones would have suited the boy. Their characters were the opposite too. He was docile, she was a bully and a renegade. His intelligence had been obvious very early, and her lack of it was also obvious. I don't want to go too far—she was not stupid. She was simply normal. That, at least, was a relief. Not another Dische freak. But her character was abnormal.

From the first day onward, she dealt harshly with any opposition to her wishes. At the hospital, an outrageous exception had to be made for her. Because again and again, if she did not get fed, she held her breath until she turned blue, and soon her arms and legs began twitching; she had a convulsion. The hospital staff had some young, impressionable nurses who were frightened by this and called a doctor. On the evening of her first day and the morning of her second, the emergency doctor came five times, because this newborn also proved to be unusually greedy. Thereafter, the baby was fed out of turn, any time she wished. She got what she wanted. This capitulation would have incredible ramifications, of course. The old nurses snorted about it, they had seen it all before, and they knew this was merely an uncommonly severe case of "breath holding," a psychiatric condition usually with a later onset, starting in babies of about six months. It is linked to extreme stubbornness. Everyone pitied the new mother. But she was naïve, and happy.

Renate decided they needed a bigger apartment. Dische thought theirs would do just fine, it was very cheap. His salary was modest, despite all of his alleged fame in his field. But the Jewish geniuses had been on sale during the 1930s, and Columbia had snapped them up. I must say that much in his favor—despite talking about money all the time, he did not chase the dollar. He simply accepted his lowly salary. He was stingy on a shoestring, and would have been stingy on a gold mine; his stinginess was not a practical matter. Renate wasn't earning much either, she was just a student. She tutored undergraduates, and spent her earnings on child care. She found an apartment larger but just as cheap, because more squalid. It had two bedrooms. Dische moved into the dining room there, Renate into the living room, and they had one room for the children and one for a maid.

She hired yet another German girl, freshly and illegally arrived in America, and because this time she got lucky and the girl was nice, she made friends with her, chatted with her, encouraged intimacies. When the maid announced that she wanted to get married, Renate did not forbid it, or even discourage it, as was proper. She congratulated the maid for abandoning her almost as soon as she had arrived, and bought her a big wedding present.

Renate was stymied. New York was overrun with Germans yearning to breathe free by earning a good living. The motherland was in ruins; anyone with any energy and initiative was trying to improve their lot by coming to America. They licked shoes gladly in exchange for a living, and yet they had standards. No one wanted to work for this weird ménage. No one would stay longer than a few months. The children had little to recommend them, they were turning out to be as strange as their parents. Little Carl started reading and writing when he was three, in two languages. But when a stranger even looked at him, he started to cry. His parents thought that all children were like that. His sister was having her breath-holding seizures daily. On my suggestion, her mother no longer paid attention. She pushed the pram to the park and calmly watched her child hold her breath until she turned deep blue, her limbs jerking, her eyes rolling. The other mothers began to scream. But Renate just smiled and watched her sunshine carry on. She knew that the child, once unconscious, would start to breathe normally again, and then she would pull out of her dramatic seizure. Little Carl was busy with his more academic interests. He started playing chess with Dische when he was four. Renate decided to enroll him in kindergarten. She had heard about excellent, highly selective schools in New York, and one September she dropped by one of them with Little Carl and asked if her son might attend. The administration was shocked by her ignorance. One applied to such a school at least one year before hoping, praying to attend. Most were not accepted. However, as the child was already there, they might as well have a look at him.

He and Renate were asked to wait in the school library. The child found a book that interested him, *Hamlet*, and sat down to read it. By the time the admissions officer came to fetch him, he was too engrossed to respond to his name being called.

He started the first grade a week later. He was scrawny for his age, and by the far the smallest and youngest and smartest in his class. Every day, he wet his pants, number one and often number two. He started taking the bus home by himself, and it freed the nanny up in the afternoon. He just walked a few blocks, got on the number 5, and rode it for about one hour uptown. If he had somehow managed not to wet his pants at school, then he wet them on the bus. He knew where to get off, and how to find his way home from there, it was just another few blocks. He would turn five soon anyway. When he got home, the nanny took off his wet trousers for him. We all agreed that he was a pathetic little boy.

By then, Renate had already received her doctorate in biochemistry, had applied to medical school and been admitted. It had been a long, roundabout route to her goal—she was determined to become a surgeon, like her father, and show him up.

🏵

CARL GAVE ME A DIARY with the title OUR VACATION embossed in gold on the cover. I started writing as our Buick nosed down our driveway. I wrote down our average speed on the New England Thruway, the temperature, the taste of the cream cheese and tomato sandwich ("very delicious"), and the temperature of the milk from the red thermos ("lukewarm"). My handwriting would be hard to read, because the car was bouncing. I finished later, sitting at my desk in the rental cabin: "We reached New Hampshire at 4 o'clock. This is our first vacation in ten years. I beseech you God: keep me from snoring this evening. Please God let Carl have a good time and sleep well at night."

God did not hear my prayers. The first night, Carl retreated to the sofa in the little living room. I woke up in the morning alone in bed. Is snoring something you can control with willpower? My mighty willpower could work miracles, but Carl had purple rings under his eyes. He went fishing, and I studied the *Reader's Digest.* He took a rowboat out onto the lake. He caught the Smiths. George and Susie. That was something. George Smith had been an officer in the American army. Not quite a general, but nearly. He was older than Carl, but very fit. Susie was as plump as I was, but more daring about showing it—she wore shorts and sleeveless blouses. Her husband showed us how, if he placed his hands around her upper arm, he could not close them. Then he kissed her, his face nearly disappeared in her jolly cheek. Their son had served in Korea, and their grandson Jack was at West Point. A picture-book grandson. I told them about Little Carl, and wished he were more like their Jack, and about Dische. They listened with sympathy. Then Susie said, "Listen, I just have to get this off my chest. George and I agree—Dr. Rother, you are the spitting image of Harry Truman!"

We were great friends by dinnertime. They both came from military backgrounds, strict Protestants, but they knew how to enjoy themselves. That evening, George and Carl smoked cigars on the veranda, and Susie and I told each other our whole lives. Of course I left out Carl's background and family. That night I did *not* snore. Carl went fishing every day with George, they shared a rowboat. We ate dinner together. During the day, Susie and I went swimming from the dock, and the men remarked that once we actually got in the water we were as graceful as seals. We laughed together about how they looked when they were out in the boat rowing vigorously, like two old walruses. Susie was a few years older than I was, but perfectly fresh. She had never really endured any hardships, and I liked that. I did not want to hear any complaints. At last, I had an American girlfriend. You can't imagine how upgraded I felt! When we were apart, her name, Susie Smith, popped into my mind constantly like a wonderful tune. And when we were together, there was not a dull moment. We filled all silence with chat and we traded magazines. When our week was over and we had to say a sad goodbye, the Smiths gave us a goodbye present of a leather address book with the title embossed in gold: ADDRESS BOOK OF THE ROTHERS, which matched our vacation book. When I thumbed through it, I found that they had already inscribed their particulars. They invited us to their house for a visit in Colorado Springs. A big house. I said, "Carl, they are well-to-do." Vulgar of me to mention their money, but he let it slide. I had chosen "well-to-do" because, unlike "rich," it was an acceptable expression. We promised to attend their grandson's graduation from West Point the following spring.

We returned home in triumph. The return drive was very hot, and the cheese sandwiches I made fell apart in our hands so we threw them away and traveled hungry. I was happy to be home, but I told Renate it was the nicest vacation we ever took.

❧

SO THINGS WERE "LOOKING UP." Our lives were improving. Having the name and address of the Smiths turned our new address book into a superior kind of passport. Susie and I wrote to each other constantly, keeping each other up-to-date on all the details of our daily lives. Faithful was also a most amusing friend to me, especially after I had him neutered and he stopped embarrassing me by licking the pavement on the street. Our biggest old worry was Dische because he was such a bad influence on our grandchildren.

It was an undeniable fact that although we were all really courageous, both Dische children were excessively timid. I discussed this with Carl, and he said fearfulness is not inherited but passed along like a viral infection. Dische was terrified of seeing blood. He was afraid of illness, infection, men on the street who were larger than he was (almost all of them). He was not manly. No surprise that his children were timorous. Particularly Irene, the willful, had a panic problem. She was a robust child, but frightened of anything you could think of besides candy, and she was even afraid of candy if it was given by strangers, because someone had told her it could be dangerous. A woman on the street offered her a peppermint, and she had to wipe the spittle from her lips as she replied, "No thanks, it might be poisoned." She was afraid of electrical sockets, of darkness, rain, thunder, lightning, of wind, of the clouds, of ghosts. She had nightmares that made her list of fears grow. After one dream involving a giant dachshund and an elevator and me, she grew afraid of her own grandmother. I saw the look in her eye. I gave her some candy and the look went away.

Renate was so stubbornly defensive about this child, she refused to acknowledge that she was a coward. Irene was even afraid of eating carrots. Why? An understandable question.

One weekend, Renate had brought home visitors for her children: two white rabbits from the laboratory. She named them Uncle and Auntie. The bunnies liked eating carrots. They were such a hit with the children that Renate brought them home every weekend. And then one day, she did not bring them. Pressed, she admitted that something terrible had happened. Uncle and Auntie, she reminded the children, were gluttons. They ate carrots without any consideration whether they were hungry or not. One day, they overate, and their stomachs burst. They died. At least they died together. From then on, you could no longer serve carrots to Irene, even if they were slathered in butter. You couldn't even put them on the table without her starting a commotion. Finally we lost our patience and told her the truth—the rabbits had been research animals, they were used for an experiment in cancer medication, which proved toxic. The medication was injected, for heaven's sake, they hadn't overeaten a single carrot. And then Irene asked, "Were they really named Uncle and Auntie, or did you just call them that because we don't have any aunts and uncles? Everybody else does."

Renate decided she had to work on her child's self-confidence. She took the girl aside and said, "You know, you are not really afraid of anything. You are like me. You are just not afraid." That did not work at all.

She tried to set a good example. She nearly severed her finger peeling apples. She calmly put down the knife and the fruit, wrapped her hand tightly in a kitchen towel, mopped up the blood so quickly that the children didn't notice, told them they would have to wait for their apples for a "few minutes," and meandered out the door. She went to the emergency room, had the finger sewn up, returned, and showed her children the stitches. "Was nothing to be afraid of," she said. "It's nothing." Didn't work either. Both children howled when they skinned their knees.

She found new and rich opportunities to demonstrate lack of fear when she bought her first car, a Rambler. This had so few frills, it didn't even have a bottom. The brake linings got drenched driving through puddles, and then the brakes simply didn't work for a few minutes. When she stepped into the brakes and there was no response, Renate would snicker loudly, steer with hoopla. She said, "That funny feeling you get in your stomach when the brakes don't work? That's eternity." She became very skillful at driving without brakes, and never had a single accident. Once, on an icy highway, the car skidded into the opposite lane, where it was narrowly avoided by a truck. More cars came barreling at them. The children started crying in the backseat. She turned around and snarled at them, judgmental for once, "Don't tell me you're afraid to die! Now jump out of the car, and stand behind the safety barrier."

"Of course I'm not afraid to die!" Irene protested, and got out of the car slowly. Because she wasn't afraid to die. She was just afraid of having her hair stand up on end just before she was struck by lightning, or being swept out to sea by a tidal wave coming in over New York Harbor, or being chewed up by a rabid dog suddenly let loose on Broadway.

But all of a sudden, I had my own worries. Carl was not working very hard. He asked me to reduce the number of patients he was seeing in order to allow him two free hours every afternoon, which he said he was spending at Englewood Hospital, taking a refresher course. At first I thought this would rejuvenate his interest. But his interest lay somewhere else. One day he told me, without referring once to my own past observation about the matter, which had earned his instant rebuke, that poor Margie had an alcohol problem. He needed to help her. He had taken away the drink and put her on a strict diet of vegetables and fruit and tea, and he had promised her that the minute she felt tempted, she could ring him, no matter what time. She did not call. She stopped by the office for injections of vitamins, and then he started stopping at her house on his way home, before coming to see me, and he gave her the injections there, in private, in order to save her the trip. Often I would wake up in the middle of the night, and he would be gone, because, he said, he had heard her footsteps on the sidewalk pacing, and he knew that she was having a bad night. It became impossible to have a conversation with him, he was so uninterested in me. When I tried to talk about our grandchildren, he yawned and said, "Have you nothing else on your mind?" I noticed that he did not like to look at me. I went to the hairdresser and ordered a new hairdo. Curls. He did not comment. If forced by circumstance to listen to something I was saying, he looked contemptuous. He told me a hundred times that I knew nothing about medicine, and nothing about dogs, and nothing about America. At night, he lay awake, and when I asked him if something was the matter, he told me curtly that I was crazy, and it was getting on his nerves. He became cruel. When Liesel made *Milchkaltschale* for the first time in years, he told me not to eat so much. He remarked that my eyebrows were turning gray. He casually announced that he had to accompany Margie to Philadelphia one weekend, where she would visit her brother. He did not trust her to drive alone in her condition. When I hazarded a protest he cut me off.

I had no one to talk to. I could not confide in Susie Smith, she would have been too horrified. Finally I admitted the situation to Renate, but she brushed it off. She even had the nerve to tell me she thought that a little female attention was good for Carl's self-confidence. He was looking better, she said. He had lost weight, and his step had a bounce in it. Renate was right. I noticed how Carl chatted with the young patients in a new tone of familiarity— as if he felt they belonged to his own generation. He suggested I was not really needed in the office, and asked for the key back so he could give it to a young assistant. I pretended I couldn't find the key. One Sunday, instead of going on a promised outing with me, he just disappeared. He didn't return until late at night. He refused to tell me where he had been, denounced my efforts to "jail" him, and went to sleep without saying another word.

I arose in the middle of the night. He was sleeping soundly. I wrote him a letter asking for a divorce, and I got in the car and drove to his office. It was 3:00 a.m., in Weehawken. The Empress was abdicating.

I do not wish this on anyone: to know the feeling of a Wee-hawken street in 1952, on a spring night. The smell of the alley. The despair that drove me to unlock the door and venture inside the office. It was a foreign place to me now. I left the letter on his desk, and returned home before dawn. Carl did not stir when I lay down next to him and waited for morning.

At six sharp, I heard him sit up. I wanted to tell him that 1952 was probably my last year, but I knew that my husband would not mind at all. Indeed, it would throw open a closed door. He would rejoice. I groaned in misery, whereupon he said curtly, "Stay in bed," and launched himself into a new and glorious day.

A few hours after he had left, I was still in bed, dozing now. The phone rang. It was a patient who lived in our neighborhood, kindly inquiring whether everything was all right, since the doctor had not come into work at all, but had left a note on his door apologizing that he was delayed until noon.

I called Renate and told her what had happened but she was entirely without sympathy for me. She did not want to discuss it.

Finally, at my wit's end, I confided in the maid, Liesel—a social abomination if you look at it objectively. And Liesel said, "That letter was a mistake."

She said it with such finality and certainty that I lost my bearings. He would be checking into his office. I began shouting at her, "Go and get it back before he comes!"

I instructed her to take my key to the office from my purse and to take the bus, and she rushed out the door.

⚜

"DO NOT HITCHHIKE," said Liesel to the grandchildren. "Never hitchhike."

She started telling them that when they were two and four years old respectively and didn't know what hitchhiking meant. It was a refrain in her conversation when she was alone with them. She could find her way to the hitchhiking warning from almost any context, even from walking down one block to the Dairy Queen to buy an ice-cream cone on a hot summer day. "Walk, but don't hitchhike. *Never* hitchhike."

"How do *you* know, Liesel? You have never hitchhiked in your life."

"You don't know everything about me."

"When did you ever hitchhike?"

"It is none of your business."

But she told them in another context.

The Power of Prayer Context.

"If you pray to God when you need help, He will help you."

"How do you know?"

"Because He helped me once."

"How."

"I had to go to Dr. Rother's office. I was in a hurry. Frau Doktor sent me. She wanted me to pick up something there. I had to be there before noon. But the bus to Weehawken just didn't come. Finally, I hitchhiked. A man picked me up. He said he would take me to Weehawken. He had another idea. He put his hand underneath my dress, on my leg. Here, on my thigh. And he squeezed very hard. His hand went up into my lap. I prayed to God to Jesus to the Virgin Mary and all the Apostles to help me. I had my hands together and my eyes closed, and he asked me what I was doing. I said,

'Speaking to God about you.' He veered to the side of the road. He opened the door and told me to get out. I was saved, thanks to the power of prayer."

LIESEL DID NOT MAKE IT to the office by noon. Dr. Rother found my letter and tore it to shreds. He returned home and raged at me. "This is what you want anyway, isn't it," he cried. "This is what you've been wanting for thirty years. You should have stayed in Germany. That is what you wanted! And you have no right to come into my office when I am not there. Probably snooping around."

And then he ran out the door, no doubt to see Margie.

Liesel thundered around the house, but said nothing. She had the authority of an angry goddess. I was impressed, but she had no influence on Carl. He did not talk to me for six days and nights. Liesel cooked the meals for us. We sat over dinner in the silence of a wake without mourners, and then I retired to bed, and he left the house. He returned late at night. But he returned.

On the seventh day, he spoke. He had a suggestion. Margie had promised herself a trip if she managed to kick the alcohol habit. And with his help, she had managed. And she was going to go to Europe. She had decided to invite us along. She would pay for everything. First-class steamer tickets. We had not been back, we could not afford a trip. Her great generosity made it possible. We would rent a car and drive anywhere we pleased. Margie had never been to Europe. She wanted us to show it to her. He, Carl, was my husband, and he would share a cabin with me. I had doubted his morals, and it had hurt him to the quick. Margie had helped him when he was in a bad situation, and he felt obliged to help her now. I was trying to stop him. I was sinning. And she was so forgiving that she was extending this invitation to me.

The boat was sailing the next week.

I WAS LEAVING RENATE ALONE, but Liesel had a good idea how to manage the Disches. Her niece Friedel was fetched from Germany on a tourist visa, and she moved right into the Dische household. She was eighteen, with brown curls, ruddy cheeks, a thick beard on her legs, and goatees under her arms. She was Catholic and church-going, and she had been raised well. Of course she was appalled by the Dische children. Liesel forbade her to complain, so she kept her thoughts to herself. They were not a mystery, though. She thought those American brats were disgusting. Spoiled. They did not have to lift a finger for the common good. All they were expected to do was go to school, come home, eat dinner, and go to bed. They did not have to milk the cows or shovel dung all afternoon, the way she had done. She gave them as many chores to do as possible, but there weren't many, because she cleaned the house herself in the morning, and she was thorough and hardworking. They didn't even have to help wash and dry the dishes after supper, because Renate usually came home then and insisted on spending some time with them, and expected Friedel to do those chores. Renate trusted Friedel because she was Liesel's niece, and left the children in her care for hours and eventually days at a time.

Soon Friedel began to hit them. She hit them in the face with her open hand. They grew used to the small hurt, and didn't mind anymore. She started using a flyswatter, which they found humiliating. She kept one handy for the purpose. She put her back and shoulder into this exercise; she hit as hard as she could. They grew used to that too. She tried various harder objects at hand, wooden spoons, a cookbook, but they got used to everything. Then her attention was drawn to a shallow closet packed full of clothing; it could be locked from the outside. If stuffed inside vigorously, a small child could still fit there. It was always nighttime in the closet. If the child screamed too loudly, then Friedel left the house.

Out on the street, she heard nothing. When she returned, the child was purple-faced and exhausted, grateful to be released from this perfectly safe confinement, and inevitably fell asleep in a corner.

Irene whined about Friedel's harshness, but for once, Renate and I agreed on something: we didn't believe Liesel's niece would ever hit the children without good reason. Proof was that only Irene complained. Little Carl behaved himself and did not get punished. The New World was forcing me to let down my guard against the lower classes, and I remarked that at last someone cared sufficiently about Irene to discipline her. Dische didn't raise a finger. He did not mind what the children did as long as they didn't disturb him. The boy started religious training and we wondered whether he might become a priest. We broached the subject of becoming pope with him. He seemed enthusiastic.

We arrived in Europe in the middle of June, in Cherbourg, after traveling in two first-class cabins next door to each other. I did not enjoy the voyage much. The food was probably excellent, and the service. I have a snapshot recollection of Margie's hand holding a cocktail glass filled with milk, the fingers bare—she had taken off the engagement ring her husband had given her. She clearly felt it didn't belong on this jaunt, paid for with his money.

We rented a Mercedes car and drove to Monte Carlo. She was determined to go to the town she said must have been named after my husband. The car was so large, it could hardly steer through the narrow streets. I sat in the backseat and prayed. I thought the lump in my throat would strangle me. My husband and his admirer felt briefly guilty; then their delight in each other overwhelmed them. Margie paid for everything, the hotels, the restaurants. She had a purse on her arm that was always full of cash. She kept saying, "Oh, I am having a whale of a time."

We stayed in Monte Carlo for nearly a month because Margie liked to play roulette in moderation. Carl joined her. I didn't care for the game. I retired early most evenings, and read the *Reader's Digest* or wrote letters to Susie Smith, or to my relatives in Germany, about what a great time I was having, although I regretted that our tight itinerary did not include the Rhineland. I agreed with everyone that Willy Brandt, who had run off and taken up Norwegian citizenship during the war, was a terrible traitor for fighting against his own motherland, no matter what the circumstances, and his newly won election to the highest public office in Germany was therefore outrageous, although frankly, I didn't care, I had more important things on my mind. The lump in my throat was now a chronic constriction, and I was losing weight. Margie praised me for this, and bought me a pink dress and a wide-brimmed straw hat. Carl thanked her lavishly and did not look at me.

One night I was lying alone in my hotel room while Margie and Carl were out playing, and they had an altercation of some kind. Carl came back gloomy and offended. I was kind to him and asked him no questions. We did not see Margie for breakfast. He did not volunteer any information on her whereabouts. We had a quiet morning.

She was there for lunch, with a tall young gentleman who identified himself before she had a chance as Count Lifschinsky. He had a Polish accent, a monocle, and Old World manners. Before opening my mouth to say hello, I prayed ten Hail Marys that he was in love with Margie.

The count told us about his beautiful spread on the Baltic coast that had been confiscated by the Reds. He said he would invite Margie there to see it for herself the minute it was returned to him. He was working hard on getting it back; he had no time for any other job. He had a castle, and two thousand hectares of cherry orchards—white cherries so sweet they made you levitate, red cherries so sour they put your feet back on the ground—and he also had ten thousand hectares of choice pasture . . . and . . . and thousands of beef cattle and . . . numerous serfs.

He insisted on ordering a very good bottle of wine, and after Carl pointedly refused to touch it, and I followed his example much against my desires, he insisted Margie share it with him and then allowed her to pay for his lunch. We left the table when Margie was already drunk. They left for a game of roulette.

We returned home soon afterward without Margie. We had to finance the train ride back to Cherbourg. The boat ride home was one of the most pleasant I ever had. I knew then that God occasionally did hear my prayers. His choice in which ones to honor, however, was a puzzle.

❧

WHEN WE GOT BACK TO WEEHAWKEN, we went right back to our routine and I declared it my valley of love and delight. Carl was hanging his head slightly, and I was humble and determined to make him utterly happy. I doted on him and insisted that all others, meaning Renate and Dische and the grandchildren, show him the respect he deserved. We bought a funny blue parakeet, named Happy, and after Faithful was run over by a truck, we bought a long-haired dachshund puppy we named Lucky. After Lucky ate Happy, and a few hours later bit the postman, we put him down. No more dogs. There was enough to do with grandchildren in the house.

We were pleased to take Little Carl on the weekends, just so he could absorb the healthy atmosphere in our house, the regular meals, the prayer, the conversations that were designed to form him. We often mentioned George and Susie Smith's grandson, with the lovely name Jack, graduating from West Point. Jack had lived with his family in Thailand, and Jack had ridden elephants there. Wouldn't that be something for you too, Little Carl? Jack was also a good tennis player. His grandfather had seen to that. We spoke about Jack in every possible context, steering Little Carl to a similar adulthood.

He no longer looked like a little monkey. He was a very sweet and pretty boy, who could do no wrong, but was pleasant and agreeable and always polite. He preferred being alone. He disappeared like a shot when the doorbell rang. He liked to rest behind the bed we had made for him in Carl's den, between the bedstead and the wall, where he would read. We worked hard to turn him into a normal little boy. We gave him candy and a bicycle. He did not require candy, and he fell off the bike. We bought him a ball and I offered to play with him, but his face grew sad. He did not like to displease me. He comforted me that his sister would love to play with me. And it was true. When Irene came, she made a beeline to the ball and forced me into hours of tossing it around, until I thought I would die of boredom. Then she co-opted her brother's bike, made me teach her how to ride it. At least I got to know the neighborhood that way, trudging up and down the hot street, holding the seat, the neighbors coming out as we passed, calling "Hi there" and smiling approvingly. The pedal scratched my leg as I walked. The wound became infected.

I was in the hospital. No more sports. I had blood poisoning. It seemed that 1957 would be my final year. Carl visited me and lavished me with concern. I recovered, but my leg was forever disfigured, the skin black-and-blue as if ink had leaked and stained it. I was keenly aware of a lack of apology. Irene had set off a causal chain of events—she had forced me to hold the bike, which had infected me. But she was determined even then never, ever to feel guilty about anything. For years afterward, I tested the waters to see if she was changing, learning to register guilt. If she was in the room, I would arrange to pull up my stockings, holding the discolored leg stretched out just for an instant, and glancing at her meaningfully. She pretended not to notice.

After I was recovered, Carl and I went to work together as we had always done before the Margie Period. Now that it was really over, no sign of Margie returning and her house next door empty, Carl began taking an interest in me again, in my appearance and my opinions. Renate and Irene were my biggest obstacles to being one big happy family, the girl because of her peculiar nature, and Renate because she did not ever put that child in her place.

Irene had terrorized everyone with her breath holding, and now she terrorized everyone with her imagination. She was always underfoot when Friedel cleaned the house, and then she was terrified of staying home alone, so Friedel had to take her everywhere. Out on the street, she seemed to lose all fear, even though that was one place where a little caution was a good thing. Friedel held her hand tightly so she wouldn't suddenly pull away and run off, and Friedel complained that her hand got cramps from holding on so tightly; bending down slightly sideways to accommodate the small child was giving her backaches. We told her that small children have flexible arms, she should stand up straight, the child's arm would accommodate after a few days.

Friedel had a few tricks up her sleeve too—she harnessed the child's imagination and told her war stories. She described how when the sirens had wailed, the American bombers had come and the tar melted in the streets. People were stuck in it, and got cooked. Those who could, fled into bomb shelters. Once, a bomb fell into the next bomb shelter, where it hit a water main, and Friedel and her mother, her sister and brothers, listened to the screams of the mothers and children drowning slowly inside. Friedel had discovered that when she told Irene these stories, the child was docile. She could run all of her errands without any aggravation. They returned home in the late morning, in time for the siren that heralded noon in New York. When that siren began to wail, Irene thought the bombers were coming. Friedel explained to her not once or twice but at least a dozen times that the sirens only meant it was twelve o'clock, but the child was so frightened that she forgot what one had told her about time. So Friedel started disappearing just before noon, either to take the garbage out or just to see a neighbor, and the child had a little fright bath. Yet it did not harden her. When Friedel came home shortly afterward, the child hugged and kissed her with gratitude for returning at all, which was nice. Friedel put lunch on the table. After that, came the peace and quiet of the Nap.

The Nap lasted two hours. The shade was drawn. Pajamas were issued. Eyes were to be kept closed. Unnecessary stirring was prohibited, punished. The child did not sleep, because she kept busy. As soon as Friedel stepped out of the room, she opened her eyes. The shade, illuminated by the afternoon sun, glowed like a movie screen. There, Irene discovered she could watch her favorite stories. When Friedel stormed back in to check on her, she learned that the film could also be screened within, her eyes closed. Friedel's regime of boredom had terrible consequences; the child learned that her imagination was always on, always running, and it was hers to administer. It could run out of control and frighten her occasionally, but mostly it proved a constant provider of amusement. And so it happened that she began watching movies in church, and missed the most important lessons of the catechism.

Of course, she was also bored, being at home all the time. She threw herself on her brother when he came home. Poor Little Carl soon misbehaved because of her. But he learned his lesson. Little Carl was *able* to learn his lesson. When Little Carl was five, in the second grade, he liked to keep to himself when he came home from school. Irene could not bear it. She pestered him. In the next room, Friedel was ironing. She said, "Little Carl, play with your sister. I have to go to the basement for the laundry." He dropped his book reluctantly.

"I'm strong!" Irene said when he came in the door. "I'm much stronger than you." She was four years old. She shoved out her jaw and glared at him. Her wispy blond hair stood straight up on her head. Then she raised her arm and made a muscle. "Look!" she commanded. "My muscles are bigger than yours."

"Oh, you're a terrible sissy," he answered calmly, as if it were a tiresome matter of fact. He gazed around the room and saw the iron, propped on the ironing board. It was turned on. He was knowledgeable about irons. "You're too much of a sissy to touch that iron."

"No I'm not!" she snapped.

"Yes you are," he said, using his tired, resigned voice.

"No I'm not!" she shrieked.

"Prove it," he said, trying not to show his excitement.

She fetched the footstool, placed it next to the ironing board, stepped up. Now she could reach the iron easily. She felt tall and masterful. "You watch," she said.

She pressed her palm flat against the iron. When she spread her fingers she could almost reach from one edge of the iron to the other—at the top of the iron, where it became narrower, her hands were that big now. She admired herself for that. And she felt nothing. "See?" she cried in triumph. She smelled the burning meat before she felt the pain.

She tumbled backward off the stool, hollering and wailing. Little Carl flashed a brief smile, ran out of the room, flung himself on his bed, and began to read. The nanny was coming in.

Irene tattled, of course. Little Carl got a hiding from Friedel. Ten beats of the cooking spoon in his face. Irene had to go to the hospital, and everyone slathered her with amused affection and attention, and no one pointed out what a fool she had been. At least, Little Carl learned an important lesson: crime does not pay. Irene did not learn a thing.

Carl and I tried again and again to help the little family, but there was only so much a mortal can do. Carl grew fed up. "Family is not everything," he said. He was protective of our tranquillity. When Jacob Rother, Carl's only surviving relative, came to New York on a visit, Carl felt it was the last straw. He did not wish the family black sheep to remind him of what had happened to the Rothers. He lashed out at Jacob's nerve for trying to contact us. "That's all I need is that thief back in our life." I argued, only meekly, that Jacob was a successful businessman in Melbourne. I pointed out that he was still young, in his early fifties, and had probably changed a lot. I remembered how handsome he had been. I did not say "He is your only relative," because of course Carl was all too aware of that. It fell to me to call Jacob in his midtown hotel and explain that Carl was too busy to see him. Jacob said, "And what about you, doll. Don't you want to see me?" My sympathy dissolved. He had no manners, and I was pleased to say, "No, Jacob Rother, actually I don't."

"I have George Smith," said Carl. "I don't need to have a brother." It occurred to me that I felt the same way about my brother Otto, so I could not argue.

THE NEIGHBORING HOUSE stood empty for over a year. One day, the lights were on again. We waited, and said nothing. A few days passed. Someone was inside the house. We expected to see Margie any minute. Carl was short-tempered and preoccupied, and I was full of dread.

Then one evening, as we were comfortably watching TV, the doorbell rang. My heart fell into my shoes. Carl was very pale. He did not move, but commanded, "Let Liesel get the door."

We heard Liesel opening the door and saying haughtily, "Residence Dr. Rother!" A male voice replied, and I heard her hesitate, and then give out a cheerful "Sure!" Without asking us whether it was all right, Liesel ushered a respectable-looking young man into the living room. He introduced himself as Margie's nephew. Margie, he told us, had passed away in Rome, in a clinic where her second husband, Count Lifschinsky, had brought her to have her incarcerated. Somehow, she had gotten her hands on drink there, and in the space of just a few minutes had emptied two bottles of vodka. This had killed her. The nephew had a letter from the director of the clinic. He rebuked the count on several occasions for supplying his patient with alcohol when she was confined in his establishment, and there was apparently no doubt in the director's mind as to the origin of the two fatal bottles. Carl listened to this without any expression. He did not move in his chair. If the news affected him, he never showed it. He was practiced at loss.

Margie had left a will, and her nephew as the executor. Alas, there was no money in her bank account at all. She had spent every penny on her romp through Europe, but she had specified that her diamond engagement ring, safely kept in Weehawken, was to be turned over to Mrs. Carl Rother. The ring was mine.

I never wore it of course. I segregated it in my box of rings, it enjoyed its own compartment. When I showed Renate the collection once, she said, "Oh that diamond is the prettiest!" I was angry about her poor judgment. And when Irene, with her utter lack of sensitivity on the subject, began selling off my jewelry, she got more for Margie's ring than for any other piece. People should pay a little more attention to the history of what they buy.

❧

IN THE MEANTIME, Renate had become a medical doctor.

She had always intended to become a surgeon, just like her father. But she had two small children and could not get a residency in surgery. This final stage of her education would have required her to work and sleep at the hospital for days at a time. No administrator in his right mind would give a mother a job as a surgeon anyway, much less accept her as a resident, no matter her gifts for it, her agile fingers and calm temperament. Since she could not enter the field in which her father had excelled, she chose the field that he had failed: pathology. She boasted to us that it was the greatest service of all in medicine: to diagnose. Without a diagnosis, a surgeon could not operate. But also, if he botched the operation, the pathologist was there to tell him that. In short, and this she didn't have to say, the pathologist was the sworn enemy of the surgeon. Carl saw the matter clearly—Renate's interest was a way of betraying him. He did not say so. He said to me at dinner, "Instead of going into the business of saving life, she is going into the business of death," and his face twisted in pain.

Liesel could not mind her own business. Dropping an alluring slice of pork loin on his plate, looking down at the meat and not at him, she stuttered, "I admire Renate for her . . . courage. She looks death in the face." Before we could contradict her, she had stalked back into the kitchen, and we were left to consider her words.

Soon, Renate left Columbia University's calm, superior academic halls and descended into the Hades of New York, the city morgue. After long negotiations with Carl, I paid her a diplomatic visit. It was autumn. I dressed up in my simple clothing: I wore my gold chains tucked beneath the collar of my black wool suit, with the plain pumps and a light gray overcoat. I enjoyed my visit. I did not mind the smell. I viewed the cadavers with interest. A woman with her soul in order and her feet on the ground does not fear or object to death. I was pleased at the way Renate introduced me to all her colleagues, the words "my mother!" expressed with pride and delight.

We went for lunch in the cafeteria. Plain, good cooking. Everyone there knew my daughter; even the cafeteria workers beamed when they saw her. Then we returned to the morgue and she let me wear a lab coat and watch while she dissected a dead middle-aged woman. I assured everyone that I found it fascinating. When she walked me back to my Buick, I said, "Renate, why don't you work as a real doctor?"

I remember her expression. She smiled the way she had done when she received the news that her concert in Leobschütz was canceled. Her eyes shone. Resistance.

"I just want the best for you," I said. "And for your children."

But Renate was stubborn, and did as she pleased. She stayed at the morgue, becoming deputy medical examiner of the city. She worked constantly, restlessly. Her children saw her in the evenings, for dinner, when she told them tales of New York. She did not censor herself, she liked reality. Oh, what wonderful lamb chops! Today we had an unidentified body with the most beautiful breasts. Is that spinach I see? May I? When we stripped her, she turned out to have a penis. The penis was real, the breasts weren't. They were made of rubber balls that were sewn under the skin. The penis had a tattoo on it. The police needed to identify her, so we had to figure out a way of pumping up the penis. Pass the salad, please. The tattoo said Abraham Lincoln.

After dinner, she often had to leave again. She was called to death scenes in the middle of the night. A patrol car came for her. Little Carl didn't appear to mind, but Irene did. She demanded that her mother stay at home nights like a "normal" mother. A few more little details would have to be changed to make the word "normal" apply. But if anyone could manage to force something on Renate, I said, then it would be iron-willed Irene. The girl screamed from her bed when she heard the doorbell ring nights. Renate ignored her. She explained that she was serving the interests of science. She left. Once, Irene opened the door and hollered after her, "I wish you were dead!"

Renate was on her way to Harlem. A child had been found dead in a chest of drawers. The family claimed that they had made a baby bed in the bottom drawer, for want of a better one, and someone had accidentally closed the drawer, so that the child had suffocated. Renate studied the preliminary case report, sitting in the backseat of the police car. She entered the tenement with two police officers and began climbing the stairs. The officers decided to have a cigarette, and let her walk ahead. On the next landing, a man was waiting. He stabbed Renate in the face and hands, but she held on to her doctor's bag.

When she got home that night, she woke Irene up and showed her the wounds. She said, "There. Your wish almost came true." But Irene's real wish did come true. After that, Renate quit the night service, saying she was not afraid, but she was not suicidal either. She began bringing her microscope and specimens home at night, and she set up shop in her living room. If the children insisted on her attention, she showed them specimens, or illustrations of diseases from her pathology book. Little Carl was easily disgusted, but Irene took to it like a fish to water.

Renate was delighted, started taking her along to the morgue whenever she could, shared the fun. Her panicky daughter had not the slightest fear of dead people. Renate was proud when Irene, measuring the stench, crisply identified the approximate week of death of a newly arrived floater. Dische tried to interest his son in biochemistry, took him along to the lab, but although Little Carl was not a scaredy-cat like his sister, he detested the smell of chemicals. Besides, he hated all the strangers he had to greet there, and being stared at for being old Dische's son, and everyone asking him stupid questions like "Are you a genius like your father?"

In a lighthearted moment, I had taught my grandchildren a trick—to look down when people tried to strike up a conversation. This generally discouraged any further words. Little Carl tried this out and has been using it ever since. He grew used to the horrible smell, and didn't mind going to the lab as much. Family life was divided into a male domain—chemistry, and a female domain—death.

But where was I? Weehawken. Margie's house was sold, and we soon had new neighbors, the Contis. Mrs. Conti was fat and jolly. Her husband built highways, he drove a limousine with the trimmings. The neighborhood was being overrun by Italians with big cars. They were too vulgar to like, but they appreciated a good Catholic doctor. The Contis came to Carl's practice, bringing their five children. We were very pleased with them, and when the back-yard fence collapsed during a hard winter, we did not bother putting it back up.

Our home was tranquil and clean as a hard-boiled egg. Liesel took care of us. I had a settee, with cookies on a Bunzlau dish in the living room. Carl no longer allowed Renate's career to irritate him. His medical practice flourished. His patients called him "our Catholic doctor," not knowing that he was still blackballed from working in a Catholic hospital. But he had a position in the state hospital as a gynecological surgeon, he was an honored resident of the area, and I could be proud to be his wife. The policeman who directed the traffic in front of the Palisades Amusement Park gave us free tickets to the rides. The butcher saved especially good cuts for us. The florist sent us flowers after his wife's uterine prolapse was resolved.

We bought a TV set, with a white glowing frame. I did not understand how the antenna worked, and was quick to be disappointed or lose my temper with it. Again, I had to cede authority to Carl, who made the decisions about which channel to watch, adjusting the antenna. I bought a Studebaker, green. We became a two-car family. We had two grandchildren, two cars, our own home in a safe Italian neighborhood, and last but not least, a plot in our church graveyard. The cemetery lay on a hillside, with a forest on one side, and the valley, with miles of open fields stretching to the horizon, on the other. Carl had picked a plot directly next to the forest. The Garden State seemed to reach the pinnacle of its beauty right there, and we felt we had finally taken firm control of our lives, a feeling close to happiness.

It was an added pleasure when Renate began to complain to me about Dische. Soon she could not stop complaining. He was uninterested in anything but his work; he was stingy. He paid for the rent, but made Renate pay for Friedel and the children's religious training. While he dutifully presented her with two new pearls on every wedding anniversary, she was sure they were fake. But she did not complain about that. She did not really care as much as I felt she should care, and apparently he often told her that he was looking forward to their tenth anniversary, so he could finally see her wearing the completed necklace. That wish of his was, on the scale of gentlemanly sentiments, as high as he ever got. The family did not take vacations, because Dische did not want to pay.

Carl said, "I will buy them a vacation house just to show Dische what a stingy father he is; we are sacrificing our own money so that our grandchildren have a place to go to in the summers." We bought a wooden house at Chadwick Beach. I took Liesel to see it, and she said, "It looks like a bomb shelter made of old tinder." I told her to keep her opinions to herself, but from then on I fondly called it our beach bomb shelter. It had one large room that contained the kitchen at one end, and four comfortable bunk beds built directly into the walls at the other, and outside, in the garage, a bathroom. It stood about five houses down from the crashing surf of the Jersey Shore. On his first reluctant visit there Dische poked around the living room, examined the bunk beds, and then calmly told us about a colleague's summerhouse that was directly on the water and had three bathrooms.

Dische considered vacations a torturous time away from his lab. What could he do all day? He did not know how to swim. He did not believe anyone could actually swim. I swam way, way out with Renate, farther than anyone else dared, while he paced the beach in terror. We laughed about his fear, and he minded. He said his fear was reasonable, as we were swimming in ice-cold water, way beyond the reach of a lifeguard. "What?" I demanded. "You think drowning is unpleasant?" For once, he had his wits about him. He said he was from inland, and he had recognized the ocean to be his mortal enemy; it had been waiting all those decades to pull him in and drown him, and he wasn't going to give it the pleasure. I liked that, his standing up to the ocean. I actually bragged about it in a letter to my best friend, Susie Smith, but she wrote back that my son-in-law sounded peculiar.

We sent the children up to the beach for the entire summer with Friedel, and just once in those three months did Dische agree to visit them. He put on a pair of sneakers for the occasion, and a pair of shorts. His legs had more varicose veins than mine. It was not a pretty sight. Carl told Little Carl not to expose his legs if they became as ugly as his father's.

THE BEACH HOUSE was as far away from the lab and the morgue as you could get. But placing a broken vase on a different shelf will not repair it. Little changed. We did our best, but everything backfired. We gave the children a black brute of a tomcat hurriedly chosen from the animal shelter. He proved to be a weak, timid creature whose fur fell out in tufts when he got excited, which was often, because other cats beat him up; he was not a good example of what a swarthy male should be. Little Carl played with the other neighborhood children, normal children, no geniuses, who answered to names like Billy and Jerry, and had fathers who were cops and contractors. But their healthy contempt for eggheads embarrassed Little Carl. For a while, though, it seemed to us he might learn at least to hide his book learning. Irene didn't have to learn. She worked hard at a dream she and I had in common: being accepted by the boys as one of their own. Friedel saw to discipline—regular meals, two-hour naps, early to bed. The big red hand. The closet. The closet in the summerhouse was smaller, tighter, because Friedel kept the blankets and laundry in there. It smelled of pine and fresh laundry and then, after Irene spent some controlling time in there, of urine. The child began smelling of urine all the time. Her pants were always wet. Friedel thought hard about how to control this. Little Carl had been so easily browbeaten out of this weakness.

She took the child down several streets to the shops. A policeman stood at one corner directing traffic. Friedel looked down at Irene, pulling the child's hand sharply upward, and said, "If you wet your pants one more time, I am going to tell him, and he will arrest you. You will be sent back to Germany." She could not think of a worse punishment.

Irene wet her pants again anyway.

It was lunchtime, and Friedel was looking forward to the two-hour nap, when she could take her own siesta. Now that Irene had soiled herself again, she would have to deliver on her threat. She had a better idea. She told Little Carl that his sister had to change her pants again, and that he could tell the other children, in case they wanted to watch.

Little Carl ran to inform the boys. They hauled some beach chairs over from the neighboring yard, climbed up on them, and peered into the bedroom window where Irene was pulling off her soaking, stained pants. Her skin was red and raw. She glanced upward and saw in the window, like monstrous butterflies that had landed on the pane, boys' faces leering at her.

That evening, Renate came for a surprise visit. She noticed that something was the matter with her daughter. A mother knows her child's temperature. The child was hotter than usual. Finally, the child confided in her mother. She was a baby again. Peeing in her pants. She blubbered and expected more chastisement. Her mother did not scold her, but took her to the bathroom and said, "Let's have a look." The child's urine was laced with blood. That same night, she took her back to the city and brought her to the hospital. She had a kidney infection. I wanted to fire Friedel. Renate would not permit it. She said that Friedel was ignorant, but she could learn. She did not say, Friedel is Liesel's niece, and therefore we cannot fire her. She did not say, I will never find anyone better.

I thought of taking the children myself. But I knew my heart was too weak. I thought of lending Liesel, and taking Friedel myself, but no, that was unthinkable. Black sin of selfishness. When Irene recovered, she was returned to Friedel's cruel regime. By then, her heart was hardened against all authority. Authority, in her eyes, was despicable, no matter how well-intentioned it was. The die was cast.

We always speculated that only a great romantic love for a sensible man could neutralize the rebellion in Irene's heart. But she didn't wait around for a sensible man. It turned out that her nature was, like Renate's, one of gross enthusiasm for boys. More about this later.

Suffice it to say that such predilections are obvious early on in life. When she was five years old, a blond, freckled boy on Chadwick Beach was caught by her radar. When she saw him, she swooned. Someone told her he was seven, older than her brother. He took no notice of her. One day, though, he came strolling along the little road in front of the house all by himself. He saw Irene playing in the yard, and he called to her, "Do you know what time it is?"

She understood that this was a great big compliment of a ruse. A seven-year-old asking the time.

Her heart played a drumroll. She did not know how to tell time, but she knew to speed over to him. She ran across the sandy yard toward the street, where he loitered. As she ran, God thumped His mighty Fist. She stepped on a nail that was waiting for the soft part of her foot, head up, and drove itself by the power of her eager footstep deep into her flesh. She screamed, she yowled. She hurled herself on the ground. The little boy was terrified and ran away. The nail was very rusty and she had an infection. She had to wear socks and shoes for the final month of that long, hot summer, and was not allowed on the beach at all. I was pleased, figuring she had learned an invaluable lesson—mark my words, it never, ever, pays to run after boys.

IRENE WAS HER FATHER'S SPITTING IMAGE, but she did not look as Jewish as Little Carl. We told her she looked like a real German girl, or even Dutch.

We told Little Carl that if anyone asked him, he should say—or maybe, in order not to lie, just indicate—that his family was Italian, or Spanish. Not Jewish. We warned him not to talk with his hands, the way his father did. We cautioned him not to speak about money, the way his father did. We begged him not to roost in books the way his father did. Every weekend, he came gladly to stay with us in our citadel in Weehawken, where we could form him. We advised him to learn to play tennis, it would put muscle on his shoulders. His shoulders were limp, and he did not like tennis. His father thought that sport was for idiots. Dische climbed the stairs six flights to his office every day, which was healthier, he claimed, than destroying his joints with jerky movement involving a ball.

Little Carl didn't like going to church, because of all the people, but he enjoyed the catechism. He knew a lot about dogma and history. He enjoyed praying with us before dinner and after dinner. He ate everything on his plate. He had good manners. He was not at all like Dische, really. Except that like his father, he was frail. His sister was muscle-bound. The pediatrician said he had never seen such stomach muscles on a small child, male or female. She was proud of it, and told me she would like to be a man. I told her that all of us women in the family wanted to be men, but God had other plans for us. Besides, if she just looked around her, she would notice that women were in fact the stronger sex.

We were covering up Carl's greatest weakness, his background. We had decided not to tell the children about it. Bad enough that Dische could not be persuaded to be quiet about his own. Indeed, he talked openly in front of the children about going to the synagogue. Why? After all, he did not talk about his family, he did not admit that his mother and sisters had been murdered. He seemed to find the fact embarrassing. He himself had run away from Europe in time. He did not talk about that either. So why discuss going to the synagogue? He could just go, and not tell the children. At any rate, he followed our strict orders, and never told the children that Carl had converted. Carl was a Catholic, and that was all. The children learned that as good Catholics, we were opposed to the Nazis, therefore we left Germany.

Our house was full of portraits of my family, in paintings and photographs. The only Rother we had along was an alabaster bust of Carl's mother. I placed this in the corner of the living room, on top of a honey-colored Biedermeier commode. The Rothers had not owned a single item of Biedermeier, but I was making up for that. When you entered the living room, Oma Rother was the first person you saw. The family coward, Irene, was frightened of the bust because it was as white as any ghost. I noticed that she always entered the living room from a side entrance, and avoided that corner.

It could not be helped that I had to leave her alone with her grandfather once. I thought it would do her good, actually. I sent her into the living room, had her sit at the edge of the sofa closest to Carl's easy chair. As Liesel and I went out the door, we could hear their voices having a friendly conversation. Carl was not very talkative, but she was, and being alone with him, she asked him if he was a good boy when he was little, and he told her about expecting a spanking from his father for some minor act of disobedience, and padding his pants with newspaper beforehand.

This amazing revelation that Carl had once been small and disobedient, and was admitting it to her, made her cast around for more intimacies. So she asked, "Who is that ugly, ugly woman?" She pointed to the alabaster bust. Slowly, his demeanor changed. He pressed backward, away from her, into his cushions. He put on his rage face. He said nothing. She remained on the sofa; there was no escape.

When Liesel and I returned, the anger in the room was as perceptible as an old corpse. Irene and Carl were ensconced in silence next to each other. He stood up when I came in, and he said, "I am glad you returned." He headed for his den, on leaden legs. I gave Irene the benefit of the doubt. After all, she was not being a ninny, she was not crying. I sat down next to her, put my arm around her, and said, "Okay, what happened?" Irene repeated the offending question, leaving out the word "ugly," and I decided to answer it. The bust was her grandfather's beloved mother, who was dead. That is why he didn't want to talk about it. He was sad, and because he was a good, kind grandfather, he didn't want to make a show of his sadness, therefore he didn't want to talk about his mother. My kind tone encouraged her. "How did she die?" asked the child. Her curiosity had all the strength and tact of a locomotive. I told her that Carl's mother was a good Catholic who had loved God, and that she died of old age in her bed, which made a total of two lies. I invited my granddaughter to a game of canasta. I cheated so that she would notice, she cheated back, and we nearly died of laughter.

It was Liesel who talked completely out of turn. She was Little Carl's confidante. He hung on to her skirts. After Irene had asked me about the bust and received such an unsatisfactory answer, she asked Little Carl, and Little Carl asked Liesel. He was following her around as she cleaned up the living room while I was out, and he too pointed at the bust, risked all, and cried, "Who is that *ugly* woman?" At that, Liesel snapped. She told him that ugly woman was his grandfather's mother, who was the sweetest woman that ever lived, and the Germans had made her dig a ditch and then they shot her and pushed her into it. Because the Rothers were Jewish.

Little Carl was deeply shocked. He sat down in Carl's easy chair and stayed put while Liesel continued her work, which gradually led her back to the kitchen. When I came into the living room, Little Carl was still sitting in the easy chair, staring at the bust. I quickly realized what had happened. Liesel rejected all criticism. She said she was sick of lying to the boy. How could we object?

After that, it was more difficult persuading Little Carl that he wasn't Jewish, because he had quickly figured out that according to the laws of the Catholic Church, and the Nuremberg Laws, he was nothing else.

🐝

LITTLE CARL COULD NOT EXPLAIN the problem of their background to his little sister, Irene, because she was not able to understand it. It frustrated him sometimes that she was so limited. At the same time, she talked down to him, because despite being a year younger and a girl, she was a brute, stronger. He had to fight back somehow.

"You will never learn to read and write," he told her. "Never. Your life will be a big fat mess. Maybe you can get by. You can recognize traffic signs by their shape. You can 'read' comics, you already do. Picture books. You can go to the movies. But a lot of things will be hard. It's called being illiterate."

She was resigned to it. Nevertheless, she had ambition: she dreamed of going to school. She did not expect to learn how to read and write there, but at least she would leave the house every morning the way everyone else did except Friedel and Liesel. She despaired of ever reaching that higher form of existence.

Renate began to worry about finding a school for Irene, now that she knew these New York institutions were selective and took only clever children. She applied for a school for Little Carl, and for the admissions interview, she just "happened" to have Irene along. He was six, and had discovered Dante. The schools did not hesitate. Irene didn't have to do a thing; they took both children.

So, finally, Irene was emancipated. But she could not keep up with the other children who could all read and write in kindergarten. Irene was convinced that if she behaved slyly, then no one would notice her deficit. When the class stood in a circle and all the children spelled their names, Irene moved around the circle one child at a time, so that the teacher could never call on her. Success: the teacher said nothing. When it was her turn to read aloud from a book, Irene invented the text and believed that no one noticed. Sometimes she spotted the looks on the other children's faces: pity, contempt. But they were a polite group, and they never giggled. A few months passed, and the school sent Renate a letter. They were concerned.

Renate took her daughter to task over dinner. "They've written this silly letter," she said. "That you are not able to read and write yet. It worries them. So you better start reading and writing, okay?"

Irene just nodded her head, and the conversation was over.

"You see?" said Little Carl after dinner. "Now everyone knows."

But Irene accepted herself as she was. That is very typical of her. She accepts her own shortcomings magnanimously, even if no one else does. She still loved going to school, and she made no attempt to fool anyone now. She just sat through reading class waiting for recess and lunch and sports and crafts and singing. One day, Friedel picked her up and the teacher made a deprecating remark to her. Something had to be done at home to encourage the child to learn the alphabet. If she knew the alphabet, everything else would fall into place. The teacher handed Friedel a sheet of paper with the alphabet on it, and told her to practice with the child.

Friedel sat Irene down on the bus going home, handed her the sheet, and said, "If you don't know these letters by dinner, I will thrash you black and blue."

By dinner, Irene could spell her name. Within three weeks, she was in the fast reading class. She did not tell Little Carl, because she thought he might still be right. And also, she vastly preferred reading comic books. She was not allowed to buy them, but when she complained about this to the other children, they felt sorry for her. They lived on Park Avenue and watched their mothers packing up clothes that bored them to give away. They gave Irene their old comics. Soon she had a huge collection. Carl and I predicted that she would never learn proper English, because the comics would burn slang right into her brain. We advised Renate to confiscate her comic books when she was out of the house. Irene got wind of the operation, and hid them. We spotted her reading one. But then, Dische held a tirade at our house over cocktails about the evils of comics, and so I changed my opinion and said that reading was not so important, certainly it didn't make one a *better* person.

Dische laughed about that. He said, of course it wasn't a question of being a better person, but a member of the reading class, which was shrinking by the day, now that everyone had television. He said they should ban the medium, it was a grave danger. Carl flashed me a look. At once, I turned on the television. Dische laughed again, and said, "Well, at least turn on the news," but I said, "In our house we always see *I Dream of Jeannie*," so he just had to go along with it. He obviously found it amusing, because we didn't hear a peep out of him for the entire program. But he refused to admit he had enjoyed himself. Tactlessly, he railed against everything we held dear, from television to our Studebaker to General Eisenhower. I put him in his place. I said, "You know, I think you're just jealous because you're too old to become a real American. Your children are real Americans. You don't want them to be either." He shut up then. Renate was angry. As they were leaving after dinner, and Dische was out of earshot in the hallway, struggling to button his coat, she hissed at us, "You have no right to condescend to my husband!" Carl answered calmly, "I always knew you were spineless. But I never dreamed you'd become so spineless that you wouldn't even defend your parents against the attacks of your husband."

Irene overheard this, and slipped her hand into her mother's hand and squeezed it, two little squeezes. Renate looked down at her with that look: here comes an ally. I saw her hand squeezing back twice. It was a signal.

For a while, Renate had excuses about working on Sundays, so the Disches couldn't come to dinner. It was peaceful in Weehawken, but Liesel was annoyed. She snapped open her purse at mass when the donation plate passed and stuffed in two dollar bills, whispering so loudly it echoed, "One for me, one for Renate." I called Renate, just said her name and nothing else, allowing her to hear from my silence that I was unhappy. She said, "All right, all right, Mops, I'll see you next Sunday." And the Disches began coming again. We even enjoyed a brief period of hope that Irene's character was improving. We grasped at straws of course. For instance, we were pleased when we discovered that the girl was musical. She had started playing the violin, and when she was still wearing pigtails in the lower school, she was drafted to play concertmaster for the high school orchestra. Unfortunately, we soon had to add Playing In Public to her long list of fears. She got so scared that she trembled, and this gave her normal sawing away a vibrato she had not mastered. This fear vibrato delighted the teachers, and all the more did she have to play in public. I thought perhaps Irene was modest, not panicky, and simply didn't like to be looked at—and that this was a virtue, at last, something to build on.

Every Sunday, after dinner, Carl looked forward to playing with our granddaughter. During the meal, he sought her attention and smiled meaningfully at her in happy anticipation. Yet she was reluctant. Like me, she was embarrassed by the way he swayed and groaned at the piano. Once, she offended him by asserting that the harpsichord was a much more beautiful instrument than the piano. "You can't get all mushy on the harpsichord," she said. He said, "Mushy? What do you mean mushy?"

Finally he thought of a way of improving her enjoyment. She

should consider it a paying job. For each session of chamber music, he promised her a dime. This paid for an illicit *Archie* comic, or ten pieces of aromatic Bazooka bubble gum. For weeks in a row, she had violent near-death episodes every Sunday morning so that dinners were canceled. Carl looked wan with disappointment. So one Saturday I called up Renate and I said, "No more excuses. You are all coming to dinner tomorrow. Don't forget Irene's fiddle."

She came. And Carl was so glad to see her that he insisted on a little practice before dinner. He sat down at the piano in happy anticipation. She disappeared. Although it was already dusk, Liesel found her in the garden, batting a baseball around the wintry yard. She was brought to the piano. "I thought you were going to earn some money," Carl said. "A dime. For just one piece."

She stamped her foot and cried, "Oh, who cares about a dime!"

Then he banned her to the dark porch to await his response to this massive insult. He had worked so hard for that dime. Finally we fetched her for dinner. We told her we would inscribe that phrase on her tombstone. We repeated it among ourselves loudly. We said, "Miss Who Cares About a Dime, do you want some more gravy?" After dinner, when we were still waiting for Carl to finish his cigar, Liesel called Irene into the kitchen. "Since you aren't playing with your grandfather, you can help me clean up!" We stayed behind in the dining room, slicing a cheesecake for dessert and agreeing that Irene was getting an apt punishment. Liesel overheard. She came back into the room and demanded, "Is it punishment to work in the kitchen? Why am I being punished?" She was enraged, but she returned to her appointed place, and stayed there, thank heavens.

❦

WHILE WE WERE RACKING OUR BRAINS about how to influence and save those two grandchildren from their genes, Friedel did battle. She had the children to herself for long weeks in the summer. She wanted to fix their fear of water, so every afternoon after their naps, she would bring them shivering to the beach, and one at a time, she would carry them out to where the water was deep, and drop them in. Then she would run back to the shore, and they would swim for their lives. This was the hour of dread. One day she threw Little Carl, who was always first because he was older, into an undertow, and a lifeguard had to be dispatched by worried onlookers to rescue him. The lifeguard wanted to go right to the police.

The boy could not bear the thought of having gotten Friedel into trouble. For once, he spoke up in public. He insisted that he had begged Friedel to drop him into the sea, and that his struggling and gasping was all just pretend. By the time the rest of the family came for our holiday, he hardly spoke at all. He did not tell us what had happened. Irene refused to take a walk on the beach, even at neap tide, she was so afraid of the waves, and she was not forthcoming either. Friedel grew more confident, and she began complaining that the children were both such cowards, they were terrified of water, and Irene now hid under her bed like a puppy if there was one distant clap of thunder. Don't worry, Friedel, I said. At the next big storm, we will arrange to take the children to the beach. When they see a really violent storm and a truly ferocious sea, they will certainly get over their fear of a little wind and water.

We were having cocktails in the living room before dinner; Liesel was sitting on the porch. She had been ordered to take a rest, but she was mutinous. She perched on the edge of the rubber lounger—sitting back would indicate too much enjoyment—darning some socks, while her niece Friedel was cooking. Little Carl sidled up to Liesel and told her that Friedel had dropped him into deep water and nearly drowned him. He had chosen the object of his tattling with customary intelligence. At once, Liesel stood up, dropped her darning. She tramped over to Friedel in the kitchen and started yelling at her. She chose English for this: "You no good!" she said. "You should go!"

Friedel left within the hour. She was pregnant anyway. Her German boyfriend already had a good job, and later, when he acquired a green card, she married him. As soon as Friedel had her own children, something happened that is sensational and rare. Without any outside coercion pressing on her conscience, she changed. She grew tender and patient with her own brood; she was an excellent mother. She and her husband soon had American citizenship, and she began shaving her legs and wearing my hand-me-downs. They bought a house at Chadwick Beach that was nicer and larger than ours, and they became staunch conservatives. But Liesel never forgave her only relative in America for almost drowning Little Carl. Blood ties are not everything.

The big storm that we needed to educate Irene finally came. Renate and I left Liesel in Weehawken with Carl, and took the children to the beach. The Red Cross began evacuating the Jersey Shore in the middle of the night, several hours before Hurricane Donna showed up there. A police cruiser traveled up and down the little streets with an excited officer yelling through a megaphone, "Please stay calm." One had to leave. One could call the precinct if one needed help leaving. A few hours later, the cruiser returned, this time silently checking that all lights were out and that everyone had gone. We two women turned off the lights and held our breaths until we were alone again. At dawn, the wind began to huff and to puff and to blow the houses down. The ocean was its ally. Soon the waves reached our front door, beating on the lower walls, sloshing through the doorsill. How Renate and I laughed! We gave the children their sand pails and told them to scoop up the water. It was daylight now. Renate said, "We're going out."

We donned our yellow rain slickers and took the back entrance, which was dry. The ocean had expanded its baseline. The street was awash with garbage and useful artifacts like toys. The sand was blowing right into us, a painful collision. We all got down on our hands and knees. Renate remembered the cowardly tomcat. She went back inside, grabbed the cat, stuffed him inside her parka with just his head peeking out, and we set off on all fours. I kept up with her. The children trailed behind, but not because they were fearful. Even Irene was excited. The cat tore loose, blew away; we watched the receding black spot. "God be with him," I prayed. And then we continued. In this manner we navigated to a spot Renate had selected earlier, a dune fortified with cement. We climbed up. From there we watched the waves cavorting with the better houses on the block, the proud houses with the views. The waves ate the houses. The storm redistributed wealth. The children soon had their arms full of expensive toys the sea had taken away from others. And from that day on, our house had an unobstructed view of the beach. Because it was the nearest to the beach now, and no one wanted to build any closer given the obvious danger, its value doubled, and on paper at least, we were suddenly wealthy. Unfortunately, Irene was still afraid of minor storms, and she refused to go swimming, and the cat, found cowering in the back of the garage, hid at the first sign of drizzle.

OF COURSE MONEY does not bring happiness, money does not matter, it is merely a convenience. One's luck comes and goes. And wishes are most valuable when they remain unfulfilled. As soon as they are fulfilled, they lose all importance, making room for another wish. At Christmas in Germany, the Christ child brings presents. When Renate could not yet read and write, I helped her prepare a list of three wishes for the Christ child. I taped this list to the outside shutter of her window. Children must learn to tolerate suspense: little Renate fretted because the paper hung there for a few days before the Christ child had time to collect it. The list read as follows:

1) A big brown horse

2) A pearl necklace

3) A farm

The door to the living room was locked. The Christ child was decorating the tree for the family. He liked to speak to the child through the door. He had a high-pitched, reedy voice, and he told Renate not to tell others in the house, not even Liesel, that He was speaking to her, because it would become Too Much, and He would go away. The child didn't tell anyone, not even me. Instead, she hung around the living room door and bantered with the Christ child, about life, and about Christmas, until the Christ child grew tired and said things like "You good little girl you, go and play in your room now," and if that didn't work, then the Christ child admonished her. "Stop hanging around this door, pip-squeak, I have work to do."

Of course I was allowed in the living room, and finally Renate asked me cautiously if I was alone in there. I admitted that I was not alone. Her eyes gleamed. "And?" she asked. So I reported to my gossipy daughter that the Christ child looked just like His picture in her prayer book. Renate was being very Good and playing with a wooden train in her room. Liesel and I warned her that we were going to the market. "You're being very nice." We hugged her. "How unusual! We will be right back. You stay right here."

After a while, the child, home alone and bored, longed for some conversation. She disobeyed. She crept out of her room and down the stairs, sidled over to the living room door, and said, "Hello, Christ child."

The Christ child was mute.

"Christ child, did you leave already?" asked the anxious child. Receiving no reply, she returned with decorous haste to her room. Soon afterward, she heard us returning, and she waited until I had gone back to the living room, closing the door behind me. Then she rushed to the living room door and asked again, "Hullo, Christ child?"

"Hello, little girl," came the reply.

In that instance, she recognized my voice.

She blushed with humiliation. She whispered, "Mama. It's just you." And I came out laughing, and kissed her.

She was not disappointed. It made no difference to her. In her eyes, I was as Good and as Kind as the Christ child.

And I did not forget her wish list. I just postponed fulfilling it.

One's fortune wanes and waxes. Our neighbor, Mrs. Conti, was even fatter than I was. She was forty-eight years old, over three hundred pounds, had five children and abdominal pain. She had heavy menstrual bleeding and then suddenly her periods had stopped. Carl diagnosed menopause and uterine polyps, and recommended she have her uterus taken out.

He removed the uterus, in a routine operation. The patient recovered nicely. The pathologist's report was a surprise. Mrs. Conti had been eight weeks pregnant.

Carl told her at once, and assured her that the operation was for the best. A pregnancy at her age and carrying her weight would have been risky.

The patient sued Carl for malpractice. She also sued him for the loss of her sexual services to her husband, because now she had no desire, and for the life of her unborn child, and for all the income he would have generated in his lifetime. We went to court. The judge congratulated Carl for having hardly any wrinkles, but agreed with the plaintiff. She won a huge settlement. The Contis moved to a mansion with a view of the river.

In America, the client is king. Carl had to take out a crippling loan in order to pay for this. We were financially ruined. Carl said, "It is like the Nazis all over again."

He closed his office. He didn't want to see any more patients ever again. He did not even want to see his best friends, the Smiths, and we canceled our summer visit to them. He devoted himself to me, to nature as seen in long walks in the woods along the Hudson, to his piano, to his stamp collection.

We sold the Studebaker. The driveway looked less splendid now. One car was enough. We sold the Chadwick Beach house for a healthy amount that was instantly relayed to Mrs. Conti's purse. I urged Carl to apply for benefits, for restitution, for the money and property that had been taken from him in Germany. He refused. He suddenly looked like an old man. He stretched out his hands, looked at his slowly stiffening fingertips, and said only a Jew would take money for his dead relatives. He offered to sell his stamp collection. I wouldn't let him, and he was relieved.

I told Liesel I could no longer afford her services. She said that was quite all right. She stayed on in her position without pay. She had spent all her money on various charities anyway; they would have to make do without her. But her power grew. When she said "my kitchen," it had a note of authority. I found myself saying thank you to her.

My heart suffered. I had cataracts. My blood pressure was very high. I weighed 220 pounds. I said, 1958 is my death year. I had made it to sixty-five. That was more than I ever expected. I refused to sell any jewelry. We lived on a tight budget. Carl committed the sin of anger countless times. He said, "If Renate hadn't married Dische, I would be happy now no matter what happened."

We had some pleasures. We established that Little Carl was not stingy; to the contrary, he had no desire for possessions at all. It was hard to give him a present that he liked. His sister was different. She liked presents inordinately. We gave her less and Little Carl more. She would whine a little, and he gave everything to her. She was contrary and greedy. One winter day she came to our house and misbehaved. After dinner, Liesel told her she should dry the dishes but she insisted that her brother share the chores. Liesel said no, it was *her* chore. Irene started screeching that she hated coming to Weehawken and that she wanted to go home. I took her by the hand; I said, "Calm down. If you do not calm down, you will get nothing for Christmas but a wooden spoon to smack you with."

But she wouldn't calm down. She screamed, "I don't want anything for Christmas anyway. I just want to go home. I will not dry the dishes."

Christmas was a week later. We laid down the law to Renate, who obeyed us this once. Under the Christmas tree, laid out with presents, was just one for Irene. She unwrapped it in a great big hurry, of course. Inside was a brand-new cooking spoon to spank her with.

She shrugged and dumped it under the tree. We made her pick it up and carry it with her or she wouldn't get any cookies. She had lost this battle. Her little face was red and sweaty with rage. We all had to laugh.

👑

CARL HAD A BACKACHE. It was a weekday morning; I was in bed, with my legs up on a pillow and my mother's rosary in my hands. I had just released a hundred souls from purgatory and was feeling pessimistic. I had sinned against my grandchild, laughing at her. The wooden spoon had been hard enough. Laughing at her satisfied me, but it would just make her more rebellious. Her will was hard to break, and we had that in common. I couldn't stop feeling bad about our mocking her. Carl came into the bedroom and I sighed heavily and said that my heart could not bear the anguish with the grandchildren and Renate, and I just knew I was not going to last much longer. He answered that he had a backache. I put the rosary down and looked at him. He never complained. His expression was strange. I asked him, Where, and how bad is the pain? And he said, It is everywhere. It is bad.

After forty years, the cancer that had first made an appearance on his hand and in his testes had returned, scuttling into his bones. He must have been in pain for a long time. When he finally reported it to me, several bones in his back had been eaten right through. Renate persuaded him to take part in an experimental trial of chemotherapy. But it transpired later that he had been blindly selected for the placebo group. Gradually, all of his bones broke. He was being tortured. "If only I could have ten minutes of vacation from pain," he said. "Ten minutes, that would be the best vacation of my life, and I would be satisfied." I thought surely God was punishing him for his behavior toward me. Let us pray. As usual, to no avail.

Carl invited his family for a last Sunday afternoon. It was one of those autumn days New Yorkers call perfect, when the trees are lit up red and yellow in a slow, cold forest fire that doesn't send a trace of smoke or cloud into the sky. A construction crew was scheduled to arrive the next morning, to begin bulldozing them down. The woods were going to be cleared for a development of towering apartment buildings. He said he hoped he would not live to see that; he was looking forward to his resting place in our graveyard. We placed his invalid chair in the back garden, and each family member was called over for an individual audience, except for Dische. Just one last time Dische was given the cold shoulder, but again, he did not notice, watching the evening news alone with a cocktail, and feeling perfectly happy. Carl had a few last words for everyone, something special, and for their ears only. To Renate he said, "Make me proud of you after all." To Little Carl he said, "I am leaving you the most valuable thing I have, my stamp collection. Do not give it to your sister," and to Irene he said, "We are very much alike. We both love music."

That evening, after Renate had left with her family, he had trouble breathing. I called an ambulance. I drove behind it, and for a while I drove right next to it so I could see him through a side window. He turned his face to me, he smiled, and he raised his hand, waving goodbye to me as if he were on a departing train. Then he died. It was 1963. He beat me to it.

Part
Three

he year of mourning began. The table was set for one less, all amusements were banned. Two great Catholics had moved on to heaven in a matter of months, Pope John XXIII at the beginning of the summer, then Dr. Carl Rother at the end of it. I was already over the average life expectancy, and I said to Liesel, "It's our turn." She was ten years younger than I, but she nodded.

I took the clock down off the television set and replaced it with the timeless—my favorite photo of Carl, a black-and-white portrait taken before the Margie episode, his smooth forehead reflecting light, his good hand on display against his cheek, his eyes probing the room. Dr. Rother, Weehawken's German doctor. I placed two candles on either side. In the evenings, after dinner, Liesel lit the candles, and instead of watching Jackie Gleason or *The Defenders*, we got down on our knees and prayed. We made no exception for the grandchildren, and Irene objected of course. She made it plain that the only reason she could bear visiting me was for the TV set. I did not bend to her will. Instead, I made her kneel with me in front of her grandfather's picture and say one rosary for him. She muttered that she was praying for the television to go on. I pretended not to hear. She prayed with great intensity. Even Liesel watched her with something that looked like an ironic smile on her harelip. I had given Irene, as a very special present, one of Carl's own rosaries, made of sparkling glass diamonds, which came directly from Lourdes. It wouldn't stay in her pocket. The rosary recognized an enemy, and disappeared. I gave her another, but just to use when she visited us. And then a third great Catholic, our president, was murdered. I turned on the TV to watch the "developments," because I was curious, being alive.

Soon the children joined me. School was adjourned until after the presidential funeral, and Irene took this to be a splendid example of getting her way, now that she could watch television again. "Now maybe you will start to believe in the power of prayer," snarled Liesel, no longer amused. Little Carl complained that it made him feel odd, sprawling in front of the entertainment with their poor departed grandfather looking down at them. This boy had stout moral feelings. Irene had only fears. Hadn't Opa's expression in the photograph changed? It had gone from benign interest—the owner of the room watching the goings-on with satisfaction—to wrath. The girl did not feel the slightest bit guilty about enjoying herself under such sad circumstances, but she trembled. I made her stay for a few nights in Weehawken, in order to work on her character. She could sleep in Liesel's bed, with Liesel dispatched to the porch to sleep on the garden sofa. The porch was unheated, but Liesel said she didn't mind. She slept under her winter coat. Irene did not say thank you. She slept in Liesel's nice warm bed and shivered with fear of the Ghost of Grandfather appearing to stare at her and mutter, "Who cares about a dime, then?"

The day after Carl died, I had taken over his place at the head of the dinner table, and I thought hard about my new role as head of the family. With his grandfather gone, Little Carl had lost his captain, the only competent guide who was leading him into an un-Dische existence. I admonished myself to work hard to be Carl's substitute. The boy was already twelve years old. He needed some trappings of power. I took him aside and declared with a pomp I deemed desirable, "You are the new male head of this family. You will have your grandfather's room. The den is yours. And your grandfather had one thing of great value, and he wanted you to have it. He expressly stated this wish in his will." And I presented him with his grandfather's stamp collection. Little Carl looked distinctly irritated. He had a good Christian antipathy to property that got on my nerves. He said that if I insisted on giving the stamp collection to him, then it was his to dispose of, and he would pass it on to his sister. She would want it. I knew she had a good nose for business; she would sell it. Out of the question.

The stamps had meant so much to Carl that he had taken them along for company and comfort when he struck out on his own. He had lost his family, but he managed to keep the stamps. I stored them in the attic, three suitcases full. Decades passed. The summer sun warmed the attic to 110 degrees, and the winter cooled it to 20 below. It rained on the roof, the roof leaked into the attic, the roof was patched, the floorboards were rotting, they were replaced, a carpet was laid, a guest bedroom and bath were installed, a window was left open and it rained in, the floor was soaked, hot cold, hot cold, and the stamp collection weathered it all, forgotten. Finally, one day, my granddaughter would discover it and auction it, as I had foreseen, for a pittance. It had some value because of the suitcases; the stamps turned out to have very little. By then, what was left of Carl's ghost had long since left the house in Weehawken and was lingering on in the outer stratosphere.

Where was I?

I needed a new wardrobe. I had never worn black before. The first Monday after Carl's death, I went to Gimbels and bought two black suits, size 22, one wool, the other gabardine. On Tuesday, I went back for the black dress I had tried on but rejected because of the expense. It was also gabardine, which the saleslady had called very "practical" and "a good buy," words with moral imperative, and I couldn't get them out of my head. I also took a silk evening dress, black, because I would need that for Christmas mass. When I reached home I realized I didn't have a proper coat, so I made plans for another trip to the city. Liesel remarked that she too would like to wear black to honor Carl, so we went back together on Wednesday, and I bought her a modest little black outfit, made of polyester and wool, an excellent combination, with a winter coat that she really needed. I found the perfect cashmere coat for myself, but I decided it needed a little mink trim on the collar to protect my ears, so I had to return on Thursday for that. On Friday, I bought myself a recliner, to replace Carl's worn-out living room easy chair. That was a stiff expense, but one needs to sit comfortably, and the recliner was an excellent buy, being on sale. On Saturday I went back for two black hats, including a pillbox hat such as the bereaved First Lady wore. And on Sunday, I rested.

For Christmas, Renate took me and the children skiing at a resort. It was really in honor of Carl, who had loved all winter sports. Dische wouldn't come, of course. He feared he would have to pay. It was the first Christmas I had not been at home. The resort owner went from table to table at dinner introducing herself; her name was Margie. Renate joked that I looked at the nice lady with hatred. On the afternoon of December 25, with the ski area decorated for Christmas with a life-size crèche, two dogs positioned themselves on the slope—right between the Oriental kings bearing gifts—and began mating. They were in a frenzy. The entire slope had to be evacuated because one couldn't separate them. This should have alerted me to what was going on behind my back.

On New Year's Eve we drove back to the city because Dische had insisted that Renate attend a party with important scientists like him. Time tends to drag in a slow, heavy current at that time of the year; you cannot break free. The children stayed with me in Weehawken. We played canasta. Liesel and I drank a little champagne. Her little beak nipping at the golden substance, and her look of interest at the taste, gave me pleasure. Soon I was in such good spirits that I grew childish. I took Carl's glass piggy bank that we had been filling with pennies in order to show the grandchildren the virtue of saving money, and I positioned it in the middle of the dining room table. I fetched a brown paper bag, and a hammer. While my small audience gaped, I placed the pig in the bag, handed the hammer to Little Carl, and said, "Bang it down." He refused. So I handed it to Irene. She couldn't believe her luck. She gave it a mighty blow. I pulled the bag off. The pig had fallen into four neat quarters of glass. A mound of gleaming pennies. "Gold!" I said. "We are rich."

I passed a careless handful of pennies to each. And then we played poker for money. Liesel tried to lose, succeeded. I played with all my wits but luck was on Little Carl's side. He became rich as Croesus, and felt guilty. We were still playing after midnight, when I finally grew tired and proclaimed it was time to go to bed. My granddaughter ran over, threw her arms around my neck, and gave me a big kiss. It crossed my mind that now that Carl wasn't there, the girl and I could grow closer.

MY LIFE BEGAN TO GIVE ME unexpected pleasure. Now that I no longer had Carl around to object, I applied for restitution from Germany. Bulky forms arrived. Many questions. I spread them all over the dining room table and filled them out. I liked placing my round letters on those rigid lines. I liked sitting at Carl's place at the table for the purpose. I played my husband, slightly changed. Soon I received answers. A small pension for Carl; a professor of medicine in Germany evidently did not merit much. Still. What fun. A success. I applied for more. For the death of Carl's parents and siblings, for the loss of all our property, for the loss of my daughter's education, a little pension for me for my work on the Front. I needed to hire a lawyer to assist me with restitution for our two beautiful houses, one on the main street of Breslau, the other in Leobschütz. For a small fee, the lawyer went to work. Soon he wrote. Our villas were in Silesia, which had been "ripped from Germany like the legs off a living man." He added, "Dear Lady, Germany is still bleeding from a thousand wounds." In other words—no dice. Just his huge bill to pay. I didn't pay it. He sent me enraged letters that I smiled at. He couldn't collect; I was in America. I kept filling out forms. I even applied for a pension for Liesel, which met with success. She had worked for decades, after all. Once again, the maid triumphed. Her pension was larger than mine. I didn't feel as bad about not paying her a salary.

I began to look at myself in the mirror again, and take an interest in what I saw. Improvements were urgently required. My face was very round, my hair lackluster. Perhaps I should buy a wig. An auburn wig. Carl had never mentioned how unbecoming my black-rimmed glasses were. If I took them off, I saw my face without any wrinkles whatsoever. That was amusing. I remembered how my girlfriend in Leobschütz, Helga Weltecke, had laid a mirror on the ground and demanded I lean over it and view my face. Of course everything hung down. And she said, "Now you know what you'll look like in twenty years." She was wrong. The truth is, I had few wrinkles, be-sides laugh lines around the eyes, which gave me, if the set of my mouth did not interfere, a jolly expression. My neck was folded up like a closed accordion. A scarf would cover that. Then I consulted the full-length mirror in a hall closet. My reflection didn't fit in it. I would have to buy a wider mirror, or step back. I had to stand at the far end of the room to fit my image into that mirror. Perhaps I should lose weight.

Life offered many new pleasures. I did not renew the *Reader's Digest*; instead I ordered a subscription to *Look*, and then to *Time*, and one evening, while switching on the TV set just to see if it worked, I happened upon Walter Cronkite speaking. I listened to him. He looked like a priest saying mass, bobbing his head up and down. I began to watch the news. In the afternoons, I watched television too. I discovered a show called *As the World Turns.* When Liesel made a caustic remark about my new habits, I told her to reserve judgment before seeing for herself what it was all about—moral choices, in fact. Every afternoon, she brought in her stepladder from the kitchen, set it down at the far end of the living room so that she had a pointedly inferior view of the television set, and we watched what we called "our show."

I was having, in short, a good time. A better time than some other members of the family. Renate was working all the time, and there was no one looking after the children. In Little Carl there were now rumblings of opposition to Dische. The boy began taking a passionate interest in science fiction. Over dinner, he said he believed in aliens. This enraged Dische. That settled it—Little Carl started a library of books about Martians and goings-on in outer space and giant bacteria. And Irene?

At "show-and-tell" once a week, the children took turns bringing in something from home and explaining what it meant to them. Once, Irene brought in a long word, "cytomegalicinclusion," the name of a disease that killed fetuses. This had not gone over very well. The homeroom teacher had said, bring in something that interests the other children. So she brought in dead babies in bottles. Renate had supplied them willingly. She had picked them out to be maximally informative, starting with an embryo, then a three-month-old fetus, then a six-month-old, and had provided a bag to carry them on the bus. Irene placed them in her locker for safekeeping before school, and when she spotted her teacher, she couldn't help bragging that she had brought in something really fascinating to all. She allowed the teacher to peek. The teacher said show-and-tell was canceled until the next day. Irene assured her that the babies could wait, they were pickled in formaldehyde. She allowed her best friends to have a look. The word spread. Soon a line of pupils formed down at the lobby telephone booth with the children calling their mothers to tell them their classmate was keeping dead babies in her locker. When the mothers hung up, they called the school and said they were taking their children out immediately. Just before lunch, the homeroom teacher handed Irene her coat and told her to go downstairs, her mother was waiting in the lobby. What a treat, to be picked up early.

Her mother was sitting in the lobby with the bottled babies. She told Irene that the school had complained, and that it must never happen again, and that this was cowardly and unscientific, but you couldn't expect any better from them, the other parents were ninnies. They went back to the morgue, and Renate finished an autopsy.

On the anniversary of Carl's death, Renate came to see me. She told me she was leaving Dische. She told me why. This ended my year of mourning with a flourish.

👑

IN HIS SIXTIES, the Jewish pathologist Dr. Sigmund Wilens was often referred to as a spinster. One did not say eligible bachelor, because who would want him? He was so extremely ugly. In medical school, his classmates had nicknamed him Moose because of an uncanny resemblance in his face and his gait. He was tall, with wide hips and narrow shoulders; his nose was long, it didn't end. His chin never put in an appearance. His eyes were small. He had no "good features" except perhaps, if you were partial to that kind of thing, his look of malice, and even as an elderly man he had a full head of steel gray hair. He had selected as his medical specialty a field reviled by most—pathology. He had been seduced in his youth, shortly after an appendectomy, by another pathology resident on a bet. She had been more partial to women. But the sight of Moose prostrate on his hospital bed and freshly operated on aroused her sufficiently to carry out her end of the losing bet. The funny thing was, he did what he was supposed to do. He had a day-old wound and an IV drip. She sat on him. When he got better, he wanted to repeat this and she found she couldn't say no. For nearly a decade, they were a couple, except that she really did prefer women. She was very upper crust, very Waspy; she traveled in circles of people who drank a lot of cocktails and had sex generously with various friends, and wrote books or painted pictures, and were famous. This circle integrated Sig, so that when she finally dumped him, he stayed a part of it. Everyone liked him fine because he was witty and cynical; his outlook on life, formed by his outlook on death, was original. Eventually, he wrote a highly amusing book about how stupid and vain most doctors were, and this enraged several of his colleagues to a point where they forgot their Hippocratic oath and sent him death threats. At parties, he handed these threats around, and everyone admired him. Over decades, Sig stayed a bachelor, living alone in a fancy apartment. He came home from work and grilled himself a steak and mixed himself a martini, and then he saw friends for more drinks, or went to bed early because he got up before dawn to write. Then he went to work, where he was an expert on various forms of violent death, and everyone was afraid of him because of his sharp tongue.

One day Dr. Dische, the wife of the well-known Dr. Dische, had an appointment to show Dr. Wilens some slides of a disputed cause of death. Sig Wilens was feeling no less cynical than usual that day. When Dr. Dische entered, he could barely manage a smile. Nor could she. She had a funny feeling when she saw him. She said her heart somehow contorted itself in her chest. She was a pathologist who knew exactly what a heart can and cannot do. She said it contorted. She found it unpleasant but undeniable. Oddly, he had the very same sensation. He asked her to have a cup of coffee with him.

After coffee, in the hospital cafeteria, he asked her for a walk, and they strolled around the grounds of the hospital, talking about

interesting cases, which led to a bit of autobiography, and then after the walk, they had dinner in a steak house across from the hospital and they talked about their families, which gave her the first
opening she had ever had to complain about Dische to another
man, and after dinner he brought her to her car, in the creepy underground hospital garage, and after she had unlocked the car door
and turned to say goodbye, he kissed her.

Sig was the opposite of Dische. He was generous to a fault. He
loved giving presents. He was attentive. He despised researchers,
and respected clinicians like himself. He was not fond of Jews, going out of his way to make a point of his antipathy, referring to
them as kikes. On his birth certificate, his name was Sigismund
Wilensky. He was a kike himself, who had enjoyed studying at Yale
even though his background placed him among the lower classes
there. No clubs, no Skull and Bones for him, despite his academic
brilliance. But, like Carl, he had been *d'accord*, he agreed that his
people talked too much about money, were stingy, and in general
deserved dislike. He became a conservative gentleman, a staunch
Republican. He must have reminded Renate of her father. Sig too
hated liberals. For some reason, he was mad about Renate. He felt
like an ugly giant who had inexplicably earned the affections of a
sweet, tiny maiden; he was grateful to the point of sentimental tears
when she held his hands and turned her dark eyes toward him. She
had a Jewish background, but that was forgivable because she was
not the slightest bit kike-ish to his mind, but worldly, and she had
a sense of humor that was rare, in his experience, among women.
Most women were earnest. They were afraid of him. Dr. Dische just
seemed used to him right away. When he became bad-tempered
and sharp-tongued, she yielded to him immediately, as his many sisters had done, except that she was infinitely prettier. He met her
every day at his apartment after work. When he learned that Dische,
whom he refered to as "that kike," believed red meat in excess was
bad for your health, he began broiling steaks for her every evening.

When he learned that Dische was particularly adamant about char-broiled meat, which he said was loaded with nitrogens, he char-broiled the steaks and Renate liked them even better. He made her Camparis, synthetic liquid concoctions that stopped cells from di-viding. He smoked a pipe and inhaled. It smelled divine. Manly. And he told her that Dische's hopes to live forever by virtue of a diet that excluded all carcinogens, all toxins, all fake products, and all saturated fats was laughable—worse, it was sheer cowardice. Dische was not a red-blooded Male.

Soon Renate could not live without Sig. But it was not easy ex-plaining her absences in the evenings, and on weekends, to the children or to Dische.

She needed an alibi, or better, an ally.

But she had one. She explained to her eleven-year-old daughter that she was in love, that she "liked" her father, but that he was ter-ribly stingy, and also talked too much with his mouth full, and there was only so much of that you could take, and Sig was just so much nicer. She introduced Sig to Irene. Sig made her the forbidden sub-stance, a charbroiled steak. And he gave her pocket money, some-thing Dische refused. All her school friends had pocket money, but Dische said it was totally unnecessary, the children would use it to buy junk food full of artificial color and hidden fats. Now she re-ceived a generous allowance from Sig, which she spent on candy and potato chips. She no longer had any appetite for dinner, except at Sig's house, where she had the steak. After dinner, she would watch TV, which was also a sensation, while her mother and Sig withdrew to another room to talk.

Then she went home with her mother and told Dische that they had been in the medical library, or finishing a case at the morgue, or what have you. Her mother rewarded her by confiding in her, she told her daughter there was no one else she trusted. What else is an ally for? Irene blossomed in her new importance. She gave her mother advice about how and when to meet Sig so that her father wouldn't find out. But her mother grew more desperate and eventually careless.

One day, when Renate was alone with Sig, and she had called Dische to tell him she was going to be late because there was a Case, the children had a big loud fight that disturbed Dische's evening, Dische suddenly felt that it was incredibly unfair that he, who needed his brains for higher purposes, should be left alone with the motley children, and he called her at the morgue to demand that she return home. Only to find that there was no Case. She came home very late at night. Dische was very unmanly—hysterical. He confronted her, she lied, he said he would have no more of her lies, she admitted everything, he started to cry. He asked her if she wanted a divorce and she said yes.

He was sitting on the edge of his single bed in the dining room, the mattress pushed off the springs, the sheets untucked and trailing on the floor. The bed looked like a sinking sailboat. Renate balanced beside him, attempting to comfort him, when the children, woken up by the sounds of a quarrel, peeked into the room and saw him bawling. They said nothing, crept back to bed. The next morning, they approached their mother together, whispering, "Why was Daddy crying last night?" And Renate answered, "He's upset because you two are so badly behaved." What good would the truth have done them? Instead, she used the moment as a windfall of opportunity to mold her brats.

The children hated their father for being such a crybaby and tried to forget the image of him, all frail and elderly, his hair already snow-white, sitting bent over on his bed, his face wet with tears, just because they had been a little naughty. Fate had been cruel to deprive them of a real father who would toss them in the air, or march them off to see a baseball game, or share a bag of potato chips in front of a television. The Ally was tempted to tell her brother about her mother's glamorous friend Sig, but that would have ruined her standing as trusted accomplice to her mother, so she didn't. She felt superior to her brother that she knew and he didn't. Sin of knowing too much.

The bill came soon enough.

✸

ANOTHER YEAR PASSED. I enjoyed my position with Renate of confidante, discussing every move with her. For the sake of the children, we ruled that the Disches should stay together until the divorce was finalized, and then they would just suddenly unsnap their relations, and start anew. Renate would not remarry for one year, and they would divide up the children. Dische could have Little Carl; Renate kept her ally. Instead of being grateful that he could keep Litte Carl, Dische protested that he didn't have the time to take care of him alone. So it was decided that Little Carl should go to a boarding school, where he would learn to be a man. I lobbied for a military school. I called up our first friends in America, the Smiths, from military stock, and asked them for a recommendation to West Point. A military education would straighten out his lamb's legs.

Predictably, Dische was opposed. I did everything in my power to change his mind. I even told him I would *pay* for the school. But he grew incensed, and began to yell at me; it was the first time I ever saw him yell. I don't even want to talk about the acoustics of this event. The sight was bad enough. His saliva sprayed everywhere. "Disgusting! No! No! I will have nothing to do with the military!"

I gave up. I inquired at the local church and found a good Catholic priory in Rhode Island. I took the matter in hand, made phone calls, did not mention the boy's father, or that the parents were on the verge of getting a divorce, told them only the child was a very good Catholic. He had been a wonderful little student, and then his grades had suddenly gone down because of a shattering crisis of faith. He needed to be in a good Catholic environment. The priory accepted Little Carl.

We decided it would be best not to tell him about his parents getting divorced. He was very upright, and the matter would no doubt bother him immensely because it meant that his mother would be excommunicated.

Irene was keeping abreast of the news; naturally, Renate discussed every detail with her. I felt that Little Carl was too good-hearted, and also more childish than she, and should be spared. She was a hussy already, though she had started sleeping with stuffed animals again, like a toddler. When Renate came home, now always very late at night, long after dinner and long after the children were in bed, she always found her daughter clutching three of these animals in her arms. Renate consulted me whether a twelve-year-old should be sleeping with toys. We agreed that they should just disappear. She asked the new German maid to throw them into the trash when the child was in school. And while she was at it, she might as well throw away Little Carl's science fiction collection. Little Carl accepted the decision gallantly, without a peep. His sister thrashed for days, accusing the new maid of theft. Finally, the maid quit. She said she had been warned in Germany about American children, how crazy and spoiled they were. She took the von Lassaulx silver with her.

❦

IT FELL TO ME AND LIESEL to tell Little Carl that he was going to boarding school. Liesel had made him his favorite lunch, *Schnittchen*, very thin buttered sandwiches of dark bread, with tomatoes and chives, or salami. He took one of each and solemnly ate them up, an introspective look of bliss on his face. He drank grape juice. Dische allowed neither salami nor butter because of the saturated fat, nor grape juice because of the mad expense. "Don't drink so fast," I protested. Liesel intervened: "The Frau Doktor Rother should let him drink as fast as he needs to, if he is thirsty."

I sent her a shocked look.

"It's my opinion," said Liesel defensively. "Anyway, I'm only sitting here at the table because I was ordered to."

Little Carl looked so puzzled that he stopped swallowing and regarded us.

"It's been decided that you are going to go to boarding school," I said. "It's a wonderful school, with priests and all boys, and you'll get an excellent education. You fight too much with your sister. You two need to be separated for a while."

He put down his glass and said, "I don't want to go to boarding school."

Liesel and I both said, "You have to."

Liesel got up heavily, and went to get some cookies. The kind he liked. She set them down in front of him and said, "I will be sending you some every week."

He minded very much, he was very anxious, but he went because he had been told to. I drove him to Rhode Island with Renate. We assured him over and over again that it was a wonderful place. The message had to sink in, if we said it often enough. When we arrived, we met his roommate, who had a lot of ugly freckles because he was from an Irish family. Renate said Irish boys are the nicest roommates you could find, as a graduate student she had had an Irish roommate once. I knew this was another lie. She may have had an Irish boyfriend. "You never told me about any Irish roommate," I muttered. She didn't hear me, so I shot her a long meaningful look. She returned it, her eyes saying, White lie, Mops.

Although it was a long drive, we hurried home because the very next morning, Renate was flying to Mexico for her divorce. She had decided not to wait a year before getting remarried. I forgot a minor detail—Sig had lung cancer. He had confided that his dearest wish was to get married to her before he died. She had wanted to take her daughter along to the divorce proceedings in Mexico, they could stay in a nice hotel and have some mother-daughter fun. But the lawyer had found Renate's idea in poor taste. And besides, Sig was meeting the plane on her return to New York and taking her directly to the registry to get married, and from there to the very very glamorous and expensive Ritz-Carlton Hotel for a week-long honeymoon, because Sig was *not* stingy. And on the morning of the eighth day of their marriage, he would check into the hospital to have his lung cancer taken out, and probably to die. He was *not* scared of dying. But she was afraid of him dying, more afraid than she had ever been of anyone dying, which she had the audacity to tell me.

I swallowed her fierce declaration of love. Irene would stay with me for a few weeks. I would use this opportunity to straighten out her lamb's legs. I found her very changed. She was no longer so timid. I thought the summer camp had done her good. Then it turned out that she had, from one minute to the next, stopped going to church.

❧

SIG HAD HALF HIS LUNG REMOVED, and was told he had been lucky, the tumor was now entirely gone. However, the lung tumor had also been metastatic. So the primary cancer was lying low somewhere. For the time being, he could live happily ever after.

He had a love nest made up on Park Avenue with the help of an expensive interior designer (I did not know what this profession was before then). There was a twenty-four-hour doorman and elevator man. Their new home had two bedrooms, one for his stepdaughter. For the first time, she had real furniture, not something makeshift. The little family had dinner together every night, usually a shrimp cocktail followed by a steak. They had a big television set. Sig helped Irene write her school essays. He was a very accomplished author, it just took him a minute to polish her sentences. Soon she had a reputation at school for being talented at writing.

Somehow, the girl was not grateful for her improved circumstances. She was very demanding of her mother's attention, and very spoiled, nothing pleased her. She complained that she missed her brother, and she gave her mother lectures about telling him the truth. Finally Renate wrote Little Carl a letter, explaining that she had divorced his father and had remarried another man whom she felt sure he would like very much, and that his father would be much happier on his own. Furthermore, everyone would still celebrate Thanksgiving and Christmas and Easter together, as if nothing had changed. Little Carl never wrote back, and when called on the phone, he admitted that he had read the letter and said he didn't wish to talk about it.

On the weekends, Irene went up to her father's apartment and when she returned, she complained about that too. She said her father was living in squalor, which was surely true, but that, said Renate, was his preference. He was too stingy to hire a maid. His fault. He was too stingy even to buy her some new furniture, so the rooms were yawningly empty. Meanwhile, in his room, the bookshelves were strange-looking because he had taken to hiding girlie magazines behind his multilingual esoterica. No comment. Renate refused to see this as a bad sign. She told Irene, you see, he is not sad that I am gone! And she had Sig give the girl some extra pocket money to buy herself whatever she liked.

All this was related to me in a bitter, self-righteous tone of voice by Irene herself, who wore a permanent frown on her brow, even though I warned her about premature wrinkles. She never did care enough about her looks. She seemed concerned only for Dische. As if Dische seriously minded the divorce as long as he didn't have to pay for it!

"When I come in the door, my father starts to cry. He is sitting on his bed, and he just sobs. He says he is so lonely," Irene told Renate and me when Sig was briefly out of earshot. On Tuesdays, they had dinner with me in Weehawken.

"Nonsense. He is not lonely," Renate replied. "He has his laboratory. That is his great love, you know. I don't know why he should be crying. But not because he is lonely. He always preferred it when we were out of the house."

"He is seventy years old," Irene said.

"And what," I demanded, "is so bad or so special about being seventy? Is the number so dreadful?"

"Move in with him if you feel so sorry for him!" said Renate. Sig came back into the room and smiled at us. He had cheated death and fallen in love, he was a truly happy man. Before they left, I took Irene aside and told her to take better care of her mother, who was under enormous strain, having been excommunicated from the Church. Irene seemed to study my face as I spoke, as if she was checking to see how I felt about the excommunication. I tried to look stricken. But I was sure God had instantly forgiven Renate for leaving Dische.

OVER THANKSGIVING, Renate and Irene fetched Dische in Renate's new Chevrolet, and then they picked me and Liesel up, and we drove with a minimum of conversation, Renate encouraging Dische to lecture us about his research in prenatal eye tissue garnered from abortions. He talked all the way to Rhode Island, where we checked into a fancy hotel, not a cheap roadside motel. Little Carl would share a room with his father, boys with boys, girls with girls, and the two old ladies, me and Liesel, together. The next afternoon, the "family" ate a festive turkey dinner in a restaurant. The dinner was strained. Renate kept getting up to use the phone, no doubt to call Sig, left home alone and feeling lonely, poor man. Dische ate up a storm, seemed incredibly pleased to be with us, and didn't notice our antipathy. Liesel made disparaging remarks about the cooking. Little Carl didn't say a word all evening, and even Irene was too reticent to pick a fight with anyone. We thought a splendid dessert would ensure that all had thoroughly enjoyed their family meal, and although the rest of us could not even look at any more food and were eager to leave, we ordered a double portion of homemade ice cream just for the children. They ate slowly.

We dropped Little Carl off at school and hotfooted it back down to New York, Irene sulking all the way. When Renate and her daughter stepped over the threshold of their Park Avenue home, Sig holding open his arms, Irene vomited at his feet. We blamed the drive, and her hysteria.

The phone was ringing. The boy had been taken to the hospital. Salmonella poisoning. The ice cream. "That's what happens when you go to a cheap restaurant," Sig said. Renate did not agree or disagree. Both of her children had been struck down. Her son did not return her phone calls. He was a stoic. He was hospitalized for three days over the holiday weekend and he didn't care to chat. He was thin, and when his sister called secretly—she was robust, and recovered quickly—he admitted to her that he was glad to lose even more weight because now the dorm father, who liked to visit his charges at night and put his hands under their covers, skipped his bed.

SIG WAS GROWING INCREASINGLY IRRITATED with Irene. At first, he controlled himself. He brought her a pair of hamsters from the laboratory, and permitted her to keep them in the pantry, which was really an entire room. Dische would never have allowed that. I would not have allowed that. Sig had a heart of gold. He was giving one segment of his apartment, that is, probably a space of a hundred square feet, to the child's hamsters, and he even allowed them to run wild there so she could study them in their natural surroundings. The girl spent all her evenings in this room, she even did her homework in the hamster room. Soon there were ten hamsters, and then twenty-four. Unlike Dische, Sig was very orderly, and although the mess and the stench were abominable, Sig held his tongue. This was proof that it really was easy enough to get on with Sig, Renate said. There was only one rule—never speak about Dische.

As soon as his stepdaughter realized this, she couldn't stop speaking about Dische, whom she refered to as *my* father, in warm tones. How smart, how original he was. How many languages he could speak.

One day, Sig asked her very politely not to speak about her father in his presence. She spoke about him anyway, in fact over a filet mignon. Irene said that her father had promised her a trip to Europe. He was not stingy anymore. Also, he was a genius. Everybody said so, everybody knew it. He was going to get a Nobel Prize. Suddenly Sig grew enraged. He said he didn't want to hear about her father at dinner. She smiled and poured herself milk. Some milk spilled onto the table, but she didn't clean it up, she just put down the milk container in the middle of the table and began to drink from her glass. He stood up, walked over to her, pulled her out of her chair by the arm, and told her to go to her room. He said to Renate, "I cannot live with that kike thing of yours anymore."

An hour later, Renate had packed all of Irene's clothing, driven her across the bridge to Weehawken, and dumped her with me. She did not bother to ask if I wanted her. I didn't. I was unsure that I liked the word *kike*. But I would do anything to help Renate. As she was leaving, she turned to her daughter and said, "You have ruined my marriage."

It was early autumn. The trees were a beautiful color, Carl would have loved them.

ONE DAY, Irene stopped doing her homework. In the mornings, when the homework was handed in, desk by desk, class by class, she just shook her head at the teacher, who said nothing and continued down the row. She sat through tests without filling in a single answer, and left her blank sheet lying on the table. The teachers said nothing. A month of this kind of behavior apparently merited no particular attention. Then Irene received a note to stop by the headmistress's office.

This invitation would not a inspire a child to celebrate. The headmistress was as remote as a distant mountain peak to the children. She had dangerously gray hair pulled back in a massive bun, she had a hunchback, and when she moved, her feet thundered. Once a month, she addressed the pupils at early morning assemblies, speaking literally over their heads when they were most inclined to fidget. She was not known to be stern, she was simply not known at all, and therefore, she was feared.

Irene had never been to her office. It proved to be modest. The lady received Irene without any ceremony. She looked smaller behind her desk. Irene did not know that a few hours earlier, she had interviewed Renate and had a grasp of the "home situation." She had no apparent opinions on the matter, evidently feeling this was none of the school's business. She had merely asked for Renate's impressions of her own child, and did not seem surprised to learn that she was obstreperous with her new stepfather. She had told Renate, "We all believe that one day we'll be hearing from Irene. But we don't know in which capacity." Renate had taken this to be a bad sign, with a promising vista nevertheless opening in the far distance. The headmistress asked about her work at the morgue, and remarked that her children had surely profited from having a working mother with such an interesting profession. Renate took this as an unexpected absolution for the dead-baby-in-bottles episode, and skipped away with a light heart.

Then the headmistress called for the errant pupil. She held up a piece of paper without showing it to her. She said, "Look at me, please," in a neutral tone of voice. "This is your semester report card," she said. "Tell me what you think your grades are."

"Flunked everything," replied the child flatly.

"Can you tell me why you want to flunk?" asked the head-mistress in her neutral voice.

"So I can be thrown out of school."

The woman regarded the girl, her gaze neither warm nor cold. If she was interested in the child, she was not showing it. She handed her the report card and said, "Look at it carefully, please."

The girl looked down. She had been given a C in every course.

"We've decided not to make it so easy for you," said the head-mistress.

Irene told me this afterward. She seemed somehow flattered. I told her it was not a compliment to be kept on as a charity case, but I was impressed—it was a good school, so grades did not count much. I knew her determination better than the teachers did. If they didn't fail her, she would leave anyway.

❦

IRENE WAS IN THE BACK OF THE CAR, screaming and frothing. Renate and I had become close, drawn together by the changes in the family order. If God could forgive her disastrous, far-reaching mistake in marrying Dische, then so could I. And this child would not destroy her new marriage, to a man as honorable a Jew as Carl. Nor my nerves. We drove along ignoring her, or rather, speaking about her as if she weren't there. "You know, Mops, I am so pleased about this school. It is supposed to be just lovely. A place like a family. And I loved boarding school so much. Why shouldn't Irene have that experience too?"

"Yes, Renate, it's such a good idea. I hope she calms down, doesn't behave like a crazed chicken when we get there."

"She will calm down when she sees how nice it is. Did I tell you that Sig offered to pay for it?"

"Yes you did. Very very generous of him, I must admit—not like Dische."

"It is such a shame that Papa never met Sig," said Renate. "He would have liked him."

The screeching in the back periodically got worse, and once, there was a rattling at the door, as if the girl was trying to open it to throw herself out. Of course she couldn't get the door open, because we were doing about seventy miles an hour in Renate's nice Chevy.

"Oh, isn't that pretty! Spring reaches here much earlier of course. Just one hour to the south, and everything is budding. How lucky Irene is!"

The school was housed in colonial brick splendor. The girls were playing volleyball on the lawn. They wore dark green uniforms, with vests, skirts, kneesocks. Very charming. She was introduced to the other boarders of her age. All Protestant children, with Mayflower kind of names, except one dark girl from the Bronx, who also had a Mayflower name but was the object of compassion; she had been in the church choir and was closer to God than the other girls, and had sex with all the boys who asked. I admit, sin of stupidity, that I was impressed. The girls had good-natured faces, including the Negro girl, whose face shone like melted chocolate. I liked the way they came out and shook hands with us and gave Irene a warm welcome. They were nicely dressed. Upon closer contact, the Negro girl smelled like burnt toast, which was not unpleasant, and they all looked like little ladies.

My granddaughter dropped her hysterics immediately, of course, and said a hasty goodbye, dismissing us.

We had a lovely, triumphant ride home.

TELEPHONE CALL FROM A PREFECT at the school, trying to find someone responsible for Irene: "The New Girl—is it your daughter? Oh, your granddaughter—well, she is in trouble. She refused to wear nylons and flats to dinner.

"The first week she was here, she said she didn't have flats. So she was taken to buy them. The second week she said she had flats but no nylons. So she was taken to buy those.

"The third week she admitted she had flats and nylons but she wasn't going to wear them. She called them 'disgusting.'" Disgusting! That is why the student council met today. To figure out a punishment for her.

"Two points that we took into consideration: One.

"She is new here, so she doesn't love the school maybe the way we do.

"And two, she is the youngest girl ever to get a summons. Ever. Oh, and also, a third point, she did not report herself, although the self-reporting system was explained to her, and she could have done so. Written a slip and reported herself. We had three self-reporting slips, they are pink, to discuss this week, two were for chewing gum in class, one for being late for class. But your granddaughter's infraction is by far the worst because she did not report herself. Perhaps she does not understand the significance of our Honor System! Anyway, we must make it clear to her. It's types like her that ruin the school."

❦

"MOPS, LOOK AT THIS."

A letter from the school.

"We are very concerned that Irene has not settled in . . ."

A phone call brought clarification. She could not make friends.

The teachers knew that it was her fault that she didn't make friends, because their girls were by and large a friendly lot, but they didn't really care about that. They minded that she was uncooperative in class. The music teacher had corrected one girl's pronunciation of Bach, it was not "Batch" it was "Baack," and then Irene had snickered and told the teacher that was wrong too, because Bach was a German composer and the German pronunciation was "—"; here she expelled something guttural, and the music teacher had told her, "I believe we are in America now, and in America we pronounce it Baaaack." The math teacher had complained that Irene read comic books in class, and when she, the teacher, wrote a problem on the board and called on her to surprise her and expose her wrongdoing, Irene oriented herself, driven by sheer malice to quick thinking, and answered the math question correctly. This was demoralizing to the other students, who all got A's for effort. And the sex education teacher, who was not a sex education teacher per se but the wife of the school doctor and therefore in a position to speak knowledgeably about the subject, reported that this girl had disrupted her class by laughing quietly when she told the class that an orgasm was like a sneeze. This laughing quietly was unseemly, it indicated that she had experience with the subject, and it had upset the other students so much that they told their parents, and then their parents complained about sex education, and it was now suspended. All because of this new girl. And the history teacher and the Latin teacher and the sports teacher all complained about her Attitude, and by the way, her Dorm Mother complained too about her messiness, and the other pupils did not integrate her, and now, back to the ending of the letter from the school—the headmistress was of the opinion that she should be seen by a competent psychiatrist.

Well, that did not sit well with Renate or me. Psychiatry is quackery, worse than astrology, for pansies, for spoiled New Yorkers and failed medical doctors who could not get a position in real medicine.

I drove to the school. I was a pretty woman in my early seventies. I had even-colored brown hair, pale skin, blue eyes, and above all, I had class. I arrived at the school grounds, not intimidated by the Pinkerton man guarding the high gates, the acres of manicured lawns, the luxurious entrance hall laid out with good Persian carpets, or the headmistress's office with her fake French antiques. I strode in with a face set in the uppermost-class position—chin up, eyes narrowed. "Mrs. Rother, I believe?"

A squeaky-clean office. The American flag behind her glowing empty desk, the photograph of the school founder. She came out from behind her desk and shook my hand. Of course I didn't much like her. She was a dumb little dictator. I told her that Irene came from a very, very good family. And that she was perhaps more talented than the other pupils in the school, and should perhaps be given some recognition for her obvious talents. I bragged about her musical ability and her head for science—well, she must have that given her background—and I laid it on thick and in the end they were ashamed. Irene was called from a Latin class to see me, but she did not look glad. She sidled into the room, wouldn't even come near me, whereupon the headmistress tactfully withdrew for a minute, thinking it was because of her that she was so stiff with me, but as soon as the door closed behind her Irene hissed, "You're responsible for stuffing me into this prison. I didn't know I was smart until I came here and got to know what stupid is." And then she snarled at me, "They shave their legs here! And under their arms! And if you don't, then they consider you subhuman." I felt sorry that I had gone to the trouble of defending her, and I wished she would have been more like Renate, who, after she was nearly expelled from her convent school, hugged me and thanked me for my intervening. That made it easy for me to see her point of view and laugh with her at her stupid teachers. And I was eager to have the same fun with my granddaughter. But Irene's bitterness oozed out of her, got underfoot; she was constantly slipping on it, she could not get her bearings in life. And I replied that she was an incredible nuisance to the entire family and I would be grateful if I didn't have to come again.

I told Renate not to see her child for a while, it would be best. Irene did manage to find some equilibrium at the school, meaning she had caved in on the stockings-to-dinner issue, and evidently she made friends with another girl, who came from a good family (Protestant). A letter came from the headmistress congratulating me on my suggestion; she had seen to it that Irene's talents were observed and encouraged, and she was doing nicely even in math class now. The mistress concluded that Irene was no doubt intelligent but other qualities mattered more—an opinion I could not help sharing.

FROM THE FRYING PAN INTO THE FIRE.

Another hot American summer. The children were sent on a bicycle trip with a youth organization, through the Canadian Rockies. Who can get in trouble there? Ten middle-class kids whose parents could afford $400-plus to send them away for eight weeks, and one counselor chosen for the position, his only qualification being that he was willing to go. He was a twenty-six-year-old gentleman named Bill Smith, who knew about bike repair and had a teaching degree. Bill was bored by the middle-class kids and he shocked them by telling them so, and also he reminisced about his back-home daily dose of what he called "balling," as I found out later, much later. On day four of their train trip from Montreal across the infinite prairie of Canada to the great tourist trap of Banff, Bill told them about free love. The boys were particularly intrigued. The girls were more reserved about the idea. Nobody had expected this kind of an educational experience when they signed up for a "mind-and-body experience for teens." Soon they were putting all their newly acquired ideas into practice. It turned out not to be so easy. Some of the kids just didn't get it at all, and some didn't want to. Bill laughed at all "slowpokes." The girl with the big breasts shared his bed for the duration of the trip. She was his best pupil, and Bill named her Cool Linda. After hearing Irene speak her first language on the phone to me, after establishing that she prefered Bach to the Beatles, after observing that she had apparently not yet realized that she was not living in Germany, Bill declared that he had a present for her. "It's called America," he shouted. "I'm giving you America." And he nicknamed her Yankee.

Bill also taught the kids other things. He led them to a deep ravine, with a lot of hard rock and a tiny sliver of river at the far bottom. As an exercise, he demanded that they throw all their pocket money down. This had been entrusted to them by their parents, always with a lecture about how hard it had been to earn, and how carefully it should be managed and spent. Three weeks into the trip, and none of the kids had spent a penny more than absolutely necessary! Now they were hurling it away. Then, part two of the same exercise, Bill ordered them to "panhandle" at the next highway rest stop for enough money to buy a Coke. He posed questions. "Why are you wearing shoes?"—"I don't know."—"Are they hot?"—"Yes."—"Take them off." By the time they had boarded the train home seven weeks later, stopping for one final night in Montreal, all the kids but Little Carl, whose morals were unshakable, had a full-fledged case of altered consciousness. Bill, always democratic, took a vote, and it was decided unanimously with a few abstentions to spend the last day's food money on drugs. If they wanted to eat something, they could panhandle. The kids threw away their shoes altogether, and hit the streets. They soon had enough cash to buy themselves beads and bells. The group spent their last hours as a unit wandering the streets smoking a narcotic. The parents rushing to Grand Central Station to pick up their darlings from their nature trip were deeply shocked. Bill snuck away before anyone could point him out, especially the suit-and-tie father of Cool Linda, but she understood that he must hurry home to the East Village where his girlfriend was waiting. Only my granddaughter managed to run after him and say goodbye. He looked at her coolly. I overheard him. "Dig you later, Yankee," he said.

✠

I HAVE FOUND the following episodes difficult to write down. However, I cannot leave them out. I did not witness them firsthand, but the details became known to me later, when I was able to bear them. This period of Irene's life would cause some of the worst moments of mine. Not only because I opposed her dissolute behavior: I also envied it.

I have labeled my granddaughter, raised in the morgue, a realist, like all of us Gierlich women. But this label is not entirely accurate for any of us. I am too much of an idealist to make a proper realist. My daughter Renate is too hopeful about others to qualify as a realist either. And as to my granddaughter—years of the reality served at home had given her a distorted perspective.

She had heard, though it would never be reported, that a politician died in the arms of a mistress. She had learned about shapely women at autopsy proving to be men; she knew about family men dying in secret rooms rented for the sole purpose of taking pleasure with a machine. They were found by the police, sitting astride the machine after it had gone haywire, perforating their intestines. Renate felt this information safe, even useful. I could not argue. But I told her, "Renate, don't scare them with sex. This they don't have to know about. Let them be little children." Renate cooperated. Irene was nine years old and had seen twice as many autopsies as her years, when she had the following conversation with Renate on her way home from school.

"Mama, I know what rape is."

Renate remembered my words, and appeared astonished. "So what is rape?"

"Rape is when the boy sticks his peenie in the girl."

"What idiot told you that?"

"Eliza."

"And how does Eliza know?"

"Her mommy told her."

"Oh, Eliza's mommy knows *nothing* about medical matters. She is just a reporter for *The New York Times*. She has no idea. Rape is when you scratch someone's eyes out. Okay? Men do not put their peenies in women. But do not tell Eliza I told you that. It will make her mother look foolish. Keep it to yourself, all right?"

To further obliterate a certain uncomfortable truth, I had personally told the children that they were born through the belly button. This certainly explained that peculiar place. It might cause certain questions to arise in the mind of a little boy as to his own ability to bear children, but those were easily brushed aside with the observation that one never saw pregnant men. I was proud to suppose that my daughter, and later my grandchildren, did not know about the existence of a vagina until they were rudely confronted with it, the girl at fifteen, when her bloodletting began, Little Carl when he read a smutty magazine at sixteen.

At the time of this narrative, my granddaughter, now answering only to the name Yankee, had known these significant details about her sex for exactly one year, not a long acquaintance. And this, in my opinion, would save my granddaughter from the most dire consequences of the Hippie, or Yankee, Period.

Part

Four

ankee was, at sixteen, plain. She emphasized it. She had long, uneven tresses that she refused to braid or pin up but wore drawn in a tattered curtain around her face. The nose that had stirred up outbursts of sympathy among the Jewish scientists when she was newborn had evolved into a simple, large "Dische nose." She had the wide "Dische mouth," and "Dische eyes," slits positioned unevenly on her face. The only feature she had from her aristocratic lineage were the eyebrows, but this was never the best feature of many aristocrats, their brows being so understated as to be scarcely visible. According to my mother, several generations of von Lassaulxs had no eyebrows at all, and didn't amount to much because they were too busy penciling them in.

I had ascertained that her figure was perhaps not bad, it was Nordic, like Renate's. This did not make her flesh any tauter, however. I wore out my voice warning her that she already had a wobble-behind because she refused to wear a girdle. Her breasts bounced because she refused to wear a brassiere. She knew full well that if she persisted in her folly, her body, if left to its own devices, would begin to hang all over the place like an African's. Yankee had seen what a female body looked like when it was old, because I had volunteered to show her. I had taken off my clothes before a bath, called her into the bathroom, and said, "Look!" I laughed heartily about what had become of my flesh. Gravity was an unbeatable foe and the best you could do was say, Well, that's how it goes, and find it amusing. Those who fought against gravity lost, and were seldom good losers. But those are the problems of later on. Yankee stared with sympathy at my body, as if it were just a curiosity, something that had little to do with her, and we had nothing to say to each other. And I thought, really, she was the personification of the puzzle of what goes on in the mind of a sixteen-year-old. Perhaps God knows; perhaps He does not. In any case, when He said "Vanity, vanity, all is vanity," He did not have in mind the complete absence of vanity. He did not mean a girl should no longer comb her hair and should run about in rags.

Her mother and stepfather, Renate and Sig, invited the family to dinner at their Park Avenue apartment the September afternoon Yankee was scheduled to return to school. A nice goodbye dinner for her. The happy New Yorkers served shrimp cocktail and something new, broiled lamb chops with a green salad topped with a sweet pink sauce, and a baked potato. New World cooking. There was nothing wrong with Yankee's appetite. After a while, the conversation naturally drifted to the topic of the girl's appearance. I felt that as the reigning head of the family it was time to make a decision. Should she or shouldn't she? Her nose could be fixed. It was done all the time. She could have a tiny little "Gierlich nose." The idea even appealed to Renate. We all agreed that we should decide the matter for Yankee, without consulting her, because it would be hard for the child to judge. She might say no, and then regret it bitterly. Yankee listened to us deliberate, and said nothing. We took her silence as submission, and then I mentioned a matter that I had been considering for a long time, and it seemed the proper moment to bring it up: Could the child's eyes could also be altered— enlarged? Repositioned on her face?

Now Yankee spoke up. She said appearance was totally unimportant. She said her nose could be twice as big, and it wouldn't matter. Three times as big. She ate three servings of lamb chops. She didn't seem to care what anyone said. Then she looked at the clock and said, "Uh-oh, time to go. Train money, please." She accepted cash from her mother, picked up her bag, said, "Bye-bye everyone!" and, without thanking Sig for dinner, who had paid for it, she ran out the door. The company sat in silence for a minute and savored the calmness and relaxation of society without her. Then Renate said, "You see, she was just longing to get back to school. She loves it there after all!" The relief grew slowly in the room. Everyone grew more talkative, more drinks were mixed.

I HAD ASKED YANKEE to call me every day, and she did. "You can call me collect," I said. Collect, no problem. I wanted to spare Renate the tumult. Yankee kept me informed. She enjoyed my struggle between horror and pleased amusement at the news of her misadventures. For starters, after extorting money for the train fare, she didn't buy herself a ticket, but boarded the train and checked into the restroom. She rode this all the way to Philadelphia. "I saved money, Granny," she boasted in a morning-after phone call. She had arrived at her destination, a wealthy suburb called the Main Line, under cover of darkness, wearing her new uniform— cutoff jeans, beads and bell, and bare feet. This would cause a commotion in daylight. She slipped into the dormitory, and sought her only friend, the Protestant Connie. Connie was sixteen years old, squeaky-clean of body and soul. It took Irene the rest of the night to persuade her that being a hippie was the only way to live. The morning dawned on a school with two hippie students. Soon there would be more. It didn't take much to show the light to the other boarders, all forlorn little girls who had been drummed from home, inevitably because their parents were getting divorced. The day students, with their swank, happily married parents, remained implacable, disgusted. The types that ruined their school multiplied like bacteria in standing water. It soon transpired that most girls had quite a natural affinity to drugs.

By virtue of not giving a damn about what anyone thought of her, Yankee became a ringleader. She was clearly the person behind the glazed eyes of the girls, their bumbling through classes. The piano practice room became her den. Passing by, the teachers heard low voices and loud giggles. But they couldn't prove any wrongdoing. Only Connie, who had been kind enough to befriend Yankee a year earlier, was silly enough to move on to bigger and bolder drugs, and was caught red-handed trying to buy heroin from a Pinkerton man.

But Yankee was a total fraud. She faked inhalation because she was afraid of lung cancer. And worse, shame upon shame, she didn't enjoy being high, not one bit. She found it a numbing rather than a clearing of her mind. She felt her defenses slide down. She was, in short, scared of drugs.

Finally, the deepest, most wretched secret of all: Yankee hated rock 'n' roll. She tried to love it, she listened to it constantly, she hummed it, but it was no use. It didn't measure up to her gods of classical music. She kept at it, she strove. She could even like Bob Dylan, possibly the Beatles. But the rest of them, the Monkees, the Beach Boys, they made her ears sick. She learned to strum chords on a guitar while looking enraptured. The schoolteachers did not hear the music. They saw the girls going to the dogs, and Yankee leading them. The headmistress summoned her once again.

The headmistress was stronger than she. The school was stronger.

She looked at Irene as squarely as it is possible to look at someone who is gazing at the floor, and stated, "You have an antiauthority complex because your father rejected you."

She was expelled. She returned to me, her granny. I castigated her. But I couldn't help wondering, What was so bad about having an antiauthority complex? And father rejection? If they saw Dische, they would congratulate her.

IN 1968, I joined Weight Watchers. And that year, when I was seventy-five years old, I became the oldest member to lose more than forty pounds in six months. Granny was no longer the Fat Lady.

I lost another 82 pounds, going from 221 to 139, in just nine months. I hadn't been that slender since 1919.

Ergo, I required a whole new set of clothes. This time I did not choose black, but all sorts of interesting bright colors. Finally I was able to wear my dream outfit, object of seven decades of intense regret and envy—a pair of trousers. Nowadays, fashion allowed ladies to wear them. And with my new shape, I could easily squeeze in. I bought myself a pair in every color and every fabric. I bought long tunics to wear over the trousers, and new pumps. In church, everyone stared and congratulated me. I learned to say "thank you," acknowledging the compliments boastfully, in the American manner. In Germany, I would have had to say, "Oh no, you are just flattering me, I don't believe you," which is a Big Fat Lie.

Now when I consulted the hall mirror, my reflection fit perfectly. My face had a lot of extra skin, though. I showed Liesel. I said, "Look, this is what I would look like if I had a face-lift," and I heaved the skin upward. Then I let go, so it cascaded down. "Frau Doktor Rother has an interesting future ahead of her," said the maid caustically.

My blood pressure had trouble dealing with the sudden loss of flesh to irrigate. It had been very high, and suddenly it fell to normal. I felt dizzy all the time. My specialist shook his head woefully. It seemed that 1968 was going to be my last year. I informed Renate of her imminent loss, and assured her that it was a relief to die slim, not stuff up the autopsy room. But suddenly my pleasure in this enterprise of controlling my immediate surroundings, which included my own body, proved short-lived. Because one day, that part of my own flesh and blood which I called granddaughter went missing.

She had been hard to overlook recently, staying with us in Weehawken. She had lazed around all day as if her ambition was simply to keep her body temperature up to normal, and every so often she would move in order to eat something. Her body was full of vitality despite this sloth. Her breasts and her behind had a heavy majesty and her hair swung in a glossy mass when she passed by me on her way to the refrigerator. I should have known that plans were hatching in her brain. One morning, she was gone.

Where was she?

I called Dische. He became very flustered, and cawed furiously at me, as if it were my fault, since I was the last person who had seen her. That did it for me. I told him that the school psychologist had called her behavior his fault because he had "rejected" her. That shut him up instantly. Then he remarked calmly that these psychologists had no idea about anything, and although this was exactly my opinion too, I denied it and said they were trained in the care of teenagers , and their verdict was not to be overruled. In any case, perhaps he would put on his legendary thinking cap, and figure out where she might have gone. To which he answered hopefully, "Chicago."

And then he gave the self-effacing laugh that was all he had in his weapons arsenal when he knew he was about to tread on the minefield of disagreement with me. "All the students are going there to demonstrate against the Vietnam War."

I interrupted. "She's not a student! She's sixteen years old!"

But he was not put out. "High school student. You do know, don't you, that the Democratic Convention is being held there now? The government is criminal. Anyone who can, should protest. I'm glad she went to Chicago."

I slammed down the receiver. Those telephones were the last ones you could use to make a point. Nowadays, this expression of disapproval has been removed from the repertoire of communication. A quickly disconnected line can mean bad reception, or a wrong movement of one's hand. But back then, one even had a choice in the degree to which one slammed the phone—savagely, or reluctantly, the other party could hear it clearly. Dische knew I was angry. But he didn't call back. I could imagine him chuckling on the other end about my bad temper and political naïveté.

There was nothing I could do but fret. Liesel and I went to church and begged God to purge all thoughts of my granddaughter from my mind so that I could relax. Liesel prayed too, that these thoughts should not kill Frau Doktor Rother. When we came home, she made me lie down in my lounge chair. It had three positions: upright, slightly reclined, and asleep. I set it to prone and began feeling more in control. It was actually extremely nice that after three months of putting up with Irene, she was no longer in my house.

Dische was wrong, anyway. Irene was not in Chicago, she was in jail.

🜲

SHE HAD LEFT WEEHAWKEN early in the morning, heading toward the Jersey Shore. She had a vague plan to settle down and live happily ever afterward on the beach. The trip was auspicious. She hiked down to the next big road. A car, heading north, was idling at a traffic light. It was 6:00 a.m. She knocked on the window and yelled, "Are you perhaps going to Chadwick Beach?"

The driver rolled down the window, and stared at her in a way she might have recognized as peculiar, had she been more observant. She was pouchy faced, more like a young child than a teenager. She wore a loose T-shirt that hid any female attribute, her eyes were blue, and her hair golden after weeks of lolling in the Weehawken sun. The gentleman behind the wheel broke into a sweat of joy and anticipation. Because he knew: she was an angel, sent by Jesus to test his willingness to make a sacrifice. He had never heard of Chadwick Beach, but he would drive there, if it took him all week. "It's in the other direction," the angel explained.

The driver had just been released from prison, where he had served a twelve-year sentence for armed robbery. During his forced stay, he had found Jesus and it had helped him endure. One afternoon earlier, he had been released from prison, with a job starting on Monday arranged by the state, and a car donated by his brother. He was on his way to morning mass in New York, to give thanks. The earlier the better, because he liked to sleep late, and Jesus was testing him. The earliest mass in Brooklyn was still a few dozen miles to go, and he was determined to arrive early. Now this. A more severe test. He didn't let his Savior down.

"Yes," he said, dazed by the responsibility. Transporting an angel is not given to every man. She climbed right in.

He drove until he could make a legal U-turn, proceeding cautiously, aware of the poor impression it would make if he had a collision. In fact, he drove way under the speed limit. But no one complained. Few cars were on the road. It was a long way. At a rest stop, he offered her some food, and to his surprise, she was hungry. He did not think angels needed to eat. Certainly he did not, being so excited. She ordered a hamburger and a Coke. Then they proceeded. He told the angel about the moment he found Jesus, or Jesus came to him, after a particularly rough brawl in the prison yard about a question of hometown team baseball, when he had nicked another prisoner slightly with his illicit penknife. Just as his knife slashed the skin, a single ray of sun had broken through thick cloud cover to shine down on the wound, on the arm, on the man in the prison yard. And the wound did not bleed. The brawlers were astonished. And at that precise moment, a host of prison guards appeared. The knife seemed to disappear altogether. The driver did not remember dropping it, nor did he get into trouble. Later, when he was back in his cell, the answer came to him. Christ had held his hand. Five years passed. He did not participate in another brawl. He was released a few days early. He was determined to give the rest of his life to the Lord. He revealed that he knew the hitchhiker was a test. The angel listened to this without surprise. Once, she asked to stop for a restroom.

When they arrived at the outskirts of the beach town, the angel asked to be let out. He stopped immediately at the curb to oblige her. He rolled down his window and beamed at her. When she tried to say thank you, he placed his finger in front of his mouth, shook his head, no, his eyes shut. He clasped his hands together in prayer. By the time he opened his eyes again, she was gone. He drove back at a quicker tempo to New York. He could still make an evening mass.

The girl, meanwhile, had headed for the sand, and was trudging along. She counted on running into someone agreeable who would help her decide what to do next. Soon enough, she saw a familiar sight: hippies on the beach. One of them strummed a guitar, others sang along. The shyest one of all recognized her. It was the young man who had once, as a small boy, called over to her on a pretext—asking her the time, when he could not make any sense of the term himself—with catastrophic results, as she had followed the romantic imperative and run toward him. His name was Kevin.

She noted his agreeable lankiness, his long, stringy blond hair, his hippie beads. She saw in these features an alternative to us. She spent the next hours with her new friends, irritating the families and working people on the beach with their singing. Slowly, it grew dark, and everyone went home. Even the other hippies had someplace to go. But Kevin stayed on without comment. It was early evening. He proved himself adept at building a fire. He had brought along brown rice and a tin pot, and soon had the rice cooked to perfection.

They squatted around the fire and ate their dinner, chewing

each mouthful one hundred times as Zen macrobiotic practice dictated. This is a scheme twice as complicated as Weight Watchers, but with similar results: exhaustion and weight loss. The chewing was too much work for Yankee. Kevin suggested that she join him in his sleeping bag to keep warm. Flesh of my flesh agreed. She crept in while he was still busying himself with the fire, and she fell asleep immediately. Later, she felt him sliding into the bag with her. He had no clothes on. She was wearing her full regalia. For some reason, he lay on top of her. She just let him. She did not object. She pretended not to notice. This seemed to confuse him. He made odd motions with his body. After a while, and by dint of turning his back to her and asking her to turn hers to him, they both fell asleep.

It seemed just a few minutes later that heavy footsteps tramped next to their heads, and flashlights shone in their faces. Slowly they woke up and took in their visitors. Three policemen. They were under arrest.

She was charged with truancy and vagrancy, Kevin was charged with statutory rape. A big crime. The police did not buy that the two hippies, locked together in a sleeping bag, had not committed sex. He went into the pokey too. It was not coed in there, and Yankee never saw him again.

❦

ALTHOUGH YANKEE INSISTED, her voice now tinged with regret, that Kevin had not touched her, the cops insisted on a full gynecological examination, and even after this proved Kevin innocent beyond a shadow of a doubt, they held on to him for a week just to be on the safe side. Meanwhile, Yankee was locked in a cell with three locks. The number of the trinity took on its just importance.

Here, at last, was a life of regularity that she had to accept. Three times a day, a changing staff of cell keepers laboriously unlocked the cell, top lock first, then bottom one, and last the middle extra-sturdy one. Three times, a tray of food was pushed through or,

if the keeper was in good spirits, placed on the little table next to
the toilet. The menu repeated itself day after day. On the first day,
she refused to eat, because she had committed herself to macrobiotic life, on the second she ate a little, and on the third she ate
with gusto, since it was what she had always longed for her whole
childhood: good institutional food, full of artificial colors and saturated fats. She had a roomy cell with a toilet in full view of any
passerby who wished to look inside. But no one was particularly interested. Finally, after days had passed, she asked to make a phone
call. She was scheduled to see the judge that afternoon. She called
me collect.

"Granny," she said, without a trace of apology or embarrassment. "I am in jail."

"Did you kill someone?"

"No, no, it's nothing like that."

I remained cool under fire. Did not let any interest show. I myself had never been near a prison. I told her that the matter of
whom this predicament belonged to was easy to clarify. It belonged
to her, who now called herself Yankee, and to no one else. Therefore there was no point in discussing it. She should take care of her
own possessions. I hung up. Liesel was consulted. For once, she was
completely on my side on all points.

"Liesel, am I right?"

"Frau Doktor Rother is absolutely right."

Stay tough on the jailbird, and inform Renate that her daughter
is her possession, and her problem. I picked the receiver up again
and dialed long-long-distance. A necessary expense. Renate was vacationing in Portugal with Husband Number Two. "Renate," I said,
"I've had a shock. My blood pressure is up to 210 over 180"—all
divisible by three—"and your daughter is in jail. I am busy dying.
Please take care of Irene, this Yankee, yourself."

It was one of those tropical days when Weehawken seems built
on the equator. Liesel led me back to my recliner. Upright, this

time. She moved all the fans in the house around the chair, and served her mistress iced drinks.

Meanwhile, in a handsome hotel room in Lisbon, Renate was quarreling with Sig, who was indignant about the child forcing them to leave Portugal early. He suggested that her father take care of it. My turn again. I reached Dische in his laboratory. He laughed when he heard the news, as if he found it amusing. It was the first time, he said, that a Dische had ever gone to prison. My sense of family superiority came up short. The Gierlichs and the Rothers had each seen a relative imprisoned for lowly crime. I decided that Dische was either lying or didn't know the truth. Then he realized what he was being asked and said in triumph and revenge that he was not Irene's legal guardian.

Renate put in a phone call to the New Jersey precinct to ask how long they would hold her daughter before releasing her on the street, but the policeman on the phone told her that she, Dr. Renate Dische, was running the risk of being charged with negligence. She had no choice. The Wilenses packed their handsome leather suitcases and returned to New York, where, after a few hours, Renate got into her Chevy and drove south. In truth, I regretted that I had summoned her. I wouldn't have minded seeing that jail for myself.

We all had the demented idea that Irene had finally learned her lesson. When Renate picked her up in jail ("It was very clean, Mops. A lot of bars everywhere. Nice sheriff"), the child was not remorseful about anything but the necessity of returning to me. Renate could not help mentioning the cost of the trip to pick her up, a nonrefundable flight from Europe, but Yankee refused to take other people's money seriously. It turned out that she had been sentenced to mandatory psychiatric day care. This turned out to be her autumn program. Every morning, she had to take the bus into the city, where she would see a nerve doctor who specialized in disturbed teenagers. I thought they had some nerve calling her disturbed but I held my tongue.

FOR HER FIRST APPOINTMENT, I brought her to the clinic. They made me wait outside while she saw the doctor. I paced up and down the room, which is better for the circulation, and popped in a hearing aid I carried for emergencies. I heard enough to last me a lifetime and Beyond.

"Do you take drugs?"
　"No."
　"Which ones?"
　"I don't."
　"Have you had sex?"
　"No."
　"How about earlier? Has anyone in your family ever touched you in a way that you didn't like?"
　"That's ridiculous. No, of course not."

But these answers only made the nerve doctors agree that it was a puzzling case.

A school for such children was recommended. It was far from the dangerous sidewalks of the city. There was a psychiatric clinic nearby for emergencies, and the great outdoors all around, and no grades to upset the pupils, who mostly did nothing. The teachers were called by their first names and had no authority. They tried to hide learning by packaging it in current affairs. Liza, the science teacher, instructed the girls about the anatomical results of not wearing a bra, how the capsule holding the breast to the rib cage gradually disintegrated, and the breast, which had nothing holding it to the body, hung. The girls still did not wear brassieres. Everything was allowed, and mischief had no outlet.

The head of the school took a shine to Yankee because of her IQ score. He called me. He told me he wanted me to be there, at least by phone, when he shook her out of her lethargy by telling her what it was.

I overheard the following conversation:

"Do you know what I have here?"

"No."

"The results of your IQ test."

"Cool."

"Would you like to know the results?"

"No."

Nervous male laugh: "Well let me tell you, it's high."

"Great. I like being high. I'm kidding."

"What do you intend to do with it?"

"I don't know what you mean."

"You are failing all your courses, which is quite an undertaking in this school where we have no grades. Zero cooperation. What do you intend to do after school?"

I heard her reply coolly, "I intend to go to Harvard."

Whereupon his temper caught fire. "You have a reality problem! You cannot go to Harvard, at this rate you cannot even graduate from high school!" he roared. Then he remembered me, listening in on the phone.

"Yankee, please leave my office for a minute. Wait outside."

I heard her footsteps, the door. He picked up the receiver. "Disturbed children, you do not yell at them," he said. "But this is really something else." He was breathing heavily. Hesitation. Then: "I have just decided to recommend a drastic course of action. I hate to lose her, but it must be. Let me call her back in again."

The door opened. He must have gestured. Footsteps. I can imagine how she was standing calmly before him, her face cast in a smirk at having caught him so off guard with her self-assurance based on absolutely nothing.

And then he spoke calmly again. "I am going to write a recommendation to your parents that you spend a few months in our good psychiatric clinic here. You need to be seen by a team of really competent psychiatrists. You're seventeen already. You're in a lot of trouble."

I heard her burst into tears. There was nothing wrong with her nerves after all. I hung up the phone.

👑

I HAD OTHER WOES.

Little Carl thought he was dead.

He was going to college but he didn't attend classes, he lay in bed all day. Renate went to see him in his freshman dormitory but he wouldn't even stir for her, much less say a word. Nevertheless she reported that he was perfectly fine, just going through a little phase of laziness. I said, "Liesel, Renate is blinded by optimism. We will judge him for ourselves." We drove downtown. When it turned out that girls were not allowed inside the dormitory, Liesel had an attack of shyness, and refused to set foot in the building. Prudery is incurable, and not responsive to argument. I left her outside on a park bench with a warning that if her presence was needed, I would summon her. I found my way to the small slovenly room Little Carl shared with another boy, who waved me to a heap lying on a cot with the words "He says his bed is his coffin." The boy added that my grandson regularly got up to pee, and dead people don't. Whereupon Little Carl piped up from his bed, "I do, and I'm dead," in a contentious tone.

I went back to Weehawken with Liesel after extracting a promise from Little Carl's roommate that he would call me collect twice a day from the hallway pay phone and give me an update. He reported that Little Carl also washed his hands after he peed, and he presumably took a drink now and again, because after a week of this, he was still alive, and death from dehydration, said the sharp boy, would have come after three days at the latest. In fact, Little Carl was studying in bed, reading psychoanalytical theory. His roommate was battling with freshman psychology while Little Carl plowed through the complete Freud like a bulldozer turning over the earth. A while later, he was getting up to take a shower, his bones showing like spikes. Soon he was going regularly to the school cafeteria, and then to the library, where he was seen hunched over a desk for several days and nights reading. After that he was back to "normal," and he told his roommate that he had recovered from a crisis that he did not name, but that Adler in particular had been most helpful. When his roommate asked him for help writing a term paper in psychology, Little Carl wrote it for him in an hour, landing him his first A. Little Carl's own grades were miserable because he didn't hand in his own papers, saying that he did not want good grades, because academic success irritated him.

In the meantime, the court-ordered psychiatrist "treating" my granddaughter had made progress. In response to the timeworn question of what she intended to do with her life, she had replied that she intended to come a professional harpsichordist. The psychiatrist knew little about the music trade, and he felt this a reasonable aspiration. He recommended that Yankee attend a music school. As soon as she enrolled, he would inform the court that therapy was no longer needed.

We were surprised, but pleased. She was quite enterprising, and found a teacher, and all that was left to do was pay her. This teacher was bored with her more accomplished pupils, and the name Yankee tripped without irony over her lips when she said, "Yankee is a born harpsichordist." She was messianic, and felt the girl must devote herself entirely to music. She had a school in mind, in Salzburg. Very expensive. Who pays? Sig will pay. Pupils had to apply and submit a tape. Mercifully, Yankee was willing to work with this woman. She believed in the child so much that in addition to the music lesson, she gave her a hot lunch every day. I told Renate, "Well, it's easy to believe in her if you don't have her around twenty-four hours a day." To the teacher I said, "Thanks for your help. But I always have known my grandchild is exceptionally talented." The school accepted her. There were no hippies in Europe. The psychiatrist signed her release.

She was seventeen years old, and had never been to the Promised Land, Germany. Renate and I brought her to the airport. We suggested that she keep her passport under close wraps because it still said her name was Irene in there, and this could confuse people. We were being sarcastic.

۰۰۰

DISCHE HAD WONDERED whether she was too young and female to travel by herself but we all scoffed. "I'd be more afraid of her than for her," Renate told him. Nevertheless, he felt moved to give her advice. He warned her about the weather. The north European gloom, he told her, was responsible for high culture. In California, the weather is bright, and no one stays indoors long enough to think hard. I slipped a few bars of soap into her suitcase because I had heard there was a shortage of this in Germany. The girl flew to Frankfurt, where she called collect to "talk" but mostly to complain that she was feeling ill. I could tell her old fearfulness was plaguing her. She was all alone in Germany. She felt she was in the most dangerous place on earth. I told her to pray, God would assist her, and she said, "Let me speak to Liesel." Liesel was already positioned next to me, and I passed the receiver to her. She listened for a while and then she said contemptuously, "Ach! Ach! Are there bombs falling on you? No! Is anyone arresting you? No! So don't be such a stupid goose! Here is your grandmother!" And she handed the receiver back to me. I said with more patience, "Follow the directions, go to Salzburg to school, and call me when you've settled in."

She didn't call again. After a few days, I rang the school and was told she had withdrawn from the course. She had asked for the tuition to be refunded, in cash.

Eight hundred dollars in her dirty little fist. A windfall.

We all conferred. Dische wanted to notify Interpol, so that settled it for me; we would not contact the police. We decided to wait it out. Indeed, after a few more days I received a telegram. It read, GOING EAST. LOVE YANKEE. The telegram had been sent from Istanbul.

"Renate," I asked, "have you ever been to Istanbul?" She had not. Nor had Sig. Not even Dische had been that far east.

I worried of course. Liesel and I went to church and lit a candle for her every single day. The reference to "going east" when you were already in Turkey was worrisome.

As it happens, she was perfectly fine. She was traveling on the back of a motorcycle through the Orient, what is to be said against that? To be sure, if you are not wearing a helmet, your hair gets very messy. So I have been told. I myself have never been on a motorcycle. I like speed, though. I picked up seven speeding tickets in my old Studebaker. I can also understand her not wanting to wear a helmet. Her escort, the motorbike driver, didn't have an extra helmet, and he didn't offer her his. She put her arms around his waist in Salzburg, which was perfectly acceptable since his back was turned to her, and they took off and drove all the way to Istanbul, and then some. She sat patiently on the back of his bike, staring at his big white helmet and his dark brown leather jacket. He was an ordinary, medium-sized young American, the kind with short hair. He told her he was AWOL from the army. He went to Harvard, he had been drafted, and they cut his hair, and then he ran away; his personality was rather plain, and yet he had a distinguished biography. His name, she revealed proudly in her weekly aerogram to Dische, was Ted Edwards. Which was not a Jewish name.

And so she passed her days in his company, on the bike, while the scenery passed like a moving backdrop: Ankara, Black Sea, Mount Ararat, Ağri. Her father received one sign of life a week—

the honor fell to Dische—posted every Monday. A certain routine
was evident. This is how I live now, she wrote to him. What do I
do? I travel. Dische used the aerograms as an excuse to visit me in
Weehawken, where he would hand over the letter right at the door
before stepping inside, as if it were an entrance fee. I let him sit
down on the living room sofa and fed him a cocktail while I sat
next to him in my recliner and read the letter, then I offered it to
Liesel, who turned it down. When she said, "I don't read other
people's mail," I stopped inviting her to read them. One day a week,
all summer, the aerograms came and I could track my granddaughter's movements. Renate lied and professed to take no interest in
them. She said, "As long as she is fine, that's all I want to know." I
found out later that she used to visit Dische regularly to read them
also. That was why my granddaughter wrote to Dische; it forced the
family to be friendly to him.

She described wayside restaurants, how at night they bedded
down in dirty roadside hotels, where Ted told the interested public
that she was his sister so they could share one room—two single
beds and a host of bugs. "This 'Ted' is just a good comrade," Dische
insisted. I was dubious, but hopeful that he was right. Predictably,
Dische was more interested in standards of hygiene than morals after she had gone into doleful detail about the squat-down toilets in
Turkey being so full of feces that one could use them only in bare
feet, because those you could wash off. Dische was disgusted and
wondered why his daughter had to go to an underdeveloped country. Later, she wrote about poppy fields in Kurdistan, the breadbas-
ket of the heroin industry, and the huge cloud of dust generated by
the motorbike. Her hair, she wrote, was so full of dust she couldn't
fit a helmet over it if she had one, and her hairstyle could be called
old floor mat. "Please tell Granny that."

More about Ted. His father was a doctor too, he came from a
small town in Connecticut. He really hated talking about himself,

she wrote. I realized that she accepted him completely with the small surface he presented to her, and this did not sit well with me. "Liesel," I said, "I hope he doesn't take advantage of her."

We prayed he wouldn't, that she would remain resolute. "I don't like it that he doesn't give her his helmet. She seems to think she doesn't need one." And Liesel said angrily, "If something happens to her, it doesn't matter! That's what she thinks!" And we disliked Ted, and prayed he would get tired of her and send her home.

They crossed the border into Iran. She did not have a visa; Ted did. "A calamity!" cried Dische. Ted had said he would have to go on without her. She could take a bus back, or something. Meanwhile, the border guards stared at her. They did not believe the age in the passport. Seventeen? Seventeen is a woman. This was a child. So wrote the girl in a bragging tone—they figured she was thirteen at most. Finally, they gave her a three-day transit visa, enough time to cross Iran and reach the Afghan border. She wrote down the whole episode for Dische's reading pleasure. They passed through Tabriz, and reached Tehran.

The rate of letters increased in Tehran, so we concluded she must be homesick. She described how Ted had decided to stay in Tehran for a few extra days although her visa was expiring. But he had fixed the visa for her himself, it was written in ink, he had simply added a zero. We discussed this, it sounded foolhardy. Dische grew tired of all the attention we were paying her. "Faked visas are very commonplace. I traveled on several of them too." He hauled out the ancient anecdotes to brag. "After the Anschluss. The first one was—"

"That was a long time ago. This is now." Liesel refuted him. "And where she stays is more dangerous." She spoke English for emphasis, "Dey all use Drogs." She wanted him to worry.

"No, we Disches don't like drugs," he replied with certainty. "We never had one alcoholic in the family." Which was more than could be said for the God-fearing Gierlichs, and annoying because it was so highly unlikely.

Before we could worry much more, it turned out that going any farther east was impossible. God had heard our prayers. The border to Afghanistan was closed, owing to a cholera epidemic, with deaths in the thousands. Ted grew tired of Tehran, and was headed back toward Europe, the girl with him.

On the Iranian border to Turkey, the border guards chattered excitedly when they saw her visa. Apparently, Ted's forgery job had been clumsy. She had overstayed, had tampered with the visa. Criminal act! They started yelling at Ted, who assured them he had nothing to do with her. They looked incredulous, but our child rushed to his defense. She was just a hitchhiker he had picked up, she claimed. Finally the guards calmed down. They told her that in order to leave the country, she must return to the next big city, Tabriz, to the police headquarters there, where she would either be locked up or get a visa extension. They could lock her up right now, but under the mitigating circumstances, that she looked like a thirteen-year-old, and also, the Americans, the Shah's best friends, were at that very moment landing on the moon, they would let the police chief decide. She wrote Dische that she had refused to allow Ted to bring her back to Tabriz, but I suspected the young man had not even offered. It was his idea that she should take the bus, while he continued on his way west. He abandoned her. But women should be strong.

"Liesel, she has caused this boy a lot of trouble," I asserted.

"He is a man. He should look after her," Liesel countered.

"She doesn't need a man for that," I said. I felt nervous but also proud of my granddaughter at least on this point. I knew that un-happiness could not stick to that girl. Soon enough, she would find being on her own thrilling, and I rested easy, certain she would talk her way out of any complications just as I always had.

Part

Five

of yourself is always very laudable, it is as good as a full act of contrition. Her own report to us made no mention of this episode, she wrote only that she was continuing back to Europe. For two weeks, we heard nothing. The silence was torture.

And then it turned out she had called her mother. Renate had not told us right away, because she felt it too delicate for a phone conversation. She came to Weehawken with the news. Liesel set the table for afternoon coffee, and I glared at my daughter, and Liesel added her two cents by shaking her head angrily. We figured Yankee had confided in Renate, knowing that Renate would not chide her. "Liesel, you sit down and listen too," I commanded, perhaps afraid to be alone in such a situation. The rundown: Ted had not traveled onward, but waited on the Turkish side of the border, fretting. He had searched through every bus coming from Iran until he found my granddaughter. He forced her to disembark and mount his motorcycle again. That night, in a small, shabby Oriental hotel room, he insisted they share one of the twin beds.

"I've heard enough, Renate," I said. "Not one more word."

"Not one more word!" commanded Liesel.

"Wait, it's all right, nothing happened. She refused."

"Thanks God!" Liesel and I said in English, in unison.

Renate enjoyed our discomfort. She went on. "She told me her beau Ted then said, 'I don't know what to make of you.'" At once, I relaxed. Renate and I looked at each other and soon we laughed proudly about that. A man should not know what to make of a woman. Liesel felt bewildered by this exchange, and stood up, leaving the room with hard footsteps.

Renate continued. The next morning, Ted had asked her forgiveness. He had lied to her, his name was not Ted but John, and his last name was Coombs. He showed her his passport. It had never occurred to her to look at it. He further admitted that he came from Poughkeepsie, had never gone to Harvard, and was not AWOL from the army.

"I liked him," she had informed Renate, "and then I didn't."

"That's what happens," Renate reassured her. The conversation from Turkey cost her nearly a hundred dollars. But it was worth every penny, Renate said. She had advised her daughter to get rid of Ted as quickly as possible.

But he wouldn't let her go. He insisted that she stay on the back of his bike, hauling her along to Europe.

And then Yankee turned to me for help. She called me collect from Trieste. I accepted the charges. It was a Sunday, and we had just returned from mass. She was asking my advice. "What should I do, Granny? He won't let me go anywhere on my own."

After establishing that she was calling from the town center, I had an idea. Where was the train station? It was right there. I advised her to board the next train without telling him. "Just take the next train! Take it anywhere!" I commanded.

Ted was waiting on the bike for her to call home, just a few meters away. She sauntered over, picked up her knapsack, and told him she needed to use the restroom.

Ah, granddaughter. You earn my respect. A high point in our relations, if I may say so. The train to Venice was just revving its engines. She just made it; with a mighty leap, she was on board. I could imagine what would happen next. He would spend several hours in Trieste waiting for her. He would contact the police. They would interview him, eyeing one another with mirth. Finally one would ask, Why had she worn her knapsack to go to the bathroom? The stationmaster had reported seeing a girl matching his description boarding a train. Which train? They thought about it with smirks. To Munich, they would say.

He would slink off, driving north to Munich, where he would sell his BMW to a dealer at a big loss and return to the United States without incident. He would recover. He would pay other women back a hundred times for Yankee's unkindness.

PLEASE SEND MONEY FOR PLANE TICKET HOME. WESTERN
UNION VENICE. LOVE IRENE.

The name "Irene" and the word "please" we noted as positive
qualities of this telegram. The word "love" was a heightened form
of "please"; it meant "very please." Renate was delighted to hear
from her. Such is mother love, I suffer from it too. Before I could
stop her, she had bounded down to a Western Union office and
wired enough for a student ticket from Milan or Rome back to New
York. The money was picked up.

And that is the last we heard from her for several whole
months. Instead of returning home to me, she had followed her
wanderlust south, boarding a boat in Naples and traveling to North
Africa.

We had no idea where she was, but Renate took the optimistic
view. She said, "I'm not worried. Irene will bite first." Just to be on
the safe side, she contacted Interpol and reported her daughter
missing. While Interpol searched a bit for the seventeen-year-old
runaway, we banned her from our concerns. We had no idea at all
that she was sleeping on Tunisian beaches or at the homes of interested locals, usually families who took her in for a few days as an ex-
otic diversion. The school year began in the United States, while
she proceeded along the Mediterranean eastward, aiming for nowhere in particular. Gradually, she lost her possessions and had her
money stolen, until she had no belongings beyond a white night-
dress that she wore during the day, rinsing it in the sea at night. She
lived like a monk from handouts, but she had no religious impulses,
she existed for the sake of existing. Without any input on our part,
she became, finally, fearless.

The world turned. An Indian summer in Weehawken proceeded with tranquillity, and King Idris of Libya left for a vacation

in Cyprus. That day, my granddaughter arrived per hitchhiking in his Kingdom, and took up temporary residence at the harbor in the capital city of Tripoli. Oriental hospitality was reliable. A few hours of loafing anywhere invariably produced invitations to eat and spend the night. But the population in the capital proved too busy to notice her. In the evening, she was still loitering at the boardwalk overlooking the harbor. She had not eaten all day, and considered it a well-earned blessing when a trio of Libyans in business suits approached her. She did not look closely at their leering eyes, or judge their expressions of delight when she proved willing to speak with them.

There is no such thing as a guardian angel. The fact is, one has only one's own bad thoughts, which create suspicion about others and offer protection. She accepted their invitation to dinner and, afterward, a tour of the desert. The night turned cold and crisp when her hosts parked on a dune, and urged her out of the car. Wild dogs howled. She was admiring the swath of stars in the sky when she felt something grab her dress. It did not take much to rip the cloth, it was worn out by the sun, but she found this condition of having her body exposed uncomfortable. Instead of folding her hands in prayer, she used them to cover her bare breasts. The men surrounded her, tearing at the dress and her hands.

The temperature in Weehawken was unseasonably hot and humid. I was planning to watch a rerun of As the World Turns and had taken a seat in my recliner. Liesel was rattling pots and pans in the kitchen. My granddaughter was not praying for help. Had I known of her predicament, I would clearly have prayed for her. But God has rarely, if ever, even answered my prayers. This has not stopped me from praying. Prayer is beneficial mostly for the clarity it bestows. Pray, and you know what you want. Those who do not pray are subject to indecision. They cannot choose. Even in the middle of such a mess, when you are pinned to the ground by three ugly little men, their trousers still on but their paws on their trouser buttons, even then, a failure to pray would indicate to my mind a certain indecision about what one wishes would happen next.

The sun baking Weehawken raised the temperature another degree. Liesel switched on a fan for me, and when I turned the TV on at the appointed hour, she toted the kitchen stepladder into the living room to watch "our show." She liked to plant the ladder down loudly behind my recliner to indicate to me the temporary nature of her enjoyment. But this time, at precisely the instant that Liesel's stepladder thundered on the floor, Colonel Qadhaffi gave a sign and his gunmen attacked the institutions of King Idris, using heavy weaponry. Yankee's companions were just prying her legs apart when the northern rim of the Sahara, where Tripoli lay, seemed to explode. The rapists had second thoughts, felt the explosions pertained to them, and let go of the girl. She was saved further harm. Was the fire and noise triggered at that moment by the mutinous colonel a Divine Response? I doubt it. I do not believe that God would pull out so many stops to spare what was left of her virginity.

Meanwhile, the rapists felt genuine regret and shame for their actions. They hurled themselves on their knees and begged forgiveness from the girl, and from Allah. Despite their well-meant apologies, the fracas grew worse. Sheets of flame shot to the heavens. The horizon was burning. They wept and wailed for Allah's forgiveness, but no dice.

In an effort to make Him reconsider, they packed my granddaughter into their car and drove her to the American sector of Tripoli, where they dumped her in the street. With gunfire blazing, she scuttled to the nearest house door and pounded on it. An American oil executive answered. Under the circumstances, he had no choice but to invite her inside in the Oriental manner, as his houseguest. He was a middle-aged, clean-cut divorcé still smarting from an expensive divorce, who resented having a woman under his roof, even if her dress was in shreds, exposing her breasts. He showed her to the guest bedroom, gave her needle and thread, and told her to sew her dress so that she was presentable. The maid would probably quit; a revolution was in progress.

Qadhaffi did not allow any news out of Libya. He threw an invisible fence up around his country, no one could come or go, and phone service was cut. Even if the evening news in the United States had mentioned a revolution in Libya, I could never have imagined my granddaughter to be there. A day later, I packed my suitcase and left to visit the Smiths in Denver. Renate left for an autumn vacation with Sig. Dische had a meeting in Europe. None of us had an inkling of Yankee's situation.

We didn't know that she was finally enjoying a regulated life. Order was maintained by strict curfew, rationing, and gunfire. But one can get used to anything; after a short while, even danger becomes humdrum. Soon, the oil executive began to worry about his yacht down at the harbor. He wanted to see that it was still afloat, still his. One afternoon, without any deliberation or discussion, he left the house. Yankee followed him. The harbor lay at the end of the street, which was no more than a lane filled with deep, hot sand that scorched their bare feet and ankles. Yet they walked with keen pleasure. The harbor was stocked with abandoned luxury yachts. They dove in, and swam to his boat, reveling in the pleasure of cool water and free movement. They climbed aboard, and the executive threw open a refrigerator full of caviar and French cheese. Yankee tasted her first chilled white Burgundy in Africa.

And then the bill came.

A ruckus began on the shore. It came closer. They stuck their heads up out of the hold, and cracking noises were followed by strange humming sounds. A boat had drawn up to theirs, a soldier on board was shaking a gun at them. The oil executive stood up very straight with his hands in the air. Yankee followed suit. I myself have never encountered such belligerence, but I believe they would not have treated a Lady like me so poorly. The soldier bellowed, "You go to shore."

"Yes but how?" shrieked the oil executive. Weak.

"Swim!" came the order.

They plunged in and swam. Bullets crashed into the water around them. No amount of swimming on the Jersey Shore had prepared Yankee for this exercise. I was just waking up in the Smiths' guest room, and saying good morning to my Lord. My granddaughter and her companion were greeted on the quay by a group of soldiers. A truck was waiting.

The back door was open, soldiers were visible inside, and someone shouted, "Jail. Get in."

A pretty hopeless situation. I was just thinking about what I would have for breakfast. I had seen a box of cornflakes on the kitchen counter. Soldiers nudged the pair toward the truck. A call came through on a walkie-talkie. More commotion. The soldier in charge turned hurriedly to the executive. "Give me watch," he demanded. The poor man had trouble undoing the Omega watchband in such a hurry. He handed it over. "You run!" the soldier ordered, gesturing at the road toward the house, and pointed his gun at their feet. They scrambled through boiling ankle-deep sand, gunfire spewing behind them.

But even then, my sissy granddaughter was not scared. As she and her companion tumbled back into the house they were giggling. I ate cornflakes for breakfast.

That evening, ten days into the revolution, Yankee fell ill. Sores developed on her legs, grew larger and bled, as if she had been hit by shrapnel after all. She was tired. She slept through days of gunfire. When the curfew lifted for a few hours, the executive brought her to the Wheelis Air Force Base hospital and said a cursory goodbye. She realized that she could not remember his name or his face. She had intravenous infusions, and when her fever went down, she begged to be sent home. She looked like a minor, but she had no relatives with her, no papers, no passport, and no shoes. The American consul declared himself puzzled, but he sent a telex

to the State Department, and birth records confirmed her identity.
She gave my house as her home address, and a telegram was
sent demanding money for a plane ticket to New York. The wife of
the consul personally donated a pair of ladylike pumps for her well-
being.

♔

LIESEL OPENED THE TELEGRAM, although it was not addressed to
her. She was home alone, growing old inside her worn blue cotton
dress from Leobschütz, with the narrow belt and the round white
collar, wearing the Stars and Stripes apron we had given her for
Christmas, her long white donkey hair pulled back into the same
bun, and her inner brow furrowed at the awesome responsibility. A
te-te-te-telegram, she would have told me on the phone. But I was
not available.

I was now on the road with the Smiths, we were taking a tour of
the Rockies, which are not as nice as the Alps, no comparison
there. The Rockies are just too wide, in my opinion, and too high,
and there are too many of them. Germany and Switzerland have
the perfect number of mountains, namely a few to each district, and
you know which district in advance. Of course I did not contradict
the Smiths when they praised the scenery—"the most amazing vis-
tas in the world." And my opinion was not quite as firm since our
last trip, when Carl had come along. He had covered up his doubts
about the New World's beauty by filming it. His commentary had
gotten him into trouble—he had called the valleys "voluptuous,"
which made Susie Smith stare strangely, and George Smith laugh
uncertainly. At that point, I had told him in German to keep his
thoughts to himself. He continued to point his camera at the
scenery. Unless they insinuated themselves into the picture, he
never filmed any people. I know now that he was merely being tact-
ful; the only way he could think of not to take a picture of me was
not to take a picture of anybody. And he didn't want me to see how

catastrophically fat I looked. But on this trip, several years later, he was not along, alas, and I was slender, I did not need help climbing in and out of the Smith Cadillac. Once again, we stayed in motor hotels which once again I found comfortable without class, but comfort was more important, a plus for America. Without Carl to upbraid me for being greedy, I collected the motel soaps.

Renate and Sig were vacationing at sea level, in wealthy Bermuda. He had taken ill again, the crab had returned, and he was scheduled for surgery when they returned. He had bad luck with his health. Dische had good luck. He was out of town at a Meeting, he had mentioned something about Bruges, which he insisted was the most beautiful city in Europe, as if this was an open question that could be settled. The telegram was urgent.

Still, Liesel had no business dealing with this matter until I was back in due time to handle it. URGENTLY REQUEST FUNDS. She had no right to make decisions of this nature. Because I surely would have made the decision *not* to send another cent. Renate had sent her money for a plane ticket. That was plane ticket number two, really, because she had a perfectly good return flight from Salzburg. Two plane tickets are enough. I would have said, Let her stay in Libya until the cows come home.

But Liesel was in command, and without even making a great effort to find me, she went and reached under her mattress where she stored her own money, and like some rich patron, she paid for Yankee's ticket home. And then Liesel traveled to Kennedy to stand at the gate, and saw the girl arriving in a white dress that looked like a nightgown, without so much as a handbag, but at least rid of her beads and bell (as Liesel noted at once). Her hair had the color and tidiness of scattered hay, and her skin was dark as a Negro's, said Liesel (without passing judgment). Her legs, from a distance, seemed to be dirty. They had big purple splotches on them. Yankee suddenly became aware of Liesel planted in the middle of

the arrivals hall, immobile, her posture alert, her button eyes re-
garding her as if she were watching out for her, the ogre of her
childhood who always made her dry the dishes, and who scolded
and scolded and scolded; and Yankee cried with relief to see Liesel
in her blue dress. Although it wasn't such an act of heroism to pick
her up at the airport, as I told the maid when she related it to me,
her stutter stretched smooth by this triumph.

Liesel took Yankee home, and put her into her own bed and
slept on the porch sofa under a light summer blanket. She smeared
an ointment she found in Carl's medical cabinet on the invalid's
legs: anti-hemorrhoid cream. She cooked for her, mended her
white nightgown properly, and told her to go back to school. When
the fever came back, Liesel brought her to the university hospital
emergency room where both Dr. Disches taught. The doctors contacted the tropical medicine people, who rushed right over to see
the patient. It was leishmaniasis, a rare disease to turn up in New
York, caused by sand flies. The medical students were sent by the
classful to her hospital bed, they might not have another opportunity to see those lesions in the flesh, and the professors lectured
them. "She's the Disches' daughter, and they don't even know she's
sick." And this proof of negligence made Yankee feel good, and
made her get well soon. She would have blue scars for the rest of
her life that she could brandish at her parents.

It was the third week of October. Renate, Sig, Dische, and I
were still traveling, so Yankee spent a peaceful time with Liesel,
who did not take any lip from her; she wouldn't let her use the
name of the Lord in vain, Yankee's specialty. Her mouth actually
did this automatically, her brain trailing behind with an excuse that
everyone else did it. But Liesel stamped her foot and forbade it, and
Yankee controlled her tongue. After a spell of coddling, though,
and the prospect of my return to Weehawken, she started wondering whether she shouldn't go back to school. She paid a visit to
the local high school, but the idea of being in the eleventh grade

when she had just been in a revolution didn't appeal to her. Yankee felt she had a certain obligation to herself now. She had a reputation, she was not just some girl. She had also made a career decision. She was going to be an Adventurer. Every year would bring her at least one new and formidable experience greater than the last experience, and she would die having succeeded in never spending more than one year in one place. She planned, right then and there, to outdo me.

I called her twice a day to scold her. I told her that it was difficult watching her blow any chances to make good, to make it up to us. I hid any admiration for her. My return home was pending, impending. Liesel warned her that she had to go back to high school, one finishes what one has started. "Your granny is angry at you!" she warned. It happened that the dean of a small elite liberal arts college was scheduled to give an introductory speech about his institution to any interested seniors at the local high school. Yankee had noticed the invitation, also that chocolate-chip cookies would be served, and because she had absolutely nothing better to do, she moseyed over. When she had eaten her fill, her attention wandered and she noticed the speaker. She listened. He spoke about new models of learning, and for a lazy pupil, this sounded promising. He had chosen to sit not at the podium, but at the front of the room, slouched in a school chair, his long legs jumbled. He was tall and fatherly, with glasses, a head of gray vestigial hair, and a slight paunch. He described his college as an experiment. After his talk, he stood up to leave. She approached him. She introduced herself as the daughter of university professors, who had lived in Africa and was about to become a high school dropout. He stopped in his tracks. He appeared fascinated. So she went on. She wanted to study but she couldn't possibly finish high school, it was out of the question, and what would he recommend?

At critical moments, Yankee always looked for an older man to bail her out. In her own mind, she was appealing to their father instincts. She didn't know that the charm of a damsel in distress for men is not necessarily her childishness, but to the contrary. The dean said his name was Ben. He invited her up to his college in Maine to look around. He invited her to stay with him and his family. He gave his hand, and his phone number. "Let me see if I can help you."

She packed up her knapsack, persuaded Liesel to release sufficient funds from her mattress to pay for a bus ticket to Maine, and disappeared in the nick of time before my return. She would be, for the rest of her life, a High School Dropout.

Her letters and collect calls home began again. Triumphal news. I could not complain. The dean had introduced her to his wife, Jane. His house in Maine matched a dream she had of comfortable living—not a single European antique, but not as cheap as Dische's taste. The couple were both passionately devoted to higher learning, and ending the Vietnam War. It was all they talked about. Their two daughters were away at college, so Yankee was welcome to stay until Christmas. Ben spoke to certain professors who agreed to give her a full course load, just to try her out, and if she did well, it was decided she could enroll as a freshman the following year. It was a great opportunity.

She was diligent. She took notes. She could not imagine how in blazes someone could take pleasure in information. And then she called me. "Granny," she said, in her first phone call after a week, her voice brittle. "Granny." It was a complete sentence, and I understood it immediately. Nevertheless, I probed for details. One evening, when Jane had gone out shopping, Ben stopped her in the corridor and told her how glad he was that everything was working out so well, how proud he was about his decision to take that small risk for her, that it was clearly paying off, what was the use of a high school degree for a girl as intelligent as she? And then he suddenly grabbed her by the shoulders and gave her a middle-aged kiss on the mouth.

"A middle-aged kiss? Have you such a lot of experience?" I asked.

"No," she said. "I haven't. I'm just guessing. But I didn't want his mouth anywhere near me, least of all on my own mouth. You understand?"

"No one understands better," I said.

Disgust had wrestled with politeness: placing her hands on his chest to push off, politeness stayed the hands; disgust shoved, politeness held back. This contest made her legs buckle.

"A married man's kiss, a father's kiss, disgusting!" I cried.

"Sloppy and wet and old, with smelly teeth!"

"Oh, oh, oh! And you didn't *do* anything?"

"I have to be grateful to him!" she cried. That was the nasty part. Luckily, he had lost his breath and withdrawn out of his own accord, only to hear a car enter the driveway. He gave her a dire romantic look, and let her go.

She rushed to "her" room, packed her knapsack once again, left through the back door, and by the time Jane had unpacked the groceries, there was one mouth less to feed and secretly to kiss in the house. Jane would decry her husband's judgment, allowing a crazy girl into the home who didn't even have the manners to leave a thank-you note before disappearing. When I called up to give her a piece of my mind about trusting her husband, she picked up the phone and said, "Your granddaughter left without saying goodbye, without one word of thank you for all we've done for her." I apologized for Yankee and hung up.

Yankee moved in with some students that she had met at the college, but they wanted rent, and of course she had to pay for her food. She couldn't tell her parents that her college career had ended before it really began. I had to keep it to myself.

So she became a working girl.

I did not feel sorry for her. America had taught me that menial labor does not necessarily place a person socially. Renate had cleaned floors when she was a student, and that hadn't dissolved her ties to the aristocracy. However, I must say that menial work posed a danger to Renate that it did not pose to Yankee. Because Renate had a weak sense of class worth. When she hobnobbed with workers, she believed she was their equal. Heavens, she was intimate with secretaries, with maids. She went to lunch with them, confided in them! If I were a psychiatrist, I would say this was definitely my fault, because I had tolerated Renate's attachment to Liesel, and also to her father's family. A compliment, at last, for Yankee: she did not have this flaw. She never got on with her nannies and maids. She hated them, and they hated her. By the time she was four years old, she saw the entire working class as the enemy. This proved to have disadvantages. Yankee was not willing to work hard at absolutely anything, she wasn't in the habit. So I thought that since she was in no danger of fraternizing with workers, a proper working-class job, like the military for Little Carl, would straighten out her lamb's legs.

I was pleased when she became a maid in a hotel. She wore a uniform, size 14 incidentally, because she was quite strong. The brawn didn't come in handy, though, it was negated by the brain. She cleaned seventeen rooms per eight-hour shift, making all the beds, vacuuming the floors, and scrubbing the bathrooms. The other maids were experienced, which means their bodies were pounded down from hard work, they looked like old nails half buried in a plank. They spoke in banging sounds, Spanish or Chinese. After three days of this, Yankee phoned her father collect. She had prepared the math for him, because he liked figures: she had twenty-eight minutes per room without a break. She could take a break, but it wasn't paid so it didn't count. Her salary was two dollars an hour. He interrupted her before she could go deeper into the numbers. He started yelling at her in his Dische way, loudly and without consideration of the impression he was making, "Maid? A maid? No relative of mine has ever been a maid! Come home instead!" And before she could protest that she had no money to come home, he had slammed down the receiver. She didn't dare call back. She called her mother. "Mom, I'm still in Maine but I have a job. I'm working as a maid—" Renate interrupted, "Well, that's wonderful! So you have money of your own now! I'm so pleased!"

Yankee did not have the nerve to ask her for money either.

So she called me, and as I was deep in my recliner, Liesel picked up. "Residence Dr. Rother," she said.

"Hi, Liesel," said Yankee. "You wouldn't believe this. I'm working as a cleaning lady." Whereupon Liesel started cackling with laughter, and called me to the phone. I offered her no sympathy, and no money.

A day later, she was fired. She was not fast enough, not diligent enough.

She became a dishwasher at $2.50 an hour. Fired after one shift. She found a job working telephones, selling health insurance that was valid only in the event that you were not ill. The boss made a pass at her. This is the truth—when you are a sunny seventeen-year-old without makeup and without any ideas of how to dress but have a pleasant appearance, nothing too exciting, nothing too awful, well then, men of a certain age have no compunction about taking a shot at you. They think: Sleeping with someone like that is not a sin. It happens, but does not happen. This kind of girl does not count. It is like a silly dream. These old men are never shy, they grab what they can. They are irritated when their dream does not go the way they order. In this case, the boss had proposed that she spend a night with him in a hotel, and then his hand settled like an embalmer's on her behind. Yankee slithered away, babbling as she went, telling him she did not like hard-arming customers about the necessity of buying insurance that was worthless in the event that you needed it—because of some clever fine print. Emboldened, she said, "Isn't it lying?"

He looked at her closely, and then shook his head sadly. He said nothing. He left the room. He called a meeting of all employees. They sat around the "conference room" in cheap plastic chairs, pale, fat elderly employees, the wretched of the earth, and the boss said, "The most important quality I seek in an employee is loyalty. Among us today is an employee who considers herself better than you, and better even than me. She questions my honesty and the honesty of this endeavor. I want to point her out to you." And his hand rose, swerved over the heads of the assembled until it found the girl sitting in the back row, dozing—and he cried, "There sits a girl who feels better than you. Morally better. Socially better. And I tell you, she is not better, she is lower! She is lower than the low. Will you please stand up, Yankee?"

She stood, not understanding.

"And now leave. Leave before we all stand up and hurl you out into the street."

She walked out as slowly as she could. Her hands and feet were trembling. When she reached the street she saw where she was, on a highway, the gas stations and shops clustered like rotten grapes on an old vine. Sobs shook her. Thou shalt not be a crybaby. She walked, crying, the hot air of the highway nearly blasting her off her feet. She reached a phone booth. Collect call to her mother. It was early evening on the East Coast. Renate answered. "I have just been fired from my third job!" she wailed.

"So get a fourth one, " replied her mother. "Don't ask me for a cent." And she hung up the phone. Her hand wet with tears, she dialed again. Collect call to her father.

"Job?" Dische cried. "What job?" for he had already forgotten what she had told him a week earlier. She summarized her misery without going into any details and he began his railing again but this time he did not hang up without promising to send her twenty dollars. It was enough to hitchhike home to me.

SCARCELY HAD SHE RETURNED to Weehawken when my honesty drove me to make a mistake. I told her that her grandfather had left her money for her education. He had saved for years. He had cared about every dime, because every dime had counted. Renate had repeated my mistake by mentioning the money laid back for her education, and urging her to use it to study. The girl wasn't impressed. She pointed out that education could be obtained in other ways than the academy and that the money could now be wisely invested in a scheme she had. The family feuded. Dische believed (loudly) that only a university could provide education. When Renate agreed with him, aligning herself with the enemy, I was forced to take a contrary position. I said the matter was for Carl to decide, and that I had thought about it, as if I were Carl, and come to the conclusion that he would in this case agree with Yankee. So I allowed her to take the money Carl had set aside for schooling and use it for her own form of education—instead of going to college, she would go to Africa and find a job there.

And within a week of returning home from the failed experiment in Maine, she was gone again. She flew standby to wherever she could in Europe, and hitchhiked south, without any worthwhile incident that she reported by aerogram, until she reached Athens. Her education was in full swing. In Athens, she wrote me a long letter. Me. It was intended to rouse my envy, and it succeeded. She had met a handsome young American on a grand tour just like hers. Education keeps no hours. They had scaled the fence of the Acropolis Parthenon at midnight, taken seats in the Temple of Athena, and played poker by moonlight. She was fully aware that she was trumping me. Soon enough, the guards appeared with guns and handcuffs. But her companion had presence of mind. He had easygoing American manners that suggested a big bank account that might be shared if the circumstances were right. He offered them cigarettes. So the arrest was perfunctory, the visit to the police station brief. They were too sleepy to do anything more than part ways, the boy continuing on to Turkey, where he would, by the way, die, die young, after a brutal assault by a bus driver. The poor lamb, his soul went to heaven, I can attest to that.

From Athens, she took a boat to Alexandria, and we tracked her via her aerograms to Cairo. Remaining ignorant of precisely what she was up to in Africa was helpful. My imagination filled in many blanks. Much later, I would realize how little I understood her in one regard—as little as I understood Renate. In short, I wouldn't have envied her romantic education, which was really more fit for the animal kingdom, instruction by an older man taking place in bathrooms and on balconies; now I know that in this respect she was worse, even, than Renate.

Because in Cairo, she managed to fall in love, something that had hitherto been missing in her résumé. She chose as the object of her stray affections a Palestinian from Lebanon, a doctor, because he was dark haired and dark eyed, and, best of all, he didn't like her too much. She really liked him a lot for that. At first, he tolerated her company, but then he slowly started getting used to her and wanted her to stay with him, and so she liked him less. He urged her to accompany him to Jordan, to the Palestinian refugee camp where he was going to help his people. He took her to one in Cairo, showed her around the slovenly poverty beneath the miles of tin roofs, and for the first time she found a place she definitely did not ever want to call home. When he blamed the camp on the Jews, she decided that the situation was too complicated ever to understand. She had a moment of Prescience and Modesty that would not reoccur in her later years, when she would claim opinions about conflicts in the Middle East that, like a marriage quarrel, only a higher force can truly understand.

The Palestinian doctor soon left Cairo to take up his position in Jordan, and she would not go with him. His heart was not exactly smashed. He was a bon vivant, and I may reveal that he ended up moving to America on a fellowship, where he sought and married a rich Protestant girl, specialized in sports injuries in a resort town, and soon made enough money to pay for his own yacht and a really splendid funeral on the occasion of his death, at sixty, after a freak accident involving a golf ball, to which his bald head had an unfortunate alignment because he had bent down to pick up a lucky penny glimmering on the field.

But Yankee wasn't thinking so far ahead anyway. Her education continued. She had found out what it means to fall in love, and what it means to fall out of love. She had established that she preferred her own company and as dangerous a situation as she could find. Now she had a choice: unrest in southern Egypt, civil war in the Sudan, guerrilla warfare in Ethiopia. In Somalia, there was only one tribe and one religion, so they really had no excuses for a civil war, but they didn't need an excuse and had a civil war anyway. Finally she flew to Eritrea, where a war of liberation raged. I received an aerogram: "I made it here and you didn't. Boy, are you ever missing something."

Later she wrote that the city of Asmara was a disappointment. It was just High Civilization in strange countryside. Churches and museums, cobbled roads, Italian coffeehouses. And Jews everywhere, good-looking ones, with sculptured tiny noses, who talked about culture and Israel. They did not talk about money, because they did not have any. They talked about their descendance from Solomon and the Bible. She felt like she was in Washington Heights.

Then, the aerograms stopped.

I was taking care of the home front. I tried to persuade Little Carl to take more part in life, as I thought of it, by joining the army. But he refused, preferring to work as a lowly assistant at Dische's laboratory. Everyone knew he had no ambition. When he came in to work in the morning, he took a seat in his cubbyhole, unfolded the New York Times crossword puzzle, and filled it out in a few minutes flat. Dische's famous colleagues got wind of this feat, dropped by to watch him perform it. Dische laughed, as if this was

something silly. I pointed out to Dische that he should try his hand
at the crossword puzzle himself. He did not think it was worth his
while. It became my goal to have him fill it out. To this end, I even
invited him for dinner with Little Carl, and presented them each
with a book of brainteasers and told them to start on page one.

Little Carl refused to compete with his father. He disappeared
into Carl's old den and did not come down again, so that I had to
entertain Dische myself, and he enjoyed himself, so the evening
was a fiasco.

We had all agreed that it was time once again not to think about
Yankee. A period of having no inkling followed in which we hardly
mentioned her except to agree with Renate when she stated, "She
bites first." I liked that description of her, and asked myself whether
I had ever given occasion for someone to say that about me.

As I found out later, Death kept visiting my granddaughter as
she traveled through Ethiopia, but she tricked him, and got away.
He kept trying. In Addis Ababa, she was invited to a wedding with
a twenty-course meal that included raw meat infested with deadly
bacteria. Trained by Dische's fearfulness, Yankee suspected it, and
the practiced liar claimed to have a stomachache that the other
guests soon had, only worse.

By the time she reached the tranquillity of Nairobi, she had
been traveling for two months. Her money was running out. I will
reveal that it was pure chutzpah and not some guardian angel that
led her by the hand to the National Museum in Nairobi, where she
simply burst in on the director in his office to ask for a job. His secretary did the shooing out. No, no job. She glared at the eighteen-
year-old with the wash-and-go polyester dress, her golden cleavage
showing. Weirdos dropped by the National Museum every day.
Kenya attracted them. This one was unusually young, but there are
all kinds. The girl resisted the instant brush-off. And in this second
asking, the insistence for a chance, her girl's voice was overheard by
the director, who yelled through the slightly open door, "Just a

minute! I *do* need someone!" Grimly, the secretary allowed her in to see her boss. He was, as it happens, world famous, the last living explorer really. The secretary was trying to protect him from other, lesser explorers, like this floozy, but he didn't make it easy.

He was sitting behind his desk, looking English, his face pale, his crafty eyes blue, wearing a crown of white hair. "What are your qualifications?" he asked.

And she replied, "I am a high school dropout."

"Marvelous," he said, clearly meaning it. He seemed astonished about his luck. "And who are you besides that?"

She let loose with her credentials, a childhood as a pre-scientist in New York, her parents both professors, her complete lack of any qualifications nevertheless. He seemed satisfied. "I have a job for you."

A day later, she took up her duties at a primate research center in the temperate hills of Kenya. That was the first we heard from her in several months—her first news in weeks came by telegram: JOB WITH LOUIS LEAKEY IN KENYA.

"LIESEL. She is safe. And she has a job!"

"Finally."

"With a famous scientist.

"Who cares about that?"And Liesel added in English, "It only matter that she working."

The aerograms began coming again, always addressed to me because she knew how much I would relish and share them. The primates lived in enormous outdoor cages that contained the whole panorama of their daily lives: trees, running and standing water, bushes, bugs. Only one thing was missing—their enemies. So naturally they were cranky and bored. They had been caged in families, with an alpha male, the inferior and juvenile males, and all the ladies. The morale among the big capuchin males deteriorated most rapidly. They became wife beaters. Separate living quarters needed to be set up for one particularly angry fellow; then he was joined by another, blood still dripping from his incisors. A third joined them soon. They spent their days trying to trick the others, and life was amusing for them. They groomed one another, and beat and raped one another, and in the between times they strutted about, and were easily the best-looking monkeys in the habitat. The scientists kept exhaustive records of monkey behavior with time sheets that listed their activities. Young hired hands like Yankee were dispatched for eight-hour shifts of placing check marks every minute on these sheets. Yankee found it dull.

"She should not complain so much. It is better than cleaning rooms," I told Liesel.

One morning, a primatologist from the United States came to visit, newly arrived on the subcontinent, with sentimental feelings for monkeys. She had dressed up for the occasion, in a smart suit and high heels. She strode up to the three male capuchins and got to know them. They hung on the bars, their gorgeous black-and-white outfits, their maleness turned toward the scientist. She spoke to them seriously about their lives, asked them what they were doing, and how they felt. She read mutual interest in their faces looking down at her, for they were hanging high up in the bars. I'd stay back a little if I were you, thought my granddaughter, but said nothing, for the visitor had shown too much awareness of her superior position in life, the ink having just dried on her Ph.D. The capuchins listened to her babble for a while; then, as one monkey, they urinated on her.

She ran off, crying.

Yankee went back to her routine, worrying that it would never be as lively again at her place of work.

That afternoon, while she was still under the impression of this pleasant adventure, her boss came to see how everyone was getting along, and he asked her a routine question—what she thought of the job—and she replied, "Well . . . I don't see any sense in it."

He did not scold her. "Why not, Miss Dische?" he asked seriously.

"These behavior categories just don't interest me. I'd rather watch them in the wild and get to know them. At the moment, the scientists are more interesting than the monkeys, and that's not the point."

She had happened on the right answer.

He told her to pack her bags, he was going to take her back to Nairobi. He had a bigger and better project for her. "Stop calling me Dr. Leakey," he said. "Call me Louis. And do you have a real name? It can't be Yankee. Irene. That's better. And you're going to have to learn Kikuyu. It's an important language."

Thus, the Yankee Period ended. Her letter to us was signed "Irene."

Part

Five

*L*iesel," I said. "I think Dr. Leakey must have a wonderful house."

Liesel and I had taken to staying seated after our TV show, and talking about various important family matters. "It is simple, and it stands right on the game park. He lives with wild animals. And a lot of servants."

My granddaughter had described the staff, knowing this would be of vital interest to me. They were all Kikuyu, his own chosen tribe.

His father had come to Africa as a Protestant missionary whose goal in life was to convert the locals to his faith. Before his father knew it, his son spoke fluent Kikuyu, preferred the Africans to the English boys. His father tried to forbid the contact, and failed; his son had a mind of his own. When he was twelve, he asked to be initiated into the tribe. The ceremony required a show of manhood. The boy sat in a cold stream for a while until he declared himself ready. He squatted, and two pebbles were placed on him, one on each thigh, and he was circumcised with a panga sword. If the pebbles left their appointed places on his legs, the initiation failed. Only one attempt was possible. Louis was initiated.

His father packed him off to England, but Louis felt a foreigner there, and he returned as soon as he was of age. When his father was murdered by the rebelling Mau Mau in a ritual slaying, hung upside down with his head in a hole in the ground and the hole filled up, Louis did not condemn his people. He insisted his British father had earned his just desserts. The Kikuyu never considered Louis an outsider. And nowhere was he more at home than in the African outdoors.

I approved. At last, here was a man who was not weak. He was as courageous as I was. No, I had to admit, he was even more courageous. I thought Irene's worship well-placed.

Her letters were detailed. He had a wife and sons who, it was said, disapproved of him, but Irene could not think why. Once, shyly, he had suggested she keep him warm at night, the way old Kikuyu warriors were kept warm by children, and she had said I don't want to, I'm sorry, and he had said that's fine, I just asked. And didn't seem the slightest put out. Collecting some skulls at the National Museum, she noticed the secretary's look, and she picked up the innuendo that he was a dirty old man, but she was sure he wasn't. She was so allergic to dirty old men, she would have noticed it. He treated her like the daughter he had never had. And he was like the father she had never had—virile, solicitous, a gentleman. He took a huge interest in everything she thought, he cooked for her, he taught her what he knew. She repaid him with an endless curiosity about everything he thought or did, and accepted his care.

For several months, which seemed like years, they settled into that marvelous thing: a routine. Every morning, they got up early and went to the big game park. He taught her how to survive there, because soon she would have to. He initiated her into the great Study of Feces. She learned to regard the ground, and never miss a pile. Which animal had deposited it, which gender, and how many minutes or hours ago? Then there was the Study of the Horizon. Louis pointed to the trees and said, "What do you see there?" At first, although her eyesight was fresh and keen, she saw nothing. He taught her to observe more closely—the slight movement of a certain branch that could be fretting monkeys, which indicated a natural enemy nearby; the vultures as tiny pinpoints in the sky, pointing out a fresh lion kill. He broke the news to her, he believed she had talent. He saw a bright future in anthropology. She would follow in the footsteps of his first protégée, Jane Goodall. He had been looking for someone to study pygmy chimpanzees. He had hoped to find someone like Jane, who had also dropped out of high school. When Irene had burst into the museum to ask him for a job, and boasted of her lack of credentials, he had blessed his luck. He gave her a monograph about pygmy chimps. There were hardly any. They mated in the missionary position.

He wrote to National Geographic, saying that he had finally found just the person for his project. It required funding.

National Geographic wrote back—the anthropologist he proposed for the task would need some kind of qualifications. "You will have to go to college," he said, breaking the news to her.

"You can come here every vacation and we'll work together. Where would you like to go to school?" And she replied, "Harvard." He did not laugh, or roll his eyes. He said, "Then you will go to Harvard."

The college could not resist the legendary paleontologist beating down their doors, insisting on this favor. Can you imagine Renate's pride? She had gone to Columbia, and her daughter was outdoing her. Renate liked to be outdone by her daughter. I said, "Renate, so what. Harvard. What does that mean in the long run?"

Liesel said it was good but not for reasons of show. "Because she will have to work there. Girls should work. Renate works hard too."

Liesel took the bus to Little Carl's apartment to pick up his washing, dragging it back to Weehawken, returning it ironed, with a month's supply of butter cookies. He was still working as an unskilled assistant in Dische's laboratory, running minor errands all day. Liesel called him "my boy." She was a stickler for good character, she knew he had that. Irene didn't, so she would have to be good at something else. She would have to work hard, make up for her moral deficits. She stayed on in Africa, due to start Harvard in the autumn, and I bragged about her to the Smiths. "My grand-daughter is on an island in Lake Victoria." I pictured her in an ex-plorer's costume, meeting natives, hobnobbing with missionaries, riding on an elephant the way the Smiths' grandson Jack had done. Jack Smith was living a presentably dull life these days, and Susie Smith said she pitied me for my worries about Africa, which must be considerable. In fact, Irene's Africa was not quite how I pictured it.

The truth is, Irene was once again bored. She was assisting at a dig for the skeletons of ancient animals, but she did not enjoy dig-ging what remained of a million-year-old mouse out of the ground with a dental pick. To while away the time, she got to know the locals, a tribe called the Luo. Nice people, who, unlike the land-locked Kikuyu, spent their days fishing. She acquired a grammar and began learning the language. The grammar was written for mis-sionaries, with practice sentences useful to them, like "Boy! There is a hair in my soup!" When she could speak well enough, she be-friended everyone.

"That is exactly what I would have done!" I told Liesel. "You see, she swims naked now, because that's how African women swim. She has gotten over her American prudery."

"I don't know." Liesel shuddered. She was very prudish herself, and I never saw her naked once, not in all those years. She did not agree with me that nudity is a natural state. She said, "God clothed us." "Liesel, what nonsense. God made us, He didn't clothe us. The Africans are closer to God than we are!" I didn't believe that my-self, but I had to shore up my position somehow. I changed the sub-ject quickly. "Finally someone around here can speak a language Dische can't understand."

Irene also took over all communication with the staff of local helpers. The scientists had no idea how to deal with the African Help. It stymied them when the Help objected to eating only corn mash for lunch and dinner, while the scientists enjoyed savory meat dishes. Irene was dispatched to talk to them. After they were promised better meals, they went to work. The scientists absolved Irene of her odious scientific duties. Instead of squatting in the field with dental instruments, she made expeditions to the mainland to buy supplies at a market. She had a whale of a time.

But this time, her rebellion did not please Leakey. She had written a letter to him in Nairobi, bragging about her exploits as a friend of the Luo, and he replied stiffly. As a full-fledged member of the Kikuyu tribe, he heartily disliked the Luo, and felt it was a waste of time learning their language instead of Kikuyu. She wrote back, arguing with him about which tribe was better. He was angry with her. He did not write back. She heard that he had left Nairobi, and was working elsewhere. She was frightened to fall out of his graces. Then she fell ill.

Any pride she might have had in outdoing me with such a serious illness, and perhaps even beating me to an early death, was drowned in misery. She hallucinated and raved, and could not walk. She was moved like a package to Nairobi, to a museum guesthouse. Leakey was still not back. When she was aware of what was happening, she was perfectly calm. She called me. Her voice was faint. She said, "Goodbye." She hung up. I didn't know where she was. They didn't have phones on the island. She must be in a town. Renate was in Europe. Dische was in the Far East. My problem! Liesel and I prayed. Did our prayers help? She knew she was going to die, and she looked forward to it. But it was taking such a long time. Her patience was strained to the limit. Die, she commanded. Sometimes she thought she was already dead.

Then she became euphoric. She staggered outside, into an Anglo-African garden, which is, on a clear afternoon, not a bad guess at what paradise is like. She gazed at the deep blue sky and marveled as it turned dark green. It took her a while to realize she was lying facedown on an impeccable croquet lawn. The servants found her, lugged her back into her room. Strangers prodded her, administered something, left her alone. After three days, she was still not dead. A tall figure in a white linen suit was standing next to her: Leakey. He had heard about her illness, and had come for her.

When he had settled her into his house, he called me. He had a lovely upper-class English accent. He gave me all the details, promised to take care of her, and assured me that as soon as she could travel, he was sending her home. He was the first real man in our lives since Carl.

Leakey nursed her himself, forgave her the sin of preferring the Luo. She capitulated and asked for a Kikuyu grammar, and when she could walk again, he called me and said he was putting her on the next plane home to me. As much as he impressed me, I had to put my foot down. I said, "Don't. It is too much for my maid. Send her to her mother. She is attending a conference in Switzerland. I will arrange it." Liesel overheard. She stormed around to show her disapproval. I said, "Liesel, there is a limit. I am all worried out."

❧

SIG HAD ACCOMPANIED RENATE to Switzerland in order to take a romantic trip with her through the Alps after her conference. After picking Irene up, Renate called me to report that Irene was really quite frail. Sig was not pleased about taking an invalid along but he had no choice. His stepdaughter was so weak, a breeze could blow her over. "I hope the girl behaves herself, Liesel," I said. "Sig is touchy." Liesel shook her head, no, no, to show that she considered this scenario more worrisome than the earlier one, when Irene was sick in Africa. Now it was a really dangerous situation. And all my fault for not having arranged for her to come home directly to us.

Sig and Renate packed Irene into the backseat of their rental car and set off. They had been on the road for two days, and she was not picking up strength as by rights she should. She was nineteen years old, she should get well quickly. She could not eat. Sig got tired of watching her stare at plates of exquisite food in the expensive restaurants he picked out of the guidebook. Over breakfast one day, when she had refused to touch the lovely offerings, he snarled at her that she was ruining his vacation. She went quietly to the car, and lay down in the back of the car and willed herself to sleep. She could not run away, she did not have the strength.

After a drive through some gloomy Austrian scenery, they pulled into the parking lot of an appointed restaurant. Sig proposed that Irene stay in the car while they ate lunch, so she wouldn't spoil his appetite. Renate did not want to quarrel with him. She encouraged Sig to go ahead and find a table for two while she made her daughter, slumped in the backseat, comfortable by draping her summer jacket over her. "Darling," she asked anxiously, "do you mind terribly, just staying in the car, since you are not eating anyway?"

By the time they returned, the patient was shaking violently with fever. They had to cancel their plans to drive on. They checked into a village pensione. The owner was an old farmer. He wasn't afraid of illness, and he disapproved of the standoffish manner of the tourist he assumed to be the sick girl's father. He scooped the girl up in his burly arms, carried her upstairs, and settled her into a big white farmhouse bed with a big white eiderdown. She was lucid enough to be incredibly pleased: She saw the panic in her mother's eye. She knew what she had, while the two doctors did not. Malaria. Obviously. Nothing serious. Just slightly out of place in an Austrian farmhouse with mountain view. "Get me some ice cream, please." When I heard that my granddaughter had asked for ice cream, I almost cried with pride. My granddaughter. Request denied. She said, "In Africa, people with malaria always get ice cream." The ice cream was brought.

That night she heard Sig in the next room. He was crying. She listened to him for a while, without understanding. Then he came crashing into the room. He was wearing his bathrobe. His pipe was in his hand. His face was soaking wet and his eyes were red. His wife followed him, stood back. He addressed Irene. He said, "I want to apologize to you. I'm sorry for what I have done to you."

But he wished her to take a plane back to New York as soon as possible. Liesel and I picked her up at the airport.

The autumn semester at Harvard started in a month anyway. Louis had told her he expected her in Nairobi for her winter break in January. But she would never see him again.

DISCHE CAME TO DINNER. He looked at Irene and announced to the company, "The bloom is off her face already." Irene smiled at him lovingly. I felt that his observation required correction. I said, "Absolutely to the contrary. Her face is just not interesting yet. A face without wrinkles is a blank piece of paper. She will be beautiful in a few years. Perhaps." I did not bring up the sore point of her nose again.

She went up to Boston, began her studies, and once again, she discovered she was not the born student. She found academic anthropology woefully boring. Really, she just wanted to have a good time. It occurred to her that she would betray Leakey, that after picking up her degree in anthropology she would switch to medicine and become a doctor. Diseases, she thought, would be more fun. She had only a few more weeks of her first semester to go. Winter vacation was coming up, and then she would fly to Kenya. But in late autumn, that wonderful man just up and died of a heart attack. The family did not inform her. Possibly Louis had kept a whole stable of floozies in his time. They figured Irene was just another one of them. She read about his death in the paper.

The very next morning, she switched majors from anthropology to literature. She was not particularly keen on literature, but she was not averse to it either. Coincidence, nothing higher, had tossed her friends who took their studies seriously, who dreamed of being Great Writers, and she played along. She was like an old woman, living pleasantly from minute to minute and not thinking about the unknowable future. At this point, though, something happened that ended her childhood.

ONE MORNING SHORTLY BEFORE CHRISTMAS, Renate phoned Irene and asked her to come to New York quickly. She needed her ally. Sig, the indestructible, the evil titan, was stricken. He lay in a hospital bed, roaring his hatred. Irene walked into the room without fear—his hands were tied to the bed. He had had his entire gut removed and he decided that he did not want to live. But he could not just bully away his life. He called for a nurse, ordered her to open a window so he could jump out. He demanded that the IVs and the tubes be removed. He had tried to yank them out. He had created a mess, so they tied his hands down. He still had his assault weaponry of words. His expletives penetrated closed doors, and volleyed along the corridor, causing much consternation, but he would not be shut up. Renate dared to approach his bed. He hissed at her. They had made an agreement—if he ever wanted to die, she would not stop him. But she replied calmly, decidedly, that the deal was off, she wanted him alive. Whereupon he shouted at the top of his megaphone voice that she was a whore and a bitch. Irene fled, Renate following her. They left him alone. He exsanguinated shortly afterward, of a bleeding ulcer that had developed very quickly. He was in his mid-sixties. Sig died of rage.

YOUNG PEOPLE! Do not gloat about your youth, because you have a long and treacherous path to negotiate before you reach the truly lovely part of life. Your first decades are one long, tiring, demeaning struggle for at least a short turn at the control lever. Every day you get savaged by your own wishes. When you finally calm down and accept your lot, you are middle-aged, and happiness most definitely lies more closely ahead, but you still have a few years to go, passing through most arduous longing and regret. And the battle between the sexes really heats up during middle age. Middle-aged men and women are afraid of each other. They recognize in their husbands or wives the decay they would rather not notice in themselves. This causes rages and car wrecks. When they see a middle-aged woman, middle-aged men accelerate, try to cut her off, pass her, anything to express their rage. In stores, they shove her aside carelessly. At parties, they refuse to be seated next to her. They pretend she does not exist. But middle age, like purgatory, is of limited duration. March on, to your goal! The magic age of seventy. Then life per se becomes a treasure.

Don't believe any whining you've heard about aching bones. While it's true that the number of pains per hour per square centimeter of one's body increases steadily with age, so does one's sensitivity to pain decline. One grows used to or largely indifferent to it. If you stuffed a twenty-year-old into the body of a seventy-year-old, sure, they would scream with agony. Many oldsters feel no pain at all, but they pretend to, as a form of polite conversation with other oldsters. Their sighs and protests affirm their pleasurable brotherhood.

After seventy, the war between the sexes ends abruptly. Peacetime. Men and women begin to look alike; they are both hairless, and even a man's breasts begin to dangle freely after he has lived long enough, while a woman's behind becomes flat as a pancake. That is as close to paradise on earth as you'll ever get.

At long last, men and women stop demanding the impossible of each other, relationships become dearer, there is no sidetrack of a career. There is only the pleasure of the other. And if there is no other, then there is pleasure, the keenest kind, in one's self—the mouthful of good food, the cloudless sky above. You must wait for decades, youth, for these mundane items to suffuse you with True Delight.

I was seventy-nine at this point in my narrative, and therefore in my prime. I had a few debilities, but they were easily overcome. In my forties, my eyesight had plagued me because I could no longer read without glasses and I was always misplacing them. In my fifties, I dreaded going blind. In my sixties, I nearly did so. But in my seventies, my eyesight became perfect for my needs. I continued to drive, although I could no longer see, because Liesel served as my eyesight at the wheel. We drove to mass every day. First I had to exit backward out of the driveway. No problem. She knelt on the front seat, turned to the rear, chanting, "Go go go," preferring English for its precision in this matter. And I would hold the steering wheel absolutely still and accelerate backward until she cried, *"Links links links,"* or *"Rechts rechts rechts,"* preferring German for this, which meant I had to rotate my steering wheel in whichever direction she dictated until she stopped chanting. When she cried, *"Schtopp!"* preferring a mixed language form for this, I heaved my foot onto the brakes. But when she sang it, *"Schtopp Schtopp schtopp,"* then I merely relaxed my toehold on the gas a little, and slowed down.

Renate said it was a calamity, "our" driving, we were endangering innocent bystanders, and my God wouldn't help me if I was aiming the Buick in the wrong direction for a fraction of a second. I always agreed to *schtopp* driving from that day on and only take taxis, but of course we didn't, we went to church every day and God didn't *have* to watch over us, because our system was a perfectly good system.

Of course I am aware that at those times I was obeying the maid to the letter, doing what she told me to do. Periodically I told her, "Don't you get any ideas about my obeying you under any other circumstances," and she snapped, "No, no, of course not," and then we both laughed heartily.

One morning, I was just coming down the staircase all set to drive to church when the door chime rang. Liesel opened for Renate and Irene, and learned the news before I did. I was halfway down the stairs, and Renate called upward, "Sig has died." She said it drily, that was her manner. At that point, gravity overcame me. I sat down on a stair, in the middle of the staircase. I put my chin in my hands and just looked at my girls. They were very calm. It just struck me as preposterous that 1972 should be the dying year of my son-in-law, earlier than my own. A shock.

Renate suffered, of course. She could not stand the loss.

She could not sleep. But she would not admit it. She kept her upper lip so stiff that it triggered gossip. She had innumerable foes suddenly. At Sig's deathbed in the hospital, the professors from the Department of Pathology paid their respects. Renate stood next to the body laughing. The pathologists were shocked. What is this? She seems happy. It was settled: poor Sig Wilens! At his funeral, various speakers waxed rhapsodic about what a wonderful, kind man Sig had been. Renate had not loved him for his kindness, but for his wit and his realism, which often made him cruel. She and Irene nearly wept suppressing their giggles. This was noticed all over the chapel. One deduced that she was a funny one. Sig's sisters became convinced she had married him for his money.

Well, she hadn't. I would be the first to criticize her for that, and it just wasn't so. He wasn't worth marrying for money; to be truthful, he didn't have much, he had spent freely. But she was not going to give up what he did leave her. She liked the security of his little nest egg. The sisters grew enraged. They circled the apartment, glaring, taking everything in, collecting knickknacks they claimed meant something to them. They took his watch, the paintings, photographs of him as a young man. "Take, take," Renate exclaimed. "Please! He would want you to have it."

But they only became angrier. Because she didn't give them the money. Hadn't she married him after he received his death sentence of terminal cancer? A shame, a sham, the marriage?

She accepted their sudden rejection. I don't like to see anyone suffer, regardless of the reason, regardless if they earned it or didn't deserve it. Her suffering was rather more than mine when Carl died. In my case, my sorrow had a component of embarrassment. He left me alone, and I was not used to it, I felt uneasy, and that embarrassed me. So I set out to prove that I could handle it. In the case of all other deaths, those losses were merely unacceptable facts that I had to accept. But Renate was, as they say, shattered. You experience that kind of sorrow, like true love, only once in a lifetime—twice, if decades lie between. The two emotions have practically the same effect: a total riveting of attention. Every minute that passed was now a minute spent without Sig. But she had lost him, not her pride. She refused to cry in public, refused to complain, refused to show her devastation. Her sorrow inflated when she was alone, never left her bedside when she tried to fall asleep, and when she tried to eat, it constricted her throat, and she couldn't swallow. She lost twenty pounds. Her figure took on some remarkable contours. An improvement. Even I had to admit that misery became her.

The crematorium inquired when they might deliver the ashes. She had ordered the cheapest container, she did not believe in wasting money on something that was going underground. She said, "Bring the ashes on Saturday night, please." Then she invited guests and threw a dinner party. It was just before Christmas, so she put up a nice big tree, and strung lights on it. She cooked a big dinner. Guests came because they felt she needed the moral support at such a bad time, but she looked like she was having a blast. Nobody noticed that she didn't eat a bite. Punctually as ordered, at 7:00 p.m., during the second course, the doorbell rang. "Just one little minute," she called. She went to the door, signed for the package, and laid it under the Christmas tree as if it were a present, then returned to the table.

She didn't invite me, she knew I would disapprove, but her ally attended. For once, her mother's insouciance unnerved her. After the guests left, Renate grew wan. She did not want to go to bed. Irene called me secretly on the phone, and whispered, "She won't sleep anymore!" I told her to hang up, I would take care of it. I called back a few minutes later. I knew not to scold. I said, "It's funny, Renate, how you never liked beds. They make you uneasy. Maybe you should sleep, as you always used to do before Sig came along, on the sofa." Sig had bought the sofa, so it was expensive, filled with down. She did not ask why I was suddenly calling about such a matter. She sank down in the sofa, fully clothed, as if she were just receiving company. And in that pose, dressed and propped up on the sofa, she could sleep a little.

It took a secretary at work to notice that Dr. Dische was suffering. She recommended grief counseling, a psychiatrist, and gave her a name and a phone number. Renate called up and asked how much it cost, and how long the therapy would take. One year was the average grieving time, said the psychiatrist, irritated by the question. Renate calculated. She canceled the therapy and spent the money on new clothing. She looked better and better, even to the experienced medical eye. Rested from her slumber on the couch, slender, dressed to the nines. Grief made her eyes shine. By New Year's, one of her colleagues noticed.

Finally, a proper Christian swain. Dr. Mallard. With a long white neck that twisted when he glanced down, his customary way of looking at anything. A high-ranking medical doctor, he specialized in Gross Anatomy; he studied hers in his office. It cheered her up no end. Gossip about her behavior made the rounds. Nobody would just admit that she was doing what was best. In the end, I let down my iron opposition to her way of handling men. My will had been worn down. Sin of negligence. Not really. I had been reading

Time magazine again, and had come to realize that sex was natural. Animals did it, but that did not make it horrid, it made it all right. And one day it just dawned on me: I had sinned against Carl, forced him into unnatural abstinence.

Father, I have sinned. But there is nothing I can do about it now.

Sig's sisters dropped by again, on the pretext of visiting their dear, dear dead brother's widow, but actually just to catch hints as to how she was spending the money. They saw the expensive clothes, and their indignation burned in their cold white faces like a winter bonfire.

They demanded that Sig be buried with them, in their funeral plot at the Jewish cemetery in Hartford. The family wanted to stay together, they said. But the Jewish cemetery would not have him, because he had married a Goy. Pollution. For once, Renate was viewed the way Carl and I had always dreamed. Sig's sisters fluttered and screeched and could do nothing. So Renate asked at our church if she could put him in the Catholic cemetery. Of course not. A Jew. Never. Pollution. Sig remained in his canister. Renate kept him in her closet, with all the new clothes.

"Renate," I said, "a spirit cannot find rest until his remains are buried."

The church cemetery no longer lay at the edge of a forest, but bordered a housing development. One night, after midnight, we all put on our slacks, except Liesel, who refused to wear men's clothing and put on her Sunday best. Renate scaled the fence and opened the gate for us. We had brought a shovel, a flashlight, and Sig. Renate cut a neat square of sod as a plug, and her shovel hit Carl's coffin. Liesel poured him in. I shed a tear. Renate said, "Oh, stop it, Mops, you don't really believe these are his ashes? They pour everyone together. This is your idea. I would have kept him in the closet."

It was my dying year, 1974. I had blinding headaches. Renate visited me often. She thought about moving in with me but I was opposed. I was afraid of the consequences. She would rule. I was not ready to give up my dominion. I had a disease; I had to take cortisone and I lost my looks. My arms became thin, truly the way I had longed for them to be. But my face was round, and my hair fell out of my scalp and instead grew on my upper lip. What a terrible time to say goodbye to the world. I was still so curious about it. One morning, I really did not wake up. I was in a coma. Renate rushed to my side, ordered the ambulance.

"How was it?" asked Liesel, when she finally got to the hospital.

"It was unimaginable. Wonderful. Top speed through rush hour. The traffic just parted for us. I felt like Moses crossing the Red Sea!"

But in fact I could not enjoy the speediest ride of my life, as I was unconscious. I received the last rites without enjoying them either. I had a small instance of clarity when someone was poking me in the abdomen, and I heard myself groaning, and I recognized Irene's voice. "For Chrissake, just let her the fuck die!" I was most grateful to her, and for once I agreed with her wholeheartedly, and attempted to say so, "Yes, for Chrissake, please," but then no one heard me whisper.

And so it happened that one day, I woke up and was not in heaven at all, but sharing a hospital room with a woman of color, who was even older than I was. I had to stay with her for two weeks. She was from Jamaica, a cleaning lady who told me she had smoked as much as she could afford and drank as much as she could steal— she was fussy about the quality of her liquor. She was nearing one hundred, and her eyes and her appetite were better than mine. She said she owed this to never having married, and I figured she might be right. We had a good time together, recovering from our maladies. We watched television and ate our meals and discussed life. When I left, though, I didn't ask for her phone number and I knew I wouldn't see her again. There are limits to some friendships.

Back at home, my strength returned. I could go to church again. My hair grew in a pretty, luxuriant mink color. "You see," I told Renate, "I never *had* to color it." I accepted her offer of a new set of clothes.

Over in New York, Sig's apartment turned gradually into Renate's home. She did not serve steaks, or even bother with regular meals. She always slept on the sofa, she slipped back into the bohemian mode. Her swain took her to hotels. She visited me often. Again, she spoke about moving in with me. I objected. She would get on my nerves. She would disrupt my routine. Just look, I thought, how I would suffer to see up close the way she was carrying on with her Dr. Mallard. And then he suddenly swam away.

This did not cause sorrow, but far worse, gave a blow to her pride, and she had several hard years. She didn't want any consolation, though, certainly not from Dische.

He had always stayed in the picture, always ready to return to Renate. He had a girlfriend of his own for a while, a north German chemist and former Hitler Youth, blond and brassy and pushing fifty, with blue eyes that looked like they were holes in a jack-o'-lantern, lit inside with the grimmest form of ambition, the one that occurs late in life. When she was young, she had been satisfied with a low-level career. At some point she began struggling to be better than others. Whatever she did now, she hoped was superior. Did she wear an apron to cook? Then those who wore aprons were aesthetically superior. Did she like stray cats? Then liking stray cats was a sign of moral superiority. Her name suited her temperament: Gertrude. I have never known a modest, kindhearted Gertrude. She wanted to be more than a middling, middle-aged chemist. Ambition drove her to this alliance with old man Dische because he gave her so many opportunities, introduced her to important people. She was a divorcée, the men were not exactly standing in line for her favors, and Dische worshipped her, referred matter-of-factly to her great beauty as a matter beyond dispute. But he said nothing about her talents. And to Gertrude, he raved about his ex-wife, her sophistication, her piano playing, and worst, he always referred to her as Dr. Dische. Then there was the other Dische, his daughter, who felt she had proprietary rights to him. Gertrude disliked the daughter because she was too much like her father. She looked like him, same face, and she dressed badly, because she was sloppy, just like he was. But not as smart. She couldn't be a biochemist.

As husband apparent, Gertude felt that Dische was a humiliation. His table manners, his stinginess. They went shopping, and in front of the cashier and other strangers, he refused to take out his money, made her pay. An old man without means is really not attractive. She had taken care of him when a moderate amount of care was required, as befitting a normal husband—cooking, a little cleaning—and he could pay back with social status. When he became ill for the first time, she dumped him. She thought, Dische unto Dische, let the other horrible Disches take care of him.

He dreamed of coming to Weehawken. He would call up and wheedle a dinner invitation out of me. For Renate's sake, I did not invite her. Dische took the bus over from Manhattan, as if I were still his mother-in-law, and he sat down for dinner, listened to grace with his head bowed to show his respect, and then tucked into the good food. He talked at me about his research, about politics, and I listened to the edges of his conversation, just enough to identify the topic, and reminded myself that this was what God wanted me to do, sacrifice an hour for Dische. And then Liesel corrected me, saying, "I don't mind spending the five hours cooking and cleaning up for him," in her arch way, suggesting that she did more. But she didn't have to speak to him.

I must admit that an hour spent on anything was scarcely noticeable now. Time had picked up its skirts and was just dashing along. The years began to pass at such a tempo that they must have caused a gale in my face, battering it like a pilot's at terminal velocity. Before long, I was in my nineties. Little Carl was living in a bachelor apartment in Weekhawken now, and it was clear that his shyness would remain untouched by all our attempts to alter it, and that he would not start a family of his own. I looked forward to his Sunday visits, he was a quiet and considerate grandson. He went to work, and when he came home, he read and kept to himself. In another life, he would have been a monk. Irene occasionally visited us too. She had a boyfriend, a brawny but clever fellow who probably insisted on sex. Once, I asked her about this, but she didn't say anything. So I shook myself and said, "Brrrrr . . . I think sex is disgusting," just to make her take a stance. She still didn't say anything. My granddaughter didn't invite confidences, but every so often, she introduced me to her friends. Once, she showed up with a very tall gentleman, a student from college. I set the table immediately for them, with coffee and Liesel's best cookies. We had a chat. It was very pleasant. When asked, I told the visitor some of my War stories, which he seemed very interested to hear. Somehow the conversation turned to crime, and I told them about my idea that the Puerto Ricans were responsible for most of the violent crime in New York. I got a little carried away. All of a sudden it dawned on me that Irene's friend might be Puerto Rican. A drawback of poor eyesight—you cannot see skin color clearly. I peered at him, and I couldn't be sure. Finally, I just asked him directly. "You're not a Puerto Rican, are you?" To my relief, he laughed cheerfully and said, "No, ma'am." The way he said it, I realized he was Colored.

Irene and I were on good terms then, she was proud of me, and she took me aside at the next opportunity and assured me that her friend had been charmed by me, even though he was vice president of an outfit called the Black Panthers at Harvard. After that, she often brought her friends to meet me, and I always set the table and made them feel at home. She encouraged me to tell stories about the past; she said I was a natural storyteller and she urged me to write everything down, but I was much too busy.

Soon after, she gave me quite a grand gift. She had paid a visit to Germany, a place she said she dreaded. I didn't care to comment on that, because I wasn't eager for her to go, but I didn't like the idea that my own grandchild should be afraid of the country where I was born and raised. I told her that if she stayed for more than a month, I would visit her. I guess she wanted me to visit, because the next thing I knew, she was marrying a German. Now, he came from a really fine family, not a drop of Jewish blood, and quite a bit of aristocracy. In fact, his family was finer than the Gierlichs had been. And he had a small nose, as small as mine, possibly even smaller. When their first child Emily was born, Irene had checked immediately, first things first, whether the father had managed to pass on his nose gene, and when she saw that he had, she called me and said, "Granny. Do I ever have a present for you!" I kept my promise. Liesel and I packed our bags, and we traveled together to Germany to see what my new family was all about. My great-granddaughter Emily would turn out very nicely, with a small mouth just like mine, and thick hair, just like mine. Unfortunately, she had freckles. But that can be altered easily. They have very simple, effective procedures now to prevent people from looking Irish.

In the meantime, Renate wanted to move in with me and Liesel. I was reluctant, because Liesel insisted that it would be nice to have Renate at home again. Liesel was always trying to get the upper hand. Finally I agreed, and we were a family of women again, as we had been in Breslau in 1937. Straightaway, Renate turned everything on its head. She insisted on buying Liesel a new bed, although the maid really fought the idea, preferring a mattress like a bed of nails. Her claim to power rested on self-sacrifice. Renate was interested in power herself; she bought Liesel the most expensive orthopedic mattress on the market, and thus she took some control. She could afford it, as a full professor at Columbia now. She was earning a lot of money, and she took care of me. We became the very best of old friends. I took pleasure in my appearance again. I was slender, and there seemed no danger of my gaining weight, because I did not enjoy eating as much as I used to. Instead, I enjoyed buying myself clothes. Renate approved. She was nearing the golden age of seventy herself, and growing wiser by the minute. She said, "For about twenty-five years, you look better without clothes on. Then for about ten years you look good either with your clothes on, or with your clothes off. Then for the rest of your life, you look better with clothes on."

"Still, there is no shame in taking off one's clothes," I said. "I am not ashamed of my body the way you are, Renate."

For my ninety-fifth birthday, Renate said, "Mops, what can I give you?" and I replied without any hesitation, "A new hat."

She took me to the finest hat store in Manhattan. She said, "Take your pick." She told the salesman, "My mother needs a hat that suits her."

The salesman was Jewish. He said, "I have just the perfect hat for your shape of face, madam." He set down a hatbox with care, as if it held the Crown Jewels. Inside lay a hat made of cashmere and mink, deep brown, the wide-brimmed style that I could carry so well. It cost eight hundred dollars. Renate swallowed. I said, "Renate, in contrast to you, I will take very good care of this hat. I will get years and years of wear out of it."

I was joking. I refused the hat, of course, but she insisted, of course. It is still a lovely hat. Irene's eye hasn't fallen on it yet. She hasn't sold it or worn it and lost it or dropped it in the mud. It is right there in my hat closet in Weehawken as I write, setting the entire closet alight with its quiet finery.

All of a sudden, though, I felt bored. It was a peculiar feeling. I had never known it before. It was one of those gorgeous late spring days they have in America, the garden was gyrating it was growing so fast, the sun poured down, birds were swooping about, insects buzzed in the house, everything was in motion but me. I didn't want

to eat and I didn't want to watch As the World Turns, or have someone watch a film for me and tell me what it was about. I was tired of
gardens, and the house, and my body, tired of my very existence,
and I really didn't care whether Renate was there or not. I was just
plain bored. I told Renate.

She was a talented doctor. She shouldn't have bothered with all
the other stuff, the biochemistry, the specialty in dead children and
heart disease. She recognized that I was not just saying I was bored,
I was saying goodbye. She kissed me. She said, "I don't kiss you often, do I, Mops, but right now I feel like it. I hope you don't mind."
Infernal sin of modesty. I did not scold her. I said, "I like it when
you kiss me."

That night I had a long, hard think about my life. I remembered, in short, my sins. There were many, and mostly, as with most
people, they were repetitions, just the same sins over and over
again. My soul wasn't a pretty picture, but it wasn't all that bad either. It was an ordinary soul. Until a tiny incident that I had completely forgotten came back to me.

I made my first confession when I was eight years old.

I had worn a white dress, and a huge white ribbon in my thick
auburn hair. I had bathed beforehand, and I have never been so
clean, or so scared. I knelt in the confessional. The priest was gen-
tle. He wasn't a scolder. He listened, emanating God's goodwill.
Bless me, Father, for I have sinned. I told him about being Angry,
and Envious, and desiring my sister's more beautiful toy. And I
fudged and I glossed. And I left out the most important, how just an
hour earlier, I had torn off my underpants in the tub, and had
touched the forbidden territory of my body with my finger, and that
it had specifically asked me to touch it in a certain way, and not to
stop, and that I had given in easily to this demand, this appetite,
and that only the approaching footsteps of my nanny had put an
end to this game. When she came in, I lied brazenly about "losing"
my underpants underwater. This sin I confessed—sin of lying—but

the priest did not inquire as to the nature of the lie, and I was too ashamed to confess more, so the black, black sin of impurity, the most dire of mortal sins, had stayed on my conscience, and I had sinned mortally again, by taking my first Holy Communion anyway after an imperfect, incomplete confession, and I never did confess that—that I took Communion on a dirty soul. For eighty-seven years I had not confessed it, so that in fact my entire Catholic life I had been living in the depths of mortal sin, and I was doomed.

But even this fact could not impart a sense of urgency to me, not enough to summon a priest and confess. Nothing. I told Renate again, with a laugh, "It's funny, I am just not interested anymore." She lay down on the bed with me, in Carl's place, and said she would read for a while, just to be near me. We had the pillow between us, with my mother's rosary on it, and after a while I took the rosary, and felt my mother's fingers on it too.

Soon afterward, I lost consciousness. Renate was right there next to me. She looked at me, and then she sighed, and she got up and told Liesel. She did not bring me to the hospital, to the intensive care unit, to life-sustaining machinery. She went downstairs into the cellar and she fetched that bottle of raspberry spirits that I had saved up for a special occasion. She couldn't budge the wax seal, and ended up blasting it off with my electric can opener. Then she took me in her arms, with Liesel's help, and fed me with a spoon. I was aware of the delirious sweet in my mouth, and the lovely burn when I swallowed it. Finally, I was like a priest, allowed to partake of the holy blood. Just as Renate expected, the spirits brought my bored old heart to a full stop. Renate—virtue of courage and kindness. My body lay in her arms, and my soul departed. So it turned out, after all that guessing, that 1989, when I was ninety-six years old, was my last year.

Life went on afterward, of course. I do not want to place a break here where none is merited, no moment of silence, no black page. As a memory, I was very powerful. Renate continued to live at my house. Little Carl soon moved in with her, but he was not particularly companionable. No amount or degree of questioning would ever wrest a conversation out of him. After work, he came home, mostly it seemed to read. He might spend every evening for a week reading a big tome with an even bigger title, but when Renate asked what it was about, he shrugged and stated that he didn't know, he had just leafed through it. He didn't like to talk, and was not sad at my funeral, because he was too unhappy about having to say hello to my friends. Irene didn't show up, she was in Germany now and suddenly so fearful again, this time about flying, that she wouldn't even travel home to pay me those final respects. Dische came, though, leaning on two crutches now, his gaze mad; he didn't like to look at dead people. But he became one himself soon enough afterward. He had an untidy death, befitting his entire life. Just a mess. He tormented everyone with his brain, now because it had gone rotten. He spent his days trying to figure out where he was, as if it were a complicated scientific puzzle—which it is, of course. When he stopped eating and drinking it was a mercy for all concerned.

His ashes were delivered as fourth-class mail to Weehawken, where Liesel clucked and then placed him on the porch among some potted plants and some old Greek plays that no one but he would have wanted to read. So ultimately he did have a triumph, because he got to stay there for years and years, as a wrapped package on the porch. And it fell to Liesel to share the porch with him when, ten years later, and also ninety-six years old, she took to her bed there, at her own insistence. She was worn out, and begging God to come for her, and angry with Him because she could no longer work. Renate paid for around-the-clock care for her, and Liesel criticized the nurses ruthlessly. Then she could no longer criticize.

Somehow word got out that during the War, while we were already in America and she was left in Breslau working for the priest, she had taken a lot of chances. She had hidden an elderly Jewish couple in the priest's basement, she had given them her meat allowance, and stolen from his pantry to feed them. The priest never found out, and the couple lived to tell the tale. A journalist came from Israel to interview her.

Liesel was miniature and fierce as ever. She sat propped up in a chair and the young man plied her with informed questions about those days in the past when she had been a heroine, but she only answered "I don't remember" to all of them, and then she cried, "What does it matter what I did?" She dismissed him: his shirt, she said, was an ugly color, yellow, horrible. Then she could no longer sit up. For five days she lay in bed singing religious songs from her childhood, and finally God took pity on her, or He couldn't bear the noise. And He gave a sign—she would share the twenty-second of November with John F. Kennedy as her final day. Her funeral was as bombastic as mine, and she was buried right on top of me, in the Catholic cemetery of Weehawken. We are packed in there. The view has disappeared. The Garden State had built yet another highway that runs right along the back edge of it, and the church had to trim away the spacious front lawn leading to the chapel, turn it into a drive to a parking lot, so that a concrete road now runs within two inches of my final resting place.

But where was I, apart from there and Here?

I must explain about Renate. I did keep my eye on her after I was no longer on Earth. When I took my last breath, she took the gold chain off my neck that my mother had worn, and she placed it around her own neck, and that gave her some physical protection, not of an unlimited nature, but some. It took her a while to get used to being without me actually there, to take over power. At first, she just wore my clothes and ran my house. She took care of Liesel as if she were not the maid but her second mother. When it transpired that Liesel had secretly consulted a lawyer in order to write a will in which she left all of her considerable savings—more than mine—

to Little Carl, Renate argued with her, she should leave it to her own flesh and blood, her niece Friedel, but Liesel said, "No!" She became moneybags to Little Carl. Really, Liesel had cunningly, quietly, held the reins of power in the family for many years, I see that clearly now. But when Liesel finally died, Renate took these reins from her, and held on tight. She became the Empress of the Family. And, resplendent, she finally reached the age of seventy. Irene had made her some grandchildren, the details are not that interesting from my perspective, but it caused Renate joy: she became a granny. Everyone adores a granny, even a bitter middle-aged man. Renate was having a whale of a time.

One day she called up Irene in Germany. Irene was still her ally and confidante from afar. Renate said, "I've met a man." Irene sighed. There had been many men traipsing around, all unsuitable. Renate said, "But all he wants is that one thing. So I'm not interested. I just wanted to tell you."

For several weeks, Renate did not call her again. Finally Irene managed to reach her. She had been worried. But Renate sounded easygoing, pleased. "Remember that fellow I told you about?"

"Yes, the one who only wanted one thing."

"Yes."

"And?"

"Well, maybe I only want one thing too."

It was my handiwork. A memory can move mountains. After a lifetime of protests, I had given in to her insatiable appetite for Jewish men, and her willingness to share her body. I had arranged the chance meeting in the laboratory hall. I had sent her a Morton.

👑

MORTON WAS THE SON OF SIMON, a porky kosher butcher, Brooklyn born, and Sarah of Glubczyce, Poland, who spoke English as if her mouth were full of boiling aromatic *Bigosz*, screwing up her eyes and allowing only a word at a time to escape through her lips, and breaking into a sweat from the strain; she was shy, she did not want to force herself on anyone. She was never heard to use the word "I." Forced, she would say a few words about someone else's cooking, the weather, about her husband's health, about her children's achievements. One day, during a Passover supper when no one was supposed to talk, she remarked very loudly, "I miss home." Everyone said she was crazy, but they meant it nicely. Simon was normal, and he loved her for being shy, and for being small. He had never met a woman as small, she came up to his shoulders; he was five feet two. Their four children were of normal stature. When they were still in grade school, the two boys towered above their parents, but cowered before them. They were under the knout of religion. Sarah disciplined them with tears, Simon with the Bible. Morton was the eldest and ordained either to become a rabbi or to take over the butcher shop. He was nice-looking, black curls on his head, a handsome face with friendly eyes. He was a flashy scholar in high school but he rebelled, rejecting the two professions open to him. His parents accepted third best—he wanted to be a doctor. He married a nice Jewish refugee from Germany who already had a medical degree and was trying to get her family to join her in New York. Possibly Morton dragged his feet about inviting her family, with all those brothers and sisters, to join them, possibly it was only her perception. But tarrying was the end of them. Instead of blaming the Nazis, his wife forever blamed Morton for the death of her kin. She would not do him the honor of having his children. She grew ever more bitter, and specialized in psychotherapy.

When Morton's father Simon died, it transpired that while dicing up meat, he had dabbled in real estate. He left a significant fortune to his wife, Sarah, who died soon afterward from grief and could not enjoy it. While still young, Morton became a wealthy man. He accepted his money as a proof of superiority, but he did not lose his respect for Hippocrates and the Calling. He was a hardworking internist. His wife disliked medicine; the human body did not interest her. She found her husband's particularly odious. His curls had receded, exposing a narrow, even pointy forehead she refused to look at. Her hair remained luxuriant and black, a wig. His flesh fell. She propped hers up and hated him for growing old right in front of her. Death surrounded him, she thought, the way he had brought on her parents' death! They moved into a brownstone on a fashionable block where she "entertained" (Morton's term) patients, and they lived on icy, cordial terms. She tried to make him feel bad about his wealth, did not succeed, but did manage to force him into a frugality that, after twenty years, became a habit. She owned one coat, a light spring coat. In the winter, she wore a bathrobe under it. She wore their tea cozy as a hat. His clothes were threadbare, but he took care of them and he had a good figure so they looked fine. She died quickly, after the crab took over her pancreas, and he missed her.

He was lonely, he had overcome his training and bought himself a new wardrobe, but he did not feel younger in the presence of a younger woman. To the contrary, he felt older, so he was not disgusted by a woman in his own age-group—all of this would make him a good match. He kept his wealth a self-important secret, still feeling superior because of it, anointed in some way. But he did not want to share his wealth. He did not flash the label on his expensive cashmere coat. He took women on dates to the cheapest, most vulgar deli in town. They smelled a rat—he was a childless doctor for God's sake, he must be rolling in it. No one even suspected the butcher's millions. All the women he invited to the deli ordered either the roast beef dinner or the chicken breast marsala, the only expensive items on the menu, so he didn't invite them again, kept on looking. Then he met Renate, and she ordered a bacon lettuce and tomato sandwich on white toast with a lot of mayonnaise, a $2.99 special with side of coleslaw. She ate this with gusto. He liked that she was German, her big nose, her happy eyes, her quick movements, and her passion for medicine. Before he realized that she was not really Jewish, he had fallen head over heels in love with her.

❧

I HAVE SPOKEN OF IT: after you turn seventy, barring some grave misfortune, life becomes as delightful as it was when you were twenty, only more so. Morton was one of many single men who took an interest in Renate at that time, and he was romantic and handsome. Furthermore, he was healthy and he never dwelled on his infirmities; he didn't even have any. He liked to go to the opera, he read *The New York Times*. Right away, he wanted Renate to move in with him, into his luxury brownstone. She agreed to marry him long before he asked. When he didn't ask for her hand, but merely her person, she called off the relationship. He begged. She refused to move in with him until they were married. She told him her children would disapprove, having a mother that lived in sin. He balked because she was a shiksa. Imagine how pleased I was!

Finally, he gave in on the condition that she sign a prenuptial agreement making no claims on a penny of his fortune, which would go instead to distant relatives. Renate was offended but she signed. Still no wedding date. Even after this guarantee of her genuine affection, he tested her daily. He refused to give her any presents. It occurred to him that she might move her children into the house, because it was large enough. He took a precautionary measure, even though it was a terrible time to sell, and sold the brownstone at a huge loss, and moved into an apartment without a guest room. He told her he would pay the rent and the bills, but that was all.

He introduced her to his family. She adored them, and they adored her. They were generous, simple people, very much like Carl's family in Leobschütz. They did not care about her background, racially impure, and she did not mind that they were uneducated. She loved their warmth, and they noted her warm heart, and that crotchety Uncle Mort smiled all the time in her presence, and they urged him to hurry up and marry her. He was in love with her, but he wouldn't give her anything.

She still wanted a pearl necklace. All her life, she had dreamed of a thick strand of pearls around her neck. Over the years, Dische had dutifully added pearls to the necklace we had started for her, but she was sure they were fake. She had not asked Sig for one, because he loved her so much that she did not need any proof, and she preferred him to spend the money on himself. Here finally was a man who could easily afford that pearl necklace. But he said no. No jewelry. Not even a wedding ring. She nagged him, and he finally relented and bought her a twenty-dollar silver ring. She married Husband Number 3 when she was seventy-two.

Then it was back to an orderly life, with a big double bed and regular meals. They forgot each other's names, but treated each other with respect. She took to his family, and he tried hard to take to hers. He was kind and grandfatherly to the grandchildren, who adored him, but he had to fight his dislike for Irene. This daughter of hers was strange, she lived in Germany, and her husband smoked. It is not easy to get used to such a stepdaughter. Renate had a big appetite for visiting them, and Morton, a family man, obliged her. Twice a year, they visited. Their relations were fine until Irene suddenly lost her fears again.

After fainting from fright in a subway that had stopped briefly in a tunnel—oh, what a ninny she was, trembling like a terrified dog in public!—Irene had fallen into the hands of a psychiatrist. She told this authority a recurrent dream she had: she was flying on a plane that landed in a concentration camp. She had no idea about such a place, and yet she dreamed about it. Outside the inmate barracks were lovely lawns, and tables set up like an outdoor café. Gestapo officers were being served afternoon coffee and cake. Suddenly, Liesel and I strolled by. She slipped between us. From either side, Liesel and I linked arms with my granddaughter. I smiled regally at the Gestapo, Liesel scowled angrily at them. Proud. Although Irene was clad as a Jew, our pride managed to blind them, and to hide her. Around us, Jews were being casually shot, while the Gestapo officers continued to enjoy their coffee. And no one paid us any attention. We strolled past them, right out of the concentration camp. When the eminent psychiatrist heard this dream, she blamed the fearfulness that had plagued Irene on our emigration from Germany. Well, even from my perspective, I thought this idiotic. We hadn't been afraid, why should she be? Renate too thought it was the silliest thing she had ever heard.

But suddenly her daughter was no longer fainting in public. And she was flying everywhere again. She visited New York often, and it became obvious to Morton that she thought of herself as something better: she hung out with fancy people although she had not a shred of money herself. She dressed carelessly, did not go to a hairdresser. And she was not a good mother, she used four-letter words in front of the children. She justified her lifestyle with a career writing storybooks, but he looked at her publications and saw that they were neither sentimental nor good-hearted, but the opposite—cynical. He said so. His last wife had been obsessed with her dead family. This wife had a *living* family, and it was proving just as bad. He had discouraged Renate from seeing Irene, simply by limiting her trips to Europe. Now that Irene was coming to New York, he forbade it.

I have always admired strength of mind in men, but I wouldn't stand for a man keeping the women in the family apart, and from far away, I meddled. I reminded Renate of her ties to me, and that her daughter was just as tied to her. The women must stick together. Renate left Morton.

She moved back into my house, with Little Carl and Irene's family from Germany. Renate was determined not to mind losing yet another husband. But Morton panicked to find himself alone. He said he was sorry. He begged, he offered compromises. He said she could see her daughter in small doses. Just no jewelry, she should stop asking him for those pearls. She conceded. She said she was too tired to fight with a man. She wanted peace and quiet. So she packed her bags one more time and moved back in with her husband. He was extremely grateful and from that day onward, he doted on her extravagantly, and they were like a young couple. He even allowed her to see Irene. Soon he had another reason to fear losing her.

Renate had been feeling short of breath. She mentioned it casually to family and friends, but when they advised her to see a doctor, she shrugged and said, "I am a doctor. I see myself all the time." One morning, she was lecturing at the medical school, and the medical students could hear her lung rustle through the microphone. After the lecture, a smart aleck said to her, "You have fluid on your lung, we all heard it. You should have it looked at." The young generation was taking power. She ceded it. Tamely, she permitted the medical student to take her to Pulmonology, where a colleague volunteered to have a look. The medical students had been right, her lungs were flooding. He withdrew fluid from her lung with a syringe, gave her a sample. Renate thanked everyone politely, and took it over to Pathology. She wasn't going to entrust the diagnosis to a lesser doctor. She looked at the specimen under the microscope. "Chock-full of adenocarcinoma," she said. Thus she proclaimed her own death verdict.

But then her hunger to stay in control and call the shots kicked in. She announced her refusal to give in, her desire to trick the crab and his boss, Death. She had devoted her life to studying Death's means and tactics. She felt she knew him well enough to escape him. Certainly, she was not the slightest bit afraid.

❦

THE SUSPENSE BEGAN. She did not consider her body her fiercest enemy, something that required control. She just wanted it cleaned up; she had an operation. She refused the standard Valium given to preoperative patients. She said she did not need it. She said, "I am looking forward to this." A priest came. She sent him away. When the surgeon opened her up and saw her heart and lungs, they took bets that she had been a professional athlete in her youth. A nurse was sent to ask the family, money passed hands. Death was taken aback; his quarry was seventy-six years old, and people were admiring her body.

She survived the operation, began therapy. She had not reckoned with the poison; her power diminished. Morton was touched. He wanted to give her something, a token of his esteem—as she would be dead any minute—and he hit upon the perfect present: he changed his will in her favor, and told her so. I am leaving you my money, darling. Two weeks later, God gave him a chop to the brain. The blood spilled into the machinery that controlled his locomotion. It took him a while to die. His last words were "Now you can buy yourself those pearls." He did not say it nicely. He died feeling cheated.

That money did the trick. Her will to enjoy it was stronger than death. She recovered. But she was not in a hurry to buy herself anything, not even the pearl necklace. Instead, she took the pearls Dische had bought her to complement the two beautiful starter pearls we had given her, and brought them to a jeweler to string. The jeweler had some interesting points to make. Twenty-two of the pearls were beautiful, really exceptional. But the first two, the big ones at the bottom, the ones we had given her, were fake. So she realized that we had tried to trick Dische into generosity, and that he was not nearly as stingy as she believed. She thought it was funny, did not replace the fake pearls, and was pleased to discover that all along, she had already owned a lovely pearl necklace. She was slender and vivacious. Her hair had fallen out during her treatment, and it grew back in the same pretty mink color mine had done. She did not use makeup, and she had a quick step. A wealthy colleague asked her out to dinner. It seemed she might marry again. But she sent the man away. "Three times is plenty," she said.

She agreed to a second mop-up operation. She walked to the hospital to save taxi money. After the operation, her behavior proved demoralizing to the other patients. In the post-op room, the nurses quickly drew the curtains around her bed. She was sitting up—the drips and drains crisscrossing her body—eating a turkey sandwich on rye and drinking a large black coffee. That was power.

Her new wealth pleased her in theory more than in practice, and she often said, "I wish my parents could see my bank account." She could not spend the money, though. She did not know how to. She was just not a lady. She refused to take taxis, she only bought goods that were on sale, she checked for bargains, she wore the simplest clothes, in restaurants she picked the cheapest items on the menu. She did not like the idea of giving her children money either, because she was afraid they would spend it. Then she fell into the hands of a jeweler named Sami, who got tears in his eyes when he talked to her because she made him miss his own mother, godblessher, living far away on Long Island. He advised her to buy jewelry as an investment. Renate began to frequent the diamond district, just to see the good-hearted Sami. She bought a cracked worthless sapphire ring from him for ten thousand dollars. My anti-Semitism might have boiled if Sami had not shared it.

Sami was a white-haired gentleman who specialized in hood-winking old ladies. His real name was Grant, and he was an Anglo-Iranian with a talent for regional accents. When he went to the jewelry fair in Colorado, he posed as an old Mexican and unloaded poor quality tinted turquoise on northerners. But his jungle was New York, and his diet monomorphic. He made a big meal of Renate. She was always a terrible judge of character, I have said that. Renate brought him some of my favorite jewelry, and *traded* it for inferior pieces. Soon she had a whole collection of flawed stones on various rings and pendants that she took turns wearing. They did give her a lot of pleasure.

At first, Irene was my avenger. She was suspicious of Sami, and quickly established that he had cheated Renate. Irene wouldn't take that lying down. She knew what that jewelry meant to me. She went to see Sami when Renate wasn't looking, because she could no longer look, and when he burst into an aria of longing for Renate, Irene quietly handed him the defective stones and said he could buy them back. He agreed to monthly installments. He paid for years and years. Long after he had paid back every penny taken from Renate, he continued paying, in a last-ditch attempt to clean his conscience. Because Sami had one. And it saved him, as I happen to know.

But then something much worse happened. Irene's appetite to clean out my collection of jewelry was whetted by this experience, and instead of stopping right there, she started giving it away by the handful. She carried it around in her pockets, and dished it out to her friends, or to a maid hired for one day to wash windows. She claimed that my precious jewelry consisted of so many pretty shackles that had to be unlocked and dumped. And what she did not give away, she sold, even though she was not starving; soon there was none left at all, and no amount of my protesting in the grave could stop her. But how much can you kick and scream when there are so many people sharing the grave with you? And by and by, there would be even more company.

Renate was rich and healthy. She had much more money than Margie ever had. But her modesty remained intransigent. When Carl's brother Jacob contacted her, she did not turn up her nose. Her uncle was in his nineties, and the only proof that the Rothers, too, had a talent for longevity. He had not taken offense when Carl refused to receive him in Weehawken. He had grown used to having friends instead of a family, and he was now a gentleman in a retirement home on an Australian beach. One day, out of the blue, he called up Renate and asked her whether she wouldn't squire her old uncle back for one last trip to Leobschütz, "to Memory Lane." Renate dropped everything. Those two had a grand reunion in Berlin, and drove to Upper Silesia, now in Poland. Jacob looked as distinguished as a professor of surgery. He was portly, expensively dressed, he had a craggy face and a first-class toupee, and he moved briskly. He was proud of his past. He bragged that he was a legend in certain circles in Melbourne. At the high point of his career, he had stolen fourteen tons of beef filet, working with stolen cranes, refrigeration trucks, and a rented warehouse. He had retired to run a widow and orphan insurance scheme for colleagues. He joked about Carl's disdain for thieves, about how all the Rothers had slighted him but me. He remembered the meals I had fed him on the sly, and how I was the most beautiful woman he had ever seen. He recalled all the details of saying goodbye to me on the village square before undertaking the trek east, by train and boat. He kept going until he felt safe from the Nazis, which was in the South Pacific. No one in the family had been willing to follow him there, they didn't even bother to reply to his letters. "They thought Australia was on another planet, Uncle," Renate consoled him.

They finally reached Leobschütz. When they drove into the village square, which was now a dusty, forlorn Polish version of the stately one they remembered, Jacob suddenly burst into loud sobs. Renate panicked. She stared at her uncle with horror. At once he collected himself. "Can we have some lunch?" he demanded.

They turned into the next restaurant, where they gorged on Polish sausages and sauerkraut. "I don't know why I got so worked up back there," Jacob said. "Probably you were just hungry," said Renate.

They were going to take a walk through town and look at their old homes, and the family graves, which were so incomplete. "We'd better not," said Renate. "Walking around here, we might get run over by a car. And can you imagine, after that sausage lunch, what a grease stain we'd leave?" Uncle Jacob chortled at the thought, and agreed, it was time to go. They turned their backs on Leob-schütz, and on the past, and drove straight back to Berlin in the best of spirits.

Jacob went back to Melbourne, Renate went to New Jersey, and they lived happily ever after. Only once did she hear from him again, when he sent her, by special post, an unusual platinum ring with a circle of tiny diamonds. He said it had once belonged to me. Indeed, it had. It was the engagement ring Carl had given me. A year into my marriage, my fingers had grown too plump to wear it, and I had put it away. I had owned and worn such a lot of jewelry in my day, I had not noticed its absence. He had stolen it. Now Re-nate thanked him mightily and often wore this ring. She called it "Jacob's ring." It seemed that nothing, not even her past, could worry her. For five years, my daughter enjoyed herself without reser-vation. She had no quarrels with anyone. She lived harmoniously in my home in Weehawken, turning it into a bohemian madhouse of books and records and bottled babies in the kitchen. Liesel's or-der just could not hold. Little Carl lived there too. Without his grandparents to guide him, his interests had followed the siren call of his blood—he took an interest in money. It was an academic in-terest really. He became very wealthy speculating on the stock mar-ket, and he did not lose his money when others did. Nor did he spend it as others did, because he was just too shy and apprehensive about other people to look for a bride, and he never did learn to take an interest in worldly possessions. Accordingly, he was a happy man. He grew ever more handsome as time passed, and he remained slen-der, his hair thick and black, and his eyes unclouded by marital woes. He spent his days reading and thinking, and never talking about himself. His sister, in rare moments of modesty, still consid-ered him her opposite in all ways, and therefore vastly superior.

To my surprise, Renate's own form of ridiculous modesty did not harm her; to the contrary, it made her beloved by all. She just never wanted to disapprove of anybody or anything. She refused to take a stand. Once, a colleague of hers went on vacation in the tropics, rang Renate in New York, and begged her for advice. "I've fallen in love with the neighbor," she said.

Now I ask myself, Why ask Dr. Renate Dische for advice about such a matter? What is going on here? What have I missed? In any case, here was her chance—her responsibility—to say no. No. Take hold of yourself. I was holding my breath, figuratively speaking, waiting for her answer.

Instead she said, "Congratulations! How wonderful! Well, you just go and have a good time, dear, just don't let your husband find out." You bet she didn't either. And I soon learned that Renate was known far and wide among her female colleagues as a source for excuses. If someone wanted to spend an evening privately, and not tell her husband, Professor Dische nonchalantly provided backup. She didn't even ask questions. She just said, "Yes of course, you are coming to my house for a little dinner, and if your husband calls I will tell him you've just stepped outside to buy something we need, don't you worry about a thing."

In her own mind, Renate was behaving altruistically, she wanted to be useful, to do something for mankind. And she did not pass judgment, not on herself, not on others. I always objected to that, but I have found that here, one considers it a virtue. She has other virtues of course; I have not skipped over them. Her industriousness never let up—she did not miss a day at the autopsy room if she could help it, even when she was gravely ill. And then she fulfilled the last two wishes remaining on the list that I had stuck on her shutter when she was very small: she bought a farm outside the city, with more land than she could have dreamed of in Germany, and she kept horses. She bought an imperial-looking piano and played the big sentimental works coolly. The Gierlich women were always unsentimental, and affectionate.

After years of strife, she and Irene began spending a lot of time together, reveling in each other's moral laxness. The two became sort of an infernal duo, always giggling about serious matters and never criticizing each other about a thing. They became, in short, the truest and staunchest allies. They had long ago forgotten any differences they had, which means they had not bowed to the popular convention that one has to *talk* about everything, which is really very unchristian by the way—either you forgive or you don't, or rather, either you forget or you don't. The two of them spoke about me so often that I couldn't resist joining them as a memory. The three of us had a good time. Actually, the four of us. Liesel always tagged along as a memory too, criticizing and warning.

I want to be fair to Carl; he was not a weak presence either. One morning when Renate was dissecting the huge, sloppy heart of a failed transplant with a group of young interns, she asked, "Does anyone want to know why the heart represents love to me?" There are no rules about what you can or can't chat about during an autopsy, but this impending intimacy took everyone aback. She continued to work, and as her fingers took apart the poor mutilated organ, she described being taken to a Baltic beach in Germany when she was five, watching other fathers build sand castles for their children, while her own father sprawled exhausted next to his wife. Carl registered her disappointment. He stood up, and did his paternal duty. He built an enormous sand heart for her, with all the vessels and ventricles carefully designed so that the waves would run through them correctly. "I guess he was a not an ordinary mortal," concluded Renate, looking up and flashing her interns one of those big fake smiles that she used to cover up any strong emotion.

The tide grew. When the heart was washed away, the girl whimpered, and her father admonished her, "Don't you cry. That's just what happens."

HER ILLNESS HAS COME BACK, and this time, no amount of strength of will to live can help her triumph. When she is in pain, she does not ask for her ally, but for Liesel. She begs Liesel to cook some *flädelsuppe*, creamed spinach, dumplings with gravy. Instead, her children cumbersomely prepare her BLT sandwiches, insisting that she like them. She is at the farm. She agrees not to sleep on the sofa, and a bed is brought into the living room. She looks out the window, and instead of seeing the rolling hills of the farm, she sees the garden in Leobschütz, the raspberry bushes, and again, she asks for Liesel.

IT IS NIGHT. It is after midnight. It is snowing. The ground is covered with snow, and more keeps coming. It is bitter cold and dark outside, but inside the house it is warm, and a yellow lamp shines on Renate's face on the pillow. She is raving. She is frantic. She says, "The Nazis . . . The Nazis . . ." She can't get the sentence out, it is too—frightening.

Renate is terrified.

"The Nazis . . . are inside me. I can't get away. They are burning me up. Help me." She has never asked for help before. Little Carl crushes morphine tablets with the back of a spoon into a paste, Irene rolls the paste on her fingers and rubs Renate's tongue with it. More, more. The dogs are miserable. They whine at her bedside. The Nazis are proving invincible, they snatch her last minutes of consciousness. Forgive me what I cannot forget. Outside, the snow is growing deeper. A tidal wave of snow drops over the house. The funeral parlor attendants negotiate through the blizzard in a battered station wagon, because no one can see in the dark. They tramp into the house wearing masks of sympathy and carrying a bill for a luxury hearse, because life goes on. They zip Renate into a black rubber bag. The dogs growl and gnash their teeth. She is coming to me now.

I AM OVERJOYED. There is no joy like the Joy Here. Because it turns out that despite the vast difference in the quality of our behavior, we've both ended up in the same place, along with my Nazi brother Otto, that horrible Nazi boyfriend Paul, Carl, all of Renate's Jewish husbands, and positioned at God's Right Hand, much closer than anyone else I know—is Liesel. They aren't the same to me, however, and what happens to Little Carl and to Irene and to her own girl, Emily, and her son, Leon, who looks more Dische than I would wish, well, actually I don't really care. I have cut a few corners here and there, anyway. Even at this vantage point, I can't be bothered to poke around in the past, or remember everything. Sometimes I have surely remembered wrong and occasionally I have embellished things—sin of lying—but this was, in all honesty, only to amuse myself, and I planned to go back and change those places. But it is too much bother now. Sin of sloth. Let others judge, I no longer want to.

I have Maria Renate here with me, and now I can relax, and end this rumination. In the blink of an eye, Irene will join us. But at the moment, I have that girl all to myself. Really, absolutely nothing beats a daughter.

Discussion Questions
for *The Empress of Weehawken*

1. How were you affected by the fact that the author and Elisabeth's granddaughter have the same last name? How is the experience of reading a novel different from reading a memoir?

2. What are the merits of Elisabeth's criteria for choosing a spouse? What was the key to her enduring marriage to Carl?

3. Did Carl's family have anything other than nationality in common with Elisabeth's? Why was Carl unenthusiastic about his relatives and their Jewish cultural identity?

4. What ultimately led to the Rothers' survival under Hitler? How did their situation differ from those in other Holocaust narratives you have read? How would you have resolved Elisabeth and Carl's dilemma over whether to flee?

5. How would you describe Elisabeth's unique storytelling voice? How does she manage to be both irresistible and outrageous? Who is the "keeper of the saga" in your family?

6. What are the traits of Elisabeth's version of Catholicism? How does the hierarchy of sins help her negotiate life? What does she fear? How does she determine whether others are worthy?

7. Discuss the parenting styles described in *The Empress of Weehawken*. How did Liesel and her niece exert control over the children in their care (and over the parents)? How does Elisabeth's mothering compare to Renate's? Was it nature or nurture that caused Irene and Little Carl to make unconventional, sometimes self-defeating, choices?

8. Has the idea of an American identity changed very much since the time Elisabeth and Renate finally reunited with Carl? What aspects of American life characterized the mid-twentieth century but have now vanished? What did the Rothers love and dislike about their American and German homelands?

9. Discuss the various husbands described in *The Empress of Weehawken*. Who did you see as the ideal man? What did Renate seem to need in a man? How do her husbands compare to her father?

10. The novel opens with Carl's determination to have a son and closes with the line "nothing beats a daughter." How do the novel's female characters learn how to define themselves as women? What were the expectations for each generation in areas such as sex, marriage, careers, grooming, and housekeeping? How do their attitudes compare to the ones in your family history?

11. How do Elisabeth and Renate approach the cycles of life? Was Elisabeth ever rebellious in her youth? How do their attitudes change when they become widows?

12. Elisabeth often tells of moments when "the bill came" and God delivered retribution. How does this point of view shape her decisions? Does Irene prove or disprove Elisabeth's ideas about the rewards systems lurking in our destinies?

13. How do the novel's characters feel about money? What does stinginess or extravagance indicate about their personalities? Who are the novel's most prosperous characters, in literal or symbolic ways?

14. To what do you attribute Elisabeth's longevity? What legacy has she left when she narrates her final, joyful scene?

CPSIA information can be obtained at www.ICGtesting.com
Printed in the USA
LVOW07s1618221014

410014LV00002B/433/P